Life After Death

Spotting someone walking around upstairs in their mansion, the Steele twins enter learning that their uncle, Professor Steele, is alive and well. He looks twenty years younger than he did before his death.

Not surprised, he welcomes the boys, greeting them with a hug wrapping each arm around his nephews. He thanks them for leading and guiding his 'Golden Eagle' Organization and Steele Corporation in his absence.

Professor Steele organizes an event entitled "Return of the King." He invites over the dark web every person who has a SuperPower which the Department of Defense Genetically Engineered (DODGE) Initiative and the Martins have learned about.

The day before the 'Golden Eagle' event, Professor Steele tells his nephews that he will be resuming as head of the 'Golden Eagle' Organization and his corporation. This announcement frees up the brothers to pursue other matters.

Before attending the planned Professor Steele's funeral, Oliver 'The Merc' Davis in honor of Rocky Steele's Across America Race runs in Reykjavik's Suzuki Midnight Sun Run at 1,800 mph taking the late Professor's special vitamins.

He easily wins in less than three minutes giving the gift certificate for 10,000 Icelandic Krona (or $80 US) to a young fan cheering wearing an Oregon Ducks t-shirt.

Nearby at the Laugardalshöll indoor sporting arena in Reykjavík, Iceland, he is invited to celebrate the lives of Rocky and Apollo Steele.

The arena holds 5,500 people. This is where the legendary World Chess Championship between "Bobby Fischer and Boris Spassky took place.

After landing at Reykjavík–Keflavík Airport, an Uber transports Pablo Martin and his wife Colette Evergreen and Salvador accompanies his wife, Jocelyn Thatcher. The group enters the small ballet backstage room that surprises the Martins since the parking lot was filled even after the race had concluded. The turnout seemed very weak at best.

The priest enters the room for a funeral mass wearing a purple cassock. It is a floor-length regalia with long sleeves having thirty-three buttons down the front. Purple signifies penance and reflection being a sorrowful color.

Although not religious, the Martins bow their heads saying a deep thoughtful prayer being the last SuperPower adversaries who saw the Steele siblings before their last breath. The two best friends shed a tear as their husbands loaned them a handkerchief.

Salvador tells his brother, "My friend Ben always tells me that the best reason to carry a handkerchief is to lend it to a lady."

Pablo nods in agreement.

The priest pours water upon the Steele siblings' closed caskets praying aloud "Our Father who art in Heaven."

Two monks in black robes enter the room sitting behind the Martins. One kneels saying, "The Spartans prayed for a 'beautiful death' while the Egyptians only asked, 'Have you found joy in your life?' and 'Has your life brought joy to others?'"

The other monk prays, "I walk through the valley of the shadow of death I fear no evil for you are with me."

SuperPower: The Ability to Fly or to Become Invisible:
The Golden Eagle Has Yielded
(Book #3)

Roger E. Pedersen

Special Acknowledgement to:

Cover Design: Ruth Adedeji, in Nigeria.
Editor: Roxana Coumans, Proofreadebooks.com in Romania.

This book is dedicated to my four daughters Michele Leslie Lock, Brooke Laurel DeMille, Megan Leigh Pedersen, and Meredith Marlowe Pedersen and grandchildren, Thanks to Ruth for her excellent series of cover artwork.

Library of Congress Cataloguing-in-Publication Data meaner

Pedersen, Roger E.

SuperPower: The Ability to Fly or to Become Invisible: The Golden Eagle Has Yielded (Book #3)

ISBN 978-1-7375351-4-0 (paperback) ***
ISBN 978-1-7375351-5-7 (E-Book)

Mr. Pedersen is a well-known video game designer who has purposely mentioned films, music and book references by name or quotes. As you read the book, keep track of every film (movie), music and book reference (note page at end of the book).

All inquiries for volume purchasing of this book should be negotiated with PSI Publishing, Inc. by email at PSIPublishingInc@Gmail.Com

After a brief pause, he continues, "Father, into thy hands I commend the spirits of Apollo and Rocky."

The purple clothed priest continues, "I ask that you watch over them in the next life. Be with all those here, giving each of us peace. Some of us have seen death and suffering. Give us peace, fill each of us with your spirit and springs of living waters."

As the entire group of mourners witness the priest removes his purple Cossack robe, he addresses the Martin twins asking them: "Do either of you know my acquaintances who I met as young street hustlers, they stole my wallet and identification. Visiting Spain, many years ago, that incident forced me to extort the young couple into acquiring famous works of art for me and my associates."

Pablo and Salvador blush being puzzled saying, "No."

The priest asks, "Really?" as the DODGE men keep steadfast saying, "We don't understand." Their wives are confused too.

The priest says, "I will turn the tables and confess to you. I discovered your parents Diego and Carmen. From poor street thieves, I created and educated them. Giving each of them millions of dollars. Telling Diego, your father to marry your mother."

The twins are shocked. He continues, "I financially rewarded them allowing them to move to San Francisco and change their identity from criminals to earning a prestigious seat as SFMoMA board members."

"Are you still confused?"

Pablo says, "We realize that the world isn't all sunshine and rainbows."

Colette appears that she has seen an apparition nervously saying, "I know who you are but that's impossible."

"Why?"

"Because you are dead. Been dead for a long time. Blown up from an exploding vehicle."

Her husband asks, "Who are you talking about?"

"This is the late Professor Steele, Your parents' mentor. Their benefactor. A world class genius, practically a demi-God."

The rest of the group says, "No way. He's dead and gone forever."

"No," she states, "people keep asking if he's back and alive. Now I see that he is!"

"You are telling us that at his nephews' funeral, he has decided to reveal to the world that he has resurrected?"

She replies, "He may never have died."

The priest exits the parlor followed by the two monks.

The Martin couples follow them into the large arena where over five thousand Golden Eagle Organization members are gathered such as the recent Reykjavik's Suzuki Midnight Sun Run winner, Oliver 'The Merc' Davis. Also, walking around the room dressed to kill is Astrid Christiansen from Norway.

The Professor greets JiJi Nkosi from Botswana who is wearing a ten-karat diamond ring and an Aurora Australia black opal from Lightning Ridge, Australia. He congratulates her on her exquisite jewelry and winning her recent election becoming the city's mayor.

The Professor sees Pamela Braga kiss her girlfriend Elaine Little and walks over. Clearing his throat, he turns a rosy shade of embarrassment. He states, "It's a party for the Steele's second coming.

There are more surprises ahead tonight. I recently became an ordained minister for my own church, the 'Golden Eagle' Eyrie Temple. If you two want to make your love official, just send me an email," as he smiles.

The Martin brothers and their wives enjoy the smorgasbord and champagne, being hungry and curious about which adversaries are present.

Professor Steele is handed the microphone. He begins saying, "I would like to thank everyone for joining me on this special occasion for me but sad for my departed nephews. Can everyone get a glass of sparkling white wine? I would like to offer a toast to my two amazing nephews, Rocky and Apollo. May they…"

The two monks in black robes who sat in the rear of the funeral mass service, march forward with their heads covered.

One monk grabs the microphone out of the Professor's hand. He solemnly explains, "We refuse to let the Steele brothers rest in peace. Almighty God, like Lazarus, raise up Apollo. Stand up again, Rocky. You are not down for the count. In the battle of life, we pray that Apollo and his brother Rocky avoid the ten counts of death."

On cue, the boxing bell rings indicating the end of the boxing round.

The two monks simultaneously remove their cowl revealing to the entire room that they are alive.

Professor Steele announces, "Oh, my. It is my late nephews Apollo and Rocky. Look! They are moving. They are alive. They are alive. They are moving, they are alive, they are alive," as the entire audience raises giving a standing ovation, clapping, and shouting, "They are alive!"

Apollo and Rocky high five the Professor, who hugs his recently departed nephews.

Pablo Martin tells his entourage, "Unbelievable! We witnessed that they were shot at close range."

Salvador Martin states, "Let us return home. Now that we know that the twins are alive, DODGE will update the Steele twins' files. There is nothing keeping us here now," as they depart to the airport.

The Steele brothers get greeted by the attendees as though they are celebrities.

Apollo shakes Oliver's hand congratulating him for his recent marathon win asking if he wants a Race Across America rematch.

The Merc laughs and looks at Rocky saying, "Anytime. Anywhere. I take my speed vitamins. Do you?"

Next in line is Brittany Barbosa who Rocky hugs and kisses on her cheek. She likes that so she spins around having him repeat the entire hug and cheek kiss as she can travel forward and backward through time,

Apollo greets her with a friendly hug asking her to put on her calendar for this year's FIFA World Cup Football competition.

She smiles and says, "You're on. Order the best seats soon."

Next, Romeo Monty and Juliet Capuletty greet the brothers with hugs and saying, "It's a good thing you're bad since only the good die young," making them all laugh.

Juliet Capuletty asks, "Is Commander John Marion and Misty here?"

Rocky states, "No. Yesterday, we chatted with the couple who's vacationing in Tahiti."

Pamela Braga and Elaine Little approach them receiving hugs and kisses saying, "Your uncle is too much, he is funny. Professor Steele is a 'joker.' He asked to marry us to be a legitimate same sex couple."

Apollo raises his eyebrows and replies, "He constantly hawks my brother and I about finding a partner too. When you are ready, on your own terms, give him a call."

Stormy Weather hugs the brothers saying, "Clear skies ahead."

A gorgeous lady approaches her. Stormy introduces the Steeles to her saying, "This is my best friend, Myrena Gorgona. She has been an international SuperModel gracing the covers of hundreds of iMagazines."

Myrena smiles and states, "Correction, it is one thousand, six hundred and ninety-three to be exact with three more on their way," having the two ladies giggle.

Rocky kisses Myrena's hand as Apollo hugs Stormy, then they switch having Apollo passionately hugging Myrena until his jealous brother breaks them up saying, "Do we need to rent a room?"

Stormy adds, "Men always react that way with her. I am guilty of wanting her too," as she laughs.

Myrena tells Stormy out loud, "These two look alike but there is a slight difference that I see. They are both handsome and adorable. Which one should I date?"

Stormy replies "I do not know. Each is charismatic and hot. Besides, for me they both have millions of dollars which turns me on."

Pamela Braga and Elaine Little stop by and begin kissing Stormy who is enjoying their attention. They tell her, "Do not rain on our three-way parade,"

As other men in the room eyeball the lesbian love action, the Steele brothers cannot look away from Myrena Gorgona.

She explains that "All my sisters and my mother, Keto are SuperModels. They all have married powerful, adoring men that they have lost their heads over."

The shape shifter Carlson Chesterfield turns himself into Elijah Moses, Jr. telling everyone to arrest the Steele brothers.

A few officers who have arrived with him apprehend them as he states, "Back to ADX Florence in Colorado, the Alcatraz of the Rockies with these defiant criminals who are enemies of DODGE."

The Professor, trying to win an Oscar, grabs Elijah wrestling him to the ground as the siblings begin to vacate the room. As they turn around about to run towards the street, Carlson reverts to his normal form having the entire 'Golden Eagle' membership laugh, aware of what was about to occur.

Heading back with the Professor to the family's mansion, Apollo says, "I call dibs on Myrena."

Rocky retorts, "To Hell with that, I saw the way she looked at me and I claim the dating right on her."

The Professor states, "The both of you will take turns dating and wooing her the best you can. We will let her decide which of you two she wants to be with."

The brothers agree but argue which one will go out with her first.

Chapter 2

IRL Dating a SuperPower SuperModel

Professor Steele gathers his nephews inside the library where he takes out Iceland's 100 Kronur coin.

He tells Apollo to call heads or tails where the nickel-brass, gold colored coin has a lump fish on its heads side and Iceland's coat of arms containing engraved pictures of an eagle, dragon, bull, and giant on its tails side.

As the coin is tossed high into the air spinning clockwise, Apollo shouts "Heads" which is precisely how the coin lands on the dark chocolate brown birch wood floor.

Rocky snaps his fingers saying "Darn! I guess, I will have to pick up the pieces of the catastrophic remains of your date."

Apollo calls Myrena Gorgona who tells him that this is her first visit to Iceland although as a SuperModel she has toured the world rarely beyond the photographer's lens range.

Apollo notes, "Between the North American and Eurasian Plates, the tectonic and volcanic environment in a rift valley occurs at the Þingvellir or in the Thingvellir National Park. Tomorrow morning, we can explore the park and afterwards visit the Strokkur Geyser hot spring which has a variety of geothermal pools. Make sure that you bring your Sports iMagazine swimsuit."

He continues, "Like your predecessor from a century ago, model and actress Brooke Shields, we have an iconic sight, the Blue Lagoon. It is a miraculous geothermal seawater pool with an in-water bar. After being relaxed and refreshed, we can dine at their Lava Restaurant."

She responds, "Sounds amazing. I can be ready at 8 in the morning."

At 7:45 in the morning Apollo arrives in his red Swedish Koenigsegg Sleipnir EV. The 4.8-million-dollar sports car with a top speed of 275 miles per hour.

As Myrena Gorgona walks out of her B&B residence, he gets a smile from the gorgeous SuperModel.

After giving Apollo a hug and a kiss, she tells him that she is wearing her tied up button short sleeve pink shirt that reveals the curves of her waist and belly button, with Fuchsia skimpy, hot Daisy shorts.

She reports that she is wearing her sturdy XXV Ultra mid 5 GTX comfortable, lightweight hiking boots. Under her outfit, she is wearing a four-million-dollar pink Angel Holiday bikini that contains 9,000 precious gemstones comprised of diamonds rubies emeralds, and yellow sapphires.

She adds, "I purposely wore this to tantalize your eyes as well as making every girl there jealous when the man in their life can't stop looking at me wearing it."

Apollo smiles and continues driving on Route 1 North towards Route 36 which takes less than an hour to get to their destination.

On their way to the park, they both exchange every city that each of them has visited starting with the top fashion cities of Paris, London, and New York.

As they have arrived, Apollo takes her hand walking towards the Strokkur geyser, He tells Myrena that "Every few minutes like clockwork the geyser erupts with its turbulent ejection of boiling water and steam that reaches up to one hundred feet.

He holds her closely flying upwards using his SuperPower as she turns them invisible.

She witnesses the explosive water smoking with its clouds of steam announcing, "Apollo, the God of Sun and Light. In mythology, he owns the powers of healing, medicine, archery, music, and poetry. Any hidden SuperPower you care to brag about?"

He answers like being in a hypnotic trance, "Just flight and telekinesis, moving objects using my mind."

Myrena states, "I can fly or become invisible at times. Whatever the situation calls for, I am blessed with ruling the world one day soon," as she chuckles.

Apollo shows her Kerid volcanic crater saying, "My uncle, Professor Steele tells me that over 3,000 years ago when he was young, this volcano last erupted," laughing with a Cheshire Cat grin.

Observing his SuperModel date, he gets a Mona Lisa smile as the two stare at the turquoise lake. Walking along the top edge of the red rock crater, Myrena expresses her happiness deciding to wear her comfortable, lightweight designer hiking shoes.

Apollo says, "In Iceland, we normally wear 1 1/2 lb. La Sportska Troender PED made of Nubuck Leather that is waterproof."

At the warm, geothermal waters of the Blue Lagoon, Myrena removes her shirt and skimpy shorts revealing her exquisite curves and zero body fat, showing off her SuperModel body.

Apollo and every male stare as their female partners smack many faces and torsos in an enraged, jealous reaction.

A few gay men comment, "Baby, you will never rue the day as the 'Supermodel of the World.' She has 'no tea, no shade' in that million-dollar bikini. She is one 'eleganza extravaganza' heather."

Apollo wearing light blue, men's Barracuda Swim Trunks does not get any public reaction. Even wearing his three hundred thousand-dollar Hublot King Power Minute Repeater Tourbillon Chronograph does not even earn a stare or comment.

Even the gay men ignore him.

After an hour of enjoyable, playful swimming and kissing each other waist deep in the warm water, they get toweled off and walk over to the Lava Restaurant. The unforgettable culinary experience is located on the west bank of the Blue Lagoon. Feeling under-dressed, Apollo is ready to hand the manager a 100-Kronur banknote but when he recognizes the SuperModel, Myrena, he immediately sits the couple.

The manager brings the couple a bottle of white wine and two glasses. He puts two shot glasses of complimentary Brennivin on their table as he asks, "Gorgeous SuperModel Myrena, please let me have a photo of the two of us to put on the restaurant's 'Hall of Fame.'" He accidentally insults Apollo asking him to take their picture.

Myrena orders as an appetizer the ruby beet salad as Apollo requests the garlic, marinated langoustine soup. As they are served their first course, they continue ordering as she requests the fish of the day from the nearby Grindavik Harbor. Apollo orders the rack of lamb.

They discuss the day's activities and Apollo touches her cell exchanging cell phone data. Between forkful bites of their meal, they look at each other's digital photos.

Driving home, they listen to the microchip iMusic singing to the latest nuclear rock iMusic from Lovegood Records.

Apollo parks his car near the B&B residence that Myrena is renting. He exits and opens the vehicle's door for her. They hug and kiss for minutes having her thank him saying, "I had a wonderful day with you. Tomorrow, I will be with your twin brother, but I look forward to our next date together." She leaves as he watches her to ensure that she is safely home. He drives away with the windows open at top speed.

Rocky sitting in the library working on his dual laptop-tablet computer, he hears the footsteps of his brother Apollo walking up the wooden steps. Rocky picks up his cell phone and calls Myrena. She answers saying, "Good evening my gorgeous Rocky. Are you getting excited about our upcoming date tomorrow?"

Rocky answers, "Absolutely. Since my brother took you on a mundane expedition which included swimming, I have decided to take you to the Sólheimajökull Glacier, followed by visiting the Skógurfoss waterfall then exploring the magical Seljalandsfoss. You will need to wear comfortable hiking boots, a lightweight, warm jacket with a hood, and gloves."

The next morning Rocky drives up to Myrena's B&B residence in his deadly, lethal Lamborghini Veneno Roadster Limited Edition EV valued at 5.6 million dollars US.

Myrena dressed in her midnight navy, Burberry leather, mixed denim trench coat with matching black leather pants. She accessorized her look with a Burberry leather fedora and black cashmere lined Italian leather gloves.

Rocky comments, "You're wearing quite an impressive outfit that looks awesome on you. People are going to think I am dating a female Indiana Jones. Or if you added a whip, you might be mistaken for Catwoman," having her laugh.

Heading towards the south coast of Iceland from Reykjavik traveling ninety-eight miles away is an outlet glacier called Mýrdalsjökull.

Nearby the small fishing village of Vík-í-ýrdal is the world-famous black-sand beach of Reynisfjara formed from the volcanic ash.

Myrena challenges Rocky to climb up the rectangular volcanic sculptured terrain which he gladly accepts.

After Myrena beats him to the top and then back down to the beach of black pebbles, they decide to explore the cave where lava formed stalactites appear to be pouring down on visitors. Just off the black sand beach in the water are large protruding lava rocks.

Rocky tells her, "Like Tolkien's 'The Hobbit' where Bilbo Baggins witnessed Trolls cooking dinner, the ancient residents believed that these black lava formations were Trolls caught in the sunlight turning into stone. Look over there in the distance are the Dyrhólaey cliffs that are 394 feet high near the town of Vík, the southernmost point in Iceland."

The two lovers walk holding hands to the Seljalandsfoss waterfall. The falls are many where the highest is 197 feet high where behind the falls are 527 steps that lead to the top.

Wearing their waterproof outfits, Myrena leads Rocky up the metal steps. They walk as water engulfs them, spraying them sideways.

In the romantic deluge, Rocky hugs, and passionately kisses Myrena looking into her green eyes.

He asks her, "Does the water, like rain turn you on?"

She replies, "I am really getting wet. And it is not from you."

Leaving the beach and waterfalls, they sit inside Rocky's Lamborghini kissing and getting to know each other until his stomach growls indicating it is time to seek nourishment.

Rocky drives to the Black Sand Vik Restaurant, a new Michelin restaurant.

The host welcomes them as he sits the couple at a window table that overlooks the ocean, town, and surrounding mountains from its hill location.

Rocky suggests having the delicious, hard to find puffin, arctic char, which is a cold-water salmon, and Skyr, a millennian old, fat free dairy product.

She says, "My stomach is game for anything new. I am adventurous."

He adds, "I know the Michelin chef here and he always makes the national dish of Iceland for me called 'Hákarl' that consists of a Greenland shark with whale meat on the side. As you might know whale and puffin meat is legal to consume in Iceland, so outsiders often try a sample. So now, you can brag to the other anorexic SuperModels about your Icelandic cuisine."

The wine steward brings Rocky a bottle of Domaine Weinbach Pinot Gris Altenbourg asking him to taste it before serving.

He does and says "AEdislegt" meaning "Excellent."

The chef himself brings the delicacies to their table saying, "Sir Rocky and Madam, 'Bon Appetit.'"

Myrena with her Icelandic virgin tastebuds eats the puffin stating, "It tastes like something between tuna and beef. I was expecting it to taste like chicken," as she laughs.

Rocky explains, "The meat of the Greenland shark is poisonous when fresh, so it is soaked in ammonia having foreigners often gag. I suggest pinching your nose before putting it on a toothpick to consume. Another rare delicacy."

Myrena tries as she is told but she is not thrilled by its taste even when resisting the urge to breathe.

Rocky points out the whale saying, "The Minke whale can be consumed either eaten raw or cooked although eating it raw can be dangerous. Try eating the whale meat as it is cooked 'au gratin,' with breadcrumbs and grated cheese."

Myrena tries the Minke whale and decides that it is quite tasty.

For dessert, the server brings dishes each with a sample selection of Skyr with blueberries, strawberries, and raspberries.

Rocky states, "Skyr is a non-dairy, plant-based blend made from protein more than sugar with a concoction of coconut, macadamia, and pea protein."

On their two-hour drive back home, Rocky gives Myrena a wrapped gift.

She smiles unwrapping it saying, "It is not Christmas or my birthday."

Rocky tells her that his father used to quote a classic film saying, "The key to a woman's heart is an unexpected gift at an unexpected time."

To her surprise it is a book entitled 'William Shakespeare's Sonnets.'

She reads out loud from Sonnet 18, "Shall I compare thee to a summer's day? Thou art more lovely and more temperate."

She kisses Rocky on his cheek saying, "That's wonderful," as a tear rolls down her cheek. She continues reading the sonnets until they pull into her semi-circular driveway.

There, Rocky opens her door and escorts her to the residence's front door. They hug and kiss. She thanks him for an extraordinary day and unforgettable dinner. They kiss for another minute or two before she enters her dwelling.

Professor Steele contacts Myrena Gorgona telling her that she has influenced his nephews as he has never seen them as happy and excited ever, especially since their funeral. He asks her to take her time in answering his next question. He asks her, "Which of my two intelligent, handsome nephews have you selected to become your partner?"

There is a pause on the phone for two minutes. Finally, she admits to the Professor, "Both are wonderful and make me feel loved and special. To be honest with you I need more time with them. So, at this moment round one between Apollo and Rocky must be considered a tie. I look forward to the next few dates with your nephews. Thank you for calling and have a wonderful evening."

A half hour later, Apollo calls Myrena excited about his next date with her. He asks when the last time was, she encountered a whale.

She laughs saying, "I ate one for dinner and I enjoyed it."

He continues saying, "I am planning to show you the west side of Iceland where there is the stunning Snæfellsnes peninsula. Then, returning here to Reykjavik's Old Harbor where the Steele family super-yacht is docked. There, we have a captain familiar with the waters who will show us amazing marine wildlife. We will get up close to Iceland's majestic humpback whales, dolphins, and porpoises. We will privately sail among the small islands in the Faxaflói Bay as our large vessel has line-balancing and stabilizers improving the travel through turbulent waves of Iceland's water."

Arriving in the Professor's $21.5 million Rolls Royce Henry Platinum Edition made of solid platinum where the Professor's car comes with a chauffeur who opens the door for Ms. Gorgona as Apollo hands her an arrangement of rare Hawaiian Bog Orchids.

He tells her, "In order to receive this rare orchid, I bought 100 acres of land of wet forests surrounded by bogs in Hawaii dedicated to growing Hawaiian Bog Orchids in special greenhouses protected against animals and weather such as hurricanes."

The limousine enters the Snæfellsnes peninsula which is nicknamed "Little Iceland" having fjords, waterfalls, lava rock cliff, caves, and beaches with white or black sand.

Apollo announces, "Our first stop on the Snæfellsnes peninsula is Stykkishólmur where chess world champion, Bobby Fischer was planning to live but he died before doing so. There in the north is Stykkishólmur Harbor that is a fishing village. Let us get out here and go for a hike."

The chauffeur opens the door for Myrena who again is wearing her sturdy XXV Ultra mid 5 GTX comfortable, lightweight hiking boots. Apollo points upwards displaying their destination being the top of the cliffs. Holding hands, the couple begins walking at a fast pace until they begin breathing deeply and slow down. At the top of the cliffs that overlook the roadway across the water, they take digital pictures of the sights and of the two of them in the foreground. Myrena dares Apollo to race her to the tiny, orange lighthouse. They start running at high speed as Myrena moves ahead but Apollo catches up passing her at the end.

The two look inside the building taking a slower pace as Apollo tells Myrena that he has the SuperPower of flight being clocked at 1,800 mph.

She smiles and tells him that she also has that SuperPower but at a faster speed. She smiles saying, "The next time we race, I won't ease off you at the end."

They sprint back to their awaiting chauffeur who drives the couple to Bjarnarhöfn where the shark-museum occupies a long white building. Hanging on steel hooks from the ceiling are jawbone of Greenland sharks. The tour guide explains the biology and fermenting process being a four to five months drying undertaking for Iceland's national dish called Hákarl.

Many of the visitors are taking photographs of their SuperModel museum guest. Most ask her to pose with them, which she does not mind as she holds Apollo's hand putting him in the picture too.

After a bite of fermented shark which tastes fishy along with a shot of the famous Icelandic schnapps, Brennivin, they leave as they are still in the northern peninsula.

Heading to Kirkjufellsfoss, also known as the "Church Mountain Falls" being a pyramid shaped mountain rising over 1,519 feet with three distinct waterfalls on its left side. The church steeple shaped mountain normally takes the average person 90 minutes to hike to the top and another 90 minutes to return,

Daring Apollo again, the two SuperPower SuperFlyers arrive at the top in a minute then take a few selfies of them together. Then, after greeting a few other hikers, they race back down in a minute.

Photos of the waterfalls are taken as many visitors as possible at the falls ask Myrena for "Fanfies" (a selfie with a celebrity).

Driving to the south, they stop at the Djupalonssandur Beach where the ocean waves and non-stop winds thunder. The large, mysterious rock formations and its breathtaking coast cliffs are picturesque.

On the beach are four "Lifting rocks" weighing 50 lbs. to 342 lbs. that evaluated the strength of each fisherperson.

Myrena challenges Apollo who initially lifts only the first two rocks waiting for the SuperModel to demonstrate her strength.

He teases her saying, "Can you reel in a minnow or a marlin?"

She lifts the first rock without any effort. Then, she lifts the second and third rock easily, On the fourth rock that weighs 342 lbs. she tries to get a good grip on the rock. She maneuvers until she has a firm hold on it then slowly lifts it up to her shoulders then places it back down.

She tells Apollo, "Can you do better than a girl? Does a SuperModel have more strength than a SuperPower leader?"

In response, Apollo grabs all four rocks in his two hands and lifts all of them above his head smiling.

He gloats saying, "Are you satisfied? That deserves at least a hug and a passionate kiss," as he asks for his just reward.

Leaving the beach having relic pieces of a destroyed fishing vessel scattered all around, they travel to the Buðir black church where pitch is painted on the church's exterior wood with a white door and window frames.

Apollo joking asks Myrena, "We can end this boxing match between me and my brother if we go inside this church and get married, what do you think?"

She looks at him as though he is either joking or insane saying, "WTF! Really? We still have a few more rounds to finish."

The chauffeur tells Apollo that he has reservations at downtown Reykjavik's Michelin restaurant, 'The Ox' that has eleven seats inside its hidden restaurant. They leave for their scheduled dinner reservation.

Once parked outside 'The Ox,' the chauffeur indicates that he will be nearby in two hours to drive the couple back home.

Once inside the Michelin restaurant, they are seated.

Apollo states, "We will be having the chef selected meal with the sommelier pairing the alcohol to the course."

Myrena smiles and nods agreeing.

Beginning with a complementary rosé champagne, the chef delivers an appetizer of spicy scallops placed back in their shell with a spicy kick of wasabi.

Then, the couple is served an unfiltered, naturally sparkling Italian wine with rye bread with a bed of pickled angelica seeds with salty butter sprinkled on top.

The sommelier brings the chatting lovers an amber beer from Lady Brewery.

As the conversation continues, they discuss their thoughts and goals in leading a well-run SuperPower Organization. They agree that it is like being a general leading an army.

Then, they are brought two glasses of dry German Riesling with a plate filled with Icelandic baked cod accompanied with mussel purée, caramelized miso, and onion sauce. The main meal is paired with glasses of red Terlan Lagrein as the chef serves them Icelandic lamb and chanterelles with red beets and Icelandic raspberries, along with a side of cured, smoked, and dehydrated reindeer heart.

Feeling quite full, the chef reminds them "There is always room for dessert especially my exquisite dessert which is coming out now. I made this surprise specifically for young lovers."

The sommelier serves sparkling orange Greek wine along with Björk Icelandic liqueur infused with a birch branch, and Ethiopian brewed coffee.

The chef serves the couple his finale which is a dessert of hazelnut ice-cream and a decadent chocolate sandwich.

After giving the host his black credit card and both unable to eat a mint candy, the chauffeur drives Myrena back to her B&B living quarters.

Apollo gets out opening the door for her. They walk to her front door having her fiddle with her keys, Apollo moves his lips ninety percent towards hers. He pauses waiting for her to come the other ten percent which she does having them kiss and hug intensely.

Finally, she indicates that another date is to follow as he watches her safely enter the dwelling.

Returning to the Steele mansion, he feels confident that she will choose him as her partner.

Rocky hears Apollo singing, "Cause she's young and I'm hers and she's so beautiful, I'm gonna be with a SuperModel."

Rocky recognizes the tracks from 'Super Model' from the classic movie, "Clueless."

Rocky presses the digits on his cell hearing the familiar sound of Myrena's cell iMusic that's Lovegood Record's nuclear version of Aqua's 'Barbie Girl.'

Then, the angelic voice of Myrena says, "Good evening, Rocky. How is my adorable, love stallion tonight?"

Rocky answers, "Excellent. You can try me anytime… Whinny, neigh, Whinny, neigh," having her laugh.

He continues, "Tomorrow's adventure for us will be my secret, but I promise that it will be an experience you will cherish forever. Dress warmly."

Rocky picks up Myrena in front of her rented house.

Driving back to the Steele mansion, she is dressed in her pink Apres ski outfit telling Rocky, "The German company that made this outfit is also the official sponsor of the German ski team. Collaborating with scientists from the Mc Murdo station in Antarctica the jacket will keep me warm as many climbers have worn a similar jacket in the dead of winter on top of the summit of Everest."

He replies, "I received my jacket as a gift from Iceland's Olympic ski coach. It is a blue, men's bomber jacket displaying the Iceland flag representing Independence Day with the word 'Iceland' in red outline by white just above the left pectoralis muscle."

She comments, "You are a very sexy, patriotic suitor."

As they head down the long Cobblestone driveway, an unexpected humming sound is heard above their car.

Landing on the Steele's front lawn is a 25 million-dollar US Agusta-Westland AW 517 helicopter.

After the whirlybird lands, the pilot greets his boss, Rocky as he is introduced to the SuperModel, Myrena.

Rocky tells her, "We bought the helicopter from the UK after the third Iraq War. It has been the 'Golden Eagle' Organization air vehicle when we do not feel like using our SuperPower ability to fly."

She declares, "I could get used to this kind of life hardship that you have to endure." They both laugh.

Rocky indicates that, "This bird can accommodate up to 24 people sitting comfortably in luxury, VIP seats."

After forty-five minutes, the pilot announces, "It's time for you to start strapping on your Pinel and Pinel limited-edition skis and poles. Looking out of the window, all Myrena sees is untarnished white snow covering the mountain.

The pilot continues saying, "This is the highest peak in Northern Iceland called Kerling which is part of the Kerlingarfjöll mountain range. I will be letting you off the basalt rock mountain on its Summit which is 5,030 feet to its base." The Agusta-Westland AW 517 hovers five feet from the snow-covered summit

Rocky jumps off into the untouched white powder as he expects to help Myrena as she jumps off the helicopter.

Instead, she flies unaided cascading down the dormant white flakes.

Not to be outdone, Rocky uses his poles to rocket down the steep mountain behind her.

As they make their marks upon the newborn snow, they feel the chill in the air as they see their breath form clouds of exhaled, warm carbon dioxide.

Rocky passes Myrena.

Then, being a competitive, 'never say die' woman, she gets ahead of him.

This game is like checkers where one jumps ahead of their opponent and goes on throughout their downhill race.

Eventually they get to the bottom having them perform cross country skiing.

Rocky points out ahead of them his snowmobile.

Removing their skis, placing them securely on to the snowmobile. Rocky helps her onto the back of the mobile, but she maneuvers herself up front driving the snowmobile across the landscape.

Ahead is a 10-mile-long glacier where the two of them enjoy racing as white billowing clouds of snow form on each side and behind the vehicle. Myrena leans back against Rocky's chest.

Both of her hands are kept warm by her Titanium brand waterproof, insulated ski gloves, and securely tied jacket hood as she steers trying to scare her passenger.

The buzzing of the snowmobile's engine traveling at over hundred miles per hour as high speed winds crashing against their Flight Deck LX snow goggles.

Eventually the snowmobile approaches the Northern Lights Seven Glaciers Restaurant.

Once sitting inside the rest stop, they order a freshly brewed coffee and a latte.

There, Rocky states, "Iceland has been drinking coffee since the 1700s. To this day, we do not have the Seattle-based coffee shop since we refuse to let foreign chains into our country. Many times, the barista will create a heart out of the cream that floats on top of your coffee."

In the field outside the coffee restaurant, the helicopter lands attaching the snowmobile to the rear of the copter.

After Rocky and Myrena are seated and buckled in, they head 155 miles to the Southeast coast of Iceland to Jokulsarloon.

Calling ahead to secure reservations at the sister restaurant of the downtown Michelin restaurant in Reykjavik. The Old Harbor Glacier Restaurant welcomes Rocky and his guest.

Upon greeting the couple, the sommelier brings over two shot glasses of Brennivin. After downing Iceland's national drink which is a clear unsweetened schnapps. Rocky orders the $1,500 bottle of Chateau Lafite Rothschild which is 'the most elegant and delicate' wine in the world.

The sommelier has Rocky taste the Rothschild Lafite expectorating the mouthful of wine into the spittoon. He smiles and says, "Excellent vintage."

He comments to Myrena, "The Chateau Lafite-Rothschild is a very sleek wine. Do I detect black tea flavor with crushed fig fruit? I also detect a subtle smoke, with a taste of incense and tar."

The sommelier smiles and says, "You have quite an astute palette, Lord Steele," as he pours Myrena a glass.

The Michelin chef who recognizes her as the iMagazine cover girl and SuperModel serves the couple his special salad with seafood that contains scallops, mussels, lobster, and crab on top of arugula, and cabbage.

Myrena asks Rocky, "So tell me what kind of fiancé would you be to me? Would you try to be too controlling or would you worship the ground I walk on?"

He replies, "I will worship you. My Sun would rise and set upon you. Your words control my every action. I would worship you putting you high on my pedestal."

As the wine glasses are refilled, the Michelin chef brings out the main course explaining, "The selection, I specially prepared for you is a wonderful medley of whale, reindeer, puffin, cod tongue, monkfish with a side of lamb meatballs and fresh goat cheese."

Myrena asks, "What is this other meat?"

The chef answers, "That's horse meat."

Myrena comments, "In New York City, we call that the 'Belmont Steaks'" having everyone in the vicinity chuckle out loud.

Rocky tells her "You have an amazing sense of humor. Gorgeous and funny, what more could a man desire?"

Having finished off the entire bottle of Chateau Lafite Rothschild, they are brought dessert menus and Iceland's famous coffee.

As they are poured cream inside their coffee, two large slices of Icelandic almond cake dessert are placed in front of each of them.

The manager of the restaurant stops by inquiring as to their opinion regarding their dining experience.

He tells them, "The last two term President Bob Yarjo and his daughter who is the current President, Roberta Yarjo have dined here on three separate occasions."

After his black credit card is handed back to Rocky, they walk outside the restaurant heading to the Glacier Lagoon. From an open field near the ocean looking at the dark, clear moonless sky,

Myrena wonders what is going to happen as Rocky tells her. "An astonishing event occurs when the solar activity that has a cloud of gas is ejected from the Earth with magnetic field mixing with oxygen and nitrogen. The result of this phenomenon located in the northern hemisphere is scientifically called the 'aurora borealis' or more commonly called the Northern Lights."

Myrena witnesses shafts of light floating across the night sky with colors of green, blue, yellow, and infrequent red.

She comments, "It feels like the American Independence Day in the New York City Harbor as fireworks explode across the night sky."

Rocky says, "This phenomenon often lasts from ten at night to three in the morning."

At midnight, the awaiting AgustaWestland AW 517 helicopter flies the romantic couple who are passionately kissing sitting next to each other in plush, comfortable executive seats.

Myrena tells Rocky, "Please call me tomorrow as I am taking the day off to do some local chores by myself."

The helicopter drops Myrena off on her spacious front lawn. After she has entered her dwelling, the helicopter then drops Rocky Steele off at his family's mansion.

At midday the next morning, Professor Steele calls Myrena asking her again, "Which one of my two handsome, intelligent nephews do you prefer to date and be with?"

She tells him, "In the second competition between Apollo and Rocky, my prince and winner of my heart is Rocky."

The Professor says, "That is fine. I will inform both of my nephews of your decision ensuring that their competition for your affection has ended."

Before hanging up, Professor Steele tells her, "I would like you to come for Sunday dinner at 1 p.m. Then, afterwards we will talk about your position in the 'Golden Eagle' Organization."

Chapter 3

Pay No Attention to the Woman Behind the Curtain

At 12:45 p.m. on Sunday, Myrena enters the Steele mansion having the Professor acquire and hang up her iBay auction purchased Errea Iceland's Olympic Women's Winter jacket. She is purposely mimicking Rocky's previous day's Iceland ski jacket.

Rocky comes down to the library. He kisses Myrena and then checks out her pendent Iceland Winter Olympic jacket.

Myrena brags that she outbid three others on iBay to win it saying, "I wore it just for you," as she kisses him again.

The Professor receives the signal that dinner is about to be served from the kitchen staff. Rocky lets Myrena sit down as he, being a gentleman, pushes her chair in for her. Rocky sits on her left across from Apollo and right of the Professor who sits at the head of the table.

The housekeeper starts with the appetizer being dates, wrapped in bacon and grilled.

Myrena says, "This is absolutely delicious." Rocky and the Professor nod in agreement. Jealous Apollo nods gritting his teeth knowing that he took second place in Myrena's heart.

The valet pours everyone a glass of the perfectly paired, red, Bordeaux, Lacoste Borie Pauillac as the housekeeper serves the Icelandic lamb, and baby potatoes.

The Professor questions Myrena about her career and how it will interfere with her relationship and marriage. He tells her, "In an interview with a journalist a love expert stated, 'Every woman has the exact love life she wants.' What does that tell you?"

Myrena smiles and contemplates this.

She assures him and Rocky that her man will understand her career and devotion to him.

He asks her what SuperPower she possesses.

To which she replies, "I have no specific SuperPower. I can adapt to whatever abilities my situation requires often better than if I was born with that SuperPower. I can outrun Apollo, become invisible like my love, Rocky. Move with my superior mind objects better than Apollo and see through any substance, even difficult items that my sweet Rocky has trouble making transparent."-

The Iceland coffee and cream circulates amongst the family. The cake is sticky taffy pudding served with Icelandic Whiskey 'Flóki,' a barley harvested with Icelandic spring water liquor.

Afterwards, he invites Myrena to speak with him alone in his private office. He expresses his concern about her involvement in the 'Golden Eagle' Organization. He indicates that when she marries Rocky, she will have thirty-three percent of the vote when issues need to be judged. She thinks about her future saying, "Since the brothers know each other and think alike I must insist on at least thirty-six percent."

The Professor says, "If you prove yourself an asset, I will give it to you."

Using her mind control, charismatic SuperPower ability, she asks, "Fifty percent since the brothers will often agree with each other negating my decision."

She continues saying in her mind, "Having a fifty percent vote I insist that on a tie, I win."

The Professor demands, "On a tie, I will determine the outcome."

Unhappily, Myrena states, "Being realistic, I will be a sparkling gem in the 'Golden Eagle' crown. Hordes of men will flock to my siren voice and Helen of Troy beauty that metaphorically sailed a thousand SuperPower ships."

The Professor tells her, "Prove your worth and on your wedding morning, I will give you, my answer."

Professor Steele tells Myrena "If you can get engaged to Rocky and by next Saturday set up an entire wedding for at least three hundred guests that includes all the trimmings then I promise that I will favorably consider your request."

As Myrena goes into the other room to convince or trick Rocky into proposing to her, the Professor contacts the Bishop of Iceland who heads the Diocese of 380 Angelica Lutheran Churches.

The Professor offers his support guaranteeing to write a blank check sending all their clergy to their worldwide headquarters of the Lutheran World Federation in Chicago, Illinois.

The Professor states, "I want every Evangelical Lutheran Church to send all members of their clergy on Thursday to Chicago, Illinois where I will take care of all the expenses including the airfare, five-star hotel, organizing all the group's meals from the Continental Hotel breakfast to their dining at Chicago's best restaurants including a Chicago Pizza-fest."

For the twenty rabbis in Iceland who watch over their flock of 350 Jewish members, that Professor states, "I want to send every rabbi on Wednesday on an all-expense paid by me seven-day trip to the Holy Land complete with airfare, hotel, meals and tour guide."

The chief rabbi says, "Mazel Tov!"

The Professor continues saying, "The tour guide has promised me to take you to the Jewish cultural and historical sites such as the Western Wall which is the most sacred place in Judaism also known as the Kotel, the Western Wall tunnels which are an excavation beneath the Western Wall, the Tower of David located near the Jaffa gate in Jerusalem's Old City, the Jewish Quarter located in the Southeast section of Jerusalem's Old City where the Hurva Synagogue and four Sephardic Synagogues are located, the City of David called 'the birthplace of Jerusalem' where King David established his kingdom, Yad Vashem which is a Holocaust Memorial commemorating the victims of the Holocaust, the Israel Museum with its model of the Holy Land and the Shrine of the Book, Masada a UNESCO world heritage site which was built in the early BC's by Herod the Great, Safed which is located in Israel's North District of the city of Safed which is the center of the Kabbalah or Jewish mysticism, Independence Hall which is Tel Aviv Independence where the signing of Israel's Declaration of Independence occurred in May of 1948."

The chief rabbi, with a tear in his eyes replies, "You are my promise and my courage, guiding my helpers as I move toward healing, guard the encouragement of simple improvements every day, praising your loving concern for Professor Steele who has faithfully restored me for your namesake."

For the forty-five Catholic priests and their bishops, he sends them on an all-expense-paid week's trip to the Vatican.

Professor Steele states, "For the Catholic entourage there is a 7:30 am early morning Vatican tour through the Vatican Museum such as the Raphael Room in the Sistine Chapel with Michelangelo's painting of the Sistine Chapel's ceiling in western wall showing the creation of Adam where the 'Hand of God is seen reaching to Adams,' and Pope Julius II who constructed the Cortile Del Belvedere. Then, at 1:00 p.m. Touring St Peter's Basilica where St Peter is buried. Next day, the tour guide will take the group to the Coliseum, the Roman Forum, the Trevi Fountain, and the Piazza Navona. With an all-day meeting the following day with the Pope and his Cardinal Vicar. After that, the entire group can visit the Vatican Library, which is not open to the general public, but our tour guide has been permitted access."

Myrena asks Rocky to join her in the library as Apollo has left the residence attending to his own personal business as he sulks.

Sitting on the couch next to Rocky, she holds his hands with hers saying, "I just got off the phone with my mother's caregiver. The doctors have confirmed that she has less than a week to live. The one thing that my mother always asked me to promise her is that she would live to see me get married."

Rocky tells her, "I am deeply sorry to hear about your mother. If there is anything I can do, please let me know."

Myrena smiles and says, "As a matter of fact, there is something that you can do for me and my mother and that is to place a 10-karat diamond engagement ring on my finger and this Saturday be prepared to have a wedding. I am setting everything up in the next few days with all the trimmings and 'no holds barred.'"

Rocky smiles and says, "Is this for real or am I being Punk'd?"

She assures him, "It is for real, and everything is legitimate. In fact, your uncle, the Professor was the one who suggested it after we both heard the news about my mother."

Rocky says, "I will ask my brother Apollo to be my best man. Even though he is mad that he lost, being my twin, he will do the right thing. Then, we will buy ourselves matching $60,000 Brioni tuxedos."

Myrena tells Rocky that she has numerous cell calls and errands to make. As she leaves the Steele residence, Rocky is on the phone calling his twin brother to meet him at the tuxedo store.

Myrena in her high-tech car verbally instructs Siri to call the bishop who heads Icelandic Angelica Lutheran Church.

The bishop seems out of breath as he says, "Hello, this is Bishop Nightfor."

Myrena asks, "Are you all right, you sound out of breath?"

He answers saying, "I am running around the church in diagonals because every one of my clergy is preparing to leave for the week to visit the Lutheran World Federation headquarters in Chicago."

Myrena asks him, "What do you mean?"

The bishop replies, "Every single member of the Evangelical Lutheran clergy has won and all-expense paid trip to visit our headquarters in Chicago where we will organize a religious three-night Illinois Youth Rally."

Pretending to cry, she declares, "I am supposed to get married on Saturday. Is there anyone who can officiate my wedding?"

The bishop responds, "Not unless you plan to get married in Chicago. Perhaps the Catholic Icelandic Archdiocese can help you."

She hangs up requesting from Siri, "Call the Diocese of Reykjavik in particular the bishop." As the phone rings, she nervously starts saying, "Pick up the phone, Gosh darn it."

A woman answers the phone saying, "Reykjavik Diocese, Sister Dolores speaking."

Myrena who is a little agitated asks, "Is the bishop free?"

The sister tells her, "You are incredibly lucky to catch us, as we are all ready to visit the Vatican. One of our secret parishioners who claims to have won the EuroMillions lottery, is sponsoring all the church leaders to attend the high Holy Mass. We will not only be listening to the new Pope, but we have an audience with him on Monday."

Myrena blurts out, "You have got to be F-ing kidding me. Gosh darn-it. Sorry sister but I need to get married on Saturday. First, it is the Lutherans, followed by the Catholics. Who is available to officiate my wedding?"

The sister jokingly says, "Have you tried calling the synagogue?"

Myrena tells Siri to hang up loudly.

Running out of options, she tells Siri to call one of the two rabbis in Iceland. Getting the rabbi on the phone, she inquires, "This Saturday I am supposed to get married and the Lutheran and Catholic churches are out of town. Not just one religious person but every single member of the church that can legally officiate my wedding is leaving town."

The rabbi replies, "Unfortunately, there is a process for us to marry you. Even if you went through the entire process, our religious day is Saturday. Besides, my entire religious staff will be going to the Holy Land this week. Mazel tov. I wish you a long and prosperous marriage."

Near the capital city Reykjavík inside Bessastaðir in Garðabær, which is the presidential residence, the phone rings.

The secretary to the President answers the phone.

On the other end, Myrena asks, "I am desperate. Please I beg you to help me. Can I speak to the President?"

She asks, "Who may I say is calling?"

Myrena replies, "Myrena Gorgona on behalf of Professor Steele."

The secretary states, "The President and his husband are in Bergen, Norway enjoying their vacation."

Myrena screams stating, "What is going on this upcoming week?"

Myrena without thinking flies using her SuperPower to Bergen in Norway. There she shapeshifts into an international terrorist arriving at the hotel, she kidnaps the President and his husband using her SuperPower ability of invisibility to move the two tied up bodies into the large, desolate forests,

Looking and sounding like a Middle Eastern terrorist, Myrena flies the President and his husband to the UNESCO's World Heritage Listed 'Bryggen' that lies within a hidden world of passages.

Myrena as an international terrorist states, "I am desperate and need to raise money for our military coup. My advisors who oversee the financial ransom demands for you are negotiating with your government."

After he leaves, Myrena returns back into herself acting like she is on an adventure hiking the mountains and forests. She pretends to stumble upon the two dignitaries, freeing them.

The President of Iceland thanks Myrena stating, "If you ever need me, just ask anything and I promise to be there for you," handing her a card with his private, confidential cell number.

She asks him, "Can you officiate a wedding?"

He answers, "Absolutely, I can. Why?"

She answers, "Could you officially marry me this Saturday? It would mean the world to me."

He replies, "I need to move a few meetings around but for you I will."

Myrena tells him that she will message him the address of her wedding venue.

Myrena on her way flying home using her SuperPower ability notices that she is about to fly over the Reykjavik Marriott.

She drops down into the front sidewalk of the hotel entering through the automatic glass doors arriving at the hotel lobby. Every member of the Marriott staff immediately recognizes Myrena Gorgona the internationally famous iCover SuperModel.

She asks to see the banquet manager who immediately appears from his office.

He greets her with, "Hello, Myrena. How may I be of service to you?"

She tells him, "I need a meeting room that can accommodate between 300 to 500 people for my wedding reception."

He tells her, "This Hotel, the Marriott Nautica is the leading Iceland Conference Center that has an excellent reputation. We would be honored to host your wedding reception."

She tells him, "I assume that you are familiar with my groom-to-be, Rocky Steele who is the nephew of Professor Steele. The family owns the Steele Corporation which is an international company amongst the top 10 businesses in Iceland."

The banquet manager nods his head saying, "Everyone in Reykjavik knows the name 'Steele.'"

She continues saying, "We can proceed one of two ways; the first way is total silence about this private event including police security. The second way, in consideration of a significant discount, I would announce your fine, reputable hotel as the location of this SuperModel's marriage to her billionaire husband. I would need the largest banquet room for up to five hundred people, including hotel accommodation for the night and the classiest reception the Hotel contracted Michelin chef can prepare. At the beginning of the reception, as the guests coming from the wedding are escorted to our reception room, the cocktail hour with unlimited top shelf alcohol with a dozen serving stations having hors d'oeuvres and appetizers for thirty minutes. Afterwards all the guests will be guided to their assigned table. Each guest will enjoy their individual wedding favors as well as being given a glass of Dom Perignon."

She continues stating, "The wedding party will join the guests at the reception from the nearby waterfalls where dozens of bridal photographs of the family taken by our official wedding photographer as well as over two dozen International iMagazines."

She instructs the manager saying, "The band should have early access to set up as the two singers are inside their private dressing rooms getting ready to perform."

Thinking of her special day, she notes to the manager, "As Professor Steele escorts my mother, Keto, to the center of the dance floor. Apollo Steele, the best man, and groom's brother walking arm-in-arm with the maid of honor, Stormy Weather. Lastly and most importantly, my groom Rocky and myself will enter to a standing ovation as the band plays 'L' Invitation au voyage.'"

She brags, "Using my new family connections, I was able to book both internationally known divas Celeste Bordeaux and Rileigh Michele. These Superstars will entertain our wedding guests as well as being eye candy for the iMagazine reporters and photographers."

Myrena and the hotel banquet manager agreed to a fifty percent discount on everything that includes the spacious reception hall as well as the open bar and serving stations, and overnight lodging with a complimentary breakfast for all the guests.

Handing the hotel banquet manager Professor Steele's business card, she instructs him to send the invoice to his email as he is funding the entire wedding and honeymoon as his wedding present.

Myrena calls the ICC, iBroadcast film and television agency to book a suitable person to be her wedding day mother since her real mother died when she was ten.

Myrena Gorgona communicates by instant message with the Professor that she has completed all her wedding tasks having the Icelandic President officiate at the Reykjavik Evangelical Lutheran Church followed by the official wedding photographer taking family pictures at the waterfalls as reception guests head toward the Reykjavik Marriott where the Michelin chef will host the open bar hour with a dozen serving stations and elegant seated reception for up to 500 guests with overnight lodging provided with complimentary breakfast.

ICC helps Myrena by getting the iBroadcast show 'The Cake Chairperson' to donate the wedding cake for 750 people. The ICC also has 'Celebrity Make-Over Show' to provide free hair and make-up for the wedding attendees for their streaming show with flowers provided in exchange for free marketing and advertising in connection to the prestigious wedding.

The Professor says, "I am overly impressed with your quick work and ability to get things organized. You have done it in a timely, successful manner. The wedding, the reception, inviting all the guests especially the members from the 'Golden Eagle' Organization and business associates in Iceland and throughout the world. Excellent."

The Reykjavik Archbishop calls the Professor reporting, "On Sunday, we all sat in the front rows of St Peter's Basilica worshipping as the Pope held a special daily mass with the Eucharist led by 'His Holiness' who said to the congregation, 'We celebrate the true body and blood of Jesus Christ Our Lord as he said 'Take, eat, this is my body which is broken for you.' Then, after the entire Church partakes of the gluten-free, unleavened wafer. The Pope stated, 'Then, Christ told his disciples, drink from my cup for this is my blood of the Covenant which is poured out for many for the forgiveness of sins.' having the entire congregation drink the grape liquid representing the blood of Christ."

On Tuesday early evening, Rocky tells Myrena, "Today Apollo and I tried on the altered Brioni tuxedos. They fit like a glove, and I am not referring to Orenthal James trial glove. These glove fits so I must admit that I am guilty of loving you and will not quit."

The Steele's chauffeur drives the couple to Pickles, a Michelin restaurant dedicated to expressing the Icelandic landscape that produces fresh, organic ingredients.

The sommelier brings them two glasses of pink champagne as they peruse the menu.

Rocky orders the goose with Kjötsúpa and a summer salad.

Myrena orders a wedge salad, potato pancakes with a very tasty fish pie. The Kjötsúpa is an Icelandic meat soup that is the national dish comprised of sheep, lamb, or mutton and an assortment of root vegetables.

After eating their salads, Myrena asks Rocky, "I did not know that you enjoy eating goose?"

He tells her, "The customary Irish pre-wedding dinner with the couple that is to be wed had the entire family gathered to celebrate. This dinner is usually held the night before the wedding. The bride's family would prepare a luxurious, succulent meal of goose that sealed the deal on the marriage."

She asks, "Are you telling me that 'Your goose is cooked?'"

They laugh as Rocky gets down on one knee magically exposing a robin egg blue jewelry box having a 15-Karat diamond ring in it.

Looking into his SuperModel fiancée's green eyes he asks, "Will you enrich my life forever and marry me?"

She pauses and says "Yes" as they kiss. She looks at her left hand admiring the large round diamond ring with smaller diamonds encircling the platinum sides.

Myrena shows Rocky how much she loves him as she looks at him kissing him passionately.

He smiles telling her, "I am all yours. Be gentle," as he laughs.

In her mind she tells herself, "I used my SuperPower ability to control one's mind having Rocky subconsciously obeying my subliminal messages to marry me. I have never not gotten my way using the mind control SuperPower. It is a good thing to realize that I can influence my husband who is one of the voting members regarding the 'Golden Eagle' Organization."

She tells Rocky, "I need to take a photo of the engagement ring and send it to my mother and Stormy." She comments, "With all my efforts to get the occasion ready for this Saturday. I needed this confirmation. The Professor demanded me to hustle assuring that our wedding be amazing and worthy of being the 'wedding of the century.'" as she begins giggling.

Rocky orders coffee for them with his dessert being salted caramel ice cream.

Myrena requests a melon sorbet with a blueberry tart.

As Rocky uses his black credit card, the entire restaurant staff congratulates the couple as cell photos are digitally shot and downloaded with the caption "This 15-karat diamond ring gets you a SuperModel fiancé."

Getting up the next day, Myrena having made sure that the library is available for her as a temporary office. Using a computer printout that she acquired using her SuperPower ability to hack electronic devices. The list contains all the 'Golden Eagle' Organization members. The beginning of the list shows all the female members followed by the male members that have ratings from one to ten indicating how loyal they are to the Organization. Starting with the SuperPower females, she tells each member the same message. Her message states, "You have been invited as a 'Golden Eagle' SuperPower member to my upcoming wedding to Rocky Steele this Saturday. The Professor has promised me that before the wedding he will give me fifty percent ownership as a voting partner. If the two Steele brothers vote against me tying my fifty percent, the agreement is that the Professor breaks the tie on every even vote. If for some unusual reason, Professor Steele changes our deal, a third SuperPower Organization the 'Lemnian Deeds Federation' with its leader being me will be formed. It is finally time to have the superior gender running the SuperPower world. For too long has DODGE and the 'Golden Eagle' Organization been headed by men while the SuperPower women out number their male counterparts. We need a woman's touch. A female at the helm. A SuperPower Federation that is no longer being controlled by men."

Each day until Friday afternoon, Myrena is recruiting SuperPower individuals to support her if things go askew as the new leader of the 'Golden Eagle' Organization.

Myrena has been looking forward to having a pre-wedding, private meeting with Professor Steele. He gave her an extremely specific, difficult to accomplish task that she not only completed but she excelled performing her tasks. She is expecting to be highly compensated for it. She is confident that he will grant her a fifty-percent voting right.

On the morning of the wedding between Rocky Steele and Myrena Gorgona, the Professor meets privately with Myrena indicating that, "After careful consideration, I cannot in good faith give you more than thirty-four percent of the 'Golden Eagle' vote especially right away. Perhaps in a year or two when I feel more comfortable with you and my baby, the 'Golden Eagle Organization.'"

At the Evangelical Lutheran Church, the President of Iceland awaits the wedding processional for him to oversee. The members of the 'Golden Eagle' Organization begin filling up the church pews.

Myrena tells Stormy that her mother died years ago and that she had hired an elderly actor to pretend to be her mother.

She tells her that like 'Maggie Carpenter" played by Julia Roberts, she is on the verge of skipping out on her wedding since the Professor refuses to stick to his agreement and promises regarding her leadership.

As the organ plays the music having Professor Steele walking her fake mother down the aisle, then Apollo waits to escort Stormy Weather. Alone, he walks past the filled church of 'Golden Eagle' members. He and Rocky are standing in front of Iceland's President who is officiating.

Myrena and the maid of honor, Stormy do not appear. All the seated wedding guests turn around looking for her to enter.

Apollo whispers, "Your 'Pretty Woman' has vanished becoming a real 'Runaway Bride.'"

The Professor, Rocky and Apollo get a video cell message of Myrena apologizing that she cannot marry into a family of liars.

Then, a worldwide iBroadcast video of the Professor promising her that if she can organize an exceptional wedding within the week, he would give her half voting rights in the 'Golden Eagle' Organization.

Then, another video clip of him praising her for doing an exceptional job organizing the wedding. Getting the President to officiate, the Marriott hotel for the reception with Michelin chef prepared food and live music by the SuperPowered Divas, the overnight lodging with breakfast, and the honeymoon being a week on the lunar surface enjoying a drive on the moon by the Lunar Roving Vehicle or moon rover. The next video of the bride saying, "Sorry to Rocky but 'Love is a many SuperPower Thing.'"

The last iBroadcast clip is a close up of Myrena to the Professor quoting, "Professor Steele, remember 'Hell hath no fury like a woman scorned.'"

The contacted SuperPower individuals who agreed to join the "Lemnian Deeds" are invited to meet Myrena Gorgona in Paris after the Fashion Show.

After the Icelandic President announces, "I guess that everyone here has noticed that the bride has left the church. I must conclude that officially the wedding is not to be. The reception is paid for so go grab an excellent Michelin lunch. Remember to vote for me."

When the Professor watches the worldwide iBroadcast showing his deceit. Myrena's words, "That he is a liar, he does not trust my ability, he is putting her on equal ground with his two male nephews."

He chuckles with a poker face saying, "You are beautiful but my curse on you is that 'you will never find love.;"

Myrena realizes that the Professor is immune to her SuperPower ability of mind control. This is the first time ever that it didn't work or backfired. Myrena is outraged which was the reasoning behind her canceling the entire wedding. She reminds herself confessing "I guess the Professor claiming to me 'my word is my bond which is harder than oak' does not mean what most people think it does. To me it makes him a liar, untrustworthy, a serpent trying to seduce the first woman, forcing me to abandon anyone with the surname of 'Steele.'"

Myrena Gorgona iBroadcasts her vow, "I shall lead the SuperPower world. Soon, I will head the 'Golden Eagle Organization' and Steele Corporation."

Chapter 4

A Lemnian Deed

Myrena explains "The iDictionary defines a 'Lemnian Deed' being based on 'revenge' where there is slaughtering of all enemies."

Lemnos is a Greek island located on the northern part of the Aegean Sea. The 'Deeds' concept is thought to have originated from the epic tale of Jason and the Argonauts. According to Herodotus, the Pelasgian women performed a barbarous act by killing all their men.

Myrena seeks to establish her 'Lemnian Deeds' Federation by recruiting all SuperPower women and the inferior men, enslaving non-SuperPower women, and murdering their disobedient males.

Her 'Lemnian Deeds' Federation preaches that both DODGE and the 'Golden Eagle' Organization are both headed by men who ignore their female members' strengths and participation.

Myrena gets support from her friend Stormy Weather who recruits Pamela Braga and her girlfriend Elaine Little.

Their goal is to recruit SuperPower individuals focusing on the females but will except any willing male.

Myrena reminds the ladies to speak always addressing each person by their first name with smiles. She has printed out a script for each of them in their enlisting endeavor.

Myrena looking at her assigned list of SuperPower people to contact demonstrates her procedure.

She says, "Hello. is this, Hillary?"

After hearing a confirmation, she continues, "This is Myrena Gorgona."

Hillary says, "Oh my, are you the SuperModel that I've been reading about on all the iCover iMagazines?"

She continues saying. "As a matter of fact, yes I am. And I am extremely interested in having you become a lifetime member of the new SuperPower Federation called 'Lemnian Deeds.' I am sure you would agree to join a Federation that empowers women and is operated by women. Is this an Organization that you would like to become a member of?"

On the other end of the phone, Hillary says, "Absolutely."

She states, "We believe that a woman with your SuperPower abilities and intelligence would rather collaborate with us than with a male centric operated Organization such as DODGE or the 'Golden Eagle' Organization. Is that the direction that women like us want to participate in?"

Hillary replies, "You're right, we should have our own female-headed SuperPower Organization."

"The 'Lemnian Deeds' Federation will be calling you, Hillary as our newest lifetime member. We sincerely appreciate having you join us."

Myrena successfully hangs up the call saying, "And that is how it is done ladies. Now let each one of us go down our assigned list one name at a time having a sincere friendly chat with each new prospective member. We are here to make each SuperPower person feel important. We will not argue, criticize, insult, or say anything negative."

The entire team using colored pens of red, blue, and black begin calling as the called person is marked off. In front of their name, a black check mark is placed next to a recruit, a blue 'question mark' gets placed next to a call not answered, and a red 'X' next to a non-receptive caller which means another attempt to recruit them will be done in the future.

After a week and a half of recruiting, Myrena Gorgona notices that ninety percent of the candidates are under the age of thirty. This age bracket is easily influenced by celebrity-endorsed products and activities. She notices that after examining the SuperPower abilities of these new recruits over 75% of them have the ability to fly. Myrena contacts all the SuperFlyers inviting them to join her in Fashion Week at South Beach Miami. She communicates with each one of them saying, "Join me for an amazing week in SoBe. I promise you an all-expense paid five-star accommodations, passes to attend the fashion festivities, amazing seafood dinners, and specialized training to help the 'Lemnian Deeds' Federation."

A few days before Fashion Week, all Myrena's apprentices arrive by air and then transported by chauffeur driven stretch limousines to their five-star beachfront resort hotel.

Meeting everyone at the pool, having two-thirds SuperPowered females and one third SuperFlying males Myrena has hired Rileigh Michele and her band to sing for at the entire hotel resort.

Using her celebrity and SuperModel status, photographers from every iMagazine and iNewspaper from Miami to across the pond representing all the European countries are covering the entire event. Giving the 'Lemnian Deeds' Federation the maximum exposure, Myrena has hired her own iBroadcast production team to stream the entire event over the dark web. Throughout the live show recruiting text scrolls across the bottom of the screen.

Displayed are phrases such as "Join the 'Lemnian Deeds' Federation," "Don't be a slave to DODGE, be free with the 'Lemnian Deeds' Federation," and "At the 'Lemnian Deeds' Federation, we eat Golden Eagles for breakfast"

Each cycle of recruiting phrases ends with a static screen showing the 'Lemnian Deeds' Federation's email address and contact number. There are verbal phrases such as "We are organized and operated by females," "The 'Golden Eagle' Organization lied to Myrena, join her to fight back," and "The best and only choice for SuperPower people is the 'Lemnian Deeds' Federation."

Myrena flies her special guest by a private charter jet from the Key West International Airport to Miami International Airport then provides a chauffeur-driven limousine to the five-star beachfront resort hotel.

In her hotel suite, the married SuperPower legend who has two daughters and a son validates with her bank that her appearance fee of a half a million US dollars has been deposited.

The next day, Myrena standing in front of her entire army of SuperFlyers says "Long ago, a young teenage girl with the SuperPower ability of flight became known as the 'angel of death,' where she would strap using a harness her victim onto her back.

Then, flying hundreds of miles off the coast of Miami towards Cuba, she would push the ejection button releasing her prey plummeting into the depths of the ocean as shark bait."

Walking out of the beach cabana, Myrena announces, "Here is the South Beach Miami's original "El Angel de la Muerte" or translated in English as the "Angel of Death," Brooke Laurel." Brooke stands next to her waving at the 'Lemnian Deeds' Federation troop.

Her entire audience begins clapping as she continues saying, "For the next few days after you learn to operate the harness, you will fly high into the air with a biodegradable mannequin attached to your back releasing it from high into the air into the ocean. As the mannequin dissolves in saltwater being filled with nutritious food for the fish and sharks that live and swim below the blue surface."

Brooke tells everyone gathered, "It has been over twenty years since I have performed this baptism: as she straps the harness on herself.

Then, grabbing a biodegradable mannequin, she hops, skips, and jumps into the air.

A digital video recording drone provides live coverage on the large screen monitor on the beach. Being iBroadcast as a live, rare transmission of Brooke Laurel simulating her infamous "Sink or swim" descent.

Myrena, Brooke and their helpers pass out to each SuperFlyer their own harnesses to practice attaching it to their body and pressing the ejection button.

The next day, Myrena appears with Brooke in front of her entire assembly watching their helpers take over teaching everyone how to strap a mannequin on to their back. After an hour viewing the new recruits practicing their newly learned skill, Brooke Laurel signs autographs and wishes everyone well,

Myrena leaves to attend her fashion press conference as well as rehearsing for her runway exhibition where she will not only model her line of clothing but will be unveiling her own SuperModel collection.

The next evening, Myrena checks on all her recruits as her helpers are having them attach mannequins to their back.

Then, in a swift, upward motion each member flying high into the air hundreds of miles off the coast South Beach Miami says 'adios' to the heavy burden on their back.

Flying back to the hotel resort beach, each SuperFlyer reports on how well their mission went. With each exercise, the candidates report getting better and better, and many enjoy their newly learned skill. At night while dancing alongside the pool, many high five each other shouting 'El Angel de la Muerte' or ' Angel of Death.'

With over one hundred trained SuperFlyers, Myrena Gorgona feels confident in her Air Force that will aid the 'Lemnian Deeds' Federation in the war against DODGE and the 'Golden Eagle' Organization.

During the South Beach Miami Fashion Week, Myrena oversees her designers putting their final changes on her array of models that strut down the runway wearing Myrena's latest fashions being revealed to the world.

The event is being iBroadcast to thirty-five countries. The Gorgona Fashion production team has livestreaming capturing the backstage preparation, interviews with the designers and their models, to the celebrity attended parties. Traveling on the heels of SuperModel Myrena Gorgona are her impressively dressed models due to her influence with her Dade County luxury stores like Gucci, Louis Vuitton, and Versace.

When not attending the fashion hoopla, the 'Lemnian Deeds' Federation members study the Peruvian martial art of Bacom or Vacon.

With its emphasis on power, each attack is designed to ruin an opponent's balance. This fighting style inflicts the maximum amount of pain on one's opponent. Using armlocks, this martial art form often results in the death of the opponent.

Myrena, who has earned her black belt in Jujitsu, which Bacom is based on, watches her SuperFlyers progress each day.

She anticipates that each member will continue advancing as she finances their training with a one hundred thousand reward upon earning their black belt. Anyone who terminates a member of DODGE, or the 'Golden Eagle' Organization will earn a quarter million dollars for each life taken.

The predominately female SuperFlyer members enjoy getting an advance glimpse of the latest fashion trends, while the males do not mind viewing the young, sexy models. Afterwards, they enjoy the fantastic food, top shelf drinks, and music where both the entourage of female and male models are willing to dance with Myrena's troop.

Beginning every morning after their complimentary breakfast, Jiu Jitsu Brotherhood Master Alarcon who tells people, "My surname means 'fortress,' as I am 'a bulwark never failing.'"

Enjoying the Fashion Week's closing ceremony and party, one of the male Superflyers comments out loud "With an endless flow of banquet servers offering all kinds of hors d'oeuvres that include sushi, sashimi, prawns, and lobster tails. Thank goodness, I am amongst size zero models that aren't eating allowing me to stuff myself as they watch" letting out a sinister laugh.

Myrena gathers all her trainees after dinner telling them all to get a "Good night's sleep. Tomorrow morning, we are all going on a humanitarian mission to feed the Nouveau Pan Creation Religious Retreat attendees in Caracas Venezuela."

The next day at 7 a.m., Myrena Gorgona and all her new recruits board a private aircraft that is 1,540 miles away from their destination Caracas. Upon landing, they immediately bypass airport immigration as they are all invited guests by the President of Venezuela which is officially known as the Bolivian Republic of Venezuela. Having diplomatic immunity, they all enter a chartered bus that drives them to the religious retreat. As the 'Lemnian Deeds' Federation sets up the food for the luncheon distributing plates, cups, and utensils on each of the picnic benches.

Myrena's local male helpers mix the two five-gallon plastic beverage dispensing jug. She specifically instructs her two trusted male volunteers that the JJ's lemonade that's in the blue beverage jug is strictly for all the males. The red beverage jug containing fruit punch is to be consumed by all the females. She explains that each of these drinks lessen the sexual desires for each gender and that mixing them up is not medically advisable.

The organizer of the religious retreat Joseph Michaels announces that it is time for everyone to "Select your seat and then take your plate and beverage cup to enter the food line, selecting each item that you wish to eat."

At quarter to noon, slowly filling up all the picnic tables, are the attendees of the religious retreat. The volunteers from the Deeds Federation welcome all their guests. Each guest holding their plate and paper beverage cup waits in line. Each person in turn, decides what items are to be added to their heavy-duty paper plates. At the end of the line, are several selections of desserts.

Handing their beverage paper cup to the Deeds Federation volunteer, they are poured the beverage based on their gender.

After each of the guests are offered seconds including the desserts and the beverage, the army of the Deeds Federation cleans up.

After thanked numerous times by the attendees and finally by the leader of the religious retreat, Joseph Michaels.

Myrena Gorgona and her entire Deeds Federation of volunteers reenter the chartered bus heading back to the airport.

Onboard the charter plane, the entire group is served prime rib with Cabernet Sauvignon. The dark colored wine full body being dry and tannic is a perfect pairing to prime rib. This cut of meat is defined as the cow's rib rack cut where the first cut uses ribs ten through twelve while the second cut uses ribs six through nine.

Two days later making headlines on all the International iNewspapers and headlining the iBroadcast iChannels,

"This is Meredith Marlowe reporting from Caracas Venezuela where at a Nouveau Pan Creation religious gathering over 1,000 men and two women have suddenly died from an undetermined cause. More to follow."

One of the trusted volunteers asks Myrena Gorgona, "Did this incident have anything to do with our humanitarian mission?"

Myrena pretending to be shocked answers, "Absolutely not."

The volunteer nods her head in agreement being brought up in her youth as a devoted Catholic.

Myrena quotes to her friend Stormy stating, "The French Cistercian Monk Arnald Amalric said 'Kill Them All. God will recognize his own.' But the quote as recorded in history is 'kill them all and let God sort them out.'"

Upon further investigation by the 'Lemnian Deeds' Federation, the two women who were cremated exchanged beverage drinks with their male significant partners as they preferred lemonade over the fruit punch. Before this information exposes blame on the Federation, Myrena Gorgona interrogates her SuperFlyers who helped pour the beverages in Venezuela. Myrena uses her obtained SuperPower to fly and become invisible travels secretly to Caracas. After flying at 1,800 mph, she invisibly lands in under ninety minutes. She stealthily enters the first survivor's house. Sound asleep, she binds her victim who is in the Land of Nod.

Myrena hops, skips, and jumps reaching over two miles above the Caribbean Sea. The Venezuelan government protects all sharks in Los Roques from commercial shark fishing. The mangroves coast in the Caribbean Sea, Myrena disposes her additional baggage.

As she returns to visit the next surviving man, the first man whose wife died from the poisoned JJ lemonade wakes up plummeting into the shark infested mangroves. Planning to repeat her activity, Myrena secretly enters the second survivor's residence. As he is sound asleep, she securely gags him to silence him. Binding him onto her back, she jokingly states, "Transportation to the beach provided by the new 'Angel of Death.'"

Again, leaping into the air, she flies back to the Caribbean Sea mangroves a short distance past her first victim's 'drop zone.'

A muffled scream is barely heard as she remarks "Bon Voyage. Enjoy your trip of a lifetime." She watches him drop, hit the blue sea, and generate a maroon-colored circle around his carcass.

Myrena Gorgona, unseen flies home for a well-earned good night's rest. The iCover girl covers up her devious tracks.

Myrena Gorgona has been invited to be the keynote speaker in Vienna Austria at the "Introvert/ Extrovert National Convention." the capital city that speaks both German and English is known by several other names such as 'The City of Music' due to its past residence being Schubert, Strauss, Haydn, Beethoven, and Mozart, 'The City of Dreams' due to it being the home of Sigmund Freud the world-renowned psychoanalyst.

As a UNESCO World Heritage Site with three million inhabitants, Vienna attracts over 6.7 million tourists a year.

Myrena and her Deeds volunteer helpers pass out her business cards to the convention attendees. Those who identify themselves as extroverts receive a card marked with the capital letter 'M' that directs them to the 'Lemnian Deeds' Federation website. Receiving a similar business card, the introverted conference attendees receive a card marked with a square inside a circle.

Ms. Gorgona's goal is to get those with SuperPower abilities to join her Federation and recruit female volunteers.

On the first day of the convention after delivering her keynote speech, she plugs her 'Lemnian Deeds' Federation website and indicates that her conference volunteers are passing out her business card.

Myrena's daily updates from her office indicate numerous registered conference attendees; many indicate that they have one or two SuperPower abilities.

Myrena Gorgona has rented a chartered bus to transport her volunteers and many females who registered on her website claiming to have SuperPower abilities.

As the bus parks outside the Arena Wein, the concert promoter greets the SuperModel. She escorts the entire bus into Austria's largest indoor arena that seats over 20,000 concertgoers.

The promoter brags, "This venue was once an active slaughterhouse. Now today it will be where the world's top nuclear punk rock band Ghoti' will perform."

Myrena tells everyone that the name of the band 'fish' is the phonetic spelling of 'tough women action."

The promoter opens the velvet rope for SuperModel and fashion designer, Myrena and her group that occupy the first three rows.

As the warm-up band plays, the group begins to dance.

Finally, the entire Arena begins to applaud as the lights turn off.

Then, with an announcement that echoes around the former slaughterhouse stating, "The Arena Wein welcomes the number one nuclear punk-rock band, Fish."

Having twenty thousand excited fans applauding and screaming, the announcer continues saying "This rock concert is sponsored by the 'Lemnian Deeds Federation.'"

The applause and shouting continue especially from those sitting in the front three rows.

Myrena Gorgona flies into Amsterdam Airport Schiphol where her chauffeur gathers her luggage transporting it to his awaiting luxury limousine. The luxury stretch towncar travels 8.1 miles to her hotel.

The concierge welcomes the famous SuperModel.

The manager checks her into her penthouse suite overlooking the canal at the five-star Hard Rock Hotel Amsterdam American,

She wakes up early the next day, heading to the Rijksmuseum, the Vincent van Gogh Museum.

Myrena and her local assistants pass out flyers trying to get volunteers to join her 'Lemnian Deeds' Federation near the Rijksmuseum,

The assistants yell out, ""Friends, Amsterdammers, unstable artists, countrymen, van Gogh, lend me your ear."

From there Myrena takes half the assistants heading down the street past the Anne Frank House to De Wallen, the 'red light' district. Inside tis district are 225 window brothels as prostitution is legal having 325 licensed workers. Photographs and drinking are prohibited but cannabis smoking is allowed. There are 164 coffee shops in Amsterdam of which fourteen are in the red-light district. Amongst the windows, there are a few blue colored ones for transgender occupants,

At night, her LGBTQ volunteers pass out flyers to recruit SuperPower individuals who live an alternate lifestyle.

Myrena has learned through her connections that the anti-LGBTQ group BLAME (Biblical Liberation of Amsterdam's Moral environment) that are an organized violent, murderous Organization.

The ladies of the district joke "I would kill for a Heineken beer: as alcohol is forbidden there.

The BLAME protesters standing outside the De Wallen red light district are yelling, throwing rocks as they drink Amsterdam's best beers.

One of the ladies with the SuperPower of invisibility gets a quart container that is filled with tetrodotoxin. Tetrodotoxin is a deadly poison, a potent neurotoxin from pufferfish, porcupinefish, ocean sunfish, and triggerfish. The pufferfish extracted poison kills within twenty minutes due to respiratory failure. Each beer drinking member of BLAME gets unseen drops of tetrodotoxin or TTX added to their Amsterdam's 'to die for' cereal grains brewed beverage.

Thirty minutes later the rocks throwing has stopped, the yelling has been silenced as the BLAME members are lying face down on the pavement.

One street lady jokes, "Tell Harper Lee and her thirty million readers 'Someone has killed the mockingbird.'"

The next day, before flying home, Myrena's office tells her that fifty thousand new registrants from the Netherlands have joined the - Federation.

Myrena states "We stopped the BLAME game dead in their tracks."

Chapter 5

Dossier on '1313'

Being accidentally born to a preteen mother who had not yet gotten sterilized by the government. Her baby daughter was placed in an orphanage and given the identification of '1313.'

At age seven, she was adopted by Mr. and Mrs. Russ where the wife desperately wanted to become a mother. Traveling by car to her new home, Mrs. Russ told her "How do you like the name 'Vivian?'

The girl called '1313' who never had a real name answers "That sounds very pretty. I like that name."

Inside the house, Mrs. Russ had decorated the room in pink with stuffed animals on top of the bed. Mrs. Russ says to Vivian, "This is your room; I hope that you like the way that I decorated it for you."

Vivian smiles and nods her head indicating 'yes.'

After living with the Russ' for six months, Mr. Russ began coming home late from work intoxicated. He would often start arguing with his wife and that ended in him hitting her and leaving the house. Vivian would hear her new mother crying in her room.

Having her first birthday party becoming 8 years old, Mrs. Russ had all her classmates come to her birthday party at Mac Burgers. In the rented Mac Burgers 'party' room, the children were entertained by a magician followed by having cake. For the first time in Vivian's life, she received and opened presents on her birthday.

At the orphanage, the children would often tell stories about birthday parties and getting presents but no one had ever seen this phenomenon occur.

A week after the party, Mr. Russ again came home angry and drunk. As history repeating itself, he began arguing with his wife and started to smack her face.

This time Vivian left her room standing between the couple trying to stop the abuse. Mr. Russ grabbed Vivian, pushing her to the side so that he could hit his wife again. As his hand clinched into a fist, Vivian leaped forward grabbing his leg.

He tries to toss her like a 'rag doll' but his leg glows crimson red. He begins to age rapidly turning into a wrinkly, grey haired old man. Not knowing what had occurred, he ran out of the house. Just as he took five steps past the front door, he keeled over. Expecting his body to hit the paved driveway, it magically disappeared leaving no trace evidence of the event.

Mrs. Russ, not witnessing the event, assumed that her husband ran away never to return. She raised Vivian by herself. Getting mediocre grades and always being shy and introverted, she refused to participate in sports, always coming home after school.

Vivian enjoyed being by herself in her own room. Her mother being abandoned, supported the family with her job as a nurse. She was happy not being abused by her husband and rarely dated even though she was asked out many times. She taught Vivian self-reliance and to distrust men.

When Vivian was a senior in high school, her mother was diagnosed with an incurable disease that is hereditary. Her mother came to her High School graduation, being extremely proud that her adoptive daughter had passed the government requirements.

During that summer, her mother got worse and her pain excruciating. She begged the doctors to euthanasia her.

Often, Vivian heard her mother tell doctors to end her pain. The pain had her waking up in the middle of the night crying.

One night, Vivian walked into her mother's bedroom. There she saw her mother laying in pain having her face covered in tears.

Vivian slowly approached her bed hugging her telling her mother that she loved her. Her mother begged Vivian to help her as the pain was unbearable. She touched her mother near her heart having her entire body glow green as she vanished.

Vivian, still half-asleep, believes that she saw a fiery chariot taking her mother up into the heavens. Rubbing her eyes, Vivian looks back at the empty bed. Her mother no longer had pain as she magically disappeared.

A few days later, Vivian receives a call from a man who called himself 'Professor Steele' asking her to join his 'Golden Eagle' Organization.

She answers, "I guess so."

After hanging up the phone, it began to ring again. Vivian picked it up, hearing the voice on the other end tell her, "This is the MT Bank. We would like to inform the resident of your property that your mortgage has been completely paid off. Also, you now have an account in your name where one million dollars has been deposited."

Vivian decides to have people call her 'Vi' which is perfectly suited for her having discovered her new SuperPowers of invisibility and instant death.

The Professor sends 'Vi' Russ, a FedUp drone that contains her new assignment,

Professor Steele using his surveillance equipment to track by communication satellites where he can track all the secret communication from the dark web due to the world-class hacker skills of the Cyber Mistress. He reads his daily reports from Washington DC's Situation Room, the DODGE headquarters, worldwide syndicates, and criminals for hire. Marked in the red meaning extremely critical, the Professor notices that a disgruntled art dealer has put up one million dollars to eliminate his friend and mentor, FA-King. Professor Steele immediately alerts every member of the 'Golden Eagle' Organization to seek out and to report back to any person who accepts this contract. Each 'Golden Eagle' member using their SuperPower ability polices the globe in search of a potential assassin.

Professor Steele posts to his membership a reward of two million dollar to report the name and location of anyone with the intent to harm FA-King and apprehend the criminal.

A report comes in that one of the members of the Miami Spanish Lords has electronically via the dark web signed on to dispose of the world-famous art curator.

Professor Steele hires Vivian Russ to invisibly shadow the FA-King and using her SuperPower ability dispose of anyone intending to harm him. Vivian invisible positions herself over a hundred feet behind the FA-King. She watches intently as a young Spanish male is walking around with a petition asking people to sign it.

Walking towards FA- King, Vivian prepares herself to tackle the young man with a deadly blow. After the FA-King politely refuses to sign his petition, the young Spanish man solicits his next petition signer.

Vivian Russ, at age twenty, observes the daily activities of FA-King. She notices a Spanish male secretly watching him trying not to be seen.

As FA-King walks around town completing his daily tasks, Vivian sees the young Spanish man following him from a distance. Vivian decides to sneak up behind the young Spanish man saying "Que pasa?"

He turns around telling her in a Spanish accent, "Perderse estúpido."

She knows the translation being "Get lost, stupid." Vivian accidentally sees a concealed weapon underneath his lightweight jacket. She pretends to trip.

The Spanish man looks down at her as she grabs his leg. His whole body turns red as he disintegrates after vanishing through the Gates of Hell.

The Professor calls Vi Russ thanking her, He jokes saying, "The 'King Midas' touch turned people into 'gold,' but your touch turns people 'old' and then they disappear forever." After a jovial laugh, he reminds her that her bank account has become larger.

The Professor learns that on the vendetta list on the dark web after the FA-King's name are the names of the Pope, the President of Iran, the leader of the Islamic militant Organization, Stormy Weather, and himself. He reports to his entire membership to report any information on the assault attempts on the Pope, Stormy Weather, or himself. The rest of those to be liquidated are on their own.

The 'Golden Eagle' hired guide explains, "On the island of Marinduque in the Philippines, the Pope visits during the Lenten festival of Moriones. This annual event lasts seven days. Amongst the Passion of the Christ story, the celebrators wearing masks and costumes representing Roman soldiers and Syrian mercenaries. The actors pretend to search for Saint Longinus for the seven days. Longinus was the blind, unnamed Roman soldier who pierced the side of Jesus with his lance, a pole weapon. Religious legend suggests that upon removing his 'Spear of Destiny' from Christ's side, some blood spurted into his face, A miracle occurred that restored his eyesight having him become a believer, a Christian. This event is the basis for his Sainthood."

As they move through the crowds, the guide continues saying, "The Pope is accompanying the religious leaders as they recreate the Stations of the Cross which is also called the Way of the Cross, the Way of Sorrows, or the Via Crucis. The participants follow the actual path Jesus walked to Mount Calvary or Golgotha where Christ was crucified on the cross."

The papal congregation walks behind the 'Christ' carrying his cross as Roman centurions forcefully tug at the connected ropes.

The Pope waves to the spectators enjoying the ninety-degree Fahrenheit weather.

The guide states, "The population of the Philippines has eighty-nine percent being devoted Catholics. The festival spectators wear shorts with many digital cameras and camcorders recording the events. We encourage web videos, Podcasts and blogs to promote our island and festival."

Unbeknownst to anyone outside the 'Golden Eagle' Organization, Vivian Russ is in the crowd walking passionately from the sidelines with the tormented 'Christ' actor. She is constantly scanning the others in the crowd believing that there is an assassin among them.

The Professor had developed a special EMF-detector to locate today's ghosts known as 'invisibility' ability SuperPower people.

Vivian awaits to feel a vibration from this device as she proceeds along the Way of the Cross.

A Roman soldier pretends to flog the cross carrying 'Christ.' As other masked soldiers laugh and poke fun at the rabbi who called himself the 'King of the Jews.'

Vivian notices that many of the Filipinos in the crowd are sweating using towels to dry themselves off as they drink cold, bottled water.

On top of a skull-shaped hill, three crosses with men appear in the air. One of the two thieves ridicules the actor 'Christ' while the other thief begs for forgiveness.

As millions are mesmerized by the performance both in person and viewing on the iBroadcast iChannels, Vivian Russ feels a strong vibration from her special EMF-detector.

She walks around the nearby crowd until the device is screaming.

As the actor in a gold costume playing Longinus blindly stabs 'Christ' in his side confirming his death, an invisible man carrying a SIG SAUER P517 micro-compact 9mm semi-automatic pistol is discovered by Vivian. Before he can get into a proper stance with his target in sight,

Vi Russ is able to grab his right shoulder. The man screams out turning his head towards her. His neck, shoulder and arm turn red as he disintegrates. His powdered remnants fall into an opened hole underneath where his feet once stood.

Quoting from the Bible, the actor playing 'Jesus,' states, "I am thirsty." The soldier placing a jar of wine vinegar soaked in a sponge puts the porous substance on a hyssop plant stalk lifting it to Jesus' lips. When he had finished receiving the drink, he said, "It is finished," bowing his head and giving up his spirit.

The Pope is kneeling in front of the dead crucified 'Christ' as other actor soldiers remove the body from the cross. The entire faithful Catholic crowd of over six million follow in respect to their religious leader by kneeling.

On the iBroadcast, the Philippine's Archbishop is heard praying, "Keep our Pope safe from my mouth to God's ears. Amen."

Vivian is praised for her efforts as the Steele brothers had desecrated the first Pope's remains under Saint Peter's Basilica.

Helping the 'Golden Eagle' Organization, Vivian Russ joins forces with the next assassination target, Stormy Weather.

Stormy tells Vivian, "No one, not even God is going to rain on my parade," as the two laugh.

The two attend a LGBTQ party where rumor has been revealed to the Steele brothers that an attempt on Stormy's life is highly possible. Throughout the affair, the two SuperPower ladies tell each other who is familiar and who is a stranger to them.

Stormy kisses one lady who jumps back. They become suspicious of her and keep a close eye on her.

Later, another lady is very friendly with her being very touchy-feely. She becomes another suspect. She hugs Stormy and kisses her many times.

Stormy tells her, "Come! We are ready for the floor show!"

All the rainbow clan gather around the transgender cabaret singer who is dressed like Dr. Frank-N-Furter from the 'Rocky Horror Picture Show.'

The sweet transvestite sings "Time is fleeting. Madness takes its toll." The entire club dances singing "Let's do the time warp again" as they step to the left then to their right. They place their hands on their hips. Then, pressing both knees together ending with a midsection forward thrust.

After the thunderous applause, the group pretends to faint having the singer state, "We certainly do not need a 'Shock Treatment.'"

Next, the entertainment performs a magician's quick-change maneuver appearing in a gold dress. They impersonate the classic Katy Perry singing "I Kissed a Girl." The audience joins in singing, "I kissed a girl, and I liked it."

Everyone takes out their lip balm tube rubbing the tip against the lips of their partner or partner for the night as the singer bellows, "The taste of her cherry Chapstick." The interested pairing begins to embrace and kiss exchanging flavors. Everyone cheers yelling, "We loved it."

Vivian chats with a gay man, Freddie who is excited to meet the legendary Stormy who got the bill passed to change one's information on government papers and licenses.

Vivian invites him to meet Stormy. She is holding his arm as they walk through the crowd. She notices that Freddie knows a lot about Stormy and her history. She fears that something is off but remains silent.

As Vivian introduces Freddie to Stormy, he smiles shouting, "Sic semper tyrannis!"

Stormy stands sideways knowing that 'Thus ever to tyrants!' was stated by Brutus as he delivered the knife blow to Julius Caesar and said to Abraham Lincoln by John Wilkes Booth.

Without hesitation, he reveals a Samurai hand forged, sharpened high carbon steel blade- with bloodgroove for a faster and lighter sword.

Stormy hits the assailant with a lightning bolt of one billion joules of energy.

Freddie yells "Oh, rat fart!"

Vivian, still holding his arm, turns his body red. His entire body glows crimson, turning into a silver color. Like mercury, Freddie is liquified flowing downward into an automatic portal to the abyss.

Stormy exclaims, "Another one bites the dust!"

Last on the assassination list is the name 'Professor Steele.' Vivian Russ moves into his mansion in Reykjavik occupying a guest room.

The Professor tells her, "I am no stranger to death; we have traveled the same roads together many times" as he laughs. The two take daily walks around the city. Many citizens greet him as he is a local hero and legend.

The 'Golden Eagle' Organization has its staff checking everyone who enters the country by land, sea, and air. A database in conjunction with the country's systems that provides passport and government identification on everyone entering and exiting Iceland. Reports are scanned daily for those lodging in hotel, motel, and B&Bs. People renting vehicles, boats, motorcycles, and bikes are relayed to the Organization members protecting their beloved leader.

The highway scanners record transportation vehicles, and every cell phone are tracked with each second's GPS position.

The Professor jokes states, "We saved the Pope, now we need to save 'God.'"

Professor Steele tells his two nephews Rocky and Apollo to pack their overnight bags as he has arranged a world class celebration.

As the twins begin packing, Vivian Russ enters the kitchen to grab a bottle of unaltered Tuocon sparkling water. The Professor updates her on his plans. Vivian with her water bottle in hand returns to her room to pack an overnight bag.

As Apollo and Rocky Steele have their Tumi extended trip wheeled packing case. Holding in their other hand, they carry their tuxedos inside their protective garment bag.

As Vivian walks down the stairs, the Professor presents her with a red Valentino Haute Couture dress with red Jimmy Choo Crystal pump shoes. The Professor helps Vivian place her dress and shoes inside a soft-sided garment bag.

Waiting outside the Professor's mansion is their chauffeur-driven limousine that will transport the four passengers to Reykjavik International Airport.

As each of them enters the back of the limousine, the chauffeur places all their luggage inside its spacious trunk.

Arriving at the Icelandair terminal, the concierge takes their luggage. Professor Steele and his three guests enter the register travel program gate that verifies their identities using biometric security avoiding the TSA line.

Walking towards their gate, Apollo Steele asks his uncle, "Can we get a hint as to our destination? Perhaps a glimpse regarding what we will be celebrating?"

The Professor remains silent handing each of them their first-class tickets.

Onboard the Steele brothers order themselves a glass of Brennivin. For Vivian, they order the sambuca-like flavor drought which has a taste of cumin, caraway, and dill. The boys who have spent many a night blacked out by drinking more than their limit having an accompanying shot of clear schnapps which is known as 'Black Death.'

The Professor has ordered in advance a $2,200 US bottle from Northeast Scotland. The bottle of Macallan Sherry Oak 12year-old Scotch is a rich body, mature whiskey having a wood spice with dried fruit aroma.

The younger generation shares bags of pretzels and chips downing their drinks.

The Professor orders a deluxe fruit plate with crackers.

Professor Steele looks into Vivian's eyes and says, "I want you to understand Vi that I see a girl that is full of life, but her life is filled with death. Always remember to keep these two aspects of you separate."

After landing at the Paris Charles-de-Gaulle Airport, the hired chauffeur gathers their luggage driving everyone to the Hotel des Arts, a five-star hotel.

After checking into the hotel and changing into their tuxedos or Valentino red dress with matching shoes, everyone meets in the lobby.

The chauffeur escorts the group to the limousine opening the rear passenger door for everyone to be comfortably seated.

The driver tells them, "We are headed to the one-star Michelin restaurant located at quaint De la Tournelle in Paris. This is the location of 'The Silver Tower.' the historic restaurant known to Parisians as 'La Tour d' Argent.'"

Claiming to be an over four-hundred-year-old establishment, the restaurant has served famous patrons where a postcard is marked with the served bird's serial number.

The Professor states, "Past palettes who enjoyed the restaurant's own farm raised ducks belong to the U.S. President Franklin Delano Roosevelt, Marlene Dietrich, Charlie Chaplin, Ernest Hemingway, father and daughter U.S. Presidents Bob and Roberta Yarjo."

Joining the Professor for an evening of scrumptious waterfowl delight are Oregon's Oliver Davis, Stormy Weather, Astrid Christensen, and a special guest, FA-King.

After a delightful dinner, Astrid morphs into a duplicate of Professor Steele. Vivian becomes an invisible scout for potential threats behind the group as Stormy rises 150 feet above the street being overhead and in front of the Steeles and FA-King.

Professor Steele tells his old friend FA-King, "My life is a series of cheating death."

FA-King replies, "Let us keep that true for the both of us."

Oliver Davis holds invisible Vivian's hand as he flies at 1,500 mph high above alongside the Parisian clouds.

In the northwestern part, above Cathedrale Notre-Dame de Paris lying in a prone position is a man holding a Thor REP517 long range rifle.

With supersonic speed, Oliver 'The Merc' Davis catapults the visible Vivian landing on top of the sniper's back. She places her hands on either side of his head having it explode like a pumpkin on gate night filled with M-80s which are large powerful firecrackers. The rifle and its solid projectiles disintegrate as the headless body lies face down.

As a joke, Oliver puts a large boulder under the cadaver's shirt between the shoulder blades or scapula to resemble Victor Hugo's 'The Hunchback of Notre-Dame.'

The Professor remarks to the FA-King, "In playing chess with Death, I have gambled claiming that 'after checkmating him, I will be set free.'"

The next morning, all the guests of Professor Steele enjoy a buffet gourmet breakfast inside the hotel's historic basement dining room that still has its original stone walls.

After the younger attendees have devoured dozens of freshly baked croissants, yogurt with granola chips, avocado toast, 'cafe crème' also called a 'café au lait' being a latte like coffee.

The Professor and FA-King enjoy a glass of Chambord that is a cognac with a raspberry, blackberry, and vanilla flavor.

Accompanying the liquor created by Louis XIV in 1685 while visiting the Château de Chambord in the Loire Valley, the older generation orders poached egg Benedict with cooked ham, several strips of crispy bacon, two Lincolnshire pork sausages, and a basket of baguettes served with sliced cheese and butter.

Everyone exits the restaurant as the chauffeur opens the rear door of the large luxury limousine.

The Professor and FA-King stay behind to properly thank the hotelier and the restaurant's executive chef.

FA-King excuses himself to use the facilities before traveling to London to lecture at the Royal Academy of Arts.

The Professor exits the building's white Lutetian limestone facade. He notices a shiny metal object reflecting the sun's glare from across the street. He looks and quietly signals in that direction. Professor Steele notices a well-dressed man wearing a suit holding a portable rocket launcher which is a bazooka like weapon. The assassin immediately launches a projectile, the rear propellant gas expelled weapon that has no axonal force from the forward rocket launching 380 mm projectile.

Everyone seated inside the large luxury limousine witnesses the large rocket projectile passing through the Professor's chest.

As all his internal organs explode covering the white Lutetian limestone facade in a 14-yard blast radius.

The hired assassin performs a ninja-like technique jumping inside a FedUp delivery truck that races down the street.

Being evaluated numerous times throughout his academic career, Professor Steele has been evaluated using the 'six-sigma' normal curve for intelligence quotient or IQ scoring the highest possible having an IQ beyond 180.

The friends and relatives of the Professor observe that where his body once stood, a large pile of ashes is present.

Suddenly the crimson colored white Lutetian limestone facade has miraculously return to its former state. Underneath the two-foot-high pile of ashes, there is something moving.

Concerned, Apollo and Rocky Steele emerge from the large luxury limousine. They see a human right hand moving upward from the pile of ashes.

Apollo grabs the hand using his two hands. As the left hand emerges, his brother Rocky uses his two hands to pull it up. The two brothers lift with all their strength.

Just like when a phoenix dies, it is reborn from the ashes, Professor Steele is once again standing unharmed outside Hotel De Arts' entrance.

Apollo and Rocky Steele carefully examine their uncle from head to toe. As everything seems to be back in order, they notice that the Professor looks twenty years younger.

The Professor sits in the front passenger seat where the limousine chauffeur closes his door. The entire 'Golden Eagle' Organization Parisian gathering is driven to the International Airport. After saying their goodbyes, each guest heads to their gate flight staff to get their ticket to fly back home.

In first class, Professor Steele sits next to Vivian and across the aisle from his two nephews. He is reading the Reykjavík Grapevine iNews and drinking his chocolate milk shake and the youth order Opal red liqueur made of herbs and liquor.

In front of her walking to the restroom, a man stops dead in his tracks staring at the Professor. Vivian realizes that he is the paid assassin that successfully disintegrated the Professor before his rebirth ability.

Stunned, the standing assassin is frozen being ignorant that Vivian, now visible, is seated next to him.

She grabs his rear end, having his entire body turn crimson before he vanishes without a trace.

Vi Russ continues to sit next to the Professor enjoying her frozen strawberry milk shake as though nothing unordinary has occurred,

The Professor smiles as he turns the electronic iNews page to read.

Chapter 6

Dossier on Star Kronika

Running down the hall Star Kronika is late for another one of her college classes. She keeps telling herself, "If I had a Star Trek transporter, I probably would still be late." She sits down in her class knowing that in the next hour the only thing between her and graduating is her final exams.

On her way back to her dorms, she listens to the iMusic nuclear band version of the old Geffen Records song by Cher "If I Could Turn Back Time." Listening, she tells herself, "That's my life's dream, to be a SuperPower person with the ability to move forward and backwards through time."

After taking her last final exam, Star Kronika waits on an exceedingly lengthy line seeking to purchase a general admission ticket to listen to her favorite nuclear band,

Standing at the very end of a line that goes around the building and through to the ticket booth. Having her left leg get restless, Star kicks it with her right leg. First kicking her right toe against her left heel. Then, kicking her right heel against her left toe. Finally kicking the side of her right foot against the opposite side of her left foot. She looks at her watch trying to estimate when she will be done so that she can get some pizza for dinner. She is confused and astonished that the clock on her wrist iCommunicator that normally increments every second has stopped. She looks add the people in front of her in line and they seem motionless. She starts to walk forward to the front of the line.

She notices that one young man has dropped his can of soda which is froze mid fall. Another couple standing in line are kissing. They seem petrified and unable to even blink. Another student who is in her English class, looks like a mannequin as Star takes out her mirror putting it under his nose. This is a tactic often used by medical professionals to check if the patient is alive where the mirror will fog up confirming that they are.

Looking at her mirror and seeing no changes, she says, "Moe Greene is dead. Although he may be frozen in time."

Star Kronika walks all the way forward to the ticket booth and stands in front of everyone knowing that she is the next person to be served.

Using her right foot to kick her left foot, her entire world comes alive again. She hears the can of soda hit the ground just as the ticket salesperson announces, "Next."

After eating two slices of pizza and a salad, Star gets an anonymous call. On the other end, a man states, "Hello, Star Kronika. This is Professor Steele."

Star says, "How in the world did you get my number?"

The Professor tells her, "Let me be the first to congratulate you on graduating Summa cum Laude. That means that your four years of undergraduate studies in all your classes you earned straight 'A's.'"

Star replies, "Really? How did I ever do that?"

The Professor tells her, "Star, you have a special SuperPower ability and to further educate you, I would suggest that on your way back to the dorms that you 'hop, skip, and jump.'"

Star says, "You say to 'hop, skip, and jump." Still on the call, she performs a hop, skip, and jump. Instantly, she rockets upward and past the clouds.

She hears coming from her phone the Professor saying, "Now that you are over a thousand feet above your campus, you realize your two SuperPower abilities; to freeze time and fly. I will be in touch with you very soon for a special mission. As soon as you can call your bank to verify your new account balance. Ciao, Star Kronika."

The day after the concert Star is on the phone with her best friend telling her, "Last night the 'Little Boy' iNuclear rock concert was out of this world. Everyone around me agreed that it was the best concert that they had ever been to. The section I purchased was standing room only able to force my way forward standing by the edge of the stage. I even got to shake hands with several members of the band."

Just then she hears a beep indicating that someone is trying to reach her. Star tells her friend that she will call her back.

Star picks up the other lines saying, "Hello?"

The caller replies, "Star, this is Stormy Weather. The Professor gave me your number. Could you meet me in Chicago at the Chicago Millennium Park Fairmont Hotel? Your tickets will be waiting at the check-in. Tomorrow at 10 a.m., an Uber will pick you up to take you to the nearest airport."

Star Kronika packs her suitcase to spend the weekend in the 'Windy City.'

Arriving at the airport, Star approaches the ticket counter indicating 'Will Call' giving the check-in lady her driver's license for her identification. Her ticket is processed by having her one small suitcase tossed onto the baggage conveyor belt with her flight information attached. Star checks her ticket and to her surprise, she has a first-class ticket with an accompanying drink and ten-dollar snack voucher.

Waiting at her gate, Star is watching a young mother with her three children wait for her husband to arrive. She looks worn out and under motherly stress.

Star feels bad for her as she watches her husband deplane kissing her and the children. He grabs the hands of his children which brings a smile onto his wife's face.

The children demand to eat at Mac Burgers to which their father tells them, "After I get my suitcase, we can all enjoy a 'jolly' meal at Mac Burgers." The happy family exits through the concourse.

The gate agent announces that "The first-class passengers may board the plane."

Star Kronika stands up as she proudly hands the agent her ticket. Getting the processed ticket and her boarding pass back, she places it with her voucher inside the paper ticket holder. Entering the aircraft turning left towards first class, Star smiles as she looks at her luxurious, spacious seat.

The flight attendant asks her, "Would you like a complimentary drink?"

Star replies, "May I have a Bailey's Irish Cream on the rocks."

The drink is brought to her as she looks over the plastic food and drink menu. Star decides in-flight to use her drink voucher to get a Cranapple Finlandia Vodka Cocktail with a turkey sandwich, fruit, and cheese plate with cheesy fish snacks.

After the pre-flight safety instructions is shown on her seat's monitor, she watches the iMusic Channel until her gratis lunch remains are disposed of as the announcement of their landing is heard.

After landing at Chicago O'Hare Airport, Star departs walking towards her flight's baggage claim. Walking through the concourse, she notices a husband kissing his wife goodbye as he boards his flight. She and her three small children wave goodbye as the man waves back disappearing down the jetway.

Star notices as the woman and her three toddlers walk past the frozen treat kiosk, the youngsters excitedly begin wanting soft serve ice cream.

She hears the mother explain, "I'm sorry but I do not have money to buy anything."

Feeling bad for the mother, Star blinks her eyes three times.

The entire airport terminal appears to be in suspended animation.

Star walks around the petrified people opening the door to the soft serve ice cream kiosk. She grabs four ice cream cones filling each one up with a soft serve swirl of vanilla and chocolate ice cream.

Then, returning into the concourse in front of the kiosk, she carefully places in each of the children and their mother's hand each cone.

As she walks away towards the baggage claim, she blinks again three times rapidly. The entire concourse comes alive.

Magically, the mother and her three young children are amazed as they begin to slowly lick each side of their delicious, sweet dessert.

Meeting Star Kronika at her baggage claim is Stormy Weather. Stormy has an Uber waiting outside the terminal to take the duo to the Fairmont Hotel for their annual LGBTQ fundraiser.

The Gay iChannel indicates that last year's Gala raised over 2.5 million dollars US.

That night, Stormy takes Star to the Gastro Pub restaurant located inside the Fairmont Hotel.

Stormy asks the waiter, "What Chicago beer would you recommend?"

He tells her, "The 312 Lemonade Shandy from the local Goose Island Beer Company is popular. It tastes like a lemon Italian ice beer."

The ladies order a glass to start. Discussing local cuisine, the duo agrees to order a vegetarian 14-inch Chicago style thick crust pizza with two Chi-Greek salads.

Stormy asks Star "Do you know why Chicago is nicknamed the 'Windy City?'"

Star guesses, "Because people get blown away by the gusts of air which I hear is an everyday occurrence here."

Stormy chuckles and states, "Although a lot of Chi-town residents believe the famous myth that the nickname was from the World's Fair since the late 1800's one of the more accurate reasons is politics. The politicians in Chicago were known to be profit centric as the competition for state feuding between New York City and Chicago grew among journalists."

Just then, arriving is their hot, aromatic Chicago style thick-crust pizza and two Chi-Greek salads consisting of whipped feta, cucumber, cured tomatoes, olives, oregano with Greek dressing.

The two hungry SuperPower members of the 'Golden Eagle' Organization slowly devour their salads followed by half a pizza pie each.

Stormy admits, "Most men are ignorant not knowing that women can eat a lot of food just not in full public view."

After downing their fourth glass of lemon ice beer, Stormy hands their waiter her black credit card.

The two of them will be selling silent auction tickets all day before they attend the black-tie dinner party for hundreds of wealthy patrons as they dance to the live entertainment.

As the hosts are successfully selling hundreds of dollars of raffle tickets and silent auction bids, every hour Stormy sends Star into the Counting Room to drop off everyone's collected money.

Star walks into the Counting Room handing the event's treasurer the collected monies from everyone working on the floor.

She gets a receipt signed by her and returns to her station after dropping off the receipt with the floor supervisor.

With two hours to go before the black-tie dinner with live entertainment, Star walks into the Counting Room.

Forcefully busting in behind her are six armed thieves wearing masks of the ex-presidents. The robber wearing ex-president Bob Yarjo's mask grabs Star yelling, "Turn over all of the cash unless you want everyone to get shot," as he fires off around of over a dozen projectiles from his laser blaster.

Star blinking her eyes three times freezes everyone in the room as every projectile appears motionless in mid-air. She frees herself from the leader's grip.

Then, she walks over to each of the volunteers who are counting the LGBTQ fundraiser donations freeing them and moving them to a safe location. Star returns sitting in front of the dozen frozen projectiles like Neo.

Star says, "Bullet time" as she laughs using both of her hands to maneuver each projectile setting them on a course in the direction of each of the six assailants.

Once every projectile is aimed at each of the six robbers, she blinks another three times rapidly.

As the unexpected fundraising volunteers begin to yell, all the projectile's launch in the direction of each of the marauders.

One by one, they plummet to the floor.

The event's security enters the Counting Room confirming that each of the assailants is dead.

Before anyone explains what happened, Star exits the room leaving behind all the latest donations.

Star finds Stormy telling her that she will be getting ready in her fanciest gown to attend the LGBTQ black-tie dinner party.

Meeting each other in the hotel lobby, Stormy tells Star that she will protect her from others who prey on "Baby dykes and Newbies."

Star says, "Thanks, but I prefer men."

Stormy comments, "We all did at one time in our lives. Relax and open your eyes to the entire world of dating," as she laughs.

Star replies, "I am open and not prejudice as I support whole heartedly the LGBTQ community. I believe and value everyone's choice. Hopefully, all will accept my choice."

They walk into the fancy gala as there are men dancing with each other. Women kissing and enjoying Latin dances.

Star sees a variety of ladies dancing with each other.

Stormy becomes her mentor verbally pointing out the diverse types of lesbians,

Stormy tells Star, "Over there is a 'femme' or 'lipstick' lesbian, Against the bar are a couple of butch lesbians. Discussing politics are your 'activist' lesbians. Hard to tell but there are a few chapstick lesbians who one day prefer to be femme and the next day are butch."

Star nods as she is being educated.

Stormy continues telling her, "Then, there are 'stone butch' and 'stone femme.' These lesbians enjoy giving pleasure but resist receiving any, then there are those more like me called 'hasbian' lesbians. We follow our own heart and desires dating both men and women as the mood strikes us. Over there are a few 'boi' lesbians. They look, dress, and act like young boys but down under they are all female."

Stormy points to a few ladies sitting near the bar wearing expensive designer outfits. She says, "The ladies over there are most likely lawyers, doctors, or CEOs being members of the 'power' lesbians."

Turning towards Star, she comments, "You could be a LUG lesbian which stands for 'Lesbian Until Graduation.' An experimenting collegiate female who may get married and have a family someday or not. The 'alpha' lesbian is your cheerleader or class president that is labeled 'cool.' Then, there is the 'lone star' lesbian who either tried a relationship with a man but came back or has only had one serious lesbian relationship."

Stormy walks around looking at her prospects for the night.

A well-dressed man approaches Star saying, "I heard that you saved this year's LGBTQ fundraiser event."

Star smiles and replies, "Who told you that?"

He says, "My name is Ronald Primrose the third. I am the CEO of a major Chicago airline corporation."

Star smiles and says, "Nice to meet you. I am Star Kronika, a recent college graduate. I am here with my friend, Stormy Weather who says she dates both men and women."

Ronald tells her, "Just for the record, I am a straight male although I fully support everyone's choice. My mother is the chairperson for this event which throughout the many years my company and myself financially support the LGBTQ community."

Star states, "For the record, I have not decided where I belong but to date, I have enjoyed the relationships that I have had with men."

Ronald asks her, "Would you like to dance?"

Star Kronika nods as Ronald leads her to the center of the dance floor.

He tells her, "As a teen my mother forced me to take dance lessons which I resisted but now I am grateful for the lessons."

On the dance floor as Latin style music is played, Star smiles as she takes her left leg forward, then back together. Moving her right leg back and then together. Swinging her hips back and forth creating the figure-eight motion. Bending one knee while keeping the other leg straight and then switching bending the other knee to an 8-count.

Ronald is pleasantly surprised asking her, "Where did you learn how to dance?"

Star confesses, "Growing up my best friend's mother owned a dance studio. I used to watch as a young child adults practicing in her studio. Memorizing every one of their choreographed steps, I was able to enter and win several competitions. Then, I enrolled for a huge discount taking classes after school every day."

Ronald and Star enjoy the entire night together and in-between each break, they enjoy the different hors d'oeuvres that the wait staff are serving while drinking champagne.

In the meantime, Stormy has brought several female acquaintances into her hotel room having the party continue.

The next day Stormy and Star take an Uber to Chicago O'Hare Airport.

Star admits to Stormy, "I am not quite sure if I should fly back to my college or back to where I grew up."

Stormy tells her, "Have you heard of the famous SuperModel, Myrena Gorgona?"

Star being puzzled states, "Of course I have. Everyone has, why?"

Stormy takes Star's hand walking her to the Parisian Airline's counter where she purchases two first-class tickets.

Stormy takes out her cell phone and dials. Star hears her say, "Bonjour Myrena. Nous venons pour une visite.'

Star who took French throughout her schooling knows the English translation is "We come for a visit."

Chapter 7

Dossier of Olympia Gort

Working in the Tokyo Robotic Laboratory, hardware genius Dr. Hiroshi Gort attempts to make a few small adjustments to their prototype AI female assistant. His wife, Dr. Yoko, the brain behind the complex algorithmic software, has just finished downloading her latest patch into the prototype's memory.

Dr. Hiroshi Gort hopes that this trial of 'Test C-2' does not malfunction like the previous three versions had done. Giving his wife the thumbs up to start running the test script that checks every possible scenario for the AI inside the female assistant.

Standing next to the female assistant robot, Dr. Hiroshi closely checks each movement making sure that the robotic assistant reacts like a human would.

Dr Yoko Gort tells her postgraduate comp sci classes, "Passing the 'Turing test' which is a test of a robot's ability to exhibit intelligent behavior equivalent or indistinguishable from that of a human."

Each step in the process as the robot proceeds through each scripted movement, Dr. Hiroshi checks his list of actions placing a check mark in front of each one.

The next few robotic actions require one foot and then the other followed by jumping in the air with both feet. He begins walking in a circle around the female robot as these actions are being performed. Suddenly, the robot missteps causing it to spark and then explode.

Dr. Yoko Gort runs into the laboratory with a fire extinguisher, but it is too late. Her husband has been completely consumed in the explosion and engulfed in the fire that followed.

A year later in memory of her late husband, Dr. Yoko Gort decides to use her husband's stored semen to impregnate her frozen eggs in vitro. Nine months later, a beautiful Japanese girl is born being named 'Olympia.'

Olympia Gort excels at school, especially in her math and technology classes where she is building high tech racing robots.

On the iBroadcast show that mimics the 20th century amusement ride called 'bumper cars,' she develops a sophisticated AI robot that's sole purpose is to destroy its opponent and become the 'King of the Hill.'

Her mother has taught her about programming and software algorithms which she is now significantly more advanced often confusing her mother talking about new theories on software and hardware.

At thirteen years old attending the University, she has teamed up with two other doctoral candidate students from the Tokyo University working on their PhD thesis in robotic research.

Each week on the international iBroadcast show, Olympia and her team dedicated to her father named 'Hiroshi,' easily defeat all adversaries that enter the 'Tobor Arena.'

Olympia claims that she can interface her human body with any energy source such as electrical, mechanical or this case, 'robotically.' If a fire breaks out like one did killing her father, she can become invisible.

For the last three seasons competing in the 'Tobor Arena,' team 'Hiroshi' has won the prestigious 'Golden Microchip' trophy.

Tokyo University has given Olympia and her team doctorates in robotic engineering even though Olympia had just turned 16 years old.

Olympia Gort as a four-year-old was always viewing on her recorded microchip by her mother Ray Bradbury's 'The Electric Grandmother' which based on his science fiction short story 'I Sing the Body Electric.' Similar recorded microchip film first by comic legend, Robin Williams playing in the original 'Bicentennial Man,' which has recently been remade with Oscar winner Robert Leach.

Olympia's lifelong dream has always been to design such an Android programmed for household tasks. She especially enjoys the fact that as the children grew older and had children of their own, the Android caregiver could still recall through playback recorded audio and microchip digital events and scenes throughout every event witnessed by the android.

Olympia Gort receives an endless research grant from Professor Steele and his 'Golden Eagle' Organization.

Dr. Olympia Gort and her team have been working on developing an 'emotional microchip.' Their goal is to get an honest, heartfelt response to the question, "How are you feeling right now," from their android.

The factory demonstration android units can already record and playback any event that it has seen, access in real time each worldwide server that hosts a yottabyte of data. Each Android accessing the latest Watson AI technology can perform simplistic to the most intense surgical operations, diagnose the most common to the rarest disease or ailment reporting immediately to the Worldwide Center for Disease Control.

Accessing the International Dental Database, any android can tend to any mammal's teeth issue and repair such as any defects such as cavities, erosion, gum disease, a broken or cracked tooth, or an abscessed tooth.

Olympia's team has made some advancements to the 'emotional microchip' such as if one is speaking harshly to the Android or slaps it on its face, rear, or hand, it is programmed to shed a cheer or two as its face turns a shade of red.

On her staff are several psychiatrists and behavioral scientists who are ensuring that each android having the 'emotional microchip' reacts and combines verbal responses with accurate body language.

Olympia gets an anonymous email telling her that there is a land that few can visit where the roads are paved in gold like the legendary city of Eldorado. There, a wizard has granted certain visitors' mechanical organs that can transform inanimate objects into living beings with functioning microchips that replace the brain and emotional heart. She enters the cyberspace wormhole following the white rabbit.

There she is confronted by a kaleidoscope of images as she falls downward. Upon crashing into a large cushiony mushroom, she stands up looking at her venue. In front of her are chess pieces blocking her every move. Olympia sacrifices her queen announcing mate in three moves. The board opens a path for her to pass by.

Olympia walks down the one-way road entering a cul-de-sac where in front of her are two locked doors. Standing in front of each door is a true miracle of modern technology where identical twin girls born in vitro stand guarding their door.

The first girl on the left states, "Good day. My name is Jackie and one of us twins always tells the truth."

The second girl on the right remarks "Salutations. My name is Jill and one of us twins always lies. There are two doors behind each of us."

Her twin sister Jackie states, "Behind one of these locked doors will lead you to your destination."

After a dramatic pause, Jill reveals, "And behind the other door, unlocking it will lead to instant death. Just like opening the Ark of the Covenant in the classic adventure film 'Raiders of the Lost Ark.'"

Jackie instructs, "If you take our challenge, you can only ask one of us twins only one question to receive the key to open either door. Asking the right question will give you the key to continue towards your destination."

Jill releases a sinister laugh commenting, "And with one incorrect question burning streams of light will consume you rapidly melting your skin and bones."

Jackie comments, "Think about your question and which of us you will ask. I always hate sweeping up the ashes of those who wrongly guess."

Olympia places each of her hands on either side of her eyebrows as she intensely thinks. Her brain is racing at the speed of light as she contemplates every scenario to properly solve this riddle. She keeps saying to herself, "What would Bilbo do?"

Inside her head, every question that she thinks about she counters with all the possible responses. She is trying to find the needle in the haystack that would give her the same answer for one telling the truth or for the other who always lies.

Finally, she snaps both of her fingers as a Cheshire Cat smile adorns her face.

Not knowing which twin always truthful and which twin is always lies, she picks the twin on the left side, Jackie.

She asks Jackie looking her straight in her eyes "Which of these two doors would your twin sister select?"

With this question, Olympia knows for certain that if Jackie is truthful and the door behind her leads to her destination, that her twin sister is the liar She would select the other door. If Jackie is the lying twin, and the door behind her leads to her destination she would not tell the truth. She must select the other door. In both scenarios, regardless of the truthfulness of Jackie, her response would be to select the door that leads to instant death. Therefore, the other door will always lead to her destination avoiding the wrath of God.

Olympia grabs the key and inserts it into the other door.

The twins kneel putting their head between their legs and covering the top of their head with their hands. In one swift movement, the door opens revealing a road entirely made of gold. The path leads to the sought-after destination.

Watching the twins dematerialize, as the voice from above the golden road Is heard saying, "The way is open. It was made by those who are analytical people. Enter, the way is open."

Along the golden streets Olympia discovers a high-tech office were lying on the help desk are various robotic parts including the microchip brain and heart CPUs (central processing units).

Olympia returns to her cybernetic laboratory with the newly acquired heart and brain microchips.

The next day, her robotic team assists her to connect the brain microchip. Olympia wires it to the central processing unit located at the head of her most advanced Android. Downloading her new cerebral software that she has spent months designing and developing. When her monitor indicates that the software has been fully downloaded, she instructs Andrea the Android to raise her left hand.

Andrea complies. Olympia tells her to raise her right hand. With both hands raised, Andrea says, "I give up," having her smile with a realistic sounding laugh.

Next, Olympia and her cybernetic team carefully places the heart microchip inside Andrea's head. Since this is not a real heart but it does control all its emotions. For the Android, CPUs can be placed anywhere that has digital access to the cerebral and nerve response circuitry. After the team verifies that the heart microchip has been correctly wired, Andrea's tests ensure that team has correctly updated the emotional and personality responses.

Olympia shows her Android a collection of 3D color photographs of the famous Professor Steele.

Andrea examines the photo. After traversing the internet and every available database, Andrea responds, "You are a very brilliant person, but my information indicates that you are a liar and a very bad person."

Olympia places a vanity mirror in front of Andrea. Immediately her electronic respond system grabs a hairbrush. She brushes her hair making it look perfect and presentable.

Then, she examines her face, standing up to inspect her shirt and how she looks wearing it. She looks at the team commenting, "Everything looks perfect. And I look absolutely beautiful."

Olympia comments to her team, " Andrea is self-aware and her emotional heart microchip is working perfectly."

To celebrate, Olympia takes her team and Andrea to the Boss Eisley Cantina. The group finds a large table that comfortably seats eight. The server stops by and takes everyone's order including Andrea who orders an unsweetened iced tea.

The manager walks past their table and tells a group of engineers wearing glasses and sporting a pocket protector. The manager tells them "I assume that you do not know ' No droids are allowed in the Cantina. Droids do not eat or drink. They take up space that could be used for paying non-droid customers."

As the manager passes Olympia's table, he comments, "Is there a beauty pageant in town?"

Jude, the team's robotic technician answers, "My platform is 'world peace.' Thank you for noticing."

The cybernetic neural scientist, Alita quietly comments "In internal system that I attached a disposable catheter bag."

Jude jokingly says, "If it's a new, sterile catheter bag then later, the drink is on Andrea," as he chuckles.

After team Hiroshi wins their fourth 'Golden Microchip' trophy, Olympia decides that time has come to retire all her doctorate teammates.

One has been offered a lucrative position as the youngest AI Robotics professor with a huge budget and laboratory. The other is the new Chairperson for Robotic hardware and circuitry, a popular graduate and doctorate program.

Olympia Gort gets a call believing that it is from the Professor or his nephews. Answering her cell, the voice is that of a female.

Myrena Gorgona congratulates her extraordinary fourth straight victory from a field of thirty-two robots without a single defeat.

Thanking her, Olympia tells her that she is busy adjusting her android.

Myrena states, "As you may know, I run a SuperPower group called the 'Lemnian Deeds' Federation, for women, run by women, and accountable to women."

"We value all the work you have done and want to financially help you in your future endeavors. We picture your human-like androids to be powerful and versatile like the historic clones of Star Wars' Boba Fett."

Olympia says, "You have my interest so far."

Myrena tells her, "Our members have two SuperPowers and are loyal. Could you use a few million dollars to continue your times like these, it is a good validation that when I built Andrea's research without Professor Steele and his tail wagging nephews."

Olympia grins saying, "Yes."

Myrena continues, "Could you imagine a SuperPower world run by women, controlled by us, and free from the 'Golden Eagle' Organization?"

Pausing for a few seconds, Myrena says, "Think about this."

Olympia with a poker face states, "I will. Thanks."

Chapter 8

Dossier of Cynane Mino

Cynane Mino, an olive tanned girl with orange cat-like eyes was named after the Macedonian princess who was the half-sister to Alexander the Great. Her name means 'warrior princess,' as she became the country's queen. She was a skilled military leader, and the commander of the entire country's forces who as a teenager excelled in hunting, sword fighting, horseback riding, and hand-to-hand combat.

Similarly, Cynane Mino studied under Grandmaster Coragus.

Coragus explains, "Pankration, which is a Greek martial art form combining weapons training, boxing, wrestling, and kicking. The Greeks belief that the mighty Hercules used these techniques to fight the Nemean Lion, the Hydra of Lerna, the Erymanthian Boar, while Theseus being likewise trained disposed of the Minotaur. Under her Grandmaster Aristotle, she mastered the spear, pharaonic sword, the short sword or xiphos, the thick, curved iron sword called the 'Kopis,' as well as the compound bow, and crossbow."

Cynane's Universal Scouting Troop went to the local amusement park enjoying the roller coasters, bumper cars, log flume ride, and Merry Go Round. The boys began teasing the girls daring them to go into the haunted house where the entire labyrinth is in complete darkness.

Accepting their dare claiming to have 'girl power,' Cynane leads a few girls through the mazes' starting point as with each step the room gets darker and darker.

Cynane just recently started complaining to her parents that when her father turned out the lights in her bedroom, she was blinded by the intense light that she saw.

Earlier at the amusement park, a fortune teller told her, "I see that you have intense psychic power with a joyous, receptive attitude being able to take on the burdens of your friends while being strong-willed, industrious, and extremely stubborn."

She continues stating, "You have an animal sign with a feline ability to see how a house cat can see in the dark, Cats like you can see in the dark due to their large corneas with the ability to view ultraviolet or black light."

Cynane began noticing at home that many objects began to glow such as light bulbs, lit candles, and even the stars in the sky.

She began studying this phenomenon which she learned is called 'electromagnetic spectrum' where radiated energy commonly known as 'radiation' normally unseen to the human eye but to insects like bumblebees, cats, reindeer, birds, rats, and goldfish.

She jots down in her notebook that Ultraviolet rays trigger the production of vitamin D as well as lowers one's blood pressure.

In the pitch-black haunted house, Cynane holding the next girl's hand leads them through as she can easily see not only the correct path heading towards the exit but each upcoming worker that either touches each visitor scaring them or dressed like a monster jumping out from their hiding place trying to scare them.

The girls who are forewarned by Cynane are hearing more screams from the boys who provoked them.

Exiting the haunted house, the girls begin to laugh having them witness the results from the teasing boys who showed fear and were screaming.

The event gave all the girls a rush of dopamine while the boys ended up peeing in their pants.

Turning sixteen, she was invited to many schoolmates' 'sweet sixteen' birthday parties. At a wealthy mansion, her classmate Sheila lived with her socialite grandmother. During the event, all the manor's electricity went off, having a black-out.

Cynane Mino, being able to see in the dark, was unaware of the event. The adults told the teenagers to stay calm and remain stationary wherever they are.

Cynane could see men wearing masks quietly walking upstairs in the dark. She followed them watching them enter the grandmother's bedroom and placing her jewelry inside their gym bag. The other burglar enters the bathroom looking for prescription drugs especially from a senior citizen.

Cynane has read that a burglary happens every twenty seconds when there is easy access, the owners are usually away but in this case a large gathering distracting everyone especially disconnecting the electric utility company's power pole to the residence set back from the road in a cul-de-sac.

In the complete darkness, Cynane's orange eyes view a large diamond ring resting on the bedroom dresser bureau. She slowly approaches the natural cherry dresser. She takes the ten karat diamond ring and placing it inside her stylish hip/waist bag.

The burglars walk into the office where several electronic equipment can be accessed and removed. Cynane looks around and finds behind a Johannes Vermeer first generation lithograph is a wall safe. For amusement, she enters the birthday girl's birthdate including her birth year's last two digits. The safe opens. She adds to her hip/waist bag a stack of hundred-dollar bills, a multi-color, pendant containing a large 11.5 carat Australian Black Opal Lightning Ridge, and a ninety carat Burmese red ruby necklace with white pearls adjacent to each ruby and dripping with oval diamonds.

She dials 911 giving the operator her location. As the burglars make their exit walking down the stairs and into the front foyer, they are unaware that three police cars are waiting at the end of the driveway for them.

The lights come back on, allowing the party to continue.

Delivered earlier to the mansion is a four-tier cake by the iBroadcast show, the 'Cake King' which is brought into the living room. The attendees line up to be served cake with sparkling apple cider while many begin dancing to the recorded microchip iMusic.

That night back in her bedroom, Cynane Mino hides her newfound wealth inside her messy closet underneath a loose floorboard.

For her eighteenth birthday, Cynane Mino walks into the local Asian Tattoo Parlor where Fan Song, the 'King of Tattooists' has his ink studio. She desires a natural tattoo of the Chinese breed of domestic cat called the "Dragon Li" on her back. The Dragon Li is a standardized breed having a golden-brown, broken-mackerel or broken-striped, tabby pattern with distinctive missing ear tip and large almond shaped luminescent yellow/green eyes.

After the work is completed and photographed for the iMagazine entitled 'Inked,' Cynane is nicknamed 'The Girl with the Dragon Li Tattoo.'

She smiles and purrs loudly as she exits waring an Italian designer baby pink backless silk dress. The international iNewspapers and iBroadcast iNews interviews Cynane. She comments "My Dragon Li Tattoo is such a bi-otch that she must have a barbed vagina. Do not cross this female unless you want your member to bleed."

Cynane Mino is watching the iNews iBroadcast iChannel where an avalanche has trapped over fifty-eight copper miners working in Denali, Alaska.

As Cynane using her iBroadcast remote switches iChannels to view the Feles Show on the Animal Planet, her cell phone begins ringing.

Picking up the phone she says, "Hello. Ciao."

The voice at the other end states, "My name is Salvador Martin. My brother Pablo and myself head an organization of SuperPower ability people like yourself called 'DODGE.' 'DODGE' is an acronym for the Department of Defense Genetically Engineered Initiative. Have you been watching the latest iNews about the tragic incident that has occurred in Denali region of Alaska?"

Cynane replies, "Yes, I was just watching the iNews report about it."

Salvador asks her, "Would you be willing to help rescue all the copper miners using your SuperPower ability to see in complete darkness?"

Before she can respond, he continues, "Pack your overnight bag quickly as in 30 minutes an Uber will pick you up and drive you to the airport. At the 'will call' counter there will be an airline ticket to Fairbanks International Airport. At the baggage claim area there will be a chauffeur holding a sign with your name on it. The chauffeur will drive you a hundred and twenty miles which should take you slightly over two hours to get to the Denali Bluffs Hotel. This is where you will store your belongings. The supervisor of the Copper Mining Company will meet you to update you on the current situation and drive you to the copper mining site. We at the DODGE Initiative will reward you with $250,000 for your participation."

Cynane remarks, "Are you for real or am I being Punk'd again?"

Salvador tells her, "Hurry up and get ready as time is of the essence. The lives of many copper miners will only be saved by your SuperPower ability."

Cynane has packed a few overnight items in her gym bag.

The sound of the Uber's horn is heard having her grab her winter three-layer-principle, insulated, waterproof, breathable arctic parka with fur hood.

Exiting the Uber walking towards the counter agent at the Alaskan Airlines kiosk, Cynane uses her passport as her identification.

Walking towards her gate she places her boarding pass and airline ticket inside of her passport book.

As the boarding process begins, Cynane checks her boarding pass noticing that she is in first class. She stands at the beginning of the line forming behind her. After showing her boarding pass, she enters the jetway onto the plane walking towards her left and to her first-class recliner-style seat.

The flight attendant hands her the first-class service menu. Cynane tells her that she will have Caprese salad with the Hawaiian sweet roll, Trident wild Alaskan Teriyaki glazed salmon with Jasmine rice and for dessert the wild Alaskan berry cobbler.

After the safety instructions have been viewed on each passenger's personal monitor, Cynane tells her that she will have Caprese salad with the Hawaiian is served her meal. Also, served to her is the ordered Cola and coffee with cream.

Landing at the Fairbanks International Airport which has four asphalt runways, Cynane walks from the second level of Terminal 1 to the baggage claim. Waiting with a sign having her name on it is her driver to the Denali Bluffs Hotel. He escorts her holding her gym bag to his Lincoln Towncar.

Listening to her iPhone58, Cynane sings with the legendary diva, Rileigh Michele hearing her song 'Schrödinger's Cat.'

At the Denali Bluffs Hotel, Cynane is met by the supervisor of the copper mining corporation who has the hotel manager hold her overnight gym bag.

The foreman tells Cynane, "The Denali was once named Mount McKinley. The mountain range is 20,310 feet, being 1.5 vertical miles from its base to its peak. In comparison, Mount Everest, the world's highest mountain stands at over 29,000 feet."

The supervisor explains, "In the mining of copper there is an awful lot of waste rock which is called 'gangue.' Inside the underground mining shafts, copper miners using axes break apart the copper ore. The rock is then crushed and ground into powder. Next is 'froth flotation' where the waste sinks to the bottom of the fluid and is discarded. The powder is heated to over 900 degrees Fahrenheit. The miners at this location extract rocks containing 0.2% to 99.99% copper."

One miner who left before the avalanche started guides Cynane into the mine being followed by a few of his fellow miners who are carrying shovels and axes. Deep inside the underground shafts, the path is pitch black but Cynane using her SuperPower ability can see as though it was a bright, sunny day. She leads guiding the team of miners into the abyss where on the other side of the fallen rock wall their fellow miners are trapped.

Cynane grabs one of the worker's iron pickaxe and begins swinging its hickory wood handle. The two-and-a-half-pound pick breaks apart the outer surface of the rock wall. After another two thrusts double-sided pickaxe, she can see in the dark a face or two of the trapped miners. As Cynane rests, her entourage of miners using their pickaxes and shovels continue to strike the rock wall.

Once they have cleared enough of the rock enclosure, they walk inside helping their fellow miners. Walking beside their exhausted trapped worker, each rescue team member helps lift them walking towards the entrance of the mine.

Cynane is the first to exit the mines. The American as well as the International iBroadcast iNews interview her asking, "Where you able to get all of the miners that were trapped out?"

Cynane who is slightly out of breath replies, "With the help of their co-workers, all the miners who were trapped are free. Many of them need medical help. I beg the media and their families to respect the fact that they need medical attention. Please let the EMTs and the other medical professionals examine, diagnose, and aid the trapped miners.

There are plenty of rescue miners who are more than willing to share their experience with the press."

The supervisor helps Cynane into his truck as he returns her to the Denali Bluffs Hotel for a delicious barbecue dinner followed by a well-deserved good night's sleep.

Cynane is that home eating her lunch when she receives a text message from her bank telling her that "A bank deposit of 125,000 US dollars is now available." She stares at the screen yelling "Where in the world is the rest of my money for the special mission."

She calls the special contact number to the DODGE Initiative. She asks the operator to "Put Salvador Martin on the phone immediately."

When Salvador answers the phone, he hears a young female voice saying, "This is Cynane. Where is the rest of my money? You promised me $250,000 to go to Alaska to help the copper miners escape from the avalanche imprisonment and all that was added to my bank account was half that."

Salvador, who is confused tells her, "There must have been a miscommunication. I will verify my notes on our agreement, and if a mistake was made, I will rectify it immediately."

Cynane tells him "You do that. After you send my bank the other half text message me right away, I can verify your deposit. Good day, sir" having her slam her cell phone against her wooden kitchen table.

As she prepares to go out to the shopping center to buy a new outfit, Cynane is heard stating, "Men, you can't live with them, and you legally can't shoot them."

Chapter 9

Dossier on Katrina Quark

Being invited to her cousin's eighteenth birthday party, Katrina Quark, who was a very obese, unattractive high school senior watched as he opened his presents. His parents had given him a brand-new metallic silver Tesla Roadster Challenger which everybody knew cost over $350,000.

Katrina had to borrow her older brother's beat up Ford to drive herself anywhere.

At the party, the game they decided to play was called 'two minutes in the closet' where a guy and girl were chosen to enter a dark closet and decide if they wanted to kiss each other.

Upon Katrina's turn, she entered the dark closet waiting for one of the male party guests to join her. Instead, she was locked inside the closet hearing everyone outside laughing hysterically.

She grabbed the handle of the closet trying to turn it in either direction to no avail. She knocked on the door yelling "The door is locked. Please open it so I can get out."

The laughing and the clapping of all those at the party got louder as Katrina began to cry. Many tricks upon her like this have happened throughout her overweight life but never had a relative like her male cousin had been a participant.

Wiping the tears from her eyes, Katrina began to blink. As she looked at the barely visible in the dark doorknob, it began to quickly move away from her. She looked straight ahead seeing a light as though she were inside a tunnel. As she began to walk forward, she realized she had supersonic speed. Thinking that she was in a field of tall grass, she looked up and saw everyone at the party still laughing but appearing to be over a hundred feet tall. It was at that instance that Katrina Quark realized that she had acquired the SuperPower ability to shrink and to fly. As she blinked another three times, she returned to her normal height.

Katrina asked everyone, "What is everyone laughing at? What is so funny?" Their laughing instantly stopped as everyone at the party was amazed to see Katrina standing in their midst.

A few days later, Katrina Quark needed to go shopping as she realized she had left her pocketbook inside her brother's car.

Walking around the vehicle she could not figure out how to retrieve her belongings inside the Ford. She tries to open the driver's side door, but it was locked. She walked around the car checking each of the doors, but they were all locked too. She became mad and upset as she desperately needed her pocketbook which contained her wallet with her money and identification.

Remembering her experience at the party, Katrina blinked three times rapidly. She began shrinking until she got to the size of an electron which she learned in school was one thousand of the diameter of a proton. An atom, being the smallest unit of matter, is comprised of a nucleus being at least one proton with several neutrons and at least one electron.

Katrina Quark propels herself using her SuperPower ability to fly towards the passenger side window. At her present size, Katrina flies past the silica and magnetized cobalt atoms and eventually lands on the passenger seat.

Blinking her eyes, Katrina returns to normal size where she gathers her pocketbook and opens the door. She continues her day as she smiles realizing that her new-found SuperPower abilities are starting to become handy.

On Friday night, as all her classmates have been invited to a senior pre-graduation party, Katrina sits home eating a hot fudge sundae with whipped cream and a cherry on top as she begins sobbing. She tells herself, "No one will ever love me. Everybody judges me on my physical not my personality."

Just then the phone begins to ring.

As she picks it up, a man's voice is heard saying "Katrina Quark, this is your new best friend Professor Steele."

Katrina puzzled replies, "Who is this?"

The Professor tells her, "I have a special gift that my corporation's pharmaceutical branch will be delivered to you soon. This gift will change your life, but you must never alter your personality or else I will have you stepped on."

Before hanging up he tells her. "Upon your metamorphosis, I will assign you special missions that utilize your new SuperPower ability."

After finishing her delicious ice cream, she hears her doorbell ring. Opening her front door, she sees a FedUp drone requiring her to identify herself with her fingerprint. After placing her index finger on its biometric reader, a package falls out.

Katrina picks up the package as the FedUp drone flies away.

Walking back into her house, she opens the package discovering a large bottle of red pills. The card next to the bottle has written on it, "My friend Morpheus says if you take the red pill, it will free you from the enslaving desire for sweet treats where your new truth of reality will make you popular only if your personality remains the same. The Steele

Corporation has developed these prototype pills. Remember, only take one red pill each day."

With three weeks to the senior prom, Katrina Quark who still does not have a date obeys the Professor taking one red pill each day. With a little over a week before the prom, Katrina wakes up on Friday morning getting ready for school.

Brushing her teeth and combing her hair, she does not even look into the mirror. Running into her room, she puts on her jeans and t-shirt. She is surprised that they are extremely loose on her.

Frustrated she runs into her brother's room knowing that he is very skinny and puts on his jeans and t-shirt which fit her perfectly. Still unaware and being confused, Katrina rushes off to school. She sits in her homeroom seat waiting for the teacher to take attendance. All her homeroom classmates endlessly tease her and throw wadded paper at her head, asking her "Who are you?"

She replies, "Katrina Quark. Quit teasing me as you all know who I am."

As the teacher enters the room and begins calling attendance, she announces, "Katrina Quark."

To everyone's surprise, the tall, voluptuous curvy girl answering says, "Present."

The teacher looks up and says, "Is that really you Katrina? What have you done to yourself as you look like you could be a model?"

Expecting everyone in the class to laugh hysterically, she is surprised when everybody begins clapping and saying, "You look marvelous!"

Throughout her day, over ten varsity football, basketball, and wrestling classmates ask her out to the senior prom. Even two of the female cheerleaders ask to go with her.

Surprised, Katrina runs into the girl's room looking into the mirror like Alice seeing the amazing transformation that is truly a Wonderland to her.

Thanks to the Professor, his daily red pill has transformed Katrina's outer beauty to match her inner beauty.

Looking at her wrist iCommunicator, Katrina realizes that she must run off to a meeting. With her brother's car key in her hand, she runs towards the front door accidentally dropping the key. She gets down on her knees looking for the key. She moves the wooden coffee table then she hears the metallic sound of the key sliding across the metal heating cover. The next sound she hears is the key hitting the aluminum vent between the grates and bouncing before resting inside the straight, aluminum pipe. Needing to retrieve the key, she blinks three times. As she begins to shrink, Katrina jokingly yells, "How about a little heat, Scarecrow. I'm melting,. Melting, Ohhh!"

Katrina shrinks to the size of a fly using her flying ability two inches between the grates. Hovering over the metal pipe she sees the key lying stationary in front of her. Having the hole in the key surrounding her midsection as she flies back out of the grate.

Once the car key is out of harm's way so as not to repeat this incident again, Katrina blinking three times grows to her normal size. Holding the key firmly in her hand this time, she exits the house heading towards her meeting.

The summer after graduating High School, Professor Steele calls Katrina Quark telling her that he has a special mission for her in Northern Korea.

After hanging up the phone, her doorbell rings. Outside her front door is a FedUp drone. Upon getting her fingerprint biometric verification, the drone dispenses a package that contains her new valid passport with a valid visa to South Korea, a first class airline ticket for her on South Korea Airlines and lots of papers that includes her itinerary and hotel information.

On the day of her flight an Uber arrives picking her up and driving her to the international airport.

Flying into South Korea's Seoul Incheon International Airport, she gets the hotel shuttle to her five-star hotel the Paradise City Oasis. The concierge greets Katrina who shows her, her reservation confirmation. After checking in, a bellhop is called to show Katrina to her Penthouse Premier Executive Suite.

After a restful night, Katrina enjoys her complimentary breakfast then disappears. She reappears wearing her wingsuit, high altitude face mask, altimeter, and Kevlar vest. She looks around to make sure that she is not being noticed.

Using her SuperPower ability to fly across the 129 miles to the missile base near Pyongyang Airport in North Korea.

She blinks three times shrinking to the size of an ant. She flies forward resting on the roof of the entry gate's booth.

Soon a military Jeep drives up to the gate showing the soldiers on duty their identification, explaining the reason for their visit.

Katrina flies onto the roof of the Jeep as it proceeds towards the nuclear missile silo. The occupants of the Jeep exit walking towards she office building.

She flies off the roof of the Jeep.

Heading inside the nuclear missile silo, she gathers Intel to learn how many people are working in the silo. Identifying those with guns and those assessing the electronics.

Flying up high where the nuclear missile has its guidance system. She uses her SuperPower ability to become microscopic the size of an electron. She enters through the metal outer layer of the rocket and into the electronic system. There, memorizing the procedures that Professor Steele's experts have rehearsed with her, Katrina programs the guidance systems.

As the last step is completed, the nuclear missile which will be programmed to launch to any of the missile's programmed geo-locations will instead land intact to the Professor's alternate geo-location.

Exiting the rocket's metal exterior, Katrina returns to her ant size state climbing on the roof oven exiting Jeep that takes her past the International Airport.

There, she becomes full size and begins walking back to her hotel room.

She showers and starts to feel hungry after an exhausting day at the missile factory. She settles for eating a delicious meal of sweet, syrupy pancakes called 'hoeddeok' with stir fried noodles called 'japchae,' she retires for the evening.

The next day the hotel shuttle returns her to the airport where she flies home. She enjoys her smooth, first-class airline flight.

The flight attendant serves every passenger a Koryo Burger that is always served stone cold.

The attendant confirms, "Straight from our fridge to your paper plate."

Another first-class passenger complains, "What the heck is this?" She points to her paper doily with an unidentified slice of processed meat in the middle.

The entire aircraft laughs as they eventually dispose of the 'hockey puck.'

Chapter 10

The Enemy of My Enemy

Myrena Gorgona travels to San Francisco California to promote her new fashion line of unisex attire. She is dressing her models who look gender neutral putting on outfits for the non-binary generation. The models have sat for make-up and hair. She selects each outfit consisting of either a dashiki or colorful shirts with matching pants. As she is putting the last-minute touches on a male model that looks very feminine and a butch female model, amongst the spectators she notices two members of the DODGE Initiative.

Myrena thinks about the fourth Century BC expression that was found in the ancient Indian Sanskrit treatise on statecraft Arthashastra.

Myrena asks herself, "Is the adage 'the enemy of my enemy is my friend.' True?"

She notices that in the crowd are the two wives of Salvador and Pablo Martin, Jocelyn Thatcher, and Colette Evergreen.

The models are getting ready to strut down the runway displaying Myrena's latest fashion trend.

She asks Stormy who has joined her in San Francisco to introduce herself to the Martin twins' spouses. Myrena further states, "Invite the two ladies to join us for dinner at the 'City Club' members-only Michelin restaurant."

Stormy approaches Jocelyn Thatcher and Colette Evergreen. She introduces herself saying, "I'm surprised to see you at Myrena's fashion debut. You probably have recognized me as 'Stormy Weather.'"

The two DODGE executive representatives look at her saying, "It was only a few months ago that we were in an air battle together. You attempted to use your SuperPower ability controlling the atmosphere and weather to take down the airplane we were on. Our mission was headed to Colorado to place your partner, Myrena's ex-fiancé inside the world's most secure penitentiary."

Stormy smiles remarking, "Those were the good old days. Thanks for reminding me. By the way, the Steele twins last I heard were sipping Cristal champagne as free men."

She smiles enjoying a sinister laugh.

After receiving an unappreciative expression on both ladies faces, Stormy continues saying, "Myrena has declared an all-out nuclear war against the 'Golden Eagle' Organization especially targeting Professor Steele and his two nephews. As you may have heard, Myrena Gorgona has organized a new female headed organization entitled the 'Lemnian Deeds' Federation."

The DODGE female representatives shake their heads indicating that they are aware of Myrena's current activities.

Stormy smiles as she repeats what Myrena had told her saying, "You ladies know that 'the enemy of my enemy is my friend.' Therefore, Myrena would like to take both of you out to dinner tonight at the three-star rated, members-only Michelin restaurant, the 'City Club.' There, we ladies can discuss the future of our SuperPower ability organizations. We seek the demise of Professor Steele and the 'Golden Eagle' Organization."

Stormy stands up and says, "Enjoy the remaining part of the fashion show and we will see you later tonight."

After she leaves, Jocelyn calls the other DODGE executives letting them know what transpired in communicating with Stormy.

Her husband tells them to join them and report back their findings and what Myrena is planning.

While waiting for their dinner meeting, they go shopping at Neiman Marcus saying "This is going to go on our expense account" as they chuckle.

Meeting her invited guests. Stormy introduces the DODGE ladies to Myrena inside the City Club of San Francisco with its Art Deco decor.

The director immediately escorts them to his best table introducing them to his sommelier who bring them a bottle of Screaming Eagle C2abernet Sauvignon pouring it into the four glasses as the server hands them the Michelin chef's planned full course dinner that he has prepared for them.

Colette Evergreen tells Stormy and Myrena that her SuperPowers are to become invisible having the second ability to negate all the SuperPower abilities that she focuses on while keeping her SuperPower abilities intact.

Jocelyn Thatcher explains, "My SuperPowers are the ability to fly, and to convert energy in one form into another. Energy can be in the form of electrical, mechanical, magnetic, gravitational, chemical, ionization, nuclear, elastic, in waves of mechanical and sound, radiant and thermal. Some of these energies, such as electrical, mechanical, heat, and light, control electrical appliances, electric motors, and electric heaters. I use my SuperPower ability to control and convert these mechanical powers. I can store up the acquired energy release it as powerful bursts of destructive energy since the mechanical input power must equal its output power."

She continues saying, "I can operate communication devices, computers, vehicles, weapons, and even energy from humans such as joggers, cyclists, and hoverboarders."

Stormy says, "You obviously know what I am capable of with my SuperPower ability. I assume that there are terabytes of data at DODGE just on me," as she smiles.

Myrena explains, "I am the opposite of you, Colette who can negate other's SuperPowers. I get all the SuperPower abilities of others that are within my range, usually within a hundred-mile radius. For instance, right now I can control the atmosphere and weather thanks to Stormy. Control mechanical items and become invisible thanks to Colette. I am well acquainted with the SuperPower ability of both Apollo and Rocky Steele. And have witnessed the SuperPower ability of the Professor which is 'to live forever' like Methuselah from the Old Testament. Other words the Professor like the Phoenix will always 'rise from the ashes' and be reborn."

Jocelyn tells them, "One of the primary objectives of the DODGE Initiative is to be the only SuperPower organization by removing the 'Golden Eagle' Organization. The capture of the Steele family being the Professor and his two nephews, Apollo and Rocky is within both our organization's best interest."

Colette adds, "The executives of DODGE foresee a world with one SuperPower Organization where all its members are registered and assigned missions to better peoplekind. We want the entire world to understand that SuperPower people are peaceful and making the world better not to fear us."

Stormy asks the two ladies from DODGE, "So what is it that I hear about you two married twins? Are there offspring bells in the near future?"

Jocelyn and Colette answer in unison, "We are just in the beginning phases of our double wedding anniversary."

Myrena responds, "Not long ago I planned a wedding that included the official, the wedding venue, and the reception hall getting the International famous singing divas for over three hundred people in less than a week. If it were not for a devious, lying Professor who every step of my plan fought against me, I would be happily married today."

Myrena still wearing her fifteen-carat diamond engagement ring stares at the two ladies straight into their eyes saying, "If you ever desire any help, my free services are at your request."

Stormy asks the ladies to show them the jewelry. Both married ladies stick out their left hand showing off their large diamond engagement rings.

Myrena jokingly says, "'Frost yourself,' and make sure you keep the ring bearer," as they all begin laughing.

Stormy says, "We are in a members-only private Michelin three-star restaurant so let's all remain having composure and be happy for the ladies whose husbands afforded them large shiny pure carbon."

After the sommelier has placed Dom Perignon in front of each of the ladies, Myrena raises her glass saying, "Let's toast true love which I have heard is 'the soul's recognition of its counterpoint in another.'"

The rest of the group raise their glasses clicking them against each other as they drink the finest champagne with hints of coffee cream vanilla, and subtle spices.

As the Michelin Chef delivers his award-winning rich, white chocolate mousse cake, all the ladies take a little bit to praise the chef for his most excellent creation.

He thanks them. Whispering to Myrena, he says, "Everything is taken care of and placed on your account."

She winks at him having him remark, "Thank you. It's always a pleasure to have your company."

Outside the City Club, a chauffeur-driven limousine picks up the two DODGE female executives driving them back to their residence. Myrena and Stormy return to San Francisco's Palace Hotel.

The next day at San Francisco's Harvey Milk Convention Center, Myrena Gorgona is getting her makeup and hair done. The producer of the 'MM Morning Show' rushes up to Myrena asking her if she is almost ready to appear on the show.

Myrena answers "Relax darling your far too young to have stress and attitude. Besides, beauty takes time and time takes beauty."

As the on-site camera crew begins rolling with the MM Morning Show theme song playing in the background, its host Meredith Marlowe the iBroadcast journalist appears on stage welcoming her iBroadcast audience saying, "Good morning. This is Meredith Marlowe with another celebrity interview from San Francisco's Harvey Milk Convention Center during the fashion technology week. I have with me today the famous SuperModel, now SuperDesigner, Myrena Gorgona."

The entire audience begins clapping as Myrena Gorgona enters from the stage left.

Myrena struts across the stage waving her right arm at the audience. She sits in the comfortable chair on Meredith's left side.

Meredith welcomes her saying "Myrena, how does it feel to go from SuperModel to SuperDesigner having your own luxury fashion line?"

Myrena answers "For the male viewers I would equate it to the home-run King who has just become the new team manager" as the audience laughs.

Meredith Marlowe requests, "I am sure that the audience as well as myself would love to see some of your new fashion styles?"

Out of the side of the stage walks out a handsome black male model.

Myrena states, "He is wearing a bold, elegant Black Panther dashiki that is a black with gold trim regal outfit having two front pockets. Ladies, this is 100% cotton and machine washable."

Next, walking out of the side of the stage is Nakia, a thin, tall beautiful African princess.

Myrena comments, "Wearing a dark gray Ankara fabric or otherwise known as 'African prints,' 'African wax prints,' 'Holland wax' or 'Dutch wax' being 100% cotton fabric. The shoulder to mid arm sleeves has a colorful design. I designed these gorgeous gowns to show off our womanly curves that will certainly turn many a head especially worn with a braided hairstyle."

As the next male and female gender-neutral models enter the stage from either side, Myrena states, "These two gender neutral models are wearing cotton floral and rainbow V-neck designer tees. The male model is wearing long designer jeans while the female model is wearing designer jean shorts."

Meredith Marlowe asks Myrena, "That was quite an amazing collection. Where do you get your inspiration from?"

Myrena smiles and says, "From anything I observe. A picture from an iMagazine, something that catches my eye while I walk the streets, something in an old movie. I express the receptive nature of my creative facility seeking to astound the fashion wearer's universe."

Meredith Marlowe stands up with Myrena hugging her, placing a kiss on each of her cheeks. She ends the segment by saying, "SuperModel, now SuperDesigner, Myrena Gorgona. Look for her new fashion gender neutral trends coming to your local designer boutiques soon," having the cameras showing the entire audience giving them a standing ovation.

Myrena walks off stage having her new BFF Stormy congratulate her.

Outside the stage door, a chauffeur-driven limousine provided by the iBroadcast TV Show drives the two of them to lunch before they are needed back at the SF Fashion Show.

Getting back to the conventions center, Myrena begins checking her booth models making sure their hair and makeup is impeccable. Stormy, who is on the carpet of the booth is amazed at the extensive line forming to speak with Myrena and her salespeople.

As Myrena checks out which fashion outfit will be worn by which model, Stormy approaches her waiting for the right moment to chat.

Myrena smiles as she is satisfied with her day's collection unveiling turns to look at Stormy.

Stormy excited tells her, "We are going to have a bright, sunny cloudless day as there are hundreds of buyers standing in line waiting for your appearance."

Myrena remarks, "This is proof that you were not the only one watching me on the 'MM Morning Show.'"

Checking herself in the mirror, verifying that her SuperModel looks, hair, and makeup are catwalk worthy she exits from backstage.

Being greeted by thunderous applause from the salespeople representing the world's most elite boutiques and luxury brick-and-mortar stores. Trailing behind her are her SuperPower army of female order takers. One by one they greet each salesperson entering their orders on their handheld supercomputer. After they take each order, they introduce each buyer to their CEO and SuperModel, Myrena Gorgona. As required, the order-taker takes a digital downloadable photo of the ordering salesperson next to Myrena. Connecting the digital photo to the order containing their email address ensures many future orders will follow.

Stormy looks around at the other vendor's booths noticing that none of them have the traffic generated by Myrena. The timely morning iBroadcast show and her SuperModel fame has brought every salesperson both domestic and international to her today.

The orders that are being generated from the San Francisco Fashion Week Show are beyond the company's expectations.

In between customer chats and photographs, every iMagazine reporter fired their questions at Myrena. Some of the reporters desperate to get a scoop, chat privately with Stormy who knows everything about Myrena and her fashion design company.

After the show, a chauffeur-driven limousine picks up Myrena and Stormy.

Delivering the two women to the Victorian and Edwardian style mansion in the Haight-Ashbury neighborhood across from Alamo Square Park.

Ringing the doorbell, Diego Martin greets them. Being escorted into the library outside the formal dining room, they are introduced by Diego to his wife Carmen.

Carmen tells her two visitors, "It is a pleasure to meet you gorgeous ladies. Like both of you, my husband and I first interacted and then worked for Professor Steele. Without his profitable missions, we would not be married and living in this comfortable residence. We would not know about art and be board members of the San Francisco Museum of Modern Art."

Diego states, "We have been kept up to date with your dealings with the Steele family. Although we are not directly DODGE executive members, we hear at every Sunday dinner the latest information about those with SuperPower abilities. Many a dinner we have heard tales relating to Stormy Weather. And recently hearing rumored stories about a certain SuperPower SuperModel first engaged to the Professor's nephew. Then, assigned a Herculean task involving her wedding."

Diego smiles almost laughing commenting, "I really like the best man, Apollo's quote 'your Pretty Woman has vanished becoming a real Runaway Bride,'" as even Stormy laughs.

Entering from the dining room into the library, is Colette Evergreen Martin holding her husband Pablo's hand. Colette introduces Pablo to Stormy Weather and Myrena Gorgona.

Next to enter the library are Jocelyn Thatcher Martin followed by her husband Salvador. Jocelyn introduces their two guests to him.

Diego Martin asks everyone to join him and his wife in the formal dining room. For this special occasion, he hired from the Golden Chef TV show, Rosalita LeFray. Diego secretly understands that his guests prefer female professionals especially those that do not have SuperPower abilities.

The sommelier pours each person Napa Valley award-winning Chardonnay. Diego complements her on an excellent choice after he takes a test sip swallowing it.

The rest of the group follows enjoying their appetizer paired wine. For the appetizer, Chef LeFray has prepared a palm heart salad stuffed with poached lobster tails.

After consuming and enjoying their seafood salad, the sommelier refreshes their wine glasses with a Napa Valley Cabernet Sauvignon. The chef serves everyone their salad consisting of thin ribbons of zucchini, arugula, tomatoes, with shallots, capers, pepperoncini, parsley with olive oil and apple vinegar dressing.

Pablo asks Myrena, "My wife tells me that your 'Lemnian Deeds' Federation would like to coexist with the DODGE Initiative."

Myrena tells him, "That is true."

Salvador continues, "We understand that your goal is like ours in removing the 'Golden Eagle' Organization from being a SuperPower alternative."

Myrena looks into each person's eyes starting with Carmen, Jocelyn then Colette. Followed by looking into the soul of Pablo, Salvador and lastly Diego. Having everybody at the table's attention, she firmly states, "I believe that together our two SuperPower Federations can have the 'Golden Eagle' yield and eventually 'Crash and Burn.'"

Stormy adds, "Not to mention either imprisoning or terminating all those with the last name 'Steele.'"

The sommelier shows everyone a Sonoma Valley Pinot Noir red wine with the subtle flavors of fresh raspberry, plum, rose, and spice.

As the main course, white asparagus in garlic, buttery sauce, breast of duck with endive, walnuts, chanterelles (wild edible mushrooms), tequila pears sprinkled with mint leaves.

Diego raises his glass encouraging everyone else to follow saying "To friendship, everlasting love, and hopefully the joining of two SuperPower Federations."

Everyone in the group in unison says, "Amen."

Golden Michelin chef, Rosalita LeFray serves each guest her world-famous Black Forest Gateau as the sommelier pours each person a cup of Ghirardelli white chocolate coffee.

Before taking a bite and sip, all the diners stand up and applaud Rosalita and her staff for a marvelous presentation and meal.

Diego on behalf of everyone says "God made our food and drink but it takes Golden Michelin Chef Rosalita LeFray to perfect God's creation" as everyone stands an applauds.

Walking their two visitors to the front door, Colette kisses Stormy as Jocelyn kisses Myrena. And then switching, Jocelyn kisses Stormy as Colette kisses Myrena.

The Martin twins shake Stormy and Myrena's hands telling them that the Executive Board of DODGE will be in touch with her.

Salvador states, "I am fairly certain that the joining of our two groups will happen."

Pablo adds, "I believe that it will be beneficial for all of us. I look forward to the day when we are rid of the 'Golden Eagle' Organization and the Steeles."

Chapter 11

Time Waits for No Woman

Brittany Barbosa explains to Stormy Weather, "I was a full-fledged 'Golden Eagle' Organization member being nominated to win the 'Steele' trophy and award money but when my hands touched the bones of Saint Peter the first Catholic Pope, my eyes were opened, and my heart was filled with unspeakable joy."

Stormy laughs and says, "Praise the Lord!"

Brittany continues telling her, "I heard an angelic voice instruct me to join DODGE and have the Steele boys pay for their sins by aiding the Martin twins. When the time came to use my SuperPower gifts, I navigated the aircraft through the treacherous tornadoes caused by yours truly, Thanks" as she gives Stormy the evil eye.

Before going to bed, Brittany gets a call.

On the other end of the phone, she hears, "This is Myrena Gorgona, Amazon Warrior Princess. Is this Brittany Barbosa?"

Tired and about to sleep she says, "Yes."

Myrena states, "Recently, my Lemnian Deeds Federation agreed to work with DODGE on destroying the Golden Eagle Organization. Have you been aware of this?"

Brittany replies, "Yes, I have been told to provide my abilities with you."

Myrena states, "Tomorrow at 1 p.m., I need you to pick up at the San Francisco Airport a 'Lemnian Deeds' VIP named Leslie Michaels. She is my especially important guest that I want you to guarantee will not be harmed as you take the BART being the Bay Area Rapid Transit.

135

You will meet her in Terminal 3 at United Airline's ticket counter. From there it is a short walk to the BART station."

Brittany tells her, "I got it all. Be there before 1 p.m. Go to the San Francisco Airport to the United Airlines' ticket counter in Terminal 3. After meeting Leslie, proceed to the BART station heading towards the Moscone Convention Center."

Myrena wishes her, "Good night and get some rest as I want you to be wide awake tomorrow," as they hang up.

Brittany returns to her comfortable bed as she tucks herself into her soft pink bamboo sheets.

Fast-forwarding again, Brittany sees herself with Leslie walking towards the BART station. Leslie points out to her an Asian, bluetail street musician playing her electric violin as many passersby throw their change inside her cardboard box.

The violinist stops playing, staring at them. She removes a Beretta handgun from underneath her gray vest. Before she can unload the twenty rounds inside of her magazine, Brittany turns counterclockwise ten times.

Reversing time, Leslie points out to Brittany the Asian female street violinist telling her, "Look at the bluetail electric violinist. She is exceptionally talented and could easily play in the city's symphony."

In one swift motion Brittany grabs Leslie tossing her behind her as she removes her pocket hammerless Colt model 58 which is a .32 caliber self-loading firearm.

As the female violinist stops playing, Brittany protecting Leslie from harm shoots the female fiddler right between the eyes.

Brittany tells Leslie Michaels, "Unfortunately I had to nail her which is too bad because I would have loved to have heard her play the 'Arpeggio' that is the first 24 caprices for solo violin by Paganini that is distinguished to be the most difficult violin piece to play," as she laughs.

Before the two women can take another step, an Asian sumo wrestler grabs Brittany throwing her against the LED billboard advertising the National Health Care Program.

As the sumo wrestler begins to pick up Brittany who is trying to again reverse time, Leslie from behind the man stabs him in the head with a high grade, stainless steel reinforced, titanium oxide coated 7-inch tactical combat blade.

Brittany Barbosa fast-forwards again, seeing that the 'Golden Eagle' Organization has captured Leslie Michaels. She is restrained and being carried into the 'World Traveling Occult' Museum that is located inside the Moscone Convention Center Western Pavilion.

The next glimpses that Brittany sees are images of her reflection walking down the exhibit's hall marked 'The Ninth Level of Hell' based on Dante's Inferno.

Getting out of her bed and after taking a shower, Brittany prepares herself a delicious breakfast consisting of three sunny side-up eggs with wheat toast and a glass of orange juice.

As instructed and foreseen using her SuperPower ability, Brittany Barbosa enters the San Francisco Airport walking to Terminal 3 as she walks invisibly past the airport security entering the concourse.

She looks at the flight arrival board seeing that Leslie Michaels' United Airlines flight is arriving at gate seven.

Sitting at the passenger waiting area in front of gate seven, Brittany waits for Leslie Michaels to depart the plane.

The two ladies greet each other having Leslie tell her, "I assume you know how to get from the airport baggage claim area to the BART station?"

Brittany smiles and says, "What's the BART station?"

After a brief pause, Britney says, "I'm just kidding, you can rest assured that you're in good hands like Allstate."

After they have Leslie's luggage, a small suitcase with wheels, they walk across the street.

Leslie nudges Brittany saying, "Look at that Asian bluetail street musician playing her electric violin. She is very good so I'm going to toss her a dollar or two."

Brittany says, "I hear that she is exceptionally talented and could easily play in the city's symphony."

As she bends over to throw two bucks into her cardboard box, the violinist pulls out a Beretta handgun from underneath her gray vest.

Knowing the future and what is about to occur, Brittany reverses time for 30 seconds, freezing the world around her.

Then, walking over to the Asian violinist where she removes her Beretta putting it inside Leslie's suitcase.

Then, she unfreezes time where Leslie is placing the two bills into the cardboard box as the Asian violinist goes to grab her Beretta realizing that it has disappeared as she is confused.

Brittany asks the Asian violinist, "Can you play 'Arpeggio' by Paganini?" as the two ladies continue walking.

Looking to her left, Brittany sees a sumo wrestler heading towards them weighing over 400 lbs.

Brittany warns Leslie that they are about to get suplex slammed by a Japanese sumo wrestler.

As he approaches the ladies, Leslie pulls out her stainless steel reinforced titanium oxide coated 7-inch tactical combat blade pressing it against the man's chest.

She tells him, "How much guts do you currently have, or should I press the blade further to find out? "

The Sumo wrestler exclaims, "I wash my hands according to the gunbai."

Then, he leaves saying, "We will fight another match at another time."

As another assassin attacks the ladies, grabbing Brittany and throwing her against the glass plate monitor screen.

Leslie, still holding her tactical combat blade, stabs him in the auricle as he falls over dead against the LED billboard advertising the National Health Care Program.

Leslie says, "My blade went through you from ear to ear."

An Asian man talking on his phone wearing leather pants and jacket begins aiming his Glock at Leslie as another man standing reading his iNewspaper reveals his concealed handgun.

He pulls out his gun as Leslie knocks it out of his hand then acquiring it shoots the first Asian man who was talking on his phone.

Then, turning towards the second man who was reading the iNewspaper, she takes out her knife and stabs him in the neck.

Another unseen man approaches Leslie from behind as Brittany reappears shooting him from the rear. Enough shots are perfectly fired severing the assassin's spinal cord so that he literally falls over in half being able to kiss his own butt.

Leslie states, "If he weren't dead, he would be laughing his butt off at his predicament."

A few other sumo wrestlers appear as one attacks the ladies grabbing them in a hook grip.

Brittany reverses time turning him around as she takes his gun. She shoots an oncoming samurai who is wielding his katana blade aiming at the top of his head killing him. Walking away from the swordsman who falls over dead.

She yells, "Tell Mac Leod there can be only one and it's me."

Then, she returns her attention to a 300 lb. sumo wrestler who is squeezing Leslie. As the wrestler regains his balance by stomping his feet, Brittany shoots each dorsum being the top of each foot.

Falling over he loses his grip having Leslie breathing hard as she escapes.

Lifting his head up attempting to get up, Brittany shoots him right in his forehead. He falls over permanently, losing the match as his entire corpse crashes down upon the ground.

They enter the three floor train station, entering in its second floor with many stores and restaurants.

Brittany Barbosa watches another purple haired female assassin in the second floor's Southwest distance shooting razor sharp spinning discs at them. She immediately grabs Leslie spinning her counterclockwise reversing time.

Then, allowing time to proceed forward repeating itself, she looks in the floor's Southwestern direction firing her Glock several times.

The purple haired female assassin can get off several spinning discs before she is hit in the arm saying, "She who fights and runs away may live to fight another day." Holding her left throwing arm, she uses her SuperPower ability to fly at a thousand miles per hour to get away.

Brittany spins clockwise advancing time. She sees the entire area frozen in time and space.

Then, she sees walking throughout the venue Star Kronika who is renown to be working for Professor Steele and has the SuperPower ability to freeze time.

Leslie Michaels witnesses the ongoings where there are people in mid-step petrified, a young boy recycling his beverage can tossing it towards the trash receptacle. The can freezes in midair, and two male lovers embraced kissing as though they were statues.

Leslie tells Brittany, "After you reverse time so that we can see Star Kronika before she freezes time, I would appreciate you using your SuperPower ability to fly to bring me closer to her."

Brittany asks, "What can you do? You realize that she's going to freeze the both of us."

Leslie remarks, "Trust me."

Brittany rotates counterclockwise reversing time then she is holding on to Leslie thrusting her forward.

Star Kronika sees the duo propelling one of them towards her at supersonic speed. She begins to blink three times rapidly to freeze time.

Leslie Michaels points her right index finger at Star who freezes, looking petrified.

Leslie smirks saying, "Tell Freddie that 'another one bites the dust.'"

Brittany asks, "What just happened?"

Leslie smiles and says, "When I was a child and someone said something mean to you, you would retort to them 'I am rubber and you are glue, whatever you say to me bounces off me and sticks on you."

Brittany says to clarify, "Do you mean to tell me that you have the SuperPower ability to use another SuperPower person's ability against them."

Leslie says, "That's a more mature way of putting it. Yes."

Brittany inquires, "Will she stay frozen forever?"

Leslie replies, "Her spell was only to freeze time for less than an hour."

On the third level, walking parallel to the two ladies on the second level is an African American assassin. He and Brittany Barbosa stare at each other with their guns held right against their midsection. Each begins shooting at each other. Each projectile just misses each other as there are pedestrians walking back and forth in front of them.

Brittany and Leslie begin running across the second level.

The large crowd of passengers block the man's view forcing him to look over the rail from the third floor to find the women.

Finally, he spots them and holding his gun close to his chest he begins shooting as they fire back. Each misses their target as a few innocent bystanders get shot in their leg or arm hitting the ground needing medical aid.

As the ladies slide down the escalator's handrail shooting the dozen standing assassins traveling up from the first level's parallel escalator who are shot dead topple over like dominoes.

Brittany and Leslie on the downward escalator spot three armed assassins coming up the first floor's escalator. Brittany shoots the first Pakistani assassin in the head as Leslie stabs the second female Indian assassin in the heart.

As both fall down the escalator dead, Brittany shoots the third assassin in the leg. As he falls downward, Brittany continues her competitive shooting gallery adventure by shooting the falling man in his stomach, then shoulder and finally between his eyes ending her session.

Walking on the lower level by the subway, Leslie indicates that there are two approaching assassins walking towards them.

Brittany reverses time then plays it back so she can shoot one assassin as Leslie, being invisible stabs the back of the neck at the base of the skull severing the assassin's spinal cord.

Brittany picks up the two dead assassins' handguns. She hands one to Leslie as she shoots the other advancing assassin in both of his lungs causing unconsciousness and death to follow.

The black man takes the escalator down to the lower level as Leslie stabs another man and Brittany shoots a female assassin firing at her across the train tracks.

As the black male assassin walks North, the ladies walk parallel waiting for the next train.

The black assassin begins shooting just as the train arrives blocking his line of sight.

From either side of the train, the doors open as the ladies enter from one side watching closely the black male assassin who enters from the other side. Slowly they each take a step towards each other avoiding the unaware, unarmed passengers. Each step, the adversaries get closer until only the two metal poles that are four feet apart separate them.

Holding one metal pole the ladies stare at the opposing black man holding an adjacent metal pole.

As most of the passengers get off the train at the next stop, the black man kicks and punches Brittany who blocks his every movement.

Leslie swings her seven-inch, straight edge fighting knife at him. Most of her attacks are blocked but a few knife caused puncture wounds begin to resemble a 'sewing machine' stitch pattern.

The black assassin continues fighting Brittany who is weakening. The man kicks her hard knocking her semiconscious. He grabs his gun and places the barrel on her forehead.

As he is ready to pull the trigger, Leslie stabs him in the internal jugular vein of his neck telling him "If you keep pressure on the blade until medical help such as an EMT arrives, you will live. Otherwise, we will see you in the next life" forcing him to drop the handgun and hold the straight edge fighting knife against his throat just missing his trachea and larynx.

Getting off the train, Brittany pushes the button for police and medical help.

Leslie picks up his Glock 68 as she removes from her suitcase another seven-inch, straight edge fighting knife.

Walking up the metal stairs to the street, they notice three vans with machine guns touting assassins heading towards them.

Across the street is the Moscone Convention Center where the 'World Traveling Occult' Museum is being held.

Brittany remembers her day's fast forward vision where they fight the three vehicles' assassins having Leslie Michaels being restrained, captured, and brought into the museum. To circumvent this possibility, she takes Leslie into the 'World Traveling Occult' Museum.

In the lobby of the museum there is a large billboard size image of a Ouija board where a hand moves the planchette around the board spelling out various words presumably sent by spirits from beyond. The current word shown is 'BEWARE.'

Nearby, an Asian man is talking to an extremely attractive, redheaded Japanese woman. They look to their right at the passageway behind Brittany. The man waves his arms as over twenty assassins stand between the ladies and them.

Brittany turns counterclockwise reversing time thirty seconds. Stopping, she warns Leslie of the impending assassin onslaught. As the Asian man lifts his arms up, Brittany and Leslie begin firing their automatic handguns at the location behind them.

Each assassin that enters the museum is immediately shot and killed by the ladies.

As their weapons are emptied, they retreat into the exhibits displaying the Salem witch trials and the legendary ghost ship stories as they reload.

Hiding inside these dark venues Leslie using her straight edge fighting knife disarms two assassins as Brittany uses her martial arts knowledge to knockout with an extremely powerful karate punch to the neck of the female assailant.

Then, spinning around using both thumbs to blind the male assassin by poking out and removing his eyes. Both adversaries are out cold dropping their weapons which each lady retrieves.

As three more assassins enter the ghost ship gallery, the ladies crouching behind the ship's bow fire away putting holes in each of their foreheads knocking each one backwards as their heads one by one hit the floor as their feet follow.

The slow-motion ragdoll motion of each assailant dying with the head over heel motion is so wonderful to behold that Brittany spins counterclockwise to view it repeatedly. Leslie laughs as she nails another oncoming enemy in the heart.

Noticing that their automatic handguns feel light, the women gather up the dead assassins' handgun cartridges.

Leslie states, "Thank God for John Browning."

Brittany examines the fine droplets of blood spattered in a backward direction from the exit wound and in a forward direction from the entrance wound.

Brittany watches as a weaponless assassin runs towards her yelling. She grabs the bald man's coat knocking him down to the floor. The man tries to grab her gun which she knocks out of his hand as Leslie shoots him from behind. He falls to his knees before kissing the tiled floor.

Leslie begins walking to the 'Dante's Inferno' gallery as Brittany follows her.

Behind them are two crazy twenty-five-year-olds wearing White Sox uniforms with painted whitefaces and carrying Louisville Sluggers with protruding metal spikes.

In unison, they chant, "Ladies, come out and play. Can we make a homerun with your heads?" They begin to laugh out loud.

Trapping the prey having their backs against a mirrored wall. The ballplayers each swing their kanabō (translated as "Metal stick") or a Samurai or studded two-handed war club at the ladies' heads.

Luckily, each 'joker' gets a strike, missing each lady. In return, each lady shoots the other's 'joker' in the crouch.

As they bend over grabbing their balls, the other lady calls the ballplayer out with a tap to his forehead. The mirrored wall behind each 'joker' gets an embedded spider web pattern where the bullet exited the occipital lobe.

Turning around, Brittany views her reflection, she reads the large sign at the entrance to the exhibit's hall marked 'The Ninth Level of Hell based on Dante's Inferno.' She tells Leslie, "Déjà vu."

Walking further into the mirrored menagerie, the two women hide between two parallel mirrors looking down the long corridor. The dozen assassins following them all freeze in place.

Leslie remarks, "Guess who's coming to dinner and it is not Sidney Poitier."

Brittany says jokingly, "Are you ready to give Star Kronika the finger?"

With her index finger extended while the two secretly hide, Star serpentines into the gallery looking at her reflection.

Walking past the two hiding warriors, Star carefully peeks into the next passageway as Leslie sneaks up behind her using Star's SuperPower freeze ability against her, turning the troll to stone.

Brittany and Leslie walk into the next passageway knowing that Star had already checked it out. As they pass the base of a statue of "The Treachery of Pelias upon Aeson," Leslie stops to hide behind it.

Brittany begins advancing as down the corridor two Nevsky sisters who were trained in Combat Sambo the deadly martial art and combat fighting style. Running between the deadly sisters is another assassin wearing a white jacket holding an automatic machine gun.

Seeing Brittany down the hallway, he charges towards her as Leslie kneeling behind the base of the statue shoots him in the thigh.

As he hobbles forward, Brittany shoots him right in the chest killing him instantly.

Leslie yells out, "That is what you get for wearing white after Labor Day. Remember everyone, you can't wear white after Labor Day."

Using their Combat Sambo deadly style, the exotic female Moscow death squad attacks Brittany and Leslie who are skilled in the counter skill of Krav Maga that they learned in Israel.

In the Israeli against Russian martial art death match, it is the Eurasian Brown Bear's elbow flying in two directions by the sisters. Fighting back hard is the Israeli gazelle with its focus on swift victory to the opponent's eyes, throat, solar plexus, groin, ribs, and liver.

As an elbow connects with Brittany's head, she delivers a hard thrust into her adversary's liver. Leslie's opponent misses her ribs as she lands her four fingers deep inside her attacker's neck crushing the larynx.

Unable to speak with a significant respiratory compromise that can cause death, she signals to her sister that they must leave immediately seeking medical help.

The two leave the museum as an ambulance with EMTs arrive taking the sisters seeking emergency care.

Three men following each other enter the next perpendicular mirrored hallway. Leslie shoots her automatic handgun that she just put a fully loaded cartridge in. Like bowling pins, she has her projectiles enter the first assassin's chest and exit the third assassin's back. Stunned, they all look forward at her then down at their chest before falling backwards on top of each other.

Proceeding into the next gallery, Leslie hides behind the statue shooting the man and woman contract killers. First shot in the leg then hitting each in their stomach.

As the man goes down to his knees pointing the gun at Leslie who grabs his arm confiscating his firearm. She shoots the woman in the head killing her, turning her attention back to the man, she flips him over her shoulders having the man hit the floor laying on his back semi-conscious as Brittany shoots him in his heart.

Then, Leslie and Brittany lie on the ground underneath the two dead assailants hiding as two more hitmen enter the room.

They peruse the entire room unaware of the fact that the two ladies have shot them in the neck. The two men keel over now aware that they are dead.

Leslie is laying in a prone position as Brittany behind another statue is kneeling. Then, two more hitmen charge into the gallery, they shoot them dead.

Another two hired killers enter the gallery slowly suspicious of how quiet things are. Leslie lying down hits his kneecap and as he topples over nails him in the head.

Brittany with her two hands holding the handgun stretched outward kneeling behind the marble statue shoots the stomach making a large round hole in his torso.

Another woman enters heading to the right of the statue as both prone Leslie and Brittany on her knees slides across the floor, both sending projectiles through her body killing her instantly.

Leslie shoots the screaming Ninja dressed in black right in the stomach then Brittany shoots him in the head knocking him dead on the floor.

In the next room assassins with their guns drawn run across the room as the women switch automatic cartridges. Each of their shots hit with deadly force as one selfish assassin begins using his partner as a shield.

Brittany sees this treachery and turning her handgun sideways not only looks cool in films but allows the shooter to 'build the castle' meaning lining up the front and rear of the handgun.

Brittany shoots him directly in the right temple forcing blood to splatter all over the white pristine mirrored walls.

The ladies aim and shoot again as the assassins are falling to the ground. The standing adversaries are shot another time in their head ensuring no retaliation.

Leslie and Brittany keep filling up their clothing with cartridges and placing discarded weapons into the suitcase

Two more men come running down the hallway towards them. The one on the left gets shot by Leslie right in the head.

Brittany shoots the assassin on the right in the stomach.

As the hitman is trying to get up, she shoots him again in the head.

Entering a room where every wall is a mirror feeling like Bruce Lee in the film 'Enter the Dragon.' They look to the right, then in front of them. They look in every direction to see if another assassin is about to jump out and attack, They begin to use their handgun grip to crack every inch of the full-length mirrors.

With the mirrored wall resembling a massive spider web, in a swift motion they plunge forward into the next room looking in every direction at each mirrored wall. Moving their fully armed handguns left to right, they hear Star Kronika's voice indicating that she is among them.

Arriving outside the museum another four highly skilled assassins get out of an Uber and run inside the entrance having their automatic machine guns drawn.

One assassin enters the mirrored gallery getting immediately shot in the head by Leslie.

He stares at her exclaiming, "I am dead. Oh wow. Oh wow, Oh wow." as his head smashes against the floor.

As another assassin walks in only to get a headshot by Brittany. Before dying he states, "That did not work the way I envisioned it."

Star states, "That is two projectiles already used. How many more do you two have?"

Leslie provokes her saying, "Stick your head out here and count my fingers."

The newly arrived assassin gets off the elevator. There are three men holding automatic machine guns and two women with Glocks. They enter the mirrored section of the museum as both Leslie and Brittany each walk with their backs against the mirrored wall.

The three men with machine guns walk down the mirrored wall hallway as the two women instruct one to go left with her while the other goes right with the other two men.

Brittany peeks down the hallway seeing nothing but her reflection in the mirrored walls.

Hiding between two parallel mirrored walls Leslie views an assassin holding a machine gun. She grabs it with her left hand pointing it away and downward as her right-hand swings like a baseball bat between the man's two eyebrows breaking his nose.

The other man using his automatic machine gun forcefully pushes Brittany backward into the mirrored wall. She uses her left leg to kick him hard in the groin forcing him to bend over.

Leslie sees her assailant spurting blood from his nose into his eyes as he tears up.

Stepping into the gallery is one of the women who has her Glock drawn not yet seeing Leslie who reveals herself from behind the temporarily blinded man. The female assassin shoots at her hitting her blinded male partner who accidentally steps into her shot. The back of his head is now missing.

Leslie jokingly states "You needed that like a hole in your head" as she laughs.

Knocking the machine gun out of the man's hand, Leslie grabs the man's head with her two hands banging his skull against the mirrored wall becoming unconscious. Seeing the hitwoman aim her weapon at Leslie, she maneuvers the senseless man as a shield. His female assassin partner makes Swiss cheese out of his back emptying her cartridge.

Leslie jokes saying, "It is nice to see your back, you spineless wimp."

Brittany shoots the female assassin as she is holding her useless empty gun falling over dead.

Entering the mirrored hallway, the second male assassin shoots at Brittany missing her.

Leslie decides to hunt down Star Kronika while Brittany ducks down the parallel hallway with her newly acquired automatic machinegun.

Brittany moves a mirrored panel so anyone entering the gallery would only see their reflection and not Brittany standing behind it.

As the second team's male assassin stands in the middle of the passageway turning away from Brittany, Brittany presses the machine gun's trigger letting a few rounds shoot through the mirrored panel killing him immediately as he falls face down.

Walking down the mirrored hallway parallel to the other corridor, Brittany crashes through the mirrored wall into the next gallery's room. She jumps through the reflective glass wall hitting the second team's female assassin knocking her down. Brittany uses her seven-inch straight combat knife plunging it into the back of her neck. She struggles to get upright dropping her automatic machinegun. Oscillating as she stands, the female assassin scratches Brittany's forearm.

Brittany blocks a poorly executed punch and right knee smash throwing her disorientated body high over her head deeming her unconscious. The assassin collides into the mirrored wall and down to the floor.

Using a figure four against the hitwoman's neck, Brittany chokes her as not receiving any blood and air leads to asphyxiation and strangulation killing her.

Brittany shoots an assailant aiming at her in the head causing him to fall from the second level with a significant section of his cranium missing.

Another Asian is running towards her using martial arts motions as she nails him causing him to slid across the floor towards her.

She remembers an old song saying, "Ricky Martin is calling telling you 'La vida loca, she'll give you lots of pain, like a bullet to your brain,'" as his head smashes against the mirrored floor spouting blood all over.

Brittany enters the last mirrored room where Star Kronika has a Samurai katana sword against Leslie's throat. Unable to convince the enemy to call a truce, Brittany spins counterclockwise allowing Leslie Michaels to use her SuperPower ability to freeze Star using her own SuperPower against herself.

Arriving at the Moscone Convention Center are DODGE personnel who lift the catatonic Star Kronika placing her lifeless, rigid body in an inescapable straight jacket.

They cart her off restrained to their secret intervention center to convince Star Kronika to switch her SuperPower organization allegiance.

Waking up being revived, Star is restrained not allowing her to move to use her SuperPower,

The DODGE interrogator explains that she is still alive so he can convince her to leave the Golden Eagle Organization and pledge her SuperPower allegiance to DODGE,

Star says, "I will think about it, but I need to know how I benefit as the Steeles have been very gracious towards me."

She is placed in a secured cell still wearing the straight jacket.

Chapter 12

Recruiting the Old Guard

Rileigh Michele is giving a one-week concert in Sydney Australia at the Olympic Park. The Olympic Stadium shows are sold out to an audience of 115 thousand 'Meow' and 'Kitty Litter' fans.

Visiting her at the upgraded, five-star Novotel Sydney Olympic Park hotel is Oscar winning actor Robert Leach.

Twelve and a half miles away, Rileigh rents out the iconic Sydney Australia Opera House. The Opera House is the home of the Sydney Symphony Orchestra. With a capacity of 2,679 seats, it houses the Sydney Opera House Grand Organ which is the largest mechanical tracker action organ in the world having over ten thousand pipes.

Music icon Rileigh Michele plays the venue's famous organ singing for Robert her current lyrics to the opening number of his next role. Leach is to portray the leading role of Rick Blaine once played by Humphrey Bogart in the remake of Casablanca that has more sexual content and less dialogue.

Sitting at the Grand Organ, Rileigh Michele has numerous pipes feeding wind into each pipe causing the air to oscillate thus producing a sound.

On the same continent, in the same city Myrena Gorgona is supervising her trendy fashion exhibit at the Australian Fashion Week.

She tells Stormy who is accompanying her "In Aussie one can mix pleasure with business. After all, when in Sydney" receiving a Cheshire Cat smile from Stormy.

Traveling for her 'Golden Eagle' Organization pilgrage, JiJi Nkosi is scheduled to land in Sydney later that day heading to the black opal gemstone mines.

It is Myrena's plan to intercept JiJi and convince her that after her Steele brothers assigned mission to join her becoming a 'Lemnian Deeds' Federation member. "After all, it is the females who do all the work therefore we should reap all the rewards."

Rileigh begins to sing to Robert saying "My tribute to your version of 'Casablanca…'"

In Casablanca in French Morocco at Rick's Café American
Everyone knows the café, and Mister Rick, the man
Drinking, gambling, and sex with French, German and Italian
Playing the small, salmon-colored piano is Sam.
Rick never mingles with customers being never impressed
In fact, the president of the largest Amsterdam money lender
is in our kitchen cooking, cleaning, and in white is dressed.
There is gambling in the back, roulette to win some tender

Sam is asked to play the tune 'As Time Goes By' again.
Play it again Sam, in front of all the ladies and men
Now in town is a married woman, his former lover.
Rick sneaks off with her keeping the affair undercover
Rick came from Paris but was born in New York City
His former lover's husband is unaware of their fling, a pity!
Inside the expensive and chic nightclub, beyond the neon sign
Adulterous lovers say 'Kiss me. Kiss me as if it were the last

time.'

He keeps saying 'Here's looking at you, kid' for the hundredth
time
Of all the gin joints, in all the towns, in all the world, she walks
into mine
Every night in his secret, private bed, It's still the same old story
The duo kisses, makes passion, often a fight for love and glory
Honestly, the day is long! When are you planning to go to bed
If we are caught 'Round up the usual suspects' I will dread.
Louie, I think this is the beginning of a beautiful friendship,
I say.
Inside of us, we both know you belong with Victor every day

Robert congratulates Rileigh, giving her many kisses. They both leave adjourning to the three-star Michelin restaurant, the Local Eatery nearby. Sitting down inside the Italian bistro where the staff is very accommodating and welcoming,

The two order caprese salad followed by the salmon special and ham and pineapple pizza.

Myrena and Stormy meet JiJi at the Sydney International Airport taking her to lunch at 'The Commander's First-Class Cockpit' being a member's only, exclusive travelers club that serves a gourmet buffet with wine and drinks.

Sitting down after they have ordered their food and drinks, Myrena explains that she was prepared and ready to become an executive member of the 'Golden Eagle' Organization.

She stresses the fact that she did everything required to become a member and the life partner of Rocky Steele.

She states, "If it were not for the lying and treachery of Professor Steele, I would be one of your supervisors assigning you to missions."

As they are being served their drinks as they are enjoying their gourmet buffet lunch,

Stormy adds, "JiJi, we value your SuperPower abilities but believe that you are being short-changed by the male dominated organization. Our organization 'Lemnian Deeds' Federation promises that you will receive ninety-five percent of the profit that you have rightfully earned."

JiJi after listening carefully responds, "The 'Golden Eagle' Organization and the Steele family have always treated me well and I have more money than I could spend in a hundred lifetimes."

Myrena smiles and tells her, "That is true. You, JiJi have extremely lined the coffers of their pockets too."

JiJi tells them, "I will think about allowing you to provide me with a trial-mission. If you can exceed what the 'Golden Eagle' Organization and the Steeles' provide such as taking care of all my expenses and arrangements. In addition, if proving to me that there will be a significant increase in my percentage then I will consider joining your Federation."

After having some Australian mountain coffee and cheesecake, a chauffeur-driven limousine picks up JiJi transporting her to her mission's destination.

Then, another private chauffeur driven limousine picks up Myrena and Stormy bringing them back to the International Convention Centre Sydney to finish setting up for the Australian Fashion Week.

A month later, under the guise of attending the Loughborough University Stashion Show, Myrena Gorgona and Stormy travel to Heathrow Airport.

They walk to baggage claim where their chauffeur gathers their overnight Tumi Titanium luggage. Heading to Terminal 2, he opens the rear door for his clients.

As he sits in the driver's seat, he states, "Are we all seat belted in? Restrained? Our drive to Loughborough University is only two and a quarter hours away. Enjoy yourselves."

Loughborough University has been crowned several times the 'University of the Year' and numerous as the winner in both the 'University Sports Facilities' and 'Sports and Societies,'

Upon arriving at the University, the committee for the Stashion Show greets the SuperPower SuperModel and her guest.

They have made dinner reservation at the Revolution Loughborough.

After a tour of the show's venue in the student union, Myrena asks the chairperson to escort them to the Michele Locke Sports Center. They walk a short distance along Union Way to Rutlands Way into the front of the Sports Center.

Meeting them inside the lobby is Zoey Chamberlain, the four-year reigning Women's World high jump record holder at eleven feet, three inches.

Zoey welcomes them saying "My name is Zoey Chamberlain."

Stormy replies, "We know who you are and the amazing feats that you have accomplished in high school and here at Lboro." Myrena nods in agreement shaking her hand followed by Stormy.

Zoey, still in awe of meeting her fashion idol says, "I own just about every fashion outfit of yours. Friends call me, 'Gorgona the second.'" as she giggles.

After a pause, Zoey continues, "I have been instructed to bring you to Coach Locke's office without further delay," as they walk the hallways. Along their path, world-class athletes wave and say, "Hello."

Upon arriving at the spacious head track coach and BOA (British Olympic Association) chairperson, Zoey knocks upon the door which opens automatically. Michele Locke stands up from her oak desk greeting her guests. As she extends her hand, Stormy hugs her followed by Myrena.

Zoey states, "And I will never forget you two, especially iMagazine SuperModel and SuperDesigner Myrena Gorgona."

Michele asks them to sit down in the cushioned oak chairs saying, "Welcome to the University of Loughborough, my home away from home and 'ala mater.' Where are you lodging during your visit?"

Myrena answers, "We have reservation at the executive suite in the Link."

Michele states, "Rubbish. You will both stay at my nearby estate. It has five master bedrooms, maids, house cleaners and an entire kitchen staff. That should suffice all of us."

Myrena replies, "That is most gracious of you. We accept."

Stormy asks, "Can we chat about your prized female athletes?"

Coach Locke smiles saying, "Businesspeople, always getting right down to it. We can discuss that later at my dwelling in private, less ears roaming around."

Myrena gets her address and cell number saying, "After our dinner with the Stashion committee we will have our chauffeur drive us to your mansion."

For dinner with the Stashion Show committee, Stormy orders the Sri Lankan Chicken Curry in a creamy coconut and tomato sauce with rice.

Myrena has the appetizers being Fire Balls which are pork chili meatballs, shredded duck in lettuce tacos, and honey mustard sausages.

After a delicious and informative dinner, the entire table orders the Millionaire's Slice, an indulgent cheesecake made with chocolate and salted caramel.

Upon ringing the doorbell of the Locke mansion, the two visitors are serenaded by the song 'God Save the King' that Michele heard after receiving her gold Olympic medal.

Beating her housekeeper to the front door, Coach Locke welcomes her guests explaining, "Before my Olympic debut in the long and triple jump, my mother was in a coma. All her life she had wanted to hear this song as I stood on the highest tier of the podium receiving my Olympic gold medal. Every time she comes and visits me, she is welcomed by this rendition performed by the British Philharmonic Orchestra."

Thinking back on those days, Michele wipes a tear from her eye.

As the music plays on, she welcomes inside her high walnut ceiling with oak walls and flooring estate's entrance.

Located in the foyer's trophy case on the top shelf is an Olympic gold medal with just below her Olympic silver medal. Around both sides of her accolades are electronic rotating color photos of her many victories in the Olympics as well as her high school and collegiate competitions.

Taking several minutes to compliment her and enjoy the rare opportunity of viewing these personal, historical treasures.

Michele invites the two ladies into her library as her house cleaner and kitchen staff leave for the night.

Inside her library, are many first editions of Charles Dickens, William Blake, John Milton, J.R.R. Tolkien, C.S. Lewis, George Orwell, Douglas Adams, Samuel Taylor Coleridge, J.K. Rowling, and her favorite author of 'Pride and Prejudice' and many other novels, Jane Austen.

Prominently displayed on top of her bookshelf is a signed copy of 'Blackthink; My Life as Black Man and White Man' written by the legendary black Olympian Jesse Owens.

Her two SuperPower guests are thoroughly impressed by her eclectic library having all of them sit on the two parallel goose down filled with central foam seat and back cushioned luxury sofas with a bronze base.

Myrena invites Coach Michele Locke to join her SuperPower Federation.

Coach Locke says, "I am too old, too wealthy, and to set in my ways. I prefer to coach and mentor the next generation."

Myrena agrees saying "As long as you supply the 'Lemnian Deeds' Federation with new recruits. The best of the best. Since offering you money is useless, we can negotiate with favors and more."

Coach Locke places three photographs on the glass coffee table between the two sofas.

She points to the first picture saying, "This is Zoey Chamberlain you have already met at the sports center before coming in my office."

Myrena picks up the picture to get a better view then hands it to Stormy. She returns it to the glass coffee table.

Handing the next photograph to Myrena, she says, "This Lboro athlete is Lillian Mae who runs the woman's track 10,000 meter. Although Lillian can run the 10km race in under 20 seconds, she slows her pace down to complete the race in under 20 minutes."

Handing the third picture to Myrena, she introduces her saying, "This is Ruth Hannah. Although she runs as fast as her teammate Lillian, she competes in the 5km race and under 8 minutes."

After reviewing and returning all three photographs to the glass coffee table, Coach Locke states "It is an historical fact as you know that I studied under your current adversary Professor Steele not only improving my SuperPower ability but to be a mentor to others discovering their SuperPower abilities and training them."

She continues saying, "These three gifted athletes that I train on the track field, I also train on the SuperPower field. I can attest that these ladies are the most gifted SuperPowers ability individuals that I have mentored."

Stormy comments, "You have never seen the skills that Myrena possesses."

Michele states, "Zoey Chamberlain is a unique shapeshifter called a 'Therianthropy.' Do you know what that means?"

Myrena looks at Stormy saying, "Not exactly?"

Coach Locke says, "Therianthropy is the term for a SuperPower ability person that can metamorphose into any animal by shapeshifting such as the stories of werewolves, dogs, cats, and flying being an eagle. The Brothers Grimm in their Fairytale collection of stories tell of the frog that transforms into a prince. Other books by J.K. Rowling's have wizards that can transform into a wolf or a dog and witches that transform into cats. Stephenie Meyer had an Indian tribe that could upon command turn into a pack of wolves, Joan D. Vinge's novel has two lovers separated by time as he's a wolf at night and she's a Lady hawk by day."

Stormy jokes, "I get the picture as I have seen all those pictures on digital microchips," as she laughs.

Michele continues, "Besides animal shapeshifting, Zoey can become invisible. She can mimic the transparent 'hell hounds' from the Supernatural stories."

Myrena remarks, "What about these other two racers?"

She brags, "Lillian Mae and Ruth Hannah are naturally faster than your adversary Oliver 'the Merc' Davis being able to fly at 2,000 mph without pills and can insert false past experiences into another's anterior cingulate cortex where long term memories are stored. I have timed both ladies in the complete darkness of night at over 1,800 mph. Imagine if they revealed that speed to the world? Oh, my, what a problem that would cause the IOC. Could you two see them tying for first in the Self-Transcendence 3100mile race being the world's longest certified footrace in one hour, forty minutes. That certainly would destroy the previous record of thirty-five days."

Myrena and Stormy say, "Wow. Amazing."

Coach Michele Locke continues saying, "Besides SuperSpeed, these two have the SuperPower ability to become cold-blooded. They are cold-blooded, not at all like James Brown who wrote the song about dating, Linda Blair who aborted their baby. These two can like animals vary their body temperature according to their environment."

After a peaceful, restful night, the kitchen staff prepares the trio a full English breakfast.

Michele Locke states, "The full English breakfast which is often called 'a full Monty' named after the British army General Bernard Montgomery who in his World War II campaign in North Africa began every day with his full English breakfast which consisted of sunny side up eggs, two bangers which are sausages, three strips of bacon, two flat mushrooms, two ripe tomatoes, a slice of buttered toast cut in half, baked beans, breakfast Yukon Gold potatoes, a cup of black pudding with freshly squeezed orange juice accompanied by an Earl Grey tea."

Chapter 13

No Man is an Island

Olympia Gort's mother Yoko gets a call on the phone telling her, "Come to the Daniel Nathan Andrews Centre to meet with Professor Steele and Dr. Andrews."

Arriving by helicopter into the top secret 'Golden Eagle' research facility, Dr. Yoko Gort is greeted outside the helipad on the building's roof by Professor Steele. The two of them continue into the rooftop entrance passing through the security detector that scans for weapons, explosives, listening devices, and hidden recording devices.

Entering the main laboratory Dr. Daniel Nathan Andrews, the chairperson and world's leading authority on cloning walks over greeting Dr. Gort, giving her a hug explaining, "I feel that I have gotten to know you through my months of experiments."

The Professor tells her, "After that fateful day when you are unable to save your husband from his fiery passing, our scientists were able to collect enough DNA samples for our cloning experiments."

Dr. Andrews leads the group into a small laboratory. He picks up a glass container showing it to Dr. Gort saying, "This is stage one where we take a single cell of your husband's DNA having it grow into a living, dividing organism."

Looking at it closely, Doctor Gort examines the specimen.

Walking into the adjacent room they passed through a door marked 'Stage 2.' Inside this room, they see various clones that are heterogeneous biological stages of Dr. Hiroshi Gort.

169

His widowed wife asks Dr. Andrews, "May I examine the clones of my departed husband?"

He nods his head stating, "Absolutely. There is no one else in existence that can better validate our scientific research."

Yoko puts on a pair of medical examination gloves as she begins examining the cranial. On some of the clones she opens their eyes saying, "Oh my, I have gotten flashbacks of my late husband. It reminded me of the way he looked at me when we first met. We dated while attending graduate school being in the same classes."

Professor Steele replies, "Although it might seem a little eerie. We urge you to keep a scientist's approach so that we can formulate the results of our current endeavors."

She continues examining the clones of her departed husband inspecting each of the clone's torso, arms, and legs.

Dr. Andrews hands her his scanner to have her capture each clone's fingerprint electronically. Then, taking her scanned images copying them to his computer he shows her that her images and the original scanned fingerprint from Gort Robotics Facility. The original image from where every day she and her husband passed through their biometric scanners that verified them using ocular, fingerprint, and voice recognition.

These two images are placed on top of each other on the monitor. The results clearly show that they are an exact match.

Continuing into the main laboratory room, Dr. Yoko Gort witnesses advanced clones of her husband exercising and learning advanced, academic studies.

Dr. Andrews requests that Yoko interact with one of the clones both physically and verbally.

Afterwards as they are having a catered lunch, she tells Dr. Andrews and the Professor, "It was like Deja Vu having the clone communicate with the same voice of my departed husband using the same body language and motions that he had."

Upon finishing their green tea cheesecake dessert, Professor Steele escorts Dr. Yoko Gort back to the helicopter telling the pilot to come back for him in two hours.

That night Dr. Yoko Gort was unable to sleep as she keeps thinking about the activities of her day and how impossible everything she saw seemed to be.

Patrick Kelly has the SuperPower to fly and to enter the dreams of others, making them seem extremely realistic.

He tells his friends that his dream is to kill the 'Warrior Spirit' in his enemies. He enjoys controlling his victims as they dream of trying to escape like a black mamba, capturing and eating a rat.

Flying high above Yoko Gort's Penthouse condominium is Patrick Kelly who is extending both of his arms and having his fingers vibrating up and down.

As the good doctor begins entering her REM sleep Patrick has been instructed to ensure that her husband truly lives through his clones.

Using his SuperPower ability, Patrick begins with Yoko dreaming of herself collaborating with her husband knowing that this test on the robot will be the final successful test. Earlier that morning, he reminded her that "Thomas Edison said he was successful on his thousandth attempt at creating the light bulb. When asked how he felt about the failures he remarked 'I now know 999 ways not to make a lightbulb' having him smile."

Yoko told her husband, "I have an amazing feeling about this test. Let's be positive and enthusiastic today."

Hiroshi gave her a hug and a passionate kiss as he walks into the laboratory to prepare his robot for the final test he labeled 'Test C-2.' He nods to his wife who is also his assistant to start her software download.

Then, as she looks up expecting her husband to be excited as everything was working perfectly, she finds him in a sea of a blazing inferno as though a backdraft had occurred.

She immediately grabs the fire extinguisher trying to put out his hot, glowing body trapped in a cloud of ignited gas. Sadly, her efforts did not help him as his chard body toppled onto the floor.

Throughout the night as she tosses and turns, she cannot escape her dream as Patrick loops Dr. Hiroshi Gort consumed in Hellfire calling out to his wife "Yoko please help me! Something went terribly wrong. Aishiteru Yoko!"

Sleep talking Yoko kisses her departed husband saying, "I love you too."

Night after night Patrick torments Yoko through her dreams forcing her to stay up all night watching the Sci-Fi Movie iChannel until she is so exhausted, she eventually dozes off allowing Patrick to continue harassing her warrior spirit until she resigns.

Then, next night, Patrick, as instructed tells the dreaming Yoko who is easily persuaded as she hears, "Yoko, I am alive through my clones. I will visit you tomorrow at the old laboratory. You must help me in fixing the robots. I now know what went wrong the last time and need to continue our project."

As though she was in a hypnotic state, she promises to do whatever he asks,

Early in the morning Yoko Gort is awoken by the ringing of her wrist iCommunicator. She answers the phone with a sleepy 'hello.' She hears a strangely familiar voice; that sounds exactly like her departed husband.

As though she was still sleeping and dreaming, he tells her "You must meet me in our old robotic laboratory in two hours. We have a lot of work to accomplish as I have figured out what went wrong the last time we worked together. I have many questions to ask you about the current state of robotic research."

As she is disconnecting from her wrist iCommunicator, she gets up to take a shower.

She brushes her hair and gets dressed. She hears her breakfast delivery service drop off her daily traditional Japanese breakfast that includes warm rice, salted salmon, miso soup and seaweed.

As she gets off her bus, she walks towards the front of the old Gort Robotic Factory that was renovated by their daughter Olympia.

Meeting the clone of her deceased husband she advises him to join her at the computer bang shop where they can sit in front of an internet terminal as she updates him on robotic technology.

A half hour later sitting in front of a 3D floating monitor she tells the Hiroshi clone, "After your tragic accident, I became lonely and missing you. I checked into a medical facility where Medical genetic engineers used your stored semen and created in vitro our daughter Olympia."

Showing him on the monitor, videos of their daughter competing in the robotic Tobor Battles winning for several consecutive years the championship. Then, turning to her university's webpages, she shows him videos of their daughter's graduation earning her diploma as a doctor in computer hardware and software. She updates her clone ex on their daughter's success in the field of robotics where she had her robot not only surpassing the Turing test but recently completing the development and installing the 'brain' and the 'heart' microchips.

After thinking about their mission, Hiroshi tells her that he will break into their daughter's office in the Robotics Factory. Then, using a portable recording device designed by Professor Steele, he will make reproductions of all the files created by their daughter, Olympia. Afterwards her two parents will use their knowledge and their daughter's research notes to recreate an army of human-like robots that with the Professor's help will have the ability to fly and bypass Asimov's Three Robot Laws.

Arriving at the Tokyo Japan Haneda International Airport is Carlson Chesterfield who has the SuperPower ability to become invisible and a shapeshifter. Since he was first discovered by Professor Steele and his 'Golden Eagle' Organization, he has been a loyal, faithful member.

Taking a taxi as he avoids all the 'shirotaku' which are illegal, unlicensed, and uninsured taxi drivers.

Meeting his clients, doctors Yoko and Hiroshi Gort as they plan to rob their daughter's factory's office make recorded copies of every research paper and patent application. The Professor has provided

Carlson to make his client invisible. If necessary, he will shapeshift into one of her lab assistants providing a reason for someone being at the office early in the morning.

Both Olympia's mother and cloned father become busy as her mother retrieves each document while the replicant of her father begins recording. He starts with the first page then turns to each subsequent page as the recording continues.

Knowing that her daughter Olympia is speaking at the Tokyo University robotics conference she keeps a close eye on the front door just in case her daughter returns to her office unexpectedly.

As the office clock chimes indicating that it is 5 p.m. Yoko Gort walks around her daughter's office and factory one more time making sure that they did not miss a single scrap of paper to record.

Just as she gives the thumbs up to Carlton Chesterfield who holds hands with her and her cloned husband Hiroshi making them invisible, the office front door opens.

The trio now invisible walks past the evening cleaning crew. They continued down the street as each hails a different cab to their destination.

The Professor staff of thirty office assistants who work in a temporary office where he has rented twenty Mitsubishi high speed color copy machines.

Throughout the night as Yoko Gort gets a good night's sleep, the Professor has his office steadily working twenty office assistants copying documents that were recorded. The remaining ten office assistants are collating and stapling the black and white and color documents.

As Yoko gets her daily breakfast delivery, an international FedUp delivery truck drops off at her front door over three dozen cardboard boxes filled with paper copies from the recordings of the documents and computer files that belong to Olympia Gort.

Her mother, amazed at the number of cardboard boxes that were delivered, says "While the cat's away, her parents will play."

After finishing her breakfast, the duplicate of her expired husband arrives. Each of them grabs a carton containing the reproductions of all the research that they will spend the remainder of their week reading.

The doctors Gort process each of the cardboard boxes opening and reading the contents. They marked pages with yellow and pink highlighters placing a pink post-it to highlight the important pages.

On the wrist iCommunicator of Doctor Yoko Gort, she answers hearing her daughter Olympia's voice inviting her to have dinner with her at the three-star Michelin restaurant Sazenka.

She agrees to tell her that she will meet her there at 6 p.m.

Meeting her daughter in Tokyo's international community, both mother and daughter walk past the bamboo trees. At the entrance of Sazenka, they are greeted by the manager in Japanese, Chinese, English, and French.

Olympia speaking perfect Japanese indicates that she has a reservation for two. Led to their table inside the famous Michelin Chinese cuisine restaurant where each dish is adorned with premium, seasonal Japanese components.

The three-star Michelin restaurant having a Michelin-starred chef that serves its award-winning seasonal dishes.

After having green tea poured into their ceremonial cups, Olympia orders for the two of them the Pheasant wonton soup with the jellyfish salad having as the main dish cooked Japanese style, a young pigeon breast grilled over charcoal.

Olympia tells her mother, "I have been worried about you having heard that you were having trouble sleeping at night."

Her mother reassures her, "Lately I have been sleeping like a baby but a week or so ago I was having nightmares about the night that your father died being consumed by the unexpected explosion.

Her daughter reaches across the table joining their hands saying, "It's good news that you are able to sleep soundly and peacefully throughout the night."

For dessert they order the specialty of the house, a souffle cheesecake topped with Fuji apples.

After a week of studying all the stolen documents and research from their daughter's three time 'Golden Microchip' Trophy Winning Robotic Factory.

The clone of Dr. Hiroshi tells his estranged wife caused by his death states, "After downloading the whole collection of your software, I need to spend a few weeks reading the documents and soldering many components to create a new robot. You will then download into the robot's memory and central processing unit all the last known software code that you had written with any patches."

After a day at her gym swimming, Yoko gets a call on her wrist iCommunicator hearing, "This is the Professor. It's been over a month since your cloned husband had left the lab. The scientists at the 'Golden Eagle' Research Center have been helping him to work on the schematics creating the perfect flying army of robots. I am pleased to tell you that using your software, we have created the perfect 'killing machine.'"

Doctor Yoko Gort states, "That is amazing. I am glad for your success that we failed to have many years ago."

Her husband's clone gets on the phone having them speak for another forty-five minutes.

Hanging up, she learns that they are building more flying, military robots every day. The Professor has been able to program each flying robot with the Asimov laws of robotics embedded in their internal software with an override switch.

The squadron of flying robots are transported to San Francisco.

Their test mission is that each robot is armed using long-range paintball rifles. Exiting the freight transport that picked up the ship's cargo from the San Francisco port and the Professor's flying robotic army stands in front of the DODGE office building.

Pablo Martin looks outside his window viewing sixteen armed mechanical robots holding military-like rifles that are aimed at his office building's top floor's windows.

Using the interoffice speaker system, he quickly announces, "We are under attack. I need everyone to hide under their desks for protection."

Immediately everyone ducks under their steel desk as the outer office windows begin bleeding translucent colors. Each window is decorated by translucent red, orange, purple and green.

The entire exterior of the top floors of the DODGE building have been covered, the entire flying robotic army propels themselves to the roof's helipad where they continue decorating the entire area in color.

Then, on command they all disappear into the freight transporter.

After getting confirmation that everybody at the DODGE office is safe and unharmed, Pablo jokes saying, "I know that my namesake Picasso painted a lot more precise and realistic than what we have observed today. Even his Cubist masterpieces are superior to these robots' graffiti."

Throughout the office clapping and laughter is heard.

The iBroadcast iNews iChannels display an army of sixteen flying, steel robots landing on the front lawn of the White House holding electro blaster rifles.

At the iBroadcast station Meredith Marlowe tells the viewing audience, "Right now, landing on the front lawn of the White House are sixteen-armed Androids. Everyone has evacuated the building as we do not know the purpose of their mission. This is really happening right now. It is not a publicity stunt for the remake of the film 'The Day the Earth Stood Still.'"

Appearing in front of the robots is Dr. Hiroshi Gort.

Meredith Marlowe is shown on the air stating "Live from Tokyo Japan we have the Tokyo University's Technology and Robotic chairperson."

On the iBroadcast iChannel, he is seen saying, "Meredith, the man standing in front of the robots, I can't believe it, is an exact replica of my deceased dissertation professor, Dr. Hiroshi Gort. If I had not been at his funeral where he was consumed by fire in a freak robotic laboratory experiment, I must say that this is an impossible event. I cannot explain what I am seeing, other than the man we are seeing on the iBroadcast appears to look like him."

Meredith says, "Thank you chairperson for comments."

Just then the man who looks like Dr. Gort walks behind the robots.

He yells out loud, "Karma wo utsu!"

Meredith says, "Our Japanese translator tells me that he just said, 'shoot at them!' meaning the White House and anyone inside."

The squadron of flying robots commence firing their blaster rifles as they become airborne firing at the front and rooftop. With huge round holes throughout the exterior of the White House, the rest of the building remains intact.

Live on the iBroadcast screen a young, female reporter states, "This is DC iNews reporter 'Foxy' Jamie Lynn on Pennsylvania Avenue near the White House. 'The White House is Down!' Let me repeat that 'The White House is Down!'"

The iNews helicopter is transmitting wide screen footage of the event. Large chunks of the exterior at the White House are exploding off the building's front and its rooftop.

As the regiment of flying robots disperses flying over 2,000 miles per hour into the sky. The Professor instructs a member with the SuperPower ability to become invisible to transport Dr. Gort away from the action before the firing is underway.

Professor Steele returns Dr. Hiroshi Gort and his flying robot unit to be upgraded by Dr. Yoko Gort in Tokyo.

For ten days the two Gort doctors upgrade each robot's software and their body to a carbon steel casing.

Standing boastfully in front of the army of flying robots are Dr. Hiroshi Gort and his wife Dr. Yoko Gort who are digitally recording their achievement.

Olympia instructs Andrea to fire the blaster at her mother and cloned father.

Andrea quotes from the Asimov Three Laws of Robotics saying, "As my designer you know that I cannot injure or kill a human, be instructed to do likewise nor harm myself."

Olympia, who has reached her boiling point especially with her intelligent but irrational mother walks away as though she has given up.

Frustrated, Olympia walks inside the nearby massive research garage, she presses the automatic door opener.

As the army of flying robots begin cheering the Gort doctors, inside the open garage is an Antimatter Photon Cannon.

Olympia announces, "It is far better to kill one hundred villains than to destroy the entire planet."

She turns the switch on as burst after burst of antimatter photons propelled forward.

Watching the horde of robots disintegrate, Olympia with a tear in her eye whispers, "I am going to miss the woman and mother I once had. Goodbye forever," as the two humans that had the DNA that created her are annihilated in a flash.

Chapter 14

Fast and Furious in Mumbai

Nagpur Regenta Central Hotel, Casino and Convention Centre in Nagpur located in the Indian state of Maharashtra having 2,500 rooms. Inside is a 50,000 square foot casino with 1,000 slot machines, blackjack, baccarat, craps, roulette, pai gow poker, and a 5,000 square foot poker room. The poker room has forty tables with twenty viewable HDTVs and free, high-speed Wi-Fi Internet.

Amongst the three million residents there are over sixty thousand millionaires. Jack Diamond knows that there are enough wealthy fish to fry at the poker table.

Before Jack heads to the poker room, he eats breakfast at the convention center's Feliz Café. He tells the waiter, "This morning I feel like having the Indian prepared eggs, Zunka Bhakar, with a hot 'Double-Chocolate Cappuccino' with whipped cream floating on top."

He tells visitors showing off that, "Zunka Bhakar is a millet flour flatbread served with stir-fry vegetables of onions, turmeric, chopped coriander leaves, parsley, dice green pepper, red chili powder, mustard seeds, and chickpeas."

Yesterday while sitting at the casino bar getting his complimentary Jack Daniels Rye whiskey, a slightly intoxicated unlucky gambler has a black bag in his hands looking at it intently until he mutters, "Perhaps selling it another day."

He unknowingly places the black bag inside Jack's leather travel weekender bag thinking that it was his. The stranger gets up saying, "I lost a lot of Bitcoin digital currency today. I hope to win it all back tomorrow."

Jack Diamond walks over to the men's room into a stall where he opens his leather weekender removing the stranger's black bag. Inside the bag is a large red gemstone that upon inspection is real.

While getting ready for bed in the hotel's complimentary gambler penthouse suite, he wants to put the gemstone into the room's safe. Looking on 'Google Image Search' the digital photo he took with his cell of the gem matches the famous 'Liberty Bell Ruby' that was never recovered although the thieves were arrested in 2014.

He realizes that he luckily obtained the 'Liberty Bell Ruby' stolen in 2011. The red gemstone is documented as weighing 8.5 thousand carats. The large ruby was shaped like the Liberty Bell for the United States Bicentennial having fifty diamonds set on it representing the fifty states.

The stranger is a world class smuggler who was visiting private gemstone collectors trying to sell the well-known ruby that is worth $3.5 million. Their deal was to commence tomorrow but now Jack has his black bag.

An Indian philanthropist tells Jack, "Hindis like me who worship Krishna, the flute playing God of protection, compassion, tenderness, and love. His devoted followers believe that the 'king of precious gemstones' known as the 'ruby' gives one the fortune in their afterlife to be reborn as an emperor."

Jack states. "If Dorothy had only known this as the band America knew that 'Oz never did give nothing to the Tin Man. That he didn't, didn't already have.'"

Early in the morning, Jack's iCommunication device with the back having the Jack of Diamond face card sticker rings playing Lady Gaga's 'Poker Face.'

On his wrist iCommunication device is Professor Steele saying "Hello Lucky Jack! Can you guess for me what would make my July fourth to celebrate America's Independence Day. A hint would start with the July's birthstone followed by fireworks crossing all fifty states from the East to the West coast."

Jack unseen grins as he hears "I am willing to bet you two to one placing my $3.5 million US that you can guess the answer as though it was safely place in your mind's vault."

Jack whispers to himself, "How does Steele always know everything?"

The Professor instructs him, "Drive like a 'Bat out of Hell' without stopping for a meatloaf sandwich. Are you allowed to eat beef in India? I know that most Indians are against it for humane and religious reasons." As they both chuckle.

Professor Steele informs the card shark "Get quickly on the 'Mumbai-Nagpur Super Communication Expressway' from Nagpur heading to Mumbai that is officially known as 'Hindu Hrudaysamrat Balasaheb Thackeray Maharashtra Samruddhi Mahamarg' where our courier awaits your delivery."

Upon her confirmation the money transfer will be added to your offshore account. Get going as others may be seeking your acquisition."

Jack Diamond sits in the Feliz Cafe having another wonderful breakfast before he begins his eight-hour journey driving down the new Super Communication Expressway between Nagpur to Mumbai.

A six-foot-tall handsome Latino male approaches his table sitting on the opposite side. Addressing the server, he asks, "Could you get me a double chocolate latte?"

She smiles at him and says, "Would you like that plain, with cream, or having whipped cream floating on top like your friend?"

He replies, "I take my chocolate latte the way I like my ladies; plain, dark with some sweetness on the side," as he winks at her.

She leaves having Jack look up at him saying, "And what do I owe the pleasure of this stranger's company?"

Putting his right fist forward he announces, "I am Dominic Miles. My friends call me 'Dom' but we are not even close to that so you shall call me either 'Mr. Miles' or 'Dominick.'"

Jack returns the gesture by fist bumping his guest back.

Dominick continues, "Professor Steele asked me to come here to drive you to Mumbai."

Jack smirks saying, "The Professor thinks I need a babysitter!"

Dominic says, "He might think that during your eight hour drive that you might need someone to bail you out. Besides, I have won Le Mans twenty-one times. To you that would be 'Blackjack, Winner, winner, chicken dinner."

Then, he makes a finger gun hand sign saying, "Ka-ching," as the server brings him his coffee.

After leaving a generous tip, the two exit the Hotel Casino. Dominic points out his ride.

Jack asks, "Are we driving in a classic soccer mom Ford Expedition?"

Dominic chuckles saying, "Get real man! The car behind the Ford."

Jack Diamond has his eyes wide open as his tongue sticks out of his mouth.

Dominic tells him, "We are traveling inside the fastest Mustang called the Shelby GT 517 EV. As you probably know it's a 1200 horsepower EV muscle car that can hit 60 miles per hour in 1.3 seconds with a top speed of 250 mph."

Jack smiles and remarks, "Cool!"

One does not need to be a fortune teller or possess a crystal ball to realize that as lucky as Jack is and as skillful a driver as Dominick is, the 435-mile road journey will have eight hours of treacherous obstacles with enemies behind every turn.

The Martin twins assign Gabrielle Chronos and Ginny Evans to obtain the precious ruby gemstone. Gabrielle Chronos has the SuperPower ability to transform or morph the properties of matter. Gabrielle explains to Ginny that she can turn a donkey into a Thrust 7 having 40,000 horsepower with a top land speed of 845 mph.

Ginny remarks, "That jackass would have an awful lot of horses behind her as she hits the mother lode."

Both DODGE representatives can become invisible.

Ginny says, "If the rubber accidently misses the road, my other SuperPower will come in handy."

Gabrielle nods in agreement.

The ladies jump into their DODGE provided Ferrari CC90 Stradale-3 EV that is the latest 1,235-hp high-tech Hyper Supercar.

Gabrielle turns the ignition on as Ginny yells, "We are cruising in Enzo's best and brightest vehicle."

Based out of the world famous Shirdi Sai Baba in Nagpur nicknamed the 'Orange City' that receives over 3,000 visitors every day are the temple's Vedic warrior class. They are masters of Shastra Vidya being the ancient North Indian martial art of the Kshatriyas. Each member is a resolute 'sadhu' or 'holy man' having the status of being a yogi. The leader of the 'Eternal Religion' and his followers' worship and believe in Krishna as the Supreme Personality of Godhead having no equal. The leader instructs the Vedic warrior class of his 'sadhu' fighters to retrieve the stolen ruby shaped like the Liberty Bell.

The temple has purchased a T-76 "Ajeya" complete with long range laser cannons and anti-aircraft rockets. The Ajeya, which has a speed of 50 mph, sits on top of a jet powered semitruck, the "Super Shockwave 5" that travels using solar power at 375 mph.

With their Ferrari stopped at a red light, appearing from underneath the Nagpur Railway Station tracks at high speed is a 'Twister Orange' Shelby GT 517 EV.

Dominick yells out to the pedestrians, "Welcome us to the 'Twister Orange City!'"

Jack chuckles yelling, "Tell Carroll, our car is lighter, faster, and both of us are far nastier."

Watching the Ford fly past, Gabrielle tells Ginny, "This will be a remake racing duel between Ferrari verse Ford," as she floors the accelerator passing the red light.

They follow the Ford Mustang Shelby from a distance through the roundabout on to Nagpur Road turning left at the monument. Next, both sports cars travel onto Zero Mile Road. After 1.1 miles both vehicles turn left onto Sir Kasturchand Saga Marg which becomes Temple Road. Then, they make a right onto Amravati Road which merges into the 'Mumbai-Nagpur Super Communication Expressway.'

Trying to be unnoticed, the Ferrari CC90 Stradale-3 cruises a mile behind the Ford Mustang Shelby GT 517.

Gabrielle asks Ginny, "Can you reach in the backseat and get my golden saddle bag."

Ginny reaches behind grabbing the gold-colored bag behind the driver's seat. Lifting it up she says, "I'm surprised how heavy it is. What do you have in here your rock collection?" As she looks at Gabrielle and chuckles.

Gabrielle replies, "The golden bag contains a few toys and trinkets that can become powerful weapons of mass destruction when I use my SuperPower that can turn a mouse into a foot soldier, capisce Cinderella."

Driving down the Mumbai-Nagpur Superhighway heading south towards Westside of the Butibori Power Plant cruising at the posted speed limit of 95 miles an hour.

As the highway turns towards the West, Gabrielle asks Ginny to hand her a color toothpick.

Looking at the green toothpick, Gabrielle blinks three times transforming the wooden stick into a B&T APC9-SD PRO 9mm Suppressed Submachine Gun with a fully loaded machine gun magazine that they jokingly say, "This is our full metal jacket."

Ginny remarks, "Is this for real? How in the world were you able to do that?"

Gabrielle tells her, "It's SuperPower magic and nothing can stand in my way! I was told that you know how to use a machine gun."

Ginny examines the gun as she says, "Fully versed in all weapons."

Gabrielle responds, "Great because we're not in Xanadu so don't let your aim ever stray."

The next section of the Superhighway connector traveling on a diagonal Southwest direction towards the south of Seloo, the Ferrari picks up speed traveling at 120 miles an hour.

She instructs Ginny to get ready to use her weapon because it might be a bumpy ride.

As the Ferrari is in the next of the three lanes driving next to the Shelby, they see the two men singing with the micro digital audio. Their lips are mouthing the words do the classic H.E.R. song 'I can't breathe.'

Ginny says, "In a few minutes you will really be telling each other 'I can't breathe. Will anyone fight for me?'"

Gabrielle instructs her to begin emptying her full metal jacket.

Aiming at the tires, she lets a few metal projectiles fly across the lane having the Ford Mustang swerve towards the far right lane hitting the shoulder as Dominick floors the accelerator as he regains control of the vehicle.

Jack Diamond yells, "I can't believe that somebody is shooting at us. Fortunately, you have the luckiest person in the world as your passenger."

Ginny continues firing breaking the back seat window and rear windshield. Then, she shreds the rear driver side lights.

The Ford Mustang Shelby GT 517 is now in the left side lane traveling at 150 miles per hour.

Gabrielle cranks the Ferrari up matching Shelby's speed as they are within two feet from their adversary's rear bumper.

As they are nearing the exit to Seloo, a gigantic semi-truck with an armored tank mounted in its trailer comes flying down the road out of nowhere.

Ginny sees this remarking out loud, "We have company in the form of a Super Shockwave 5 with a T-76 Ajeya which is the Indian version of the Russian Super Tank."

Gabrielle maneuvers at high-speed her Ferrari passing the Ford Mustang on the far-right lane.

As the Super Shock Wave 5 travels at over two hundred miles per hour, it fires from its long-range laser cannon at the Ford Mustang Shelby.

Dominick anticipated their strategy as he steers the vehicle into the far-right lane behind the Ferrari as Ginny turns around.

He smiles at Jack saying, "Lucky for us, I was the champion drifter in Tokyo."

Looking out of her passenger window, she begins firing her 9mm Suppressed Submachine Gun knocking out the bright orange Ferrari's front windshield. Then, she shoots the passenger and driver side lights as her clip is emptied.

Continuing to head on a diagonal towards the Southwest, the cars and the truck are headed north of Wardha.

Ahead of them in the far-right lane traveling at the posted speed limit of 95 miles an hour is a car transporter containing brand new models of the Ford Mustang Shelby GT 517.

As the disheveled Shelby driven by Dominick attaches itself to the transporter, they exit trading Shelbys, their Twister Orange Shelby for a brand-new Velocity Blue Shelby.

Gabrielle yells seeing the disheveled Twister Orange Shelby, "Dude, you crashed a car with Jack inside."

Jack yells at the driver, "Make sure that you tell the Professor 'Thanks from Ruby Tuesday.'"

The driver yells back, "You mean, Goodbye 'Ruby Tuesday.'"

Now inside their Velocity Blue Shelby, Dominick proceeds passed the Ferrari yelling, "We are going to bury Ferrari. This is not about those le 'chicks.' It is all about us le 'mans.'"

Blasting their micro digital audio that is playing The Kingsmen's hit song 'Money That's What I Want' as the men sing loudly. Traveling at 120 mph they scream, "Professor, now give me money, that's what we want," as they laugh.

Passing southward Shamput heading west towards the North of Pulgaonas as one of the Vedic warrior class of 'sadhu' fighters jumps from the Super Shock Wave 5 onto the rear of the Ferrari.

Ginny holding another red toothpick that Gabrielle transforms into a Samurai Katana sword. She points the sharp blade at the temple fighter saying, "Hold it right there, buddy or you'll become a eunuch."

Removing the face mask or balaclava reveals that there is nothing to be removed as Ginny states, "Mother of pearl, the Vedic warrior is a beautiful, young lady!"

She tells them, "I am Sushmita priestess of Krishna seeking the red gemstone. We bring you ladies no harm as we seek the treasure inside the Ford Mustang," as she somersaults back onto the speeding Shockwave 5.

Continuing their westerly high-speed drive, they pass the exit for Pulgaon heading towards Devgav, Dhamangaon.

The T-76 "Ajeya" keeps firing missiles at the Shelby as Sushmita drops flying drones and motorized ground drones programmed to target the Velocity Blue Mustang.

The "Super Shockwave 5" gets off at the next exit towards Devgav knowing that the drones will finish them allowing their second team driving a Nissan GT-R Blazing Falcon to sort through the wreckage retrieving the precious ruby.

Witnessing the drones firing electro-laser blasts at them, Dominick swerves avoiding any damage.

Jack notices the upcoming motorized ground drones trying to get underneath their car. The flying drones circle around attempting another attack.

Dominick accelerates heading towards what appears a few miles ahead of them, to be a parked Grabber Lime Ford Mustang Shelby GT 517.

As they approach the Grabber Lime vehicle, Jack Diamond, holding his leather bag jumps onto its trunk. Close behind, following him is Dominick who lands on its hood. The Velocity Blue Shelby continues down the highway as a wedge was placed on the accelerator. The drones from the air hit the unmanned vehicle as the ground drones get underneath the chassis.

Now sitting in their new Grabber Lime Shelby, Dominick and Jack watch their- previous ride evaporate as the drones complete the mission.

Luckily, the Professor had this car in just the right location and its key in the ignition having its solar powered batteries fully charged. The lime green Mustang takes off at full speed as the Ferrari approaches the flaming soon-to-be junkyard vehicle.

Traveling at 100 mph, the Ford is followed by the Ferrari traveling northwest then north as they pass the exits towards Ambapur, Amravati, and the northside of Karanja.

Heading southwest to Jaina, which is 180 miles away, the Martin twins send help as a Mclaren Orange Hennessey Venom GT-2 traveling at 200 mph is seen in the Ferrari's rear mirror. Seconds later, the Venom GT-2 catches up with CC90 Stradale-3.

Waving at Gabrielle and Ginny are Lily Mae and Ruth Hannah. he track stars wave displaying their wrist 'God of Thunder' tattoo being the mascot of Loughborough University.

Lily Mae yells out, "Truth."

Ruth Hannah shouts, "Knowledge."

They both scream in unison, "Work."

Recklessly, both passenger and driver each give their elders two thumbs up. As Lily drives, Ruth lifts her Electro-Blaster rifle getting a thumbs up from Gabrielle.

The two high performance vehicles travel on the communication superhighway for over seventy miles in a southwest direction from North of Malegaon Jahangir to Mehkar.

Catching up to the adversary's Grabber Lime Ford Mustang Shelby, both Ginny and Ruth unleash projectiles upon them.

The glass windows explode, and its steel reinforcement fiberglass body gets significantly dented.

As the ladies keep following the swerving Shelby firing their weapons from two directions, ahead of them before the exit to Mehkar is a vehicle transporter. As the war-torn green Shelby has seen better driving days, the transporter blocks the DODGE members in pursuit.

Dominick tells Jack to jump onto the front of the cab. He counts to three and jumps landing by the open passenger door. He climbs over to the trailer as Dominick joins him. They move themselves across the steel ramp to enter their new Kona Blue Shelby watching their dented, shot at steel reinforcement fiberglass Grabber Lime Mustang go off the road hitting the superhighway's guardrails.

As the car carrier turns off at the exit, the two DODGE high performance vehicles see the Kona Blue Shelby speeding down the highway surpassing the 95 mph posted speed limit. They follow shooting their weapons but to their surprise this Shelby thanks to the Professor is bulletproof. The 9mm Suppressed Submachine Gun and the Electro-Laser Blaster does not even dent the Kona Blue exterior or the glass signal lights.

At the Shendra exit, a truck cruises next to the Ferrari having a mechanic check the tires and exterior. After validating that everything is working in exceptionally good order, she checks the Hennessey Venom GT-2 giving both vehicles the thumbs up.

The service truck exits by Hotel Grand Kailash, there, the driver, and his mechanic stop into the Players Resto-Bar to watch sports as they hear hypnotic ambiance music while drinking Kingfisher beers.

At the Palshi Village in Aurangabad, the Kona Blue Ford Mustang Shelby enters at 120 mph the 328-yard tunnel. Right on their tail is the Ferrari and the co-ed's Hennessey Venom GT-2.

Both Lily and Ruth start joking around by howling having Ruth comment, "Our teammate Zoey Chamberlain would respond to our beastly howls," as they laugh.

Ginny remarks, "I wonder if I was that crazy as a college coed?"

Quickly driving past the next exit where the road sign states, 'Aurangabad Caves ahead," the Ferrari and Venom GT-2 stay close behind the impenetrable Kona Blue Shelby that Lily says, "Looks like a one of the fifty shades of gray to me."

Driving as though they are racing, the three high performance cars head in a diagonal southwest direction towards Maujudabad Village in Gangapur Tahsil located in the Aurangabad district of Maharashtra.

Gabrielle signals to Lily as they both accelerate around both sides of the Shelby taking over the lead.

High overhead a Cessna aircraft hired by Professor Steele flies over the highway dropping nanobots. When a substantial number of nanobots accumulate on an object they form a nanobot aerial mine that explodes.

The Ford Mustang slows down allowing the Cessna to dusk the nanobots onto the DODGE driven vehicles. The Hennessey Venom is at its maximum speed of 250 mph. It avoids the nanobot by its speed and Lily's swerving from the far-right lane across to the far-left lane and back. Repeating this billiard ball collision driving style is working saving them from having the vehicle's exterior explode.

Not so lucky is the Ferrari as Gabrielle's driver's side tire explodes sending her flying through the air. She hits the pavement as Ginny grabs the wheel then jumps into the driver's seat, she brakes stopping the Ferrari.

Running from the CC90 Stradale-3, Ginny examines her partner Gabrielle's vital signs which do not appear to be good.

Verifying that Gabrielle is dead, Ginny uses her SuperPower ability to start her resurrection. Blinking her eyes several times with chest compressions to the heart, Ginny feels a slight murmur. She keeps it up until her driver's ghostly white corpse begins to turn a rosy hue.

Finally, Gabrielle opens her eyes saying, "What happened?"

Ginny responds, "You could say 'the rubber accidentally missed the road' and not having the SuperPower to fly, you flew thirty feet out of the driver's seat. Luckily, the Ferrari received no severe damage."

Getting back into the Ferrari, Ginny takes over as driver accelerating in 1.5 seconds to 65 mph. She keeps her foot pressed against the pedal hitting 250 mph as they catch up to the Venom.

Ruth Hannah yells out, "We were about to start the party without you two. Glad to see that you are here."

Approaching Nashik where there is the five-mile long Igatpuri Tunnel through a mountain having three lanes in both directions. With the 95-mph speed limit, the two roadsters travel at 120 mph each in their own lane with their lights on.

The ladies witness at Ghat which is the highest point of the upcoming 1.1-mile bridge the Ford Mustang Shelby flies.

Just like a stunt in an action movie, the car driven by Dominick soars over 80-feet, slamming into the road below. Jack Diamond yells, "Tell Uncle Jessie and the Duke boys that our car generally flew over the Fulahar River."

Following them, the pair of DODGE racing vehicles together fly over sixty feet. Lily yells to the Ferrari "I almost soiled my Daisy Dukes from either the excitement or the laughter afterwards."

Gabrielle states, "That jump we all made today has got to be a new record."

Coming from Shahapur is a Ram TRX-7 truck complete with a driver and rear cargo passenger holding an antitank rocket launcher that is also referred to as a bazooka.

Sprinting to 60 mph in 3.2 seconds, the Ram TRX-7 positions itself a mile in front of the Shelby. The Vedic warrior aims the 60mm M6 rocket at the bulletproof greyish blue Mustang Shelby. The shot hits the passenger's front bumper making Jack yell, "Darn! That was too close for comfort. Let us try to avoid that happening again."

The Vedic warrior reloads the bazooka as the Shelby is much closer this time. He fires again hitting the muscle car directly at the center of the front grille. The engine gets cracked having the vehicle slow down till it rests on the shoulder.

As the Ram truck disappears from whence it came, another bulletproof Iconic Gray Mustang Shelby arrives by tow truck by the Yewai ramp. Running a quarter mile on the shoulder, the Professor's team climbs into the front seat of the running vehicle.

In less than two seconds, the new replacement Shelby is cruising at 90 mph.

The Ferrari and Hennessey Venom are racing ahead of their foes blocking them at Thanes where the three lanes of the 1.25 mile Bhatsa River Bridge heads to Mumbai.

The latest, acquired Iconic Silver Ford Mustang Shelby approaches 200 mph aiming between the two rival cars.

The bulletproof silver high performance vehicle crashes into the side of two cars pushing them apart.

Traveling through the gap, Dominick drives past the DODGE teams towards the Mumbai Airport's private jet terminal.

After the Shelby is parked in front of Steele's Aerion CP513 Super Sonic Business Jet, Jack Diamond exits the car meeting Rocky Steele.

He introduces Dominick to his boss as he hands him the bag containing the 'Liberty Bell' ruby gemstone.

Rocky Steele shows the duo that he has transferred into each of their bank accounts $1.5 million US.

Jack tells Dominick, "Let's go get drunk on Corona beer."

Dominick replies, "Now you're talking. I always say, 'drink any brew as long as it is a Corona.'"

On the wrist iCommunicators belonging to the Loughborough track stars, Myrena is heard telling them, "Whomever shoots Rocky Steele dead earns $5 million. Any other shot that injures him earns you a half million dollars."

Speeding into the private airstrip before the Ferrari, Ruth Hannah and Lily Mae exit their vehicle armed.

As Rocky Steele walks up the stairs to pilot his jet, the co-eds begin shooting hitting him in his left leg.

Rocky shouts, "Darn, someone just shot my left foot. Now there will be blood to pay for this disrespect."

Lily yells at him, "Now you and my boss Myrena have cold feet, or yours will be cold and blue soon."

Seated in the pilot's seat the co-pilot begins his preflight inspection as Rocky says, "No time for this. Let's get up in the air already."

The Aerion CP513 Super Sonic Business Jet lunges forward heading toward the runway and back to Reykjavik, Iceland.

Lily Mae tells Myrena, "Ruth and I shot Mr. Steele several times hitting his left leg with a few bullets. He left limping and bleeding as he cursed at us over and over. I believe that he has the Liberty Bell ruby."

Myrena responds, "You young ladies had a very eventful day. I am extremely proud of both of you. For your arduous work, especially wounding that wimp, my ex-fiancé I have placed in your bank accounts $750,000 each."

Lily exclaims, "We can eat unlimited Ferrero Rocher and Lemon Cheesecake gelatos at Delfino's."

Ruth smiles saying, "Now we can dance every night this weekend and buy alcohol at Lboro University's nearby pub 'The Asgardian.' I might even drink a beer from the Nottingham's Liquid Light Brewing Company."

Chapter 15

Smear Campaign on Myrena and Her Deeds

As the on-site camera crew begins rolling with the MM Morning Show theme song playing in the background, its host Meredith Marlowe appears on stage welcoming her iBroadcast audience saying, "Good morning. This is Meredith Marlowe with another exciting iNews 'Trending Story.' Today we have the President of SPALD, Joseph Prince."

The camera zooms in on Joseph seated on Meredith's right wearing a Dior Homme luxury men's fashion statement.

As the camera cuts to a wide shot of Meredith and her guest, she asks him, "What does SPALD mean?"

Joseph looks directly into the camera and Meredith's eyes stating, "SPALD is an acronym for SuperPower Anti 'Lemnian Deeds.' We are mostly men that are against Myrena Gorgona and her small, minded followers who worship celebrities like her. We at SPALD are educated, SuperPower individuals that seek equality between genders accepting all. Our members can have or not have SuperPower abilities, can be from the straight or LBGTQ community, from rich cities to the poorest towns. We have no preconceived requirements to join our organization."

Meredith inquires, "Why are you anti 'Lemnian Deeds?' What do you have against SuperModel, SuperDesigner Myrena Gorgona?"

Joseph pauses and states, "Myrena formed the so-called federation after calling off the wedding to a true gentleman from an amazing family 'Rocky Steele.' I personally have known the Steele family for over ten years. I have eaten Sunday dinner at their residence on several occasions."

As the camera moves in for a close up of Joseph, he continues, "This entire merger with DODGE is a ruse to get revenge on the 'Golden Eagle' Organization, nothing more."

Meredith smiles saying, "Are you equivocally stating on the record that SPALD was formed believing that 'Hell hath no fury like a Myrena scorned."

Joseph separates his two arms with his palms upward with a serious look in his eyes confidently saying, "Absolutely. And remember the old adage 'the enemy of my enemy is my friend.' That is the only valid reason that her so called organization joined forces with DODGE."

Meredith asks, "Is the rumors that you and your group are entirely financially supported by the Steele family and their corporation?"

Joseph emphatically states, "No. As I previously mentioned, the Steele family and I go back many years as friends but there is no truth to any connection between our two organizations. We get our support from donators and philanthropists that agree with our philosophy."

Meredith tells her live audience, "That is today's 'Trending Story.'"

As both Meredith and Joseph stand and shake hands while the audience applauds as an iCommercial airs.

Entering the guest's green room, Joseph Prince receives an order of Chinese food that has two egg rolls with Kung Pao Chicken.

Joseph tells the delivery girl, "I believe that this is the most popular Chinese meal that contains peanuts. I am extremely allergic to them having my entire face swelling up like a balloon. I often go into anaphylaxis having my throat and chest close requiring someone to inject me with an epinephrine pen; otherwise, I could cease to exist."

The delivery girl removes the chicken as Joseph devours the egg rolls.

Resting on the couch, he plans his next endeavor to destroy the 'Lemnian Deeds' as he suddenly cannot breathe.

Trying to take a breath, he quickly gets up opening the green room's door. In the hallway, he sees several PAs or production assistants that he points to his throat and then at his jackets inside pocket.

One PA that has an allergy to bee stings checks Joseph's expensive suit as he passes out onto the floor. Finding the epi-pen, the PA injects the show's first guest with epinephrine that is a chemical which constricts the blood vessels opening the airways in the lungs.

After Joseph Prince opens his eyes, one of the show's producers places a glass of chilled water by Joseph's mouth having him drink a few sips. Slowly, getting up he takes a deep breath.

He thanks everyone for the help saying, "That was a narrow escape. I do not understand what happened."

Joseph Prince's cell phone begins buzzing. He answers it saying, "Hello, this is Joseph Prince."

On the other end a familiar voice states, "Don't you know that egg rolls are always made using peanut butter to hold the cabbage and other of its ingredients together?"

Then, the caller laughs stating, "Perhaps the next time you have Sunday dinner at the Steeles, you can brag how Myrena and her 'Lemnian Deeds' almost terminated you."

Stormy Weather hangs up on him as his elevated blood pressure turns his face and neck an angry shade of crimson red.

After taking a few minutes to calm down, Joseph exits through the show's backstage door where a mob is waiting for him.

A spokesperson asks him, "Where can all of us sign up to join your SuperPower Anti 'Lemnian Deeds' group."

Joseph hands out the SPALD business cards with their website address.

One compulsive supporter of SPALD says, "The card has an understated off-white color with perfect thickness. I absolutely cannot believe it; the card even has a SPALD watermark."

Leaving the studio secure parking lot in his aureolin (or 'cobalt yellow') McLaren Speedtail 6, his cell phone buzzes.

On the other end, the Professor says, "Joseph, how are you feeling after the Myrena attempt on your life?"

He replies, "Feeling better. We need to discuss our revenge on her ASAP."

Professor Steele agrees saying, "And how is the $2.4 million cobalt yellow McLaren Speedtail 6 driving? I did not mind writing the check for that donation," as he chuckles.

Having dinner at the Professor's house on a Sunday afternoon Joseph Prince tells Apollo and Rocky Steele, "How do you feel about me removing one SuperModel and Super Designer from the world's runway forever?"

Apollo says, "She is nothing special. Even James Bond would toss her aside and shoot her."

Rocky adds saying, "At our wedding, she really embarrassed me. Then, I realized that she is profoundly and irreversibly screwed up. She seeks power at all costs. Myrena is a pain in my neck so decapitate her for all I care."

The Professor rubs his forehead with his right hand thinking intently. He looks up at Joseph saying, "I have the perfect SuperPower assassin to help you in this most urgent and important mission. His name is Matthew Poncelet. I have used Matthew many times to rid the world of my SuperPower enemies. After dinner, we can go to my home office, and I will give you his private number as we enjoy a new bottle of Hennessy Beautè du Siècle Cognac together."

Myrena gets up in the morning as her housekeeper places in front of her herbal detox tea which is a blend of maté and green tea with a bowl of raw honey with strawberries and blueberries mixed with her Greek yogurt.

She gets a call on her wrist iCommunicator. After answering she hears, "Ms. Gorgona, this is Carmella, the manager at your Fashion Warehouse. The material for your upcoming fashion show that was ordered in 'Sunny Yellow' has just arrived but the color they sent is 'Bubblegum Pink.'"

Myrena tells her, "I'll be right over. Leave everything where it is and have everybody work on the order for the 'Live Clothing UK' stores."

Walking into her eight-car garage Myrena gets into her 4.2 million-dollar Lykan HyperSport 2 that is a furiously fast car deserving of a hero, having rear wheel steering 780 horsepower luxury car capable of speeds 245 miles per hour. The most impressive item on the HyperSport is not its speed but on the headlights are four hundred and twenty 15-carat pure white diamonds and rubies adorning its headlights.

The HyperSport car also has a holographic display system.

After traveling a few miles over the speed limit, Myrena arrives at her fashion warehouse that is her design factory and manufacturing operation.

Carmella greets Myrena taking her to the delivery area.

Carmella shows her all the delivery boxes containing the fabric for her fashion show's apparel. The Gorgona collection includes women's fashions for a special night out as well as travel clothing to wear on that luxury cruise liner.

After looking at the wrong ordered fabric, Myrena calls the vendor to get a half price discount. She decides to have the inhouse fashion designers provide her with a few samples immediately.

Each designer takes a different fashion piece by looking at the draft of the design and cutting the new bubblegum pink fabric and sewing each garment together with their decorative ornamentation such as buttons, sequins, and trimmings.

After finishing her bottle of plain Toucon sparkling water, Myrena examines each of the designers' work.

Meanwhile, back at Gorgona mansion Matthew Poncelet has snuck inside adjusting Myrena's Blu Chiaro Ferrari 1200 Supercar. He drastically increases the tire pressure on all four tires. Matthew plans to use a Glock 19 generation 12 which is a 9 mm pistol, to deflate one of the tires as Myrena is driving.

He positions himself down the street where the wooded area leads by a gravel path to a public park that has a 1.5-acre pond filled with fish.

Driving home from her fashion factory, Myrena feels confident that her day was well spent solving what could have been a potential disaster.

Now, her upcoming fashion show and the sales to the chain of UK fashion stores will set a new trend in fashion. The result will be that everybody who's a jetsetter will attribute this latest look to its innovator, Myrena Gorgona.

Myrena briefly stops into her residence switching her outfit into her gym workout activewear.

Wearing her bright yellow sports outfit consisting of solid crop top and shorts, she jumps into the driver's seat of her Blu Chiaro Ferrari 1200 Supercar.

As she passes the park where she often jogs around the 1.5-acre pond, she hears what sounds like a neighbor's car backfiring.

Matthew Poncelet realizes that his first bullet has bounced off the over pressured rear tire as he says, "Darn! That has never happened to me although I have heard rumors and seen that happened in movies."

He aims at the front tire having another shot which pierces the over inflated front tire.

Myrena hears the front tire explode as she tries to regain control over her vehicle.

To avoid hitting several pedestrians with their children, she crashes her car into several bushes and is stopped by a tree.

Many of the pedestrians who saw the accident are running towards her car in case she needs help.

Myrena removes her seat belt and exits the car. Her emergency system in the car has already notified her emergency assistance provider.

Heard over her car's navigation system is the operator letting her know that a tow truck is on its way.

One of the onlookers says to Myrena, "Oh my, look at the damage to your beautiful, expensive car."

Myrena replies, "Sir, when you buy three multimillion dollar Ferraris, they give you this $300,000 version for free."

After the tow truck drives off to the garage with the Ferrari 1200 Supercar, Myrena opens her garage getting inside of her $5.4 million Pagani Huayra Imola which is a hypercar named after the famous race circuit. The 800 hp limited-run super-exclusive Paganini can hit a top speed of 238 miles per hour and is able to withstand a 2 G lateral acceleration.

Myrena asks Vivian Russ to shadow her during the day as her life has been threatened several times this week.

Vi Russ sleeps over Myrena's mansion in one of the upstairs guest rooms.

At 2 am, Matthew Poncelet skillfully opens the locked front door to Myrena's residence. Walking over to the alarm system being one which he is quite familiar with disarming.

Once the coast is clear, he enters the kitchen where he removes from his pocket a syringe containing lethal tetrodotoxin. Trained sushi chefs are trained when preparing poisonous blowfish sushi to remove the toxins. The tetrodotoxin is an odorless, tasteless, and colorless neurotoxin that has no known cure or antidote.

Matthew empties the syringe into Myrena's herbal organic tea. Verifying that the poison is ample to kill a rhino, he is satisfied that tomorrow will be her last day on Earth. He exits the residence.

A few hours later, Matthew waits in the wooded area by the neighboring fishpond.

Early the next morning, Vivian goes jogging before breakfast around the fishpond.

Upon seeing Matthew Poncelet waiting in the wooded terrain, she says, "Hello."

Matthew replies, "Good morning. It is a lovely day for a jog. A day for one to be grateful to be alive."

Then, he not realizing who he is chatting with jokes saying, "Not unlike the SuperModel, Myrena Gorgona's day will become."

Acting like she is infatuated with him she asks, "What about that overstated Myrena?"

Bragging Matthew states, "Soon, she will have lowered blood pressure as she has diarrhea and vomits. Then, her nervous system will fail causing problems with her neurologic and gastrointestinal systems. Finally, a loss of sensation, then paralysis, respiratory stoppage, and eventually death. Do not ever drink the poisoned tea," as he chuckles.

After hearing his plans on her friend, Vi Russ states, "Men are so trusting and very stupid."

She bends over pretending to tie her sneakers as she grabs both of his legs telling him, "'Dead Man Walking' or not." His legs turn red and disappear as his torso hits the ground.

She continues joking saying, "My lawyer tells me that you do not have a leg to stand on. As your judge, I convict you to life without breathing," as she watches his entire body evaporate.

Then, she puts each of her hands on either side of his neck.

She smiles saying, "Finally, you are ahead of everyone but only a head," as his face turns red and vaporizes into a cloud of smoke.

Running back to Myrena's residence, she alerts everyone to Matthew's devious scheme.

They call the police who send over their best detectives.

The forensic team discovers the lethal amount of poison in the container of herbal organic tea.

They ask about the perpetrator and their whereabouts to arrest them.

Vivian laughs saying, "He is 'gone with the wind.' As God as my witness, Matthew Poncelet moved with a blanket of gray smoke never to return."

The chief detective states, "Then, the case is closed. Thank you, Ms. Gorgona, for your hospitality. Thank God, nothing worse had happened to you lovely ladies. Good day."

Chapter 16

Dog's Hell Outside the 'Happiest Place on Earth'

Cynane Mino is visiting Tokyo Japan on her vacation. For the last three days she has visited Tokyo's Disneyland enjoying the attractions such as 'Pirates of the Caribbean,' 'Jungle Cruise,' the 'Enchanted Tiki Room,' the 'Country Bears Theater' as well as the 'It's a Small World' boat ride and 'Cinderella's Fairy Tale Hall.'

She was thrilled at the high-speed journey through the galaxy on 'Space Mountain.'

The next day, she enters the park visiting Tokyo's DisneySea where she travels on 'Soaring' as though she is using her SuperPower to fly.

Then, she takes a gondola ride through the romantic canals of Venice. Next, she boards the spinning watercraft in 'Aquatopia.' Seeing the silver screen attractions, Cynane continues her sea adventure as she visits Nemo on the 'SeaRider.'

Then, to experience the force of gravity she enters the 'Twilight Zone's Tower of Terror,' then watches the 'Indiana Jones Adventure' and rides the shooting gallery tram through 'Toy Story Mania.'

Thanks to the famous SuperModel Myrena Gorgona, Cynane resides in one of the Disney family's rooms inside Cinderella's Castle.

She takes a break from the happiest place on earth as she gets a bus to downtown Tokyo.

Cynane is dropped off in front of the Imperial Palace Gardens which was once the home of the Emperor of Japan.

She then goes to Tokyo's Ginza shopping district where she buys a Louis Vuitton handbag along with a beautiful handmade kimono and one of 2,500 styles of chopsticks.

Believing that she is on the bus headed back to Tokyo Disneyland, she gets on without paying. The entire bus is filled with men dressed in expensive suits. A few of the men asked her for her name which she replies "Cynane." Each man introduces themselves to her as being either a veterinarian, a lawyer, or a medical doctor. Every person compliments her on her exotic beauty, having olive skin and orange eyes.

After the busy day, Cynane rests her head against the window and falls asleep.

She is unaware that the bus has traveled two hours northeast of Tokyo to a small farming town. Walking past her, all the passengers get off the bus.

The bus driver taps Cynane on her shoulder saying, "Miss wake up, we are at our destination."

Still groggy, she exits the bus seeing farmland for miles. Looking around, she sees all her bus mates examining each animal inside their cage.

She walks towards the cages seeing inside various breeds of dogs. As she looks carefully every dog has cuts and injuries indicating that they have been abused. She asks one of the men, "What is wrong with these dogs?"

The well-dressed Asian man tells her, "This is the 'East Tokyo Dog Fighting Association,' and we are at their monthly competition. This month, we are lucky to have several events occurring."

Puzzled and angry she says, "Isn't this kind of activity against the law?"

The man tells her, "Outside of Tokyo there are many prefectures that have no permits or licenses to organize dog fighting competitions."

Amazed she replies, "Are you for real?"

Smiling the man says, "I am a veterinarian in Tokyo who loves to gamble. At this location, there are over two hundred and fifty dogs competing to be the champion. In these cages are Pitbulls, Bully Kutta, Neapolitan Mastiff, Korean Jindo, Doberman Pinscher, Rottweiler, Akita, Caucasian Shepherd dog, and Shar Pei. Truly fine specimens of aggressive canines."

After they both walk amongst the fans and gamblers, the veterinarian points out his acquaintances that were not on the bus who are locals working as farmers, miners, laborers, and even a couple of CEOs.

He tells Cynane that he has his eye on an Old English Mastiff and that he is placing a double bet on the 200 lb. massive beast.

She asks, "A double bet?"

He responds, "Yes, one for me and the other for you."

During the next four hours, the men bet and cheer as Cynane chats with one of her girlfriends on her wrist iCommunicator.

On the grass sitting around her are the local families grilling chicken which they call 'Yakitori,' cooking salmon while drinking green tea as watermelon is passed around for dessert.

The dogs fight inside one of three 12 feet wide wooden octagon pits having a folding chair where a judge sits. Above the octagon are two large steel platforms on opposite sides where the dogs' owners view shouting their commands.

The dog fighting venue has temperatures exceeding 100 degrees Fahrenheit.

Inside the arena, one dog, a Japanese Mastiff sinks his teeth clamping down on his opponent's neck. After confirming the winner, a pressurized water hose blasts into each dog's face as plastic wedges force both of their mouths wide open. Once both dogs are separated the winner returns to his cage as the other receives from the venue's veterinarian basic medical attention.

The bus driver, seeing Cynane chatting on her wrist iCommunicator tells her, "Very soon everybody will be returning to the bus. Then, I will drive you and them back to downtown Tokyo."

Cynane returns to the bus sitting in the front seat opposite the driver.

Getting up early the next day, Cynane leaves her room in Cinderella Castle and enters Crystal Palace to have a buffet breakfast consisting of omelets, buttermilk and cheddar bacon biscuits, seafood, and prawn soup. The Asians eat ridiculously small portions, but Cynane is not from this country. For dessert she enjoyed the many cakes and fruit dishes.

As she waited for the Disneyland parade to start from her perfect viewing station, she calls the DODGE headquarters talking to the computer half of Rileigh Michele.

She explains to Rileigh all about her previous day's experience she says, "I was witnessing the horrible mistreatment of canines and dog fighting which is not only legal but viewed in Japan as a family outing.

It was almost like being in Vegas or Atlantic City without the animal cruelty."

Rileigh Michele tells her, "I will have Elijah Moses Jr. send you some backup in the form of a new DODGE member named Zoey Chamberlain."

Loughborough University's woman's track coach, Michele Locke hangs up the phone after speaking with DODGE's Elijah Moses, Jr.

She then calls the dormitory room of Zoey Chamberlain telling her, "This is Coach Locke calling on behalf of DODGE and Elijah Moses Jr. We need you to immediately pack your bags and passport for a few days trip to Tokyo Japan."

Coach Locke continues saying, "Within an hour a chauffeur-driven limousine will be parked outside your dorm to drive you to the International Airport for your mission. I have been told that you will be compensated at least $125,000 for your SuperPower abilities. Remember, the training instructions I mentored you girls on."

Zoey stands in front of the ticket counter of Japanese Airlines, she says, "Hello," to the ticket agent.

The ticket agent asks for her identification having Zoey hand her, her passport.

The ticket agent processes her boarding pass and hands her a package containing her documents from DODGE.

After handing her suitcase to the baggage counter personnel, she walks towards her gate. Then, proceeding through the automatic ID security line, she sits down on a bench and opens her document package. Inside the package are her instructions for the upcoming mission as well as tickets to Tokyo's Disneyland.

Being provided these tickets confuses her as she smiles thinking about visiting Minnie and Mickey.

She arrives at her gate with enough time to grab a large, iced tea.

The other passengers begin to line up to board the plane, Zoey looks at her ticket noticing that she is in first class.

Zoey asks the flight attendant, "How long is the flight to Tokyo?"

The flight attendant tells her, "From Birmingham International Airport to Tokyo Haneda International Airport it takes 14 hours and 20 minutes."

Zoey says, "Wow! and how far do we travel in that time?"

The flight attendant replies "We fly traveling 5,928 miles. If I were you sitting In first class, I would enjoy your free food and drinks, watch the hi-def monitor catching the latest movies and iBroadcast shows, and possibly take a quick nap so that you are completely rested when we arrive."

Zoey begins checking out all the available movies and iBroadcast shows available for her to watch.

The flight attendant stops by asking her, "Would you care for a Japanese sake? We have 'Sha-raku' and 'Ho-oh Biden' and 'shochu' that you might call distilled liquor such as 'NakaNaka,' 'Tomi no nouzan,' and Tsurusora.'"

Zoey thinks for a second saying, "Perhaps I could have one of those when you bring me my delicious first-class meal. For now, could I have an orange juice with a can of ginger ale on the side?"

She watches a few movies and eats her gourmet meal before dozing off.

Hearing the announcement that the aircraft will be landing soon, she awakes finishing her remaining cold sake.

At the baggage claim, she sees a man with a sign that says, 'Zoey Chamberlain.' Excited, she tells him "Hello, I am Zoey."

After gathering her bag, they walk to his limousine having him open the back door for her.

Forty-five minutes later, they arrived at the front gate of Tokyo Disneyland's entrance.

Holding her bag, she tells the security guard after passing the metal detectors and x-ray machines that she is a celebrity guest staying inside the Cinderella Castle.

After checking his list and getting verification from the park's chief security officer, a golf cart driven by another security officer arrives to pick Zoey up.

Downstairs waiting for Zoey is Cynane who introduces herself.

The two enter the castle where she shows Zoey her new princess's residence.

She tells the new Disney princess that for today they will roam around the park. As a special treat Myrena Gorgona has arranged for the two of them to be crowned 'the royal princess of the day' by Mickey and Minnie on top of the parade's float.

After a restful sleep, Zoey tells Cynane, "I have not slept so peacefully in a long time."

Cynane jokes saying, "You are lucky that the housekeeper has checked underneath the bed for peas. You do not want Hans Christian Andersen writing about 'Princess Zoey and the Pea.'"

After a delicious breakfast inside the Crystal Palace, the two SuperPower women take a bus to downtown Tokyo.

They walk around the shopping center until the bus headed to the countryside arrives.

Getting on the bus the two ladies sit in the front seat across from the driver.

The driver recognizes Cynane saying, "Welcome back."

She replies, "Nice to see you again. I brought my friend this time."

As the bus fills up, many of the passengers recognize Cynane including the veterinarian.

He tells her, "This time I want you to pick the winner," as he finds a seat behind hers.

The farm where the championship dog fighting occurs, Cynane shows Zoey the dogs in the cages as the men walk around examining each dog looking for a winner.

Using her SuperPower, Zoey communicates with the dogs telling them, "Fight and you, dogs may die. Tonight, come with us and you will live. Remember, the word 'freedom.'"

After walking around the farm, Cynane tells the bus driver that she and her girlfriend are getting a ride back to Tokyo with one of the handsome ASIN doctors.

Then, they head into the fields hiding until nightfall.

As the farmland is dark, Cynane, who can see in pitch black, guides Zoey to where the caged dogs are by holding her hand.

Zoey tells her, "With my SuperPower ability I can transform into any animal or bird. You do not have to worry as I am in complete control and will never harm you."

Zoey metamorphosis into an eagle soaring high into the air to verify that all the attendees of the dog fight competition have left leaving only the caged dogs behind to return to their owners later the next day.

As they get close to the area where the cages are, Zoey transforms herself into a 200 lb. gray wolf.

Cynane says, "Even though it is twilight, you can feel my presence,"

Zoey states, "I guess the wolf's out of the bag. Watch out, Red Riding Hood!"

Cynane walks in the darkness as though it were a sunny day as Zoey the gray wolf behind her is guided by her smell.

The gray wolf softly barks at every dog in their cages telling them what is about to occur.

She has each fighting dog promise not to harm her human friend, Cynane.

Cynane in complete darkness opens each cage allowing its prisoner to escape into the appointed location in the fields that Zoey has barked at, "We will lead everyone to freedom."

The field now filled with every caged dog follows Zoey still in her gray wolf form guided by Cynane.

Walking southwest on the road leading to the Tokyo Haneda International Airport, a large delivery truck opens its rear door allowing all the fighting dogs to travel to the airport.

Driving the delivery truck and parking it outside the private jet terminal, the driver opens the tailgate allowing all the fighting dogs to exit onto the tarmac.

The private jet's flight attendant opens the ramp into the cabin which is filled with bowls of oatmeal, cut up salmon, shrimp, and tuna which is easy to get in Japan.

The Martin twins have arranged for all the dogs to be flown to Chicago O'Hare Airport.

Before reverting to her human form, Zoey instructs every fighting dog to enjoy their trip in the jet for the next 10.5 hours. The cabin is stocked with water and bowls of meat and 'pork hides' otherwise known as 'pig skin' which are rich in protein and easy to digest.

As the jet lands at O'Hare Airport, a large mobile home transports all the dogs to Megan Leigh's 'Animal Shelter' and 'Puppy Farm.'

Megan Leigh was a key SuperPower ability member helping the Professor during his $3.5 billion museum masterpiece acquisition night in New York City. With her earnings, she purchased an old 70-acre horse farm in the south side of her hometown of Chicago. After renovation and construction of new buildings, Megan opened an animal shelter and kennel.

Megan Leigh goes back to college graduating from University of Illinois College of Veterinary Medicine in Urbana in Illinois earning her doctorate in Veterinary Medicine specializing in farm and domestic animals.

Megan comes out to welcome her new guests. She pets every dog as it exits the large recreational vehicle saying, "Welcome home!"

One of the dogs turns to Zoey barking, "Is this paradise?"

Zoey barks back in her human form, "Don't you realize that 'all dogs go to Heaven!"

Megan and her staff make sure that every dog has their plush dog bed, access to the toy room, water, food and is shown where the flexible flap is located to get into the grassy backyard if needed.

Megan invites her two human guests to spend the night in her luxurious farm mansion.

Chapter 17

Every Man Must Do His Duty: Join SPALD

Joseph Prince follows Myrena Gorgona's fashion schedule starting in New York, then London, Paris, and Milan. Financially supported by the Steele Corporation, Joseph intends to have public crusades for SPALD rallying against Myrena Gorgona and her 'Lemnian Deeds' Federation.

Professor Steele has hired the fashion industry's best designers paying them three times their normal fee to create SPALDwear. At each fashion show, the male and female models will strut across the catwalk displaying the SPALD creations by legendary fashion designers as Joseph Prince is heard at the microphone verbally expressing his "Anti 'Lemnian Deeds' Federation" rant.

At the SoHo (South Houston Street) in New York City, Joseph Prince sees Stormy Weather walking down the path in St. John's Park. She looks at him in disgust saying, "I did not know that 'pigs' were allowed in the park."

He states, "The men of SPALD are instructed to 'fight fire with fire.'"

Stormy laughs saying, "Tell the Professor that it would have been less expensive if he had given Myrena half of the control of the 'Golden Eagle' Organization."

He replies "I will send the Steeles your love and devotion" blowing her a kiss as she continues walking.

Seeing many well-dressed men at the park, Joseph hands out his SPALD website cards. Each one upon reading the business card comments on the most excellent font, card thickness and especially its watermark.

Joseph Prince walks back to the SoHo fashion show where world class fashion designers are checking each of their pieces that their models are wearing. As both the female and male models walk back and forth in front of them, each designer instructs them how to properly display their creations.

Outside in the front of the building Joseph preaches to the fashion industry about the evils of the 'Lemnian Deeds.' He tells everyone who passes by, "Myrena Gorgona is a scorned woman who did not know how to keep a handsome, rich bachelor like Rocky Steele satisfied. Instead of wanting love, all she saw was dollar signs. When their uncle the Professor saw her evil doings, he called her out on it. Unable to confess her true intentions, he tossed her out of the Garden of Eden calling her the Serpent's toy."-

As Joseph preached, his army of SPALD team members passed out their website's business card as they signed up new members.

Each night the Professor got updated on the day's activities.

As the fashion show in New York City's SoHo District commenced, both from the runway SPALDwear appearances and fashion buyers coming to their booth, the tremendous sales put what could be called a half-smile on to the Professor's face.

Joseph Prince and his SPALD team's recruiting effort added thousands of new members to their rosters.

The Professor looks at the daily sales reports of all the fashion design companies at the fashion show noticing that his SPALDwear topped the list and Myrena Gorgona's numbers where is slightly below the middle line.

He comments to himself, "I started this endeavor saying, 'even if went broke as long as I destroyed that treacherous, evil woman it would be worth every krona.' Luckily, as faith sometimes happens it has turned into 'Good Fortune' both financially and in membership."

The Professor flies the entire New York entourage including the world-famous designers and their staff in his confidential business jet to the London Fashion Show.

The chauffeur-driven limousine transports Joseph Prince's entire entourage down the road past the River Thames to the Palace that once was the residence of the Duke of Somerset. Parking on the south side of the Strand on the east side of Waterloo Bridge.

The world-renowned designers are backstage in the SPALDwear assigned area, preparing their gender-neutral models that are getting their hair and makeup worked on.

Each designer supervises their makeup artist and hairdresser collaborating with the models wearing their creations.

The London Fashion press are busy interviewing each of the Professor's world-renowned designers as their photographers are snapping digital photographs every two seconds.

Joseph Prince walks around backstage reporting back to the Professor the ongoings of not only the SPALDwear activity but the lack of activity at the Gorgona backstage area.

Joseph makes reservations inside the 'new wing' of the Somerset House at the award-winning Michelin restaurant Spring.

Arriving for lunch, all the team members of SPALDwear sit around the table where not a single designer sits next to his competition.

To start the lunch off to an excellent start, Professor Steele has the sommelier pour everyone a glass of Blanc de Blancs 'Extra Brut' 1er Cru from the Artéis and Company from Champagne, France.

The Michelin restaurant Spring charges $314 a bottle as the Professor's generosity has pre-ordered a minimum of twenty bottles.

The world-famous designer Andrea Warhol remarks "It is obvious that this champagne is an exquisite dry wine with a hint of the scent of apple combined with a citrus intermingled with a slight mineral texture."

Joseph Prince stands up in front of everyone raising his glass high. As the entire table follow suit, Joseph states, "To everyone here, let's toast to another amazing industry fashion show and to our benefactor the Professor."

As everyone taps their crystal toasting flute containing one of the world's best champagnes with their neighbor, they all say "Cheers."

The wait staff begins serving the three-course lunch starting with the house salad having greens topped with grape tomatoes, pomegranate, honey walnuts, goat's curd and rose harissa.

Next, it is proceeded by a spice-rubbed quail with sweet potato, followed by mackerel with beetroots and tomato.

For dessert they are served almond tarts with cream fraiche and their choice of tea.

At the opening ceremony, all the Professor's designers take center stage having the entire audience of fashion insiders respectfully give them a standing ovation.

Getting her models ready as she checks and rechecks each model's outfit, hair and makeup making sure everything is beyond perfection.

Myrena tells Stormy, "Would it be possible for you to strike Joseph Prince twice with a bolt of lightning proving that lightning can strike twice in the same place."

Stormy smiles at her and laughs knowing that she is half joking.

She says, "If you'd like, I could rain on his parade."

The entire London Fashion Show audience gives the Gorgona fashion collection an enthusiastic reception.

Following her showcase, Joseph Prince walks down the runway announcing the unisex SPALDwear collection. The gender-neutral models both male and female display the amazing creations from their world-renowned designers. As each pair of models struts across the runway, the entire LFS audience rises giving them tremendous applause.

Joseph Prince begins walking towards the front of the building to help his SPALDwear team pass out their website business cards as well as preach against the 'Lemnian Deeds' Federation.

Passing Myrena Gorgona in the backstage hallway, he tells her, "Myrena, it's not just business, it's also personal," as he begins to walk away laughing.

Myrena retorts saying, "I am so bored with you! The iNews and photographers are saying how brilliant I am, and my new fashions are 'splendid' and 'striking.' Without further ado we must be cracking. Hopefully, we will not be seeing each other again."

After leaving the London Fashion Show, the entire SPALD delegation heads over to Paris to prepare for their next fashion showcase inside the Louvre.

Joseph Prince tells one of the designer's assistance, "I was thinking that at the Paris Fashion Show, I might be a little bit more lenient towards Myrena Gorgona. After all it isn't her fault that she was born extremely beautiful, talented, and highly intelligent. And outside Rocky Steele's inherited wealth there's not a lot that he would have brought to the marriage. I believe that most people would agree with me."

The assistant just nods his head in agreement as he really couldn't care less.

At Stormy's request, she and Myrena take the Chunnel also known as the Eurotunnel that is a 31.35-mile railway from Kent, England beneath the English Channel at the Strait of Dover to Calais in France.

From there they take the train to Paris traveling forty-seven miles, taking them two hours.

Traveling on the Chunnel, Stormy confesses, "Remind me to tell you after the Parisian fashion show about the naughty thing that I had done."

Myrena tells her, "Can't you just give me a little hint?"

Stormy says, "Something that is from a book by Voltaire."

Myrena says jokingly, "You either are going to surprise the fashion show with a song from 'Les Mis' or you have stolen all the baguettes in Paris."

As a chauffeur-driven limousine picks up the two ladies from the Paris train station, they are dropped off in front of the Louvre. They walked towards the backstage area where the Gorgona fashion booth resides watching their hair stylists and makeup artists busily working on their male and female models.

Myrena catches something in the corner of her eye having her turn her head facing that direction. Seeing nothing she turns to Stormy saying, "Oh my, I could have sworn I just saw Astrid Christensen walking towards the SPALDwear booth."

Stormy replies, "Really? I believe that she's in Oslo as we just talked a few days ago."

Myrena tells Stormy, "I will be going back to our penthouse suite in the hotel to rest before tonight's opening ceremony."

Walking into the reception area, dozens of photographers take digital shots of Myrena Gorgona who is escorted by her best friend, Stormy Weather. Before entering the opening ceremony, Stormy seas the iBroadcast Fashion iNews reporting on the latest trend called 'SPALDwear.'

Stormy grabs Myrena's hand dragging her over to watch the iBroadcast Fashion iNews.

Myrena keeps saying, "I don't want to see anything to do with 'SPALDwear.' And I definitely do not want to see Joseph Prince ever again."

Stormy raises her voice saying, "I believe that you might find this fashion report to your liking."

In front of all the cameras having a worldwide audience, Joseph Prince is bragging about his wonderful world-famous designers showing images of their astonishing creations that they previously showed in London.

Suddenly, he stops talking and moves past the cameras towards Myrena Gorgona.

Holding Myrena's hand, he introduces her to the world saying, "I would like to introduce you to my incredibly good friend. She is not only the world-famous SuperModel but now one of the world's best SuperDesigners."

Kissing her hand, he continues saying, "The founder and president of Gorgona Fashion, my friend and competitor in the fashion industry, Myrena Gorgona."

Astonished Myrena says, "Thank you, Joseph Prince. That was quite an unexpected and out of the ordinary introduction."

After a few seconds of having all the cameras focused on her, she goes into the Paris Fashion Show's opening ceremony with Stormy.

Myrena sits in the front row by the runway still in shock by the iBroadcast hearing the unusually kind words of her number one adversary, Joseph Prince.

The next day, as Gorgona Fashion has its models walking down the runway showing off their new fashion line, sitting in the front row applauding is Joseph Prince.

Later in the day, iFashion iNews shows a photograph on the first webpage of Myrena standing in front of her models as Joseph Prince hands her an orchid containing a bouquet of red, lavender, fuchsia, shocking pink, light pink, and lavender.

That night the Professor calls Joseph asking him, "Have you gone crazy? The entire world has seen you honoring that 'crazy witch.' Tell me what you were thinking?"

Joseph replies, "It is all part of my grand plan. First, I get her on my side before I destroy her and her little Federation too" giving out an evil laughter as he hangs up.

Waking up, Joseph goes to the Maison Sauvage to eat breakfast amongst the spectacular floral arrangements and wild foliage. As the music in the background is playing Celeste Bordeaux's 'Morning in - Paris,' Joseph's breakfast arrives. He begins to eat his breakfast having avocado toast, an acai bowl with fresh fruit with a cup of hot café-au-lait.

As Joseph walks into the Louvre for today's Paris Fashion Show, he notices that there are two detectives from the Paris Police Prefecture. Sitting down in front of them in a sturdy wooden chair chatting away is the real 'Joseph Prince.'

Turning back into her non-shapeshifter self is Astrid Christensen who walks over near the Parisian detectives. Joseph is explaining to them that he has been kidnapped for several days.

He claims, "A fan of Voltaire had placed him inside an Iron Mask. Each day that he was imprisoned, delivery people brought him lunch and dinner, but they could not free him."

Finally, two Parisian auto technicians found him. They used their tools to unmask him and broke the lock holding the chains that restrained him.

The Professor is heard on the phone saying, "I am glad to have the real Joseph Prince back. I suspected that there was something not quite right the last time we spoke and now I understand the cunning, twisted mind of that evil, serpent witch. Although I cannot prove it, this scenario has all the markings of her bony fingerprints."

Joseph and all his designers and their apprentices head to the Milan Linate airport which is only 6.8 miles from Milan's city center.

The last of the big four fashion weeks is in Milan at Spazio Cavallerizze located at the Leonardo da Vinci National Science and Technology Museum. Other venues for the Milan Fashion Week are the Palazzo Reale's Salla delle Cariatidi and inside the Scala Ansaldo Workshop at the Padiglione Visconti.

Each of the designers are extremely excited to show off their new creations that will redefine Italian fashion.

As he looks over Myrena's fashion booth, it appears to be a rehash of her previous three exhibitions.

He stands in front of her fashion booth as her decorators are setting it up commenting, "How truly unoriginal. Perhaps next time she'll exhibit at the Milan Furniture Fair instead of in da Vinci's courtyard."

Walking back to the SPALDwear fashion booth, Joseph sees various iBroadcast iChannels interviewing each of his world famous designers who are explaining their innovative, high fashion ready to wear creations that every buyer, fashion influencer and attending celebrity are calling 'absolute genius,' 'the hottest trend in fashion history' and 'the perfect blending of iconic fashion designers producing a single brand's unique identity.'

Ranting to the international press, Joseph Prince excitedly explains, "This is a brand entitled 'SuperPower Anti-Lemnian Deeds' and it is directly attacking the company's founder and CEO, Myrena Gorgona."

The Professor instructs Joseph Prince to make reservations at Milan's three-star Michelin restaurant, Enrico Tortona.

As the entire SPALDwear team of designers, assistants, hair, and makeup artists sit down. Everyone is greeted by the restaurant manager as the highly experienced sommelier pours everyone a glass of their favorite red or white wine. Each guest has handed the 'B classic' menu.

One of the designers comments, "Imagine this. In central Milan there's an Italian restaurant serving Italian food."

The assistants, hair and makeup artists and Joseph all laugh.

The chef and his staff bring out the various award-winning Italian dishes. First, the chef oversees the first waiter bringing out a dish of tomato, liquorice, and almond appetizer.

That is followed by plates of spaghetti, toasted lemon, whiskey, and caviar.

The wait staff passes to each of the guests a large dish of Santa Margarita shrimp that has been smoked with thyme on top of risotto with black cherries and green peppers. The next large dish has Mediterranean turbot with sea snails and beetroot.

After emptying every single plate and enjoying each wine pairing from the sommelier, the chef has his waiters pass out to each guest the traditional zabaione which is an Italian custard dessert served with sliced fresh fruit and berries.

Then, several servers follow, handing each guest a bowl of pistachio homemade ice cream with bits of bitter orange.

Joseph Prince asks the Michelin chef and his staff to join his entourage for a glass of Italian champagne, Prosecco. Standing next to the table are the chef and his staff all holding crystal fluted glasses of Prosecco as Joseph and the entire team stand giving them an ovation.

The chef thanks everybody asking them to come back anytime.

Back at the Milan Fashion Show the buyers keep placing orders as the fashion influencers digitally record the SPALDwear creations as they blog to their millions of internet followers.

The Professor reports to his two nephews Rocky and Apollo, "The four major world fashion show weeks were not only a financial success but a devastating blow to the Gorgona Fashion Corporation and its founder and leader Myrena."

After a few seconds pausing he continues, "I am positive that Myrena was able to do some business but not nearly what she had anticipated before all of the shows began. We on the other hand we're not expecting anything except to tick her off. Our designs exceeded our expectations in sales and in worldwide publicity."

He pours each of his nephews and himself a Glencairn Whisky Glass of $100,000 Glenfiddich Janet Sheed Roberts Reserve 1955 that is one of the eleven bottles ever made.

Chapter 18

The African Queen Meets Little Women

Visiting New York City to attend the American Museum of Natural History inside its Halls of Gems and Minerals, JiJi Nkosi is the guest of honor having her large privately-owned gemstones on display. After watching the curators set up the exhibition with her diamonds, sapphires, and black opals, she walks down Fifth Avenue looking in the luxurious designer shops' window displays.

Down the street there's a well-dressed woman talking on her phone to her husband saying, "Honey, I know that the dress I want cost $20,000, but I want to wear it to the charity fundraiser that you will be speaking at."

After a pause, she continues saying, "I know. Yes, I know. But what if I can get it for a little less, will you let me buy it? Okay I'll try. Thanks. Love you too, Stephen."

Seeing JiJi, a young black casually dressed lady walking towards her, she asks in her Latina accent, "Pardon me, Miss but could I ask you to do me a big favor and I promise that it'll be worth your while."

JiJi, being curious replies, "Ee."

Not knowing that she just said 'yes' in Tswana the language spoken in Botswana, the wealthy woman continues asking, "Do you speak any English?"

Growing up in the Republic of Botswana that historically was a British protectorate, JiJi speaking using her British accent says, "Of course, darling. Are you going to invite me over for some tea and crumpets?" as she giggles.

Surprised, the wealthy lady says, "I would like to buy this dress in my favorite Fifth Avenue designer boutique. But my husband who is a billionaire doesn't think I should spend that kind of money. He has agreed that if I get a discount, he will let me buy it. I was wondering if you could help me?"

JiJi says, "Sounds like fun. I will try to help you."

The woman says, "I am Gisele Goldberg. What is your name and where are you from?"

"My name is JiJi Nkosi from Botswana in Africa."

Gisele points JiJi to her favorite designer boutique as the store's security guard opens the door for her.

She watches her new Botswana friend enter the boutique.

Walking around the store looking at all the clothing and each price tag the black girl in jeans wearing a New York City t-shirt is followed by one of the female salespeople.

The salesperson asks JiJi, "Is there something that I can help you with?"

Using her African accent, she replies, "No thank you. I am waiting for my friend who is supposed to meet me here."

The female salesperson responds, "Are you sure that she said to meet you in this designer boutique?"

Not even looking up as she examines one of the most expensive dresses, JiJi answers, "Ee."

As JiJi continues looking at each of the expensive clothes, the salesperson asks her, "Are you looking for something in particular?"

JiJi responds, "Just looking as I am waiting for my good friend."

Looking at a very colorful expensive dress that looks like it would fit well at any Botswana event, JiJi asks, "How much is this beautiful dress?"

The salesperson signals the boutique's security guard by pulling on her left earlobe. The guard is watching both ladies, especially JiJi.

The salesperson replies, "I don't think that particular style would fit you?"

Just then the security guard puts his left arm around JiJi pushing her towards the door as he says, "I would like to talk to you outside the store. Please follow me, Miss."

As the security guard is opening the front door forcefully escorting JiJi towards the sidewalk, Gisele Goldberg enters the store. Gisele who is well known in all the Fifth Avenue designer stores asks the salesperson, "What in God's name are you doing with my good friend, JiJi Nkosi from Botswana in Africa?"

The salesperson stutters as she says, "She, she, she's, your good friend, Mrs. Goldberg?"

Gisele says, "Yes, I told her to meet me here."

As the owner of the designer boutique comes running out of her office apologizing to them.

Gisele Goldberg introduces to the owner, "This is my good friend, Princess JiJi Nkosi from Botswana in Africa."

The owner shakes her hand telling her how sorry she is for her salesperson's rudeness that might be mistaken for racism by a more common person.

JiJi using her British accent remarks, "You are making me feel like Julia Roberts in the classic film 'Pretty Woman.' I shall tell all my relatives in the royal families throughout Africa not to shop here. I find the rudeness and racism that I have been treated with to be beyond any acceptable level even for a commoner like you."

The designer boutique's owner pleads with them to stay saying, "Please I want to make up for it. I will do anything to save our reputation."

Turning to JiJi she asks, "What could I possibly do to satisfy you so that the entire African nations' royal families will consider this shop when they visit us in New York City?"

Pausing and looking intently at her, she says, "I would like you to give my friend and myself today 50% off everything we purchase."

The designer boutique owner agrees as she personally brings various outfits for both ladies to try on. As other shoppers try to enter the boutique, the security guard tells them, "Please come back later as this is a private shopping spree."

After getting her $20,000 dress for half price, Gisele Goldberg thanks her new friend.

Leaving the designer boutique, JiJi holding the boutique's shopping bag containing her three new outfits tells the rude, racist salesperson, "Your store owner straightened out your mistake. Huge mistake. A tremendously big mistake," as she smiles showing off her black credit card.

JiJi tells Gisele that she is worth over twelve billion dollars US having her gemstone collection premiered in NY City,

JiJi hands Gisele two VIP guest invitations for her and her husband to come to the opening ceremony on Friday night at the American Museum of Natural History inside its Halls of Gems and

Minerals. She tells Gisele, "On display are over 1.5 billion dollars of my diamonds, black opals, rubies and sapphires."

During the opening ceremony inside the Museum's Gems and Minerals Hall, JiJi is introduced to Carlton Chesterfield who was asked by Professor Steele to validate her allegiance to the 'Golden Eagle' Organization.

Carlton tells her, "Everyday there is an increase of SuperPower people are joining DODGE and the 'Lemnian Deeds' Federation, especially the women. Although he is not saying it, I believe that the Professor is starting to get worried. He sent me here to contact you and then help him on a few missions that are vital."

She tells him, "Nothing has ever changed between us. As long as I get paid well for my gemstone missions. My allegiance is to the Botswana pula and the Swiss franc."

Giselle Goldberg tells her husband, "Stephen, this is JiJi, the lovely African lady from Botswana who helped me get the one of a kind $20,000 designer dress for half price. JiJi this is my husband, Stephen Goldberg."

Stephen tells her, "I am extremely glad that I do not have to have business dealings with you against me. By the way, your collection of gemstones is truly remarkable. You have quite the eye for finding the largest, most valuable, polished stones."

JiJi shakes his hand thanking his compliments.

She tells his wife, Giselle quietly, "I almost peed in my pants when you told the designer boutique owner that I was an African Princess because Botswana is a constitutional, multiparty, republican democracy with an elected President."

They both laugh as the server brings everyone a crystal fluted glass of French champagne.

Carlson Chesterfield flies into Pittsburgh International Airport taking a limousine to the Carnegie Mellon University campus.

Upon arriving in the parking lot of The Robotics Institute, the chauffeur opens the door for his passenger to exit. Coming out of the limousine is not the shapeshifter Carlson but a doppelganger of Salvador Martin.

According to the iMagazine 'Robotics Scientific Journal,' Carnegie Mellon's Robotics Institute is the world's most advanced robotics research facility and furthermore stating, "The best center for robotics research and education."

Carlson asks one of the students to show him to the office of the director of the CMU Robotics Institute.

Standing in front of the director's office, Salvador Martin knocks on the wooden door.

Hearing the director say, "Enter at your own risk" as laughter follows.

Entering his office, he sees Dexter Barnes the African American computer whiz from Baltimore and says, "It is you, Dexter?"

Seeing the head of DODGE standing in front of him, Dexter remarks, "Mr. Martin, sir. I certainly did not expect to see you today."

Salvador tells him, "Please relax, Director Barnes. I am merely here to pick up the AI62 computer chips from Beijing China that are for Olympia Gort's robotic research facility."

Dexter tells his benefactor who has donated hundreds of millions of dollars to the CMU Robotic Institute facility, "I have been personally training one of my doctorate students who has a unique SuperPower ability."

On his intercom, Dexter says, "Echo, could you come into my office for a minute."

Walking into the director's office is a beautiful Indian girl with dark skin and long black hair.

Looking at Salvador Martin, he says, "This young doctorate student is Echo Singh."

Removing a hand mirror from his desk, Carlson turns it towards Salvador who views his own reflection in the mirror.

Turning to Echo, he asks her to show his guest her unique SuperPower ability.

Blinking three times rapidly, Echo disappears.

Salvador looks into the mirror expecting to see his reflection but instead he sees the face of Echo.

Dexter says, "Her SuperPower gift is truly amazing as she can transport herself into a mirror, a painting, a photograph or any two-dimensional surface."

Laughing, Salvador states, "It this an altered state version of Oscar Wilde's 'The Picture of Dorian Gray?'"

Turning to Echo, he says, "Thank you. You may go back to your research."

Echo tells Salvador Martin, "It has been a pleasure to meet one of the executive board members of DODGE. Hopefully, we will meet again soon," as she walks back to her lab.

The real Salvador Martin sends two of his female SuperPower members to pick up the AI62 computer chips that were shipped from

Beijing China. He will personally deliver to Japan with his twin brother to Olympia Gort at her Tokyo robotic research facility.

Entering the Carnegie Mellon University campus are Katrina Quark and Pich Sok.

Katrina has the SuperPower abilities to shrink microscopically as well as the ability to fly.

The young Martin SuperPower trainee Pich Sok can control other people's minds as well as become invisible.

Katrina tells Pich, "We should survey the situation before presenting ourselves to Mr. Barnes."

Pich uses her SuperPower ability to become invisible as Katrina holds Pich's hand as the duo becomes invisible flying into the Robotics Institute.

Walking around the labs, Dexter Barnes shows Salvador each lab doing robotic research for agencies such as DODGE, the Steele Corporation, DARPA being an acronym for the 'Defense Advanced Research Projects Agency,' the Army, the Air Force, and the Navy.

At each student's lab station, he has the doctorate student explain their research. Many of the professors that get their grant financing from DODGE introduce themselves to Salvador Martin discussing their department and the important research that is being conducted. They thank him for his support and stress the need for continuing funding in their specialized area.

At the same time, Katrina and Pich enter a microwave lab getting caught inside an experiment where the team is outside the room wearing protective goggles.

Realizing the possible danger, Katrina, holding Pich's hand uses her SuperPower transforming the duo to a microscopic size where they fly between microwave's electrons and into an air vent in the ceiling to escape. Flying into a closet, the ladies resize into their normal size and walk down the hallway pretending to be students.

Katrina upon other students looking at young Pich states "It is taking my daughter to work day" getting a "That's totally Rufus" response. Sometimes, Katrina pointing at Pich says, "She is a new transfer student from Tokyo, young but brilliant."

Walking inside the DODGE research lab room, Dexter Barnes introduces Salvador Martin to their resident AI specialist Dr. William Know.

Dr. Know worked with Olympia's mother, Dr. Yoko Gort, in setting up the microprocessor software.

The doctor tells Salvador that he has copied his entire AI program code onto 500 CPU chips. He places the bag of microprocessor chips inside an orange tote bag that he had received for free earlier in the day.

Salvador thanks Dr. William Know "In this bag is the future of robotics as we know it. The late Doctors Gort last endeavors before their demise will not be in vain because of these AI microchips."

They start walking back to Dexter Barnes office, as they stop at the cafeteria where all the CMU Robotic Institute's professors and students are waiting to present Salvador Martin, their benefactor, with a luncheon. The local Pittsburgh eateries have delivered "The "Pittsburger" which is served in wax paper a burger piled high with French fries and coleslaw.

For dessert, each attendee is given Pittsburgh's dubbed, "The Greatest Cake America Has Ever Made," the burnt almond torte.

Dexter Barnes announces to everyone attending the luncheon, "In honor of our benefactor from DODGE, whom I can now call my friend. In his honor, I present a lithograph of his namesake's masterpiece the Salvador Dali's most famous work of art, 'Persistence of Memory' in the hope that he never forgets his visit to the world's greatest University that was founded by Andrew Carnegie, a friend of the Mellons. We present a lithograph of Dali's work as well as a t-shirt which contains the logo for CMU Robotics Institute."

As he hears their tremendous applause from the faculty and students, Carlson, looking like the third twin of the Martin brothers, thanks everyone as he walks around shaking everyone's hand.

Continuing back to Dexter Barnes' office, they pass the shipping room where Dexter suggests giving them a lithograph of Dali's 'Persistence.'

Salvador Martin hands the shipping clerk the gracious gift from the CMU Robotic Institute faculty. The clerk asks Salvador to provide his shipping address on the FedUp laptop.

Salvador enters the actual address of Carlton Chesterfield's current fake address for non-traceable deliveries that he knows will eventually appear at his real address' doorstep.

Dexter Barnes asks Salvador Martin "This afternoon Dr. Pascale who just won the Nobel Prize in Medicine will be lecturing on 'The Similarities Between Robotic Messaging and the Neurons in the Human Brain.' He is known for not only being a brilliant scientist but a very humorous one. His lecture today should be something that no one on campus should miss."

Carlson looking like Salvador's replicant says, "Luckily, I have plenty of time and being on campus makes me feel like a college student all over again. Where do I go to hear the lecture?"

Back in his director's office using his intercom he messages Echo Singh.

She arrives at the director's office.

Dean Barnes queries Echo, "Will you be attending Dr. Pascale's lecture that will commence in the next 15 minutes?"

Getting confirmation, he continues saying, "Would you be so kind as to take Mr. Salvador Martin with you?"

Looking at the handsome benefactor, she smiles saying, "Of course, I will."

Turning to Salvador, she says, paraphrasing her favorite classic movie 'The Matrix,' "Follow me says the white rabbit" as she nervously giggles.

Katrina and Pich continue walking as they explore all the lab research rooms. They start to notice that everyone they pass is walking towards the Grand Lecture Hall. Wondering what is happening Katrina tells Pich, "I do not know what is going on but let's follow the crowd" having her young partner nod her head in agreement.

Sitting inside the Grand Lecture Hall, Katrina is amazed that she sees what appears to be Salvador Martin sitting next to a beautiful Indian female. She has just spoken to both Martin twins last night where they were telling her that they plan to spend the day with their wives. They were excited to have an adventurous picnic at the

Golden Gate National Recreational Area with amazing views of the Golden Gate Bridge.

She tells Pich, "Do you see that man that looks exactly like your 'Uncle' Salvador Martin?" having her nod her head in agreement.

Continuing she says, "Last night he talked to us on the cell. He told us that he was going on a picnic today in San Francisco California which is 2,580 miles away. That person obviously has the SuperPower ability as a shapeshifter. For some reason, he is impersonating our beloved DODGE leader."

Telling Pich to save her seat, Katrina shrinks to a microscopic size as she flies ten rows forward landing on Echo's shoulder. She begins looking around as the only thing she sees out of place is a bright orange tote bag. She flies towards the tote bag that is resting on the floor between the legs of the Salvador Martin doppelganger.

With her dust particle size, she flies inside the tote bag. Soaring inside the bright orange tote bag, she notices a transparent plastic container with numerous black computer chips inside.

Shrinking even further to the size of an electron, Katrina maneuvers herself around the circuit board realizing that this might be the AI technology that Doctor Olympia Gort is expecting.

As the lecture begins, the fake Salvador Martin is listening to his opening statement that has a humorous anecdote that has both he and Echo laughing hysterically with the entire audience.

Since the shapeshifter is being distracted, Katrina touches the container containing the microchips which become the same size as she is. Holding on to her newly acquired treasure, she flies back to her seat revealing to Pich what she has obtained.

As the lecture concludes, all the attendees give Dr. Pascale a standing ovation.

Carlson. Chesterfield, mimicking the DODGE Executive Board member, picks up his bright orange tote bag realizing that it is completely empty. He looks around the Grand Lecture Hall looking for the thief that absconded his ill-gotten 500 AI microchips.

He tells Echo that he has to run to the restroom.

Standing by the only exits to the Grand Lecture Hall, he examines closely every attendee that walks out of the two double door exits.

As the young Pich walks past him, he begins to become suspicious as she is not your typical college doctorate student.

Following behind her is a more senior lady who is carrying a container of five hundred black microchips.

As Salvador's lookalike, Carlton sees Echo Sigh approaching him, and he says, "During the lecture a SuperPower lady stole my 500 AI microchips. I will point her out to you so that you can obtain these important items by placing them on this photograph of my dog."

Walking down the hall, they walk at a fast pace until they are behind Katrina and Pich.

Salvador points to the left hand of Katrina where she is holding a transparent plastic container of black microchips.

Echo holding the photograph supposedly of Salvador's dog touches the plastic container with her right hand.

Immediately the photograph of a dog is filled with five hundred black rectangles.

Echo hands Salvador his photograph back.

Looking at the new photograph, he smiles seeing the many black rectangles.

Remembering that his Dali lithograph is inside the shipping room, he takes Echo to that room. Seeing that his 'to be delivered' lithograph is resting where he put it. He asks Echo to transfer the five hundred black rectangles from the photo of a dog to Salvador Dali's lithograph of his 'Persistence of Memory.'

Echo blinks three times rapidly touching in her right hand the photograph of the dog. As the five hundred black rectangles disappear, she touches with her left hand the Dali lithograph which suddenly contains the five hundred black rectangles. She tells him that when the Dali reproduction arrives at his residence, the five hundred black microchips will automatically reappear in front of him.

Leaving the room, he thanks Echo for her help and kindness throughout the day.

As he gives her a kiss on the cheek and a hug, the shipping clerk walks by saying, "I will be processing your FedUp package, right now. Director Barnes has told me to ship it overnight to you."

Waiting outside CMU Robotics Institute is a chauffeur-driven limousine Dexter Barnes has arranged to take Salvador Martin back to Pittsburgh International Airport.

As the DODGE delegates begin walking out of the building, she looks inside her bag noticing that the plastic container is empty.

As she looks around the hallways, every single attendee at the Nobel prize-winning laureate's lecture is holding the exact same bright orange tote bag matching the one where the microchips were discovered.

While Carlton Chesterfield who looks exactly like he sees every morning as he shaves and brushes his teeth, boards the plane to Reykjavik Iceland. He walks forward preparing to relax, having his free drinks and meal as he sits in first class.

Back at CMU Robotics Institute, Katrina with Pich is on a conference call with the Martin twins and connected long distance with Dr. Olympia Gort. They are interrogating Dr. William Know on what happened during transferring of the 500 AI microchips to the shapeshifter who look exactly like Salvador Martin.

Dr. Olympia Gort demands from Dr. Know that he immediately reproduces by copying his AI code to another 500 AI microchips.

He explains that he may need a couple more days as he must get a new FedUp shipment from Beijing, China.

Pablo Martin has major political connections in the northern capital that was once the People's Republic of China.

Disappointed with their mission's outcome, Katrina flies back to San Francisco with Pich.

On the flight sitting in first class drinking carbonated beverages and eating snacks, they watch the latest 'Mission Impossible' movie starring Robert Leach.

After dropping Pich off with her adopted parents at the baggage claim, Katrina decides to travel to Dallas to shop at the 'Buyer's Club' and visit with some friends.

Chapter 19

Stopping the World's Fastest Human

Driving a Devel 517 with the incredibly fast speed of 375 miles per hour is Oliver 'the Merc' Davis.

Following close behind him, driving a Koenigsegg Astrape Ultimate is Myrena Gorgona with Astrid Christensen beside her.

The two women traveling at 350 miles per hour in a balanced modified vehicle are in pursuit to capture the world's fastest human.

The executive members of DODGE have parked special trucks throughout the city where each truck has a SuperPower person with the ability to negate the SuperPowers of others on which they are focusing. Their plan is to immobilize Oliver Davis as they try to convince him to switch allegiance by joining DODGE.

As the high-speed pursuit entails, the entire Metropolis police force clocks the Astrape Ultimate traveling well beyond the posted speed limit. The ladies are trying to catch Oliver's Devel 517 while avoiding the sixteen traffic law enforcement officers attempting to stop them.

Turn after turn throughout the city often making hairpin turns left and right having a few of the blue and white police cars crashing into parked cars and unaware of oncoming traffic.

Finally, Astrid tells Myrena, "Let's end this pursuit and pull over."

Myrena slams on the brakes having the Koenigsegg Astrape Ultima spin a 180 degrees.

The remaining police officers exit with their handguns drawn.

First, Myrena gets out of the vehicle with her hands held high.

The officer in charge is heard over his patrol megaphone saying, "Oh my God, it's Myrena Gorgona, SuperModel."

Next stepping out of the passenger side is shapeshifter, Astrid Christiansen.

Loudly exclaimed through the patrol megaphone is heard, "Oh my God, it is US President Roberta Yarjo."

As a chauffeur-driven limousine surrounded by police officers on motorcycles arrives at the scene, the city's mayor exits the vehicle before the chauffeur opens his door. The mayor waves his arms back and forth instructing everyone to leave the scene.

Pablo Martin who is owed many favors by former President and now Vice President, Bob Yarjo calls the city's mayor on his unlisted personal cell phone.

Upon answering his phone, the mayor hears, "This is Vice President, Bob Yarjo. The White House Situation Room is monitoring the whereabouts and activities of President Roberta Yarjo and Myrena Gorgona. Mister mayor you are on our national surveillance radar. Have a wonderful day," as he hangs up.

The mayor tells his assistant, "Today I am not going to arrest the President of the United States. No one has been injured by a horse as with the arrest of Presidents Franklin Pierce and Ulysses S. Grant."

As all the law enforcement vehicles vacate, Myrena and Astrid who resembles the current US President return to their Chili Red Koenigsegg Astrape Ultima.

Salvador Martin, who is monitoring the current whereabouts of Oliver Davis, updates the ladies to continue their shadowing quest.

The special trucks have trapped Oliver's Devel 517 with no foreseeable way to get onto the highway. The Koenigsegg Astrape Ultima arrives to record Myrena apprehending 'the Merc' Davis.

Behind the Devel is a Carnival cruise ship, the Carnival Escape docked at the port with miles of ocean behind the ship's stern.

As Myrena being seen on iBroadcast iNews getting out of her vehicle, Oliver uses his SuperPower ability to fly at an incredible speed to catapult above the red farcus funnel ship's 'Sky' deck. Not realizing what had just occurred, Myrena opens the driver's side door expecting to find Oliver Davis inside, but she is recorded as being ghosted by him. With a surprised expression on her SuperModel face the iNews cuts to an iCommercial.

Myrena and Astrid lead the entire surveillance team to board the Carnival ship entering from 'deck 0' near the medical center. Taking the elevator to the top deck, Myrena and Astrid pursue Oliver.

As the rest of her team investigates each deck searching for him. The ladies walk around the deck. Myrena walks along the starboard or right side of the ship as Astrid scouts on the port being the left side of the ship.

Looking one deck down, they see Oliver standing at the bow which is the front of the ship.

Oliver noticing that several passengers waiting to begin boarding on the dock below him have high-def cameras recording him, he states "The stunt you are about to see is performed by a professional, so for your safety and the protection of those not here, do not attempt any of the following stunts you're about to see."

Noticing that the 'Lemnian Deeds' leaders have discovered his whereabouts, Oliver smiles yelling, "I am the king of the world," as he jumps off the ship.

Normally, an action like this would trigger shock but the female duo knows that Oliver has the SuperPower ability to fly and to land safely.

Looking over their deck's bow, they observe that he landed on the US Coast Guard's fast response boat having the acronym 'FRB.' Oliver grabs each coast guard using his super speed tossing each coast guard one at a time into the water.

Now alone, he takes control of the vessel having it cruise at 50 knots which is 57.5 mph. Getting away he heads towards the open ocean waters as Astrid signals all the surveillance teams to regroup and strategize capturing Davis. Oliver smiles singing, "I am 'the skipper, brave and sure.' Now, off to 'The Merc Davis Island.'"

Myrena orders one of the senior coast guards to captain the Mercury Racing 400XS motorboat that cruises at over 100 mph.

Joining them is Astrid who has obtained long range military binoculars.

As some of the teams join the coast guards who have called in reinforcements with FRBs, the other team members get back into the special trucks in case Oliver becomes land based again.

Oliver Davis realizes that the Mercury Racing 400XS is too fast compared to his borrowed FRB, so he jumps out using his SuperPower to walk on water at 1,800 mph. His personal high speed is significantly faster than the hunting Mercury as he heads to the populated island.

The surveillance team with the coast guard return to base.

There one of the local teens sees a submarine used to film shark attacks. He asks the coast guard, "If one were to use the submarine and the shark cage could we dive deep and from a submerged position surface underneath Oliver capturing him?"

The coast guard thinks hard imagining several scenarios and says, "I believe that your plan has a seventy-five percent chance of success."

The teen tells everyone, "Let's go capture a 'man-eating Merc.'" as the group laughs.

After docking the Mercury Racing 400SX at the island's pier, Myrena and Astrid walk along the beach as the coast guard stays with the fast response boat performing a routine inspection.

Astrid transforms herself into a doppelganger of Oliver Davis. Along the beach Myrena pointing to Astrid as Oliver asks everyone, "Has anyone seen my friend's identical twin brother?"

Astrid jokingly tells her, "Would it hurt you to say, 'my boyfriend' instead of 'friend?'"

Myrena raises her eyebrows saying, "No sane person would believe that Oliver Davis can have me that way. He is not that handsome and not at all in my 'wealth' range."

Walking along the shops, Myrena and Astrid looking exactly like Oliver 'the Merc' Davis asks each person they pass if 'anyone has seen this person?' She points to himself commenting, "He is my identical twin."

With only 'no' as their answer, they continue traveling deeper towards the residential district. Walking by the inlet, they pass several fishermen carrying their daily catch to sell to local restaurants.

Seeing Astrid, one of them stops dead in his tracks saying, "How in the world did you get here ahead of us?"

Myrena asks, "What do you mean, sir."

He tells her, "We just saw this man walking past us as we fished heading up to the highest mountain on our island." He points in that direction.

Astrid speaking with Oliver's voice says, "You must have seen my identical twin brother for which we are searching. Was he alone? How long ago did he pass you?"

Another angler states, "Yes, he traveled alone and boy, was he in a hurry."

Astrid thanks him asking, "What is the 'catch of the day?"

One teen boy answers proudly, "We caught many yellowtail and white sea bass. Tonight, the out of towners will feast on grilled yellowtail in garlic sauce or eaten raw as sashimi. Some will enjoy the grilled white sea bass with roasted potatoes."

Leaving their newfound friends, Myrena and Astrid swiftly walk in the pointed direction traveling along the water uphill until only a grassy steep incline exists.

As the elevation increases, they see in the distance Oliver waving at an approaching helicopter.

They begin to run up the mountain as Oliver begins climbing up the dropped helicopter rope suspension which is often used to rescue or extract military ground forces.

Just as they get to the top of the highest island location, the helicopter with Oliver hanging from the top rung of the rope ladder takes off heading back to the city.

Myrena and Astrid walk disappointedly back to town.

There they rejoin the Mercury Racing 400SX having the coast guard return them towards the city.

As the Mercury gets into the deep ocean, the coast guard, seeing Astrid still in her Oliver Davis form, pushes him over the side of the vessel. The surveillance team launches their 'shark cage trap' powered by the submarine catching what appears to be Oliver Davis but is the shapeshifter, Astrid Christensen.

Upon raising the cage above the water, everyone witnesses that the person inside the shark cage is a beautiful female not an Oregon Duck runner. The team leader apologizes to Astrid in her normal form, freeing her. Drenched in her clothes, she climbs back onto the Mercury having that coast guard apologizing repeatedly to her.

Astrid dries off saying, "It was entirely my fault as I forgot that I was still shapeshifted as Oliver Davis, the number one DODGE enemy."

Back in the city, the remaining DODGE surveillance team waiting in their special trucks are on high alert as Myrena has communicated that Oliver has returned into the city.

Being dropped off from the helicopter, Oliver notices that the Devel 517 is now chained to the top of a tow truck ready to be carted off. He begins walking looking for a busy section away from the water.

Oliver quickly enters an Army-Navy store along the boulevard. Looking around the store, he finds a navy-blue pair of pants and short sleeve shirt like the coast guards that have been chasing him all day long. He tops off the uniform with a navy-blue US Coast Guard adjustable cap complete with emblem that hides his recognizable face.

Exiting through the back door without paying he avoids the DODGE surveillance trucks and team members looking for him.

Walking through the streets looking at the ground, he enters a full public bus sitting in the back near the aisle.

The Martin twins use their influence having the iBroadcast iNews reporting Oliver Davis as a terrorist that the Federal authorities are desperately trying to apprehend.

As passengers get on the bus at each stop, a few young adults watching their handheld monitors playing the latest shooter view "An important interruption." The iBroadcast special report clearly shows Oliver 'the Merc' Davis hanging from the rope ladder as he escapes with the Steele provided helicopter. All at once the entire gang of young videogame players yell out, "There he is. That's the terrorist "Oliver 'the Merc' Davis," pointing at him.

Without answering back, Oliver runs out of the bus just before it continues to its next stop. The DODGE surveillance team learns of the bus incident convening upon that section of the city.

The DODGE team SuperPower members that could negate Oliver's SuperPower of flight and to walk on water begin concentrating fixated on him.

Unaware of DODGE's strategy Oliver tries to run at 1,800 mph but he is unable to swiftly move. Next, he tries to fly up into the sky, but he falls onto the grass. Running towards the water, he jumps off the pier believing that his SuperPower to walk on water is intact. The DODGE members watch him sink having his Coast Guard navy blue uniform take on water.

Arriving inside a city police vehicle is Elijah Moses, Jr. who greets Myrena Gorgona and Astrid Christiansen. As the real Coast Guard officers handcuff the floating, wet former Oregon Duck, the DODGE celebrities report on the iBroadcast iNews that the subversive Oliver 'the Merc' Davis has been caught and will be incarcerated.

The DODGE board members will hold Oliver a prisoner keeping his SuperPowers negated as they try to convince him to either join DODGE or remain their prisoner.

Oliver keeps repeating, "I am a member of the 'Golden Eagle' Organization. We will guard thee on and on. Gather around and cheer chanting the glory, roaring the praises of their warriors."

Pablo Martin tells the group, let's reconvene tomorrow morning as this mighty Oregon Duck has been brainwashed. He is paraphrasing his alma mater's 'Mighty Oregon' University's chant.

Chapter 20

Countdown: The Final Curtain Call

Elijah Moses Jr. calls down to Dr. Ben King Neptune-Dolittle. He asks the aquatic veterinarian, "How are you and your husband, Dr. Rex Dolittle-Neptune doing?"

Ben answers, "We are doing very well. Our relationship is blossoming as we have never been happier. What can I do for you?"

Elijah asks him, "Could you fly back to Macau China where your old friend Jack Diamond has won the Macau Poker Invitational winning himself fifty million dollars. Our best SuperPower members stood around behind him negating his lucky SuperPower. It is unbelievable but he won the championship using only his skill and bluffing strategy. Besides going back to Macau, would be like a mini vacation for you and your husband."

Ben asks, 'What's in it for you and DODGE?"

Elijah answers, "We need to know the whereabouts of the Steele family."

Getting off the plane in Macau China, Ben and Rex exit their first-class seats heading to the baggage claim. As they gather their overnight luggage, their chauffeur takes two bags. After opening the backseat door for the two gentlemen, he places their luxury leather bags inside the limousine trunk.

Driving to the MGM Macau's Grande Praca, the chauffeur hands the hotel's concierge their bags.

After the two doctors hand the chauffeur a generous tip, he returns to the limousine and drives away.

The concierge tells the two doctors that they are already checked in as VIP guests. He brings their bags to their penthouse suite. The concierge uses his key card to open the penthouse suite door.

Then, he places their overnight bags inside the room. After they give him a generous tip, he exits closing the penthouse suite door.

They kiss each other as Rex says, "Let us walk into the casino and see what Jack Diamond is up to?"

At the Texas Hold'em table, everyone antes up $1,000 US and is dealt their first two cards.

The flop or next three cards are placed face up in the center of the table. The cards are Ace of Diamonds, Ace of Spades, and King of Diamonds.

Angela looks at her two-hole cards seeing that she has the Ace of Clubs and the King of Hearts giving her a full house Aces over Kings.

She bets $5,000 US having everyone fold but Jack Diamond who places his chips to cover the current bet. Then, with a straight face he raises her $20,000 US looking at her as he says, "This is a No Limit table."

Angela matches her chips to the current raise amount.

The fourth card to be dealt up in the center of the table commonly known as the 'turn' is the ten of Diamonds.

Again, Angela bets $50,000 US telling Jack, "Like you said, it's No Limit!"

Jack removes from his huge rack of chips $150,000 US and says, "Let me see if you're still smiling now."

Not to back down Angela places $300,000 US in chips on to the table where the dealer counts them.

Jack matches the current bet in chips.

The last card to be dealt or the 'river' is a Two of Clubs.

Angela announces that she is 'all in' having the dealer count her chips.

The dealer tells Jack that the current bet is 1.5 million dollars US which he hands to the dealer to verify.

Angela looks at Jack and says, "I'm sorry to say I have a full house Aces over Kings. Hit the road, Jack!"

She continues saying, "I might have to rename this casino as Angela's Casino."

Jack Diamond knows that the odds of a full house in Texas Hold 'em is 36 to 1.

With his serious Poker Face, Jack Diamond turns over his cards showing the Queen of Diamonds and his namesake the Jack of Diamonds.

With the odds of around 650,000 to 1, Jack has revealed a Royal Flush of Diamonds completely bankrupting Angela's chip count.

She walks away screaming, "F you, Jack Diamond!"

Throughout the casino, they see millions of dollars being gambled. Sitting at the bar buying drinks for an unbelievably beautiful, voluptuous Asian woman is Jack Diamond.

They walk over to him saying, "Hello Jack, long time no see. In fact, the last time we did see you, you lost a fortune."

Jack, a little disturbed asks, "What do I owe the pleasure of you two lovebirds?"

Ben tells him, "Rex believes that I can beat you at Texas Hold'em for a $10,000 Buy in."

Wanting to get back to hopefully his bed partner for the night, Jack tells him, "Show up here at noon tomorrow and bring the cash that I will happily take from you."

They leave heading back to their penthouse suite for the night.

The next day as Ben hands the dealer a casino credit slip for $10,000, he sits down ready to play. Jack is sitting at the table having already given his money to the casino.

As the dealer shuffles the cards, Ben tells Jack that he wants to add to the bet.

Jack Diamond agrees saying, "What are your added terms?"

Ben tells him, "When I win, I want to know the current hereabouts of the Steele family."

Jack says, "I agree. Now, let's play."

For the next 45 minutes, the chip count has gone back and forth. Currently it is exactly equal just like when the match began.

Rex who has been watching the whole time, plays on Jack's 'never lose and never-say-die' attitude saying, "I guess since you are doing so lousy today, playing like a 'whale' it would behoove you to add to the pot half your Macau Poker Invitational winnings to help feed hungry mouths of Madagascar. Whom I am told 'are starving so much that they do not have the resources to even cry about it.' So, Jack, ' do you feel lucky, punk?'"

Jack replies, "What do I care about starving children in Madagascar? Now let's play Punk!"

Jack tells the dealer to make the bet $30 million US saying, "I can do better than half of my recent poker winnings, here."

Rex asks Jack, "I thought that your family enjoys helping the less fortunate, especially the hungry children. Don't you desire to help the less fortunate?"

Surprised about the question, Jack responds honestly saying, "My mother, she volunteers for 'The Worldwide Feed the Children Foundation.' Why do you ask?"

Approaching the Texas Hold'em table where Jack is playing Ben, he looks in disbelief as Tritony Neptune-Dolittle is escorting Jack's mother.

Rex again asks Jack, "Would you reconsider, giving $30 million US of your Macau Poker Invitational winnings to help feed hungry children of Madagascar."

Jack's mother says, "Jack's a good boy and he would do anything to help the poor little children of Madagascar. Isn't that right, son?"

Jack reluctantly declares, "Yes mommy."

Without looking at his cards, Diamond Jack declares, "I fold."

He stands up telling the casino pit boss to give the promised Macau victory winnings to Tritony saying, "This round is over as I declare myself the winner," as he leaves the casino with his mother.

Harrison joins his family. They all go out to dinner; Rex with Ben and Harrison with Tritony.

Ben jokingly tells his cohorts, "Winner! Winner! Are we having chicken dinner?"

After dinner, Ben gets a text message from Jack that reads, "The Steele Corporation under Professor Steele is sponsoring the 'Eight Tea Days Around Europe' race. Good luck, donkey."

He forwards the message to Elijah Moses, Jr. at DODGE.

Chapter 21

Prelude 'Eight Tea Days Around Europe' Race

Sponsoring and organizing the 'Eight Tea Days Around Europe' automobile race, Professor Steele decides to begin and commence the entire race from the southeast town of London England.

Marking the roadway in bright yellow paint is where all the participants will start the eight-day race. The yellow line marks Greenwich Meridian or to cartographers known as 'zero degrees longitude.'

At exactly teatime being 3 p.m. Greenwich Mean Time, the Professor will lead the entire pole position of participants from Observatory Road in front of the Royal Observatory.

The Professor and his two nephews travel in a custom-built Tesla SUV complete with bulletproof windows and reinforced steel covered wheels that is protected from armor-piercing projectiles.

Behind the front passenger seat is a kitchenette with a large refrigerator freezer, supply cabinet and a Cloud-9 Queen size memory foam bed.

Arriving in Greenwich the day before the race begins, Apollo and Rocky shop inside Greenwich Market that is a covered shopping center having a farmers' market inside where they fulfill the Professor's shopping list for their eight-day adventure.

The shopping list is organized for their breakfast, lunch, and dinner as well as snacks and drinks throughout the journey.

Stored in and near the large refrigerator and freezer by the backseat bed are the wine bottles in a rack, placed inside the refrigerator are juice and beverages. In the market, the brothers pick up many fruits, freshly cut meats for sandwiches, and freshly made cookies and cakes.

On the iBroadcast prerace special show, Roxanne McLaren begins meeting each racing team, Professor Steele entertains at a private, catered luncheon for the racing teams and dignitaries who have come to Greenwich to witness the start of the race. The Professor has humorously called the long-distance race based on his favorite book by Jules Verne published in 1873, the 'Eight Tea Days Around Europe.' Beginning the race at 3 p.m. which is high tea or afternoon teatime that in the UK that is typically celebrated between 2 p.m. and 5 p.m.

Throughout the day are the sixty-four participating teams standing near their vehicle.

The Professor stands in front of all the racing teams stating, "Each of the participating teams had been selected by the Golden Eagle HQ committee. Each vehicle can have up to four team members that includes a driver and three passengers. The team decides when to switch their driver. As each team registers their vehicle and the names of their team members. The Golden Eagle staff will hand out a racing package that contains a detailed map with all the cities that they are to visit and historical sites that are along the way."

He continues saying, "The rules are clearly stated inside each package. Some of the rules are 'upon arriving at each city, they are to report to that city's listed venue where a race official validates that every vehicle on the Professor's list is accounted for.'"

Professor Steele says, "Another rule is that teams may substitute another vehicle for the one that they were previously driving only after calling or emailing the 'Golden Eagle' Organization who will alert all the race officials. As the Golden Eagle HQ will be carefully monitoring the race, they will dispatch a new vehicle quickly if the current vehicle is incapacitated, Team members may substitute the other team members with a driver, A team may add another passenger after registering that person with the 'Golden Eagle' HQ having a maximum of four members in the vehicle. Each vehicle has a GPS device, an iCommunication device that links to the iBroadcast iChannel with the Golden Eagle HQ that can be set to public or private, and an electronic toll payment device."

The Golden Eagle HQ race judge Judy Gayle says, "The international E-road network was developed by the United Nations Economic Commission for Europe or UNECE where the network is numbered from E1 upward crossing national borders. The UK has roads beginning with 'M-.' The 'A' roads are primary like highways that are fully connected within the primary road network. The 'B' roads are regional, mainly used to connect areas of lesser importance. Every vehicle racing and replacement vehicles have European Electronic Tolling Service devices that electronically pay the tolls."

Each racing team has met in a confidential meeting venue to plan out their strategy for the Eight Tea Days Around Europe race.

The night before the race starts the entire entourage of racers wearing matching t-shirts convene for a Michelin restaurant feast. Catered by 'Champagne, Beer Plus Fromage' in Greenwich are gastronomic delights from their covered and heated alfresco tables.

One table serves a variety of cheeses, freshly cut meats, with Italian black olive and kalamata olive tapenade along with cornichon, being a small, pickled cucumber.

The 'Welcome Ceremony' banquet wait staff distributes pale ale, bitter ale, and brown ale beers as well as champagne.

Trying to fit in with the rest of the racers, the Professor with Apollo and Rocky are wearing black t-shirts with a Golden Eagle on the front and on the back of each shirt is the name 'Steele.'

One of the members of the Ferrari family, Mario, whose team is driving a high-performance Ferrari EV SUV named the Purosangue Model 7.

Mario Ferrari comments seeing the black and gold shirts "I can see that your team can switch shirts at any time during the next eight days without a problem" as he walks away laughing.

Apollo replies, "My uncle has bought each of us ten of these shirts for our eight-day victory."

As Mario is still within hearing distance, Rocky says, "And to you Mario Ferrari, you can't live off your ancestors' credentials."

Roxanne McLaren walks around greeting each Eight Days Around Europe racing team. She stops in her tracks as she notices a familiar celebrity face

As the camera turns to the man standing next to her, she continues, "Sir, I understand you are racing in tomorrow's big event. Can you tell my worldwide iBroadcast audience your name and why you are racing in this Eight Tea Days event."

Turning towards the camera and removing his sunglasses he says, "I am Francis Fellini, the two-time Oscar-winning director. I have formed a racing team to compete. I have just signed a multimillion-dollar directorial contract to work on the 'European Cannonball Run' movie."

Roxanne McLaren says, "What an exciting scoop straight from the horse's mouth, What do you expect to learn from this racing experience?" as she giggles.

Fellini replies, "After the race, I have made excellent contacts with these professional racers that I intend to interview about their strategy and insights. They might be hired as extras too."

Roxanne inquires, "I look forward to going to the theater and seeing your 'European Cannonball Run' movie. After that project, what is on your next horizon?"

Francis states, "The reason for me to work on this sequel is to raise enough capital to finance my Oscar-worthy film called 'Return to Camelot,' where Lancelot has bedded Guinevere they have twins, a boy, and a girl. The boy is destined to be King with the help of his unbeaten swash buckling sister. I promise it will have amazing fight scenes showing the twins as the greatest masters of the sword."

Roxanne McLaren now zoomed in by her cinematographer comments, "We look forward to your next few films. Thank you, Francis Fellini, the legendary director."

Walking over to Team 5 standing next to its leader Elowen Redington, Roxanne McLaren states, "Greetings, Ms. Elowen Redington."

Elowen smiles and responds, "Nts'e dit'ae?"

Roxanne says to her worldwide iBroadcast audience, "That pronounced "Nn-tseh dit-aah" a traditional Alaskan tribal greeting, my researcher tells me."

Elowen responds, "Correct."

To her listening iBroadcast audience she continues, "Ms. Redington, you are the ninth generation of Ididarod champions, is that true?"

Elowen says, "Yes. The Iditarod is nicknamed 'The Last Great Race' and is an annual sled dog race in Alaska along the Iditarod Trail in Alaska with around 1,000 miles between Anchorage and Nome. Each sled operated by a racer or musher pulled by a team of fourteen dogs that race for eight or nine days."

Roxanne states, "Although this race is similar in its number of days the fact is this distance of the Eight Tea Days Around Europe is much further."

The cinematographer scans her teammates Lazer Cannon and Callon Ferrel as they pet their mascot an Alaskan Husky.

Lazer answers her, "We have won quite a few ice-cold week plus races before and we are ready to add another victory to our collection."

His teammates state in unison, "Mush! Mush! Mush!"

Turning toward the camera, she says, "This is Roxanne McLaren with Team 5 'The Ididarod Squad.'"

"This is Roxanne McLaren reporting from the Golden Eagle iBroadcast at the opening ceremony of 'Eight Tea Days Around Europe Welcome Extravaganza' hosted by the Steele Corporation."

A wide shot of the teams enjoying the party's libations and regal buffet as she continues saying, "The 64 three to four person teams' race, beginning in Greenwich UK then crossing every country around Europe for eight days and finishing back here in Greenwich. Unlike the famous Jules Verne book, we drive electric vehicles around Europe and not the world."

As the camera shows a close up of Roxanne, she says, "Each day every team during the afternoon must stop for their tea break recorded by their vehicle's camera and GPS that confirms the mandatory hourly break."

Professor Steele walks around shaking every competitor's hand wishing them, "Good luck and safe driving. The Steele team won't be seeing your team until after we cross the finish line."

Team 3's Darcy Austen driving an Aston Martin Maxi EV Supercar with the word 'Pride' on the frunk of her car and the word on the trunk 'Prejudice.'

Before being interviewed by Roxanne, Darcy introduces her Team 3's members Jubilee Perez and Romy Ruiz.

With the Ashton Martin supercar in full view for the iBroadcast audience, Roxanne asks, "Ms. Austen, can you tell us about your unique detailed supercar."

Darcy explains, "Our plain Jane Ashton Martin is reminiscent of my favorite book 'Pride and Prejudice,' Our EV vehicle represents the old adage. As everyone knows 'Pride goes before the fall.'"

The DJ 'Cool Runnings' states, "Here's a tune from 'Bunny Wailer' who was born Neville O'Riley Livingston, a Jamaican singer-songwriter and percussionist being a reggae group member of the Wailers along with Bob Marley. Later, Bunny's 'Electric Boogie' was successfully recorded and performed by Marcia Griffiths. We all know the song and how to dance to it."

The DJ 'Cool Runnings' plays Lovegood Records latest version recorded just for this event,

Roxanne McLaren finally reconnects with Professor Steele.

She asks him, "Are you excited about the upcoming Eight Tea Days Around Europe race?"

With a straight face he says, "Indubitably, I get to spend the next eight days with my two favorite nephews before we win another race."

She continues asking, "As a successful entrepreneur do you agree with the saying that 'money can't buy you happiness?'"

Looking directly at the camera the Professor remarks, "Yes I do, Roxanne. Last year the Steele Corporation and I earned over $50 billion. I was as happy last year when I made $40 billion."

Roxanne states, "Professor, where is your crystal flute glass of champagne?"

Professor Steele smiles at the camera saying, "Roxanne, champagne is for the winner's podium. Ciao."

Apollo Steele returns to his hotel suite. Hanging outside of his door is a 'Do Not Disturb' sign. Being curious as to why the sign has been placed on his suite's door, he knocks loudly.

As the door slowly opens, Apollo is surprised to see his recently acquired paramour, Amelia Kristjánsson.

Amelia greets him with a hug and passionate kiss. After the long embrace she says, "I've missed you so much that I had to come here to see you before the 'Big Race.'"

Apollo replies, "We saw each other just two days ago in Reykjavik. We attended your family's 'seafood extravaganza' dinner."

She smiles, giving him another hug and passionate kiss.

Looking into her eyes Apollo says, "So my love how in the world did you manage to get into my hotel suite?"

She chuckles saying to him, "As intelligent and good looking as you are, you should realize that I have the female power ability to control the minds of others. I can be very persuasive even without a SuperPower gift."

Apollo kisses her back telling her, "To me, you are not only the most beautiful woman but with your family's fortune in the double-digit billions, I honestly know that you are not after the Steele family fortune."

Apollo kisses her again and excuses himself to use the bathroom.

Upon exiting, he is pleasantly surprised to see his lady in his bed waiting to make love to him.

After waking up and leaving his room to join his uncle, the Professor and his brother Rocky, Apollo arrives at the breakfast table with Amelia a few minutes behind him.

Rocky jokes saying, "It is my assumption that one of us brothers did not get an awful lot of sleep last night. Although, I am quite certain that both of us were happily enjoying our comfortable beds last night."

Amelia tells her soon-to-be family, "Góðan daginn" which translates to 'good morning.' She then kisses Apollo telling them "We had a wonderful night celebrating. Today, we are excited to start the 'Around Europe' race. May I suggest that Apollo spend the first eight hours of the race resting from a night of passion."

On all the European iBroadcast iChannels, the iNews is reporting heavy traffic going into France. The two-hour delay is a major surprise to everyone but Myrena Gorgona and her 'Lemnian Deeds' Federation whose evil plans are underway.

After leaving the 3 p.m. Greenwich tea ceremony, the racers head from Dover, UK to Calais, France taking their automobiles across the English Channel. Each vehicle participating in the 'Across Europe' race has chosen closed envelopes indicating how their vehicle is to cross the Channel. Some teams may enter the P&O ferry that enters France in 90 minutes having a one-way cost of $190 US. Alternatively, other teams open their envelopes indicating that they must travel through the EuroTunnel or Chunnel with your vehicle which costs $120 US one way.

The EuroTunnel trip, which under normal circumstances takes 35 minutes but thanks to Myrena and her Deeds there is an unexpected delay.

Each racing team is discussing their new strategy to travel into the 'Hexagon' as it is often referred to as the 'L'Hexagone' due to the shape of the country.

Inside the DODGE European headquarters, Myrena Gorgona and Stormy Weather are organizing a "Stop the Professor" campaign. communicating with their European consortium of SuperPower connections, Myrena proudly states, "Our mission is to assassinate Professor Steele with minimal collateral damage."

She adds, "Unless it is his nephews, Rocky and Apollo. I can live without them in the world," as she laughs.

Supplied with the stolen "Eight 'Tea' Days Around Europe" race package, they assign lethal assassins throughout the route supplying each with unlimited finances, weapons, and supplies.

Myrena and a few Lemnian Deeds Federation board members begin recruiting SuperPower individuals to join the "Stop The Professor!" campaign.

Scotland's Delilah Craine, the daughter of Sofia Fraser and Martin Craine follows in her mother's footsteps to stop the Golden Eagle Organization using her SuperPower ability to fly and to control mechanical devices.

Marseille, France's Ruby Bordeaux Chardonnay, the daughter of Celeste Bordeaux and Robert Chardonnay who has the SuperPower ability to transform objects from one form to another and to become invisible has joined the Deeds.

Italy's Antonio Ferrari, the adopted son of Deborah Ferrari and Bianca Ricci has vowed to stop his boarding school rivals, Rocky and Apollo Steele using his SuperPower of invisibility and to manipulate the internals of any vehicle.

Studying physics at the Autonomous University of Barcelona, Spain and recruited by Stormy Weather to "Stop the Professor!" is Jonathan Barbosa, the younger brother of Brittany who has the SuperPower to become invisible and, like his sister, manipulate time.

Rolex Kronos, the brother to Gabrielle is also a hyperjacker with the SuperPower ability to become invisible.

Olympia Gort has joined the Lemnian Deeds Federation to observe and cause havoc to the racers in Eastern Europe. The Deeds value her programming robotic skills, having her stock up on explosive flying droids that are programmed to disable the racers.

Zoey Chamberlain from the UK, who considers herself a friend of Marina Gorgona and Stormy Weather having the SuperPower ability of 'therianthropy' meaning that she can metamorphosis into any animal by shapeshifting and to become invisible.

Chapter 22

Saturday: 'Eight Tea Days Around Europe' Race

The iStudio camera assistant says, "Three….Two." as she mouths silently, "One."

Roxanne McLaren appears on the Golden Eagle iBroadcast. She reports, "Good day viewers, it's Day One, you are watching live Eight Tea Days Around Europe racing iNews. There is one mission, one race, one city at a brief glance."

Roxanne continues saying, "I have a new co-host joining us, Stephen Griswald. He will provide interesting and historic commentary as the teams travel throughout Europe."

Stephen remarks, "Thank you Roxanne. Salutations everyone. We will be commenting giving the viewers the distance to the upcoming cities and the traveling time to drive there under normal speed limits."

Roxanne speaking for her iBroadcast audience replies, "You are very welcome and do not drop the mic," as she giggles.

Stephen Griswald says, "Driving 67 miles from Dartford to Dover down Highway M-20 passing Rochester, Faversham, Canterbury into Dover."

Roxanne states, "Then, each racing team has chosen lots that tells them whether at Greenwich, UK to travel across the English Channel by Chunnel or take the Port of Dover ferry."

Stephen remarks, "Once the teams are in France, they must travel on Highway A16 towards E40."

Roxanne states, "The European route E40 is the longest European highway extending 4,971 miles long, connecting Calais in France to Kyrgyzstan."

One By Land

The Professor and his two nephews along with a few of the other 'Eight Tea Day' racing vehicles take M-20 using the exit heading towards the Le Shuttle (or Channel Tunnel also referred to as the Eurotunnel). The Professor is followed by the other drivers down M-20 taking the exit at 11A until there are signs indicating 'Entering the Channel Tunnel.'

As an exhausted Apollo sleeps in the back of the vehicle on top of an extremely comfortable queen size bed, his brother Rocky who is driving sees a white sign in front of the blue security check booth.

Rocky tells the Professor, "The sign states 'drive through Europe.'"

He chuckles remarking "We are going to 'fly through Europe' with our pedal to the metal."

Professor keeps a calm, straight Poker Face ignoring his nephew's youthful comments.

Rocky keeps driving down the road with markings in white stating 'France.'

The Professor tells Rocky, "Slow down, we are entering the 'Passport and Security Controls' checkpoint."

A little way past the checkpoint is a large poster of Europe in green with the words, "Welcome 'Eight Tea Days' Racers" in red.

In exceedingly small blue letters are the names "Samuel Adams, Paul Revere, William Molineux, Thomas Hutchinson, Myrena Gorgona."

The Lemnian Deeds Federation has authorized Katrina Quark to delay the Le Shuttle so that the Professor and the other participants in the 'Eight Tea Days Around Europe" race will arrive at the same time as the ferry.

Accompanying Katrina is Leizi, a blonde-haired Chinese SuperPower teenager who can fly and to control the atmosphere.

Katrina has a backpack filled with nitrocellulose ping-pong balls that are each filled with trouble.

Before the next Channel Tunnel shuttle leaves, Katrina flies through the entire lower level throwing into the air, one ball at a time as Leizi using her lightning technique where a giant spark of electricity ignites the mildly toxic smoke bomb bouncing balls.

After getting confirmation from dozens of security guards that all the shuttles on the lower level are filled with smoke, the Terminal Control Center announces, "Attention all passengers! Due to an unforeseen situation Le Shuttle I'll be delayed up to an hour. Hopefully, we will be going soon as scheduled. Thank you for your understanding and continued support."

As the Professor listens to Mozart Symphony number 40 in G minor, he pours himself and Rocky a cup of Sri Lankan black tea.

With an air of distinction, Professor Steele states, "The American British author, Henry James put it best when he said, 'there are few hours in life more agreeable than the hour dedicated to the ceremony known as afternoon tea.'"

Rocky takes a sip saying, "The author of 'The Hitchhiker's Guide,' Douglas Adams once said 'A cup of tea would restore my normality."

The Professor stares at his nephew shaking his head back and forth. Apollo responds with a Cheshire Cat smile having his uncle take a bite of his scone as he washes it down with hot tea.

Inside the Eurotunnel, Rocky drives the vehicle into the carriage until the door closes in front of him.

At this point, they wake Apollo up. The three Steeles get out of the vehicle to stretch their legs and use the facilities that are located under the stairs.

No one had ever verified whether the Professor had any SuperPower other than being an elderly, creative genius with an appetite for knowledge. Also, no one alive could say how old he was as he never gave a year confirmation when celebrating his birthday, Even his birth certificate had never been found as he only had an Icelandic passport from its President sans birth year.

Apollo, the eldest one of the two twins, discovered years ago that he had the SuperPower ability to not only fly but had the SuperPower of telekinesis or more commonly known as the ability to move objects with his mind.

Rocky learned while he not only had the SuperPower ability to become invisible, but he also had the SuperPower ability of X-ray vision where he could see through solid objects such as walls, boxes, and inside any object.

An announcement is made telling all vehicle occupants that they have arrived. After Apollo returns to the vehicle's resting place, Apollo and the Professor grab a few snacks and beverages. Rocky drives the car forward. A road sign reads "Entering Coquelles (Hauts-de-France), France."

Two By Sea

The other racers that had been selected by lot to travel by ferry from Dover to France driving down the highway.

Above the two-lane highway are blue and white signs indicating that the ferry departure is in this direction. Passing on the left beside the mountain truck weighing station. And continuing down the highway are large blue signs indicating where to "Check in." The ferry cargo lanes are on the left.

The highway then splits into four lanes where the second lane from the left is marked 'P&O Ferry' check in. On top of a long yellow cement foundation is a glass toll booth for 'check in and ticket sales' that stops the vehicle as a barrier is lowered in front of every vehicle entering the ferry.

At Dover heading towards Calais, France, the 90-minute ferry ride requires vehicle, driver, and passenger verification at two passport immigration stations where the first station checks for vehicle-borne improvised explosion devices or VBIED and the second verifies occupants' passport ID and ticket purchase.

The P&O Ferry travels across the channel carrying 180 lorries, being a small cart or a 24-foot wagon.

Upon exiting into four lanes, the traffic turns towards the left underneath the highway. Even with large white letters indicating 'slow' where the Eight Tea Days racers accelerate through the patchwork paved two lane road heading left down an eight-lane highway that ends in a steeply sloped bridge where each vehicle is 'welcomed onboard the P&O Ferry.'

Continuing forward, each vehicle is guided by a parking attendant as to where to park and vacate the ferry vehicle parking area.

On the ferry, all vehicles must be vacant for passengers who go to the main level. Some of the racers walk towards the free telescope to admire the Dover White Cliffs that extends 315 feet above the port of Dover. This symbol of England is the first and the last view that the ferry passengers see when departing or arriving.

After viewing the waves and busy Channel traffic due to its narrowness and connection of the Atlantic Ocean to the North Sea, every driver in their crew hears the announcement to return to their vehicles. The parking attendant wearing a bright orange vest instructs each driver to proceed forward and down the ramp onto the bridge to Calais, France. Passing overhead large blue signs indicating the exit towards the highway. Even though the speed limit signs indicate "50 kilometers per hour" or 32 miles per hour every racing vehicle is traveling at twice that speed.

Placed inside every competitors' vehicle is the 'GPS locator' which is a patented device that Professor Steele invented at 13 years old. In the old days of running marathons in New York City and Boston, runners had to get certified at checkpoints but today using the young genius' GPS locator, the Eight Tea Days Around Europe Race can be monitored inside the Golden Eagle Mission Control as all the major iBroadcast iChannels transmit the event worldwide.

As the participants get off the ferry or EuroTunnel driving behind Professor Steele and his two nephews, they begin chanting, "Stop the Professor. Stop the Professor. Stop the Professor, now."

Then, they in unison beep their horns as they smile and chuckle.

Myrena Gorgona and her Lemnian Deeds members view the iBroadcast of the Eight Tea Days Around Europe racers starting their journey in France. Myrena announces to her assassins, "Welcome to the 77th Hunger Games, Professor!"

From the Golden Eagle iBroadcast studio, Roxanne McLaren introduces, "Good day my faithful racing iBroadcast audience. This is Roxanne along with my new co-host, Stephen Griswald."

The camera shows the iBroadcast booth having the two reporters on screen.

Roxanne reports, "The Golden Eagle HQ has just handed me the following, 'Everyday between noon to 4:30 p.m., each vehicle's team must stop for an hour to drink tea. All the recommended daily tea stop venues have nearby EV charging stations that takes at least 30 minutes to fully charge near empty EV vehicle. While the electronic vehicle is recharging, its team can enjoy their daily tea stop.'"

Stephen smiles remarking, "If we are going to have tea shouldn't there be a March Hare and the Mad Hatter to join us?"

Calais, France to Dunkirk, France

As the camera show the current map of France, Stephen states, "The racing teams from both the EuroTunnel and ferry will drive on A16 for 27 miles taking 35 minutes until they hit Dunkirk, France."

The camera has a close-up of Stephen who states, "Dunkirk is a small town on the coast of France. It was here that during World War II the Battle of Dunkirk was fought. That battle was a massive military campaign between the German forces and Allied troops where forcefully the Allied troops had to evacuate into England."

In his theatrical voice he continues saying, "With some relevant changes from the classic film Dunkirk, 'I remember a similar film about Dunkirk that was "[The racers] shall fight on the beaches. [The racers] shall fight on the landing grounds. [The racers] shall fight in the fields and in the streets. [The racers] shall fight in the hills; we shall [WIN!!]"'"

Roxanne says, "That was exceptionally good, Stephen. Live from the racing action we see that the Steele Tesla is in front of the pack as they race."

Stephen states, "Right behind the Tesla SUV EV is Mario Ferrari driving a Ferrari EV SUV Purosangue Model 7 wearing his black and red cotton vintage F1 Ferrari Racing Jacket."

Roxanne reports, "Breaking iNews. Team 17 has just passed the Ferrari EV SUV Purosangue and Steele Tesla where driver Paul Silverberg has their Dodge Challenger 55 EV racing fast and furious into the lead position."

Dunkirk, France to Bruges, Belgium

Stephen updates saying, "At A16 from Dunkirk, France heading to Bruges, Belgium continuing on E40 takes 53 minutes traveling for 46 miles."

Roxanne states, "Breaking iNews. Now in third position is Team 10's Porsche Taycan Sport Turismo 9 driven by Pamela Baywatch as her two teammates Holly Woodland and Parker Peter rest."

Stephen gives commentary saying, "Near the city of the Providence West Flanders, Belgium is its capital, Bruges. This Flemish region is known amongst castles with lace-making canal boat tours. To my religious listeners, the Basilica of the Holy Blood houses the blood of Jesus Christ collected by Joseph of Arimathea who allowed Jesus to lay to rest in his tomb."

Roxanne interjects, "When I think of Belgium, I think of Belgium Chocolates."

Stephen agrees, "Then, you must visit the Chocolate Museum to have the chocolate experts discuss and help you make sweets in a workshop. Speaking of museums, the FA-King tells our researchers that the Church of Our Lady houses Michelangelo's sculpture 'Madonna with Child.' There is the Salvador Dali Museum Gallery and works of art by painters John van Eyck and Hans Memling."

Driving behind the pack to Dunkirk France in their Hennessy Venon G17 Revolution are Katrina Quark and in the passenger seat sits Leizi , a Chinese blonde haired SuperPowered collegiate age teammate.

Alongside them is Delilah Craine, the daughter of Sofia Fraser and Martin Craine, who like her mother has the SuperPower ability to fly and to control mechanical devices.

Ahead mid pack is Delilah driving her orange flame Bentley Continental eGT9 that accelerates to 60 mph in 1.5 seconds with a top speed of 275 mph.

Leizi, who has the SuperPower to control the atmosphere,

begins what appears to be a typical day in Dunkirk by casting a shower of heavy rain upon the nearby vehicles.

Soon it is as though the highway has become a river with cars hydroplaning across the highway .

As each of the drivers regain control of their vehicle, they continue the race at a slower pace.

Katrina laughs and says, "I'm sure you can do better than that!"

In reply, Leizi magically starts with large hailstones and lightning where the bolts hit the highway.

In front of them, Team 18 driving a Corvette Stingray 7 EV with driver Bob Faulkner and passengers Richard Charles and Leanne Harper are getting bombarded by hailstones and swerving around intermittent blinding lightning bolts.

Then, a lightning bolt hits the Purosangue Model 7's windshield imploding upon Mario Ferrari who gets wet with safety glass all over his shirt and trousers,

In a flash, a second lightning bolt hits his chest temporarily blinding him as he swerves off the highway and into the forest crashing into several trees incapacitating the Ferrari EV SUV.

The Golden Eagle HQ transmits to the local hospital, Mario's GPS location where upon checking his vitals determine that he must be admitted for overnight observation.

Delilah Craine races down highway E40 causing commuter vehicles to block or crash into the Eight Tea Days racers

Inside of her Bentley Continental eGT9, Delilah drives behind Team 61 in their British racing green Jaguar Q-type Supercar EV emptying their battery having their vehicle stop on the side of the highway.

Then, coming up on the General Motors EcoJet that is driven by Denzel Portier who has the nickname 'The Black Peregrine Falcon' and is driving the 'Hollywood Cannonball.' Sitting next to Denzel is Francis Fellini, the Oscar winning director.

Commenting from the back seat is Tom Handkerchief who remarks, "I thought you charged the GM before we left. You know the other drivers don't do this. The guys with the white EVs are still driving on the road. How come it's always you black falcon guys? And I don't mean that racially!"

Continuing down the highway Delilah sees ahead of her, Team 45 in their Mercedes AMG 4 EV. She disconnects the fuses that protect the electronic circuits and battery causing an electrical fault that overloads the electrical system. As the Mercedes pulls over to the shoulder, the Bentley Continental drives by.

Coming upon Team 38 inside their Draco Motors Dragon Hypercar, Delilah significantly damages the electronic wiring inside the EV causing a fire.

Team 7's driver, Mork Williams remarks, "Zarth, Raven, and Marsh. Are you guys seeing this fire breathing dragon heading onto the highway shoulder? Marsh, do not get too close because they might mistake you for a marshmallow. "

In the next car ahead is Team 25 racing inside their China's BYD Company an acronym for 'Build Your Dreams.' Pure Yellow Yangwang V3 Supercar that is driven by Kennedy Johns and passengers Lincoln Abrams and Ford Geralds.

Avoiding the hailstones and life-threatening lightning bolts, Ford exclaims, "If we get hit by lightning, I might have to yell out 'You've killed Kennedy! Oh, my God you've killed Kennedy!' Or if the hailstones shatter the windshield, I might have to exclaim 'Lincoln is dead! The glass has been shattered on 'my American Cousin' inside Ford's automobile.'"

The two 'Dead Presidents' namesakes laugh as they perform the 'signum crucis' being the sign of the cross.

Restoring the weather back to its sunny day appearance, the Hennessy Venon G17 Revolution passes Team 25 having Katrina throw a couple of nitrocellulose ping pong balls under their Yangwang Supercar where they explode scaring the entire team as the car swerves back and forth onto the highway's shoulder.

The two girls working for the Lemnian Deeds Federation laugh hysterically as they drive past them.

Katrina states, "We should find a Belgium Chocolate Factory and load up as my mother use to tell me 'chocolate is a feel good food.'"

Leizi states "There's no place like home, except for the chocolate factory, of course."

Bruges, Belgium to Ghent, Belgium

Roxanne states "On the way from Bruges, the racers pass Ghent, Belgium driving for 47 minutes along the 30 miles E40 highway towards Ghent."

Stephen notes "Over one and a half million people live in Ghent with a major floral export business. The Flemish architecture has impressive Catholic bells and castles. The FA-King has communicated to us that the voor Schone Kunst museum houses impressive art works of the Flemish Masters."

The Golden Eagle Organization informs all racing teams, "High speed tires that have been damaged must be replaced by a brand-new high-speed tire as most service stations will not repair a high-speed tire for fear of lawsuits."

Katrina tells her teammate, "I need to use my SuperPower to fly and shrink microscopically to remove the tire valve stem. I must not go supersonic and enter the Quantum realm like the iComic film heroes Ant-Man and the Wasp," as she giggles.

Seeing Team 8's Volvo XTC90 EV with driver Pelton Nordic and passengers Joloc Michel and Zelda Arwen.

Katrina states, "It is time for me to travel like a rocket but as small as a .44 caliber with a diameter of 0.429 inches to flatten the Volvo EV's tire."

She thrusts towards Team 8's Volvo at 1,500 feet per hour puncturing the side of the tire and removing the entire tire valve stem causing driver Pelton to swerve then regain control of the vehicle bringing it to a stop on the highway's shoulder.

The Golden Eagle HQ immediately sends the service station mechanic to Volvo's GPS location with a brand-new tire from the local warehouse.

Team 8 waits in a safe location off the highway for the tow truck as the Hennessy Venon G17 continues down the highway towards Ghent.

Delilah Craine accelerates catching up to Team 26's Praga Bohema Copperhead Hypercar.

As the highway passes a lake, Delilah controls a semi-truck in the right lane forcing it into the left lane where it collides with the Praga Bohema.

Team 50's Johnny Leno driving his Czinger 51CM tells his passengers, "I recently read on the net that to kill a copperhead, one could use a snake trap, a glue trap or submerge the copperhead by drowning it. Seeing that the Praga Bohema Copperhead Hypercar is now floating in the lake, it will either die or get replaced by the Golden Eagle HQ."

Delilah Craine contacts the Lemnian Deeds Federation speaking to Myrena giving her an update on her activities and which vehicles she has disabled requiring replacements.

Myrena says, "On behalf of the Lemnian Deeds and me, we thank you for helping. On a personal note, tell your mother Sophia that I am a huge fan of hers both on the iBroadcast weather reports, earning her numerous awards, teaching and publishing endeavors, and her SuperPower activities. It has been a pleasure working with you as I expect to continue our relationship in the future."

Ghent, Belgium to Brussels, Belgium

Roxanne McLaren states, "As the race team speed along southeast on A10 from Ghent, Belgium for 52 minutes heading to Brussels that is 36 miles away."

Stephen Griswald reports, "Roxanne, fun fact the vegetable 'Brussels sprout' is not native to Belgium but was brought here by the French colonists and given the Belgium city name."

Roxanne reports, "Brussels is the capital of Belgium and the home of the European Union administrators. Brussels is in the shape of a pentagon."

Stephen continues, "I have just been handed an email from the FA-King who notes 'It is the home of several museums such as the Royal Museums of Art and History and the Royal Museum of the Armed Forces and Military History."

Roxanne interjects, "Brussels is well-known for its food such as the Brussel sprout, chocolate, waffles, French fries and beer."

She continues reporting, "There are two lane highways in each direction having a grass medium between the two highways. Some of the surrounding highways have a great deal of farmland."

Inside the Tesla bulletproof SUV, the Professor tells his nephews, "Brussels, Belgium has several excellent Michelin starred restaurants including two two-star and four one-star Michelin restaurants. I have personally eaten at one of the two star and at three of the one-star Michelin restaurants."

Leizi states "The Deeds' intel reports that Team 6's Kia Stinger EV has four victims who are Took Lux its driver with passengers Tuile Horvath, Ember Azer, and Rangod Hyksos.

She continues saying, "How should we attack them?"

Katrina Quark thinks and replies, "I can fly under their Kia Stinger and disable the electric vehicle."

With Leizi driving the Hennessy Venon G17, Katrina diminishes to a fly's size as she soars towards her target.

Under the Kia Stinger, she jokingly uses her SuperPower to engrave the words 'Movement that Demoralizes' to negate the Kia's motto of 'Movement that Inspires.'

Then, she disconnects the auxiliary power, pulls out the kill switch, and waits ten minutes for the capacitor's energy to dissipate.

She flies back to the Hennessy Venon G17 Warner Bros. Pictures. sits in the passenger seat watching the Kia slow down resting on the highway's shoulder.

Rangod Hykos sits on the grass saying to his teammates, "Tell the Venon to shut the front door!"

The Golden Eagle HQ immediately sends out a dispatch to the local Kia mechanical team to figure out the problem.

The venomous snakes inside the Hennessy laugh as they feel exhilarated with their current successful mission.

Brussels, Belgium to Luxembourg, Luxembourg

Roxanne states, "Driving from Brussels Belgium to Luxembourg takes 2 hours, 21 minutes on A4 for 131 miles."

Stephen says, "The official name for Luxembourg is the Grand Duchy of Luxembourg that is the smallest ruled country of Europe. The country has granted partnership rights to the LGBTQ community for marriage and adoption entitlement."

He continues, "The FA-King tells us that 'MUDAM, an acronym for Musée d'Art Moderne or Luxembourg Grand Duke Jean Museum of Modern Art has in its permanent collection works by one hundred artists, which includes Andy Warhol, Bruce Nauman, Julian Schnabel, Thomas Struth, and Daniel Buren.'"

Leizi states, "Let's see if we can force a vehicle crash incident just to witness how that team responds."

In front of them are Team 11's Rimac Nevera B2 EV Hypercar with driver Charlie 'Cheating' Chester who is steadily gaining on the two teams in front of his team's vehicle.

The Rimac tries to pass Team 36's Mercedes AMG 4 EV with Australian driver Sheila Dundee.

Then, Team 12's Lotis Lightning EV with driver Speed Demon Sam Forest and her passengers Van Kilmer and David King maneuver past the dueling vehicles passing them both.

Experienced driver Sheila Dundee weaves around her adversary 'Cheating' Chester who in turn loops back regaining their position.

The Rimac attempts to pass again, almost colliding with Team 36's Mercedes forcing driver Sheila onto the right highway shoulder.

'Cheating' Chester gets behind the Lotis Lightning EV, forcing its driver Speed Demon Sam Forest to accelerate.

As Team 36's Mercedes AMG 4 EV is back on the highway speeding up to the competitors, Sheila Dundee watches her competition collide waiting for her turn to pass them safely.

Leizi cooks up a multiple-vortex tornado that has multiple spinning funnels inside each other causing the Lotis and Rimac to circle each other tossing their passengers onto the soft shrubbery while intertwining the vehicles to mimic a classic John Chamberlain automobile sculpture.

When the tornado dissipates, the Mercedes AMG 4 EV speeds up leaving the wreckage and Hennessy in the dust.

The Hennessy Venon G17 EV stops to examine the twisted vehicle sculpture while the Golden Eagle HQ has a car hauler trailer sent to deliver a brand-new Lotis Lightning EV to Team 12, and to Team 11 a brand new Rimac Nevera B2 EV Hypercar.

Leizi states, "You get extra points for that in the game!"

Chapter 23

Sunday 'Eight Tea Days Around Europe' Race

"This is Roxanne McLaren reporting from the Golden Eagle HQ iBroadcast of the Eight Tea Days Around Europe Race. Good day viewers, it's Day Two, you are watching live racing iNews."

Stephen Griswald says, "As British former racing driver from Scotland, David Coulthard once said "Racing drivers have balls, unfortunately, none of them are crystal.""

Luxembourg, Luxembourg to Cologne, Germany

Stephen Griswald states, "One thing for sure is that race car drivers are super competitive! From early this morning, the teams began their second day journey from Luxembourg to Cologne, Germany that takes 2 hours, 35 minutes traveling 120 miles on B51 to A3 also known as the 'Autobahn.'"

Roxanne states, "Along the way, there are a few 360 degree turns starting with Notterheimer Barraere."

Stephen says, "The classic Android videogame 'Driving Zone' has racers speeding down Germany's highway E29 in their virtual life. Our racers will drive on it in real life."

Roxanne says, "The Cologne Cathedral is a Gothic church and a World Heritage Site that houses the Shrine of the Three Kings and their relics who are the Three Magi that are the three wise kings that followed the bright star that we sing about at Christmas. We three kings of Orient are…"

Stephen adds saying, "The FA-King notes that 'Museum Ludwig, located in Cologne, Germany has one of the largest Picasso collections in Europe and works by pop artists Andy Warhol and Roy Lichtenstein. The Classical Modernism art of Marc Chagall and Otto Dix plus the most comprehensive collection of early Russian avant-garde artworks outside Russia."

Team 4's Estrema Fulminea VII Hypercar with driver Caspian Prince propels at 225 mph with teammates, Quentin Marron and Torin Shepherd who review the day's itinerary and historical sites that they won't be seeing.

The vehicle can get to 60 mph in 1.4 seconds with a top speed of 265 mph.

In front of them is Team 19's cherry red Lamborghini Sián Supercar that can hit 60 mph in 1.45 seconds having a top speed of 250 mph with driver Morris Williams and his teammates Dallas Worthington and Wesley Adams.

In his rear-view monitor, Morris sees that an Estrema Fulminea VII Hypercar is trying to pass so he counters by jumping in front before that occurs.

The Estrema Fulminea VII Hypercar anticipated that reaction staying in the right lane and thrusting forward passing them.

Caspian remarks, "Darn that Lamborghini Sián Supercar! I forgot to 'Expect the unexpected!'"

He accelerates the Estrema Fulminea VII passing the Lamborghini Sián saying, "My buddy Julius Caesar once said, 'No one is so brave that he is not disturbed by something unexpected.'"

Not to be outdone, Morris Williams jets forward saying, "In Shakespeare's Julius Caesar play 'Beware of the Ides of [Sián],' Princess," as he laughs.

For over two hours, the two vehicles alone on the highway battle it out for position at high speeds.

Cologne, Germany to Stuttgart, Germany

Roxanne states "Racing from Cologne. Germany to Stuttgart, Germany takes 3 hours, 48 minutes traveling 228 miles on A3 at suggested Autobahn speeds."

Stephen Griswald remarks, "Team 36's Mercedes-AMG 4 EV and Team 10's Porsche Taycan Sport Turismo 9 EV knows Stuttgart, Germany as it is known as the birthplace of Mercedes Benz and Porsche."

Roxanne states, "Amongst the most mountainous terrain lies the highway called the Autobahn that has no posted speed limit. Can our racers beat the speed record measured on the Autobahn under normal conditions of 280 miles per hour?"

The Porsche Taycan Sport Turismo 9 EV can hit 60 mph in 1.5 seconds like most EV vehicles today with a top speed of 325 mph.

Holly Woodland states, "Our baby, Taycan is back home in Stuttgart. Willkommen zu Hause!"

An unauthorized removal from the Mercedes-Benz HQ showroom occurs as alarms alert security. Zoey Chamberlain drives away with a yellow Mercedes AMG RP 58 EV Roadster.

Myrena became friends with Zoey on her visit to Loughborough University campus visiting Coach Michele Locke where she learned that the SuperPower track star has the unique SuperPower called a 'Therianthropy' where she can metamorphose into any animal by shapeshifting and become invisible.

Mercedes AMG RP 58 Roadster can cruise to 60 mph in 1.4 seconds and has a top speed of 250 mph. Zoey drives 3.8 miles accessing the Autobahn at Des Bundes, the Federal State House.

She then accelerates the AMG RP 58 Roadster to 225 mph since there is no speed limit on the Autobahn.

With over 7,500 miles of expressway. Autobahn drivers dream of going full throttle without speed limits. Collegiate teen Zoey is no exception as she realizes in a deadly crash situation, she will become invisible avoiding death.

Joining Zoey by the Federal Building is Llobro track teammate, Ruth Hannah.

Ruth has the SuperPower to fly at 1,800 mph and can insert false past experiences into her victim's anterior cingulate cortex where long term memories are stored.

Driving at 200 mph is Team 39 in their 18K gold plated Hermes 3 Flying Wings Hypercar driven by Sheldon Parsons with passengers Amy Farrah and Simon Wolowitz. The team is comprised of Physics PhDs.

Simon says, "The other racers are jealous since our team has doctorates from École polytechnique fédérale de Lausanne. The EPFL is the only university in the world to operate a fusion reactor, a nuclear reactor, a Gene/Q Supercomputer, and P3 biohazard facility."

Ruth Hannah uses her SuperPower to create a false reality making the entire team believe that Oppenheimer's atomic bomb together with the codename Manhattan Project is about to explode with a big bang,

They clearly hear the film's script, "They won't understand it until they've used it. Theory will take you only so far."

Unable to believe what they clearly see and hear, the 18K gold plated Hermes 3 slows down to 40 mph in the right lane as the Mercedes AMG RP 58 Roadster soars passed them.

The girls laugh at the misled scientists yelling at them "Bazinga!"

Stuttgart, Germany to Munich, Germany

Roxanne reports, "Driving on the German Autobahn from Stuttgart to Munich, Germany takes 2 hours and 28 minutes. Our racers travel this leg on highway A8 for 138 miles. As they drive past Ulm where the world's tallest church, a Lutheran Church named the Ulmer Minster. Then, passing Augsburg where the Gaston Krone, a typical Tyrolean building and ski lodge. Augsburg is known as a university town, which has major companies such as Siemens, Amazon, NCR with a UNESCO World Heritage Site being its Water Management System."

Closing in on Team 58's Ocra GT Tri-Coat paint Alfa Romeo Giulia Quadrifoglio IV supercar EV with legendary Formula 1 car driver Paul Georges, is the never publicly displayed Mercedes AMG RP 58 Roadster that was stolen from the Mercedes HQ Test Factory by Zoey.

With Hannah now driving the Mercedes Roadster, Zoey transforms into an eagle flying at SuperPower speed towards the Alfa Romeo.

Then, she transforms into a mouse and crawls under the Alfa Romeo's chassis.

As a mouse, Zoey chews through the 4-prong connector of the power wiring harness and its plug that leads to the back of the boost gauge.

Zoey the mouse's efforts causes the Alfa Romeo Giulia Quadrifoglio IV Supercar EV to seriously malfunction causing a fire with smoke forcing the vehicle to slide past the shoulder colliding with dozens of shrubberies until it stops.

The Golden Eagle HQ informs the local service station to deliver a brand-new Alfa Romeo Giulia Quadrifoglio IV Supercar EV to Team 58's GPS location.

Munich Germany Teatime Ceremony

Roxanne reports, "The Golden Eagle HQ suggests for afternoon tea 'The Victorian House Munich Tea Bar, located in Munich's lively Schwabing district, furnished as a traditional Victorian House style with its walls covered in old oil paintings, having a selection of over eighty loose leaf teas, various homemade cakes, baked according to original English recipes. The scones can be made with raisins, walnuts, chocolate chips, or plain with strawberry jam or clotted cream."

Stephen says, "The types of tea served are English breakfast, Lady Grey, Rooibos, Ayurveda herbal, King Charles black, Chinese golden monkey black, Dajeeling black, Pu Erh, Earl Grey, Moroccan mint, Chai, Ceylon, Jasmin green, coconut macaroon green, candy cane, gingerbread, mango, passionfruit, herbal, oolong many of which are available in decaffeinated, organic or regular."

Roxanne states, "My favorites are the pastries that are baked on site. The Tea Bar has zucchini walnut cake, chocolate brownie, coffee walnut cake, apricot and almond cake, lavender cake, pistachio cake, London cheesecake, apple olive cake, and pineapple cake. Now, I am getting hungry!"

Stephen states, "For the sponsored racing teams the Golden Eagle HQ reports 'The Nymphenburg Room of the Royal Bavarian Hotel in Munich has an exceptional Afternoon Tea that changes every month and is well worth the price.'"

As Team 3 and Team 18 sit in The Victorian House Munich Tea Bar waiting for their ordered tea and pastry selections, Darcy Austen asks, "So tell me Richard, is your entire racing team Yanks from the Americas?"

Richard Charles says, "I believe so as we all have won the Indy 500 thrice, the Ididarod several times and several other NASCAR events."

Jubilee says, "Let me ask you, Bob Yarjo was twice the POTUS and now that his daughter is POTUS, is he now called the VPOTUS? When you meet him do you call him Mr. President or not?"

Richard replies, "Out of respect, I would call him that, yes. Hopefully, DC keeps the United States electronic dollar strong. I leave politics to the politicians, and we Yanks will kick your butts across Europe for the next few days," as his entire team laughs.

His teammate, Bob Faulkner says, "We Yanks will kick your butts from sea to shining sea."

The Royal Bavarian Hotel's general manager tells the Professor and his two nephews, "Welcome to the Nymphenburg Room of the Royal Bavarian Hotel in Munich. This is our executive sommelier Wolfgang who will make sure your visit is excellent."

The general manager tells the staff, "These are my special guests. Treat Professor Steele and his nephews like you would treat the owner of our fine hotel."

Wolfgang greets his notable guests as a few more racing teams enter the establishment.

Wolfgang approaches the table saying, "Our British afternoon tea is served in handmade Nymphenburg porcelain. The Royal Bavarian Hotel offers a selection of over 30 different teas."

Wolfgang introduces his server saying, "This is Annalise who will take care of everything. Annalise, these are our special guests from Iceland. You might have seen them recently on the iBroadcast iChannels."

Annalise says, "Welcome to Nymphenburg Room for Strawberry Afternoon Tea. Today our first course will have sandwiches with sea food roll with whipped egg, roast beef, crayfish salad with garden cress, quail eggs, grilled cold green asparagus, tartelette, and strawberry relish."

The sommelier presents a list of tea types saying, "Sirs, my I present our fine tea selection from black teas like Earl Grey and Assam, herbal teas like chamomile and mint, green teas from China, Japan and Korea."

Each Steele places their tea order as the first course is served.

After the teas are delivered and sipped, the delicious food on the porcelain plates have soon become sparse.

Apollo says to the beautiful server, "The food mysteriously disappeared, Someone needs to call the Batavian 'Earl of Sandwiches.'" as he laughs.

Annalise returns unamused saying, "For the second course of the Nymphenburg Room's Strawberry Afternoon Tea, we have strawberry yogurt mousse, strawberry meringue, strawberry tarts, candied rose petals, strawberry pistachio financier, strawberry chocolate, vanilla pudding, and a glass of strawberry Dom Pérignon Champagne with a strawberry garnish on top of the flute."

After finishing everything, Rocky says, "I am filled with strawberries as I could die in a strawberry field."

The Professor tells everyone stating, "The Liverpool Salvation Army orphanage named 'Strawberry Fields' was where young John Lennon who had lost his father would go to play with other children."

The racers begin to sing.

Cause I'm going to strawberry fields
Nothing is real
And nothing to get hung about
Strawberry fields forever

After having a scrumptious afternoon teatime, the Professor hands the cashier his black credit card.

The Steele nephews thank the entire staff as they exit high fiving the other racing teams in attendance.

Munich, Germany to Zurich, Switzerland

Roxanne states, "Zürich, Switzerland is a hub for railways, roads, and air traffic having over 2.3 million inhabitants."

Stephen states, "Driving from Munich, Germany to Zurich, Switzerland takes 3 hours and 47 minutes traveling 192 miles on A96."

The two Lemnian Deeds girls in their Mercedes AMG RP 58 Roadster travel behind Team 7's Toyota Rocket X EV with driver Mork Williams and his teammates Zarth Kilroy, Marsh Etang, and Neoma McKenzie.

Every Eight Tea Days Around Europe racing team needs to take an hour tea break so Hannah has Team 7 believe that they have missed their 'Tea Break Stop.'

Mork begins to cry saying "Nanu" as his teammates are yelling at him, blaming him for their situation which will disqualify them from the race.

As the Mercedes Roadster is ten miles ahead of Team 7, the illusion has vanished as they realize that their restroom and tea stop is just a half mile in front of their vehicle.

Roxanne McLaren reads aloud, "The FA-King reports that 'The Kunsthaus Zürich is a museum containing Switzerland's most important art collections, having around 4,000 paintings and sculptures such as Impressionist and Classical Modernist paintings from Monet, Picasso and Chagall, Kokoschka, Beckmann, and Corinth. There is Pop Art from Warhol and Hamilton alongside artists including Munch, Rothko, Twombly, Beuys and Baselitz.'"

Making their High Tea stop, Team 9's leader Leonidas Spartan exits the driver's seat as his race team members Rain Donner and Priyanka Patel go inside to use the restroom.

Leonidas watches as an ebony Chevy Camaro 69 EV enters the parking lot. From the passenger backseat emerges Team 16's Bayberry Fields and Elijah Baggins who nod at him.

Then, like an angel, its driver rises out of the vehicle. The jet-black haired supermodel, Raven Poe.

Leonidas speaks loudly saying, "Yours is almost as sexy as mine is."

Raven looks at him and says, "My eyes do not detect anything sexy in my field of vision."

Leonidas laughs and says, "I was talking about our hypercars."

Raven rolls her eyes giving him an unobstructed view of her right hand's middle finger.

Being rarely rejected he continues, "Let me know if we can talk privately after our tea break."

She responds, "Remember these words ' Nevermore said the Raven.'"

She passes him to join her team inside the restaurant.

Leonidas remembers his English literature class and quotes Edgar Allan Poe saying, "Here is some of my Poe-try, 'Deep into the darkness peering, long I stood there, wondering, fearing, doubting, dreaming dreams no mortal ever dared to dream before,'" as he chuckles to rejoin his teammates for their 'tea break.'

Finished in the washroom, Rain Donner and Priyanka Patel rejoin Leonidas to get served tea and scones.

Zurich, Switzerland to Bern, Switzerland

Roxanne McLaren states, "Traveling from Zurich, Switzerland to Bern, Switzerland takes 86 minutes to travel 78 miles on A96 with an autopay toll."

Stephen Griswald reads a note "The FA-King tells the iBroadcast producers 'The Zentrum Paul Klee is a museum dedicated to the artist Paul Klee, located in his birthplace Bern, Switzerland, The museum features about 40 percent of Paul Klee's entire artwork.'"

He continues saying, "The Museum of Fine Arts in Bern, with artwork from the Middle Ages to the present including works by Paul Klee, Pablo Picasso, Edmond Jean de Pury, Ferdinand Hodler, Meret Oppenheim, Ricco Wassmer and Adolf Wolfli. The Einsteinhaus is a museum in Bern and a former residence of Albert Einstein."

Roxanne says, "Near Bern is where my favorite Swiss cheese has a factory in Gruyere and the Swiss chocolate factory."

The Mercedes Roadster heads to Bern where the girls listen to their stolen Golden Eagle iCommunicator of Roxanne's iNews reporting. Once in Bern, they enter the Bern Toblerone Chocolate Factory singing 'The Candyman Can" song from the classic "Willy Wonka and the Chocolate Factory."

Hannah uses her SuperPower to get the salesperson at the Toblerone Chocolate Factory to believe that they handed her a sack of money in exchange for the entire store's chocolates.

With the salesperson and Zoey's help, Hannah loads the chocolate treats made from milk chocolate with white nougat, almonds, and honey packaged inside a triangular shape box representing the Matterhorn in the Swiss Alps/Italian Alps into their Mercedes Roadster.

Back speeding down the highway, Hannah, and Zoey sing, "The candyman can cause he mixes it with love and makes the world taste good."

Bern, Switzerland to Lugano, Switzerland

Roxanne states, "Traveling on A22 from Bern Switzerland to Lugano, Switzerland has a distance of 244 miles that takes 3 hours, 24 minutes."

Stephen states, "Lugano host the Swiss National Sound archives and in the Palazzo del Congressi is where the Performing Arts Center houses the Orchestra of Italian Switzerland. The Lugano Festival has jazz in July, The Long Lake Festival in August and the Blues to Bop Festival in late August to September."

Roxanne remarks little Guyana is big in sports having they're Hockey Club in the National League being their top tier and football team plays in the Swiss Super League that has held two World Cup matches inside their Stadio Comaredo Stadium. Lugano's Basketball Club, the Tigers play in the Swiss National League winning several championships. Lugano has held the International WTA tennis tournament, World Chess Olympiad, Water Polo Championship and 12 mile race walk grand prix."

Driving in front of the girls is Team 19's cherry red Lamborghini Sián with driver Dallas Worthington and her passengers Wesley Adams and Morris Williams.

The dimwitted Wesley asks, "Are we heading to our next destination?"

Morris the brain replies, "I heard it said that 'All roads lead to Rome.' or at least towards Italy."

Hannah has the team inside the Lamborghini Sián believing that their vehicle is crossing the alp mountain range bumping up and down for the entire 3.25 hours as she and Zoey laugh.

The girls open their window pretending to be Central Alps herders who yodel. The traffic that is encountered hears multipitch "yelling" from their vehicle as the team inside the cherry red Lamborghini Sián are screaming from terror.

Dallas cries saying, "I feel like I am in the old classic film 'Downhill Racer' without that hunk Redford anywhere around."

Lugano, Switzerland to Milan, Italy

Roxanne states, "Traveling on A2 from Lugano, Switzerland to A9 heading to Milan, Italy has a distance of 48 miles that takes 1 hour."

Stephen states, "Milan is the city in northern Italy, capital of Lombardy. According to our art professor, the FA-King 'Milan is famous for its historical figures such as Virgil, Pliny the Elder, Ambrose, Caravaggio, Claudio Monteverdi, Antonio Stradivari, Cesare Beccaria, Alessandro Volta, Alessandro Manzoni, and Popes John XXIII and Paul VI.'"

Roxanne states, "Milan is also regarded as one of the fashion capitals of the world, along with New York City, Paris, and London. Milan fashion highlights the Italian prêt-à-porter industry, headquartering the world's most famous Italian fashion brands, such as Valentino, Gucci, Versace, Prada, Armani, and Dolce & Gabbana."

Stephen says, "The city hosts La Scala opera house. The opera critics agree that it is one of the world's most prestigious opera houses."

Joining Zoey and Hannah in their Mercedes Roadster is Vivian Russ in her brand new Ivory Aspark Owl EV Hypercar traveling at 225 mph.

The Lboro track ladies wave pointing ahead at the black Huracán Sterrato which is their target that can accelerate to 285 mph hitting 60 mph in 1.4 seconds.

Sitting in the front passenger seat is the legendary director, Francis Fellini with driver Denzel Poitier nicknamed the 'Black Peregrine Falcon' which like him is the fastest bird flying at 242 mph. In the back seat are Fellini's favorite actors, five-time Oscar winner Mary Louise and four time Oscar winner Tom Handkerchief.

Vivian cruising towards the Hollywood filled Huracán Sterrato s joined by Hannah who has flown into her Aspark Owl's front seat.

Fellini tells Denzel, "The Black Racing World is a codename for a family of covert racing vehicles."

Denzel states, "You gotta be who you are in this racing world!"

Mary Louise remarks, "My race car driving instructor took me to a private sitting room, ordered food. I noticed that he had changed. Once he was full of smiles and laughter, but I knew at once that he was being insincere."

Tom says, "Can you hear the heartache in her voice? A voice filled with harmony and life."

Fellini states, "Let's put the pedal to the metal or the white Owl will school us Falcons at driving."

Vivian puts her Hypercar in cruise control as Hannah, using her SuperSpeed thrusts the two of them forward.

Vi Russ touches the black Lamborghini Huracán Sterrato turning it red and destroying the EV engine beyond repair.

Hannah yells at Fellini saying, "Red is the new black."

As they pass the black Lamborghini Huracán Sterrato which has died thanks to Vivian's Midas touch of Death, Hannah yells, "Your vehicle is unusable sitting 'beyond the concrete' highway."

Fellini states, "Those college age girls just trounced our vehicle."

Denzel remarks, "Everyone tells me 'it is not personal. It is business.' That's what everybody keeps saying. 'I'm just a professional.'"

Tom states, "Now we wait for the tow truck to deliver our new vehicle. The best thing about entering the race was the Steele's party with free food and drinks!"

Fellini states, "Remind me later that I need to attend this year's Academy Awards in my Oscar De La Renta Tuxedo."

Mary Louise seeing signs indicating 'Milan Ahead,' sings

Milan, Milan, Milan
Armani, Versace,
In the fashion designer's world!

As the transport vehicle trailer with six replacement vehicles are traveling in front of Vivian in her Ivory Aspark Owl EV Hypercar, she touches the rear beaver tail turning the entire trailer red.

Inside the trailer cab, the transport driver views that the six replacement vehicles have disappeared. He pulls over onto the right shoulder and parks. Getting out of his cab, he notices an Ivory Aspark Owl passing him with a young female driver who says, "Watch where you walk as reality is fleeting into oblivion."

He states, "The craziness of youth" as he notices that not only have the six vehicles vanished, but his entire trailer is gone too.

He scratches his head saying, "I thought that the owners of the replacement cars were having a bad day. My day just topped theirs as the worst day ever."

The transport driver calls the Golden Eagle HQ saying, "You are never going to believe what just happened. The six replacement vehicles along with my entire transport trailer has vanished. Completely, gone. Nothing left to deliver."

He is instructed to return to the warehouse to pick up a new transport trailer as they are preparing six new replacement vehicles to store on it.

The transport driver states, "Thanks. I will be there as soon as possible."

While waiting for their second replacement GM EcoJet to arrive, Denzel the 'Black Peregrine Falcon' states, "I believe In fairness, honesty, and being an equalizer. "

Mary Louise begins singing *Once, twice, three times a lady.*

Tom Handkerchief says to Denzel, "I told my mama that I love you, like a brother, and as you know the 'City of Brotherly Love' is called Philadelphia."

Chapter 24

Monday 'Eight Tea Days Around Europe' Race

Stephen Griswald states, "Salutations and welcome to the Golden Eagle HQ iBroadcast of Day Three of the Eight Tea Days Around Europe Race."

"Roxanne McLaren reporting on Monday, you are watching live racing iNews."

Stephen states, "One thing for sure is that race car drivers are super competitive!"

Roxanne says, "Legendary American NASCAR racing driver and racing team owner, Kyle Busch once said 'if you're a race car driver you want to succeed and be the best in your realm of racing.'"

As Team 19 approaches the second-place car just behind the Professor and his nephews, Dallas Worthington loudly remarks "Holy smokes Batman! I forgot to mail out my payment for my monthly bills."

The driver Wesley Adams says, "Relax, I have never paid my bills on time. In fact, I am always buying myself an extra week or two. Instead of using the net to pay my bills, I old school the process by using snail mail, For the last ten years, I have never mailed any of my bills with a stamped envelope."

Without saying a word, Dallas gives her friend a puzzled look.

Responding proudly Wesley confesses, "What I do with all my bills is in the upper left corner of the envelope I write the address of the payee. In the center of the envelope, I put my address as though the payee is sending me the letter. When the post office receives my correspondence and notices that no stamp has been placed in the upper right corner of the envelope, they returned the envelope and its contents to the address in the upper left corner indicating that insufficient postage needs to be placed on the envelope to be delivered. Obviously upon being returned to the payee of my bill, they open it to find its contents which is my bill's payment."

With a Cheshire Cat grin on her face, Dallas states, "You're lucky that the racing committee doesn't know what I know. That it won't be long before you get your driver's license."

They both are looking into each other's eyes as they let out a sinister laugh.

Cruising in Eight Tea Days Around Europe race, Team 45 the Evangelista family enjoys playing mental games as they pursue the Professor and his nephews, inside their Pontiac Firebird Trans Am Mark 6 Hypercar, the Evangelistas are in birth order, Matthew, Mark, Luke, and Joanne.

As they continued their high-speed, the religious brother Matthew asks the other passengers, "In the Bible only four of the archangels are named."

The other passengers look at him nodding their heads in agreement.

He continues saying, "Their names are Michael, Raphael, and Gabriel. What is the fourth archangel's name?"

The others in the car begin discussing the presented dilemma possibilities.

The English literature professor, Mark begins discussing John Milton's 'Paradise Lost.'

They begin discussing the fact that is well known that Michael and Gabriel are the archangels, and that Raphael was mentioned in the deuterocanonical Book of Tobit and recognized by the Catholic and Eastern Orthodox churches.

Luke begins digging deeper saying, "I am bringing up that archangels according to Islamic texts are Jibrael, Mikael, Israfil, and Azrael. In Jewish literature noted in the Book of Enoch, Metatron is described as an archangel."

The questioning religious brother, Matthew keeps smiling saying, "The noted archangel's name will have you banging your head against the wall."

With each named archangel, Matthew states, "That's a good point but it is not listed in the Bible. Think deeper to get warmer" as he laughs.

Joanne guesses, "Jesus' mother, Mary, Abraham's wife, Sarah, King David's grandmother, Ruth, or Rahab."

After ninety minutes, the others in the car say sadly, "We give up, who's the fourth named archangel in the Bible?"

The laughing questioner exclaims, "Created as an archangel called by God as 'the morning star' or 'shining one,' is Lucifer, now known as 'the devil.'"

The rest of the car hits their forehead with an open hand as they groan turning into a laugh.

The iNews is showing several back and forth between Team 12's Lotis Lightning EV with driver Speed Demon Sam Forest and Team 11's Rimac Nevera B2 EV Hypercar with driver Charlie 'Cheating' Chester.

Sam's teammates Thunder Blitz, and Newt Harper begin taunting Team 11 chanting, "Ram the Rimac!"

Team 21's Liquid Petroleum Aston Martin Valkyrie Tarantula EV has an all-female team having its members DemiLeigh Sedgefield, Iris Lille, and Bonnie Houston enter the sweets area of the store.

The Rimac Team 11 members enter the convenience store as the ladies Giana Rossi, Keara Karlson and Theris O'Leary use the powder room.

Sam Forest walks over to the empty three-passenger, limited production EV Supercar, the Lotus turns around to check out Team 21's Supercar. She notices that the Liquid Petroleum Aston Martin Valkyrie Tarantula EV has a tight fit with a third seat behind the passenger seat and a transparent, removable roof.

Speed Demon Sam looks in the store's window seeing that 'Cheater' Chester is purchasing a few boxes of Dutch chocolates.

Team 12's members Thunder and Newt leave the Lotus to enter the store to purchase snacks,

As 'Cheater' Chester walks over to use the restroom, Sam sneaks up behind him noticing that he is holding the Rimac Nevera B2's laser cut key in his left hand. As Chester is disposing a large paper bag in the overflowing garbage container, on purpose Speed Demon Sam slams into Chester causing the garbage to fly onto the floor as Rimac's transparent laser key falls into the mess.

Laughing, Sam and Team 12 quickly leave the convenience store.

As Team 12 rejoins her, she floors the accelerator of the Lotus out of the parking lot, Speed Demon Sam laughs as Chester is still sifting through the piles of garbage looking for the vehicles' laser cut key.

Milan, Italy to Innsbruck, Austria

Stephen states, "The race from Milan, Italy to Innsbruck, Austria takes 4 hours, 5 minutes traveling 59 miles on A1 having an autobilled toll."

Roxanne says, "Innsbruck, Austria the capital of Tyrol which was the site of the 1964, 1976, 2140 Winter Olympics. Innsbruck name means 'brook over the inn.'"

Stephen reads a note from the FA-King stating, "Inside the Tyroler Landesmuseum Ferdinandeum houses a valuable Dutch collection of works by Rembrandt and Brueghel as well as Oscar Kokoschka, Egon Schiele, Albin Egger-Lienz and Max Weiler.

Roxanne says, "Inside the Hofkirche or Court Church is the tomb of Emperor Maximilian I which is empty since Maximilian is buried in the Wiener Neystadt Castle," as she chuckles.

Stephen continues, "The FA-King adds 'inside the Hapsburg Portrait Gallery amongst the 200 paintings on display are the works of Lukas Cranach, Tizian, van Dyke and Diego Velazquez.'"

Italy's Antonio Ferrari, the adopted son of Deborah Ferrari and Bianca Ricci has vowed to stop his boarding school rivals,

Through family connections, Antonio is given a metallic blue Ferrari Enzo 517 Supercar EV that can accelerate to 60 mph in 1.45 seconds having a top speed of 250 mph.

Antonio has the SuperPower of invisibility and to manipulate the internals of any object like a vehicle or computer.

Antonio using his SuperPower to control Team 9's Tesla Road Warrior VI EV, first turns on its windshield wipers, followed by his iRadio loudly playing Rileigh Michele's 'Schrödinger Cat!'

As Team 9's driver Leonidas Spartan tries to turn the iRadio down in the wipers off, Antonio continues his SuperPower harassment by slowing the car down to 30 mph and then in less than 2 seconds have the car up to 60 mph accelerating to 100 mph.

The passengers of Team 9 Rain Donner and Priyanka Patel, get concerned and they begin yelling at him saying, "Leonidas, what is going on? Have you lost total control of this vehicle? Perhaps one of us should take over the driving responsibility."

Leonidas replies, "It's not me doing anything it is the vehicle, I swear that something is going wrong inside its electronic system."

Throughout the four hours, Antonio continues turning the wipers and iRadio on followed by vehicle slowing down and then going full speed.

Team 12's Lotis Lightning EV with experienced driver Speed Demon Sam Forest being cheered on by her passengers Van Kilmer and David King fly past Team 9's Tesla Road Warrior VI EV.

As Team 9's vehicle approaches the Innsbruck, Austria's border, they veer off the road parking on the shoulder allowing Antonio's Ferrari to drive past them at 180 mph.

Spartan gets back on the highway remarking, "Tell that crazy maniac in the Ferrari that Spartan promises 'You're gonna regret this the rest of your life. both seconds of it.'"

Innsbruck, Austria to Ljubljana, Slovena

Roxanne states, "Ljubljana, the capital of Slovenia has a 15th century Ljubljana Castle that stands on Castle Hill above the downtown city."

Stephen says, "Ljubljana Cathedral or Saint Nicholas's Church is a Gothic church that was in the early 18th century replaced by a Baroque building, a recognizable landmark having a green dome and twin towers that is located near the Ljubljana Central Market and Town Hall."

Roxanne states, "Leaving Innsbruck Austria traveling to Ljubljana, Slovena takes 4 hours and 51 minutes traveling 141 miles on highway A2 with an autobilled toll."

Team 12's Lotis Lightning EV with experienced driver Speed Demon Sam Forest passes Team 5's Ford Mustang EV Ididarod Edition by the new Continental's concierge.

Antonio says to himself, "I can see the Iditarod's only survivor seeking vengeance quote the film saying to me 'Yeah, well, because he destroyed our Ford Mustang EV, and, uh, he killed our dog.'"

Antonio's metallic blue Ferrari Enzo 517 Supercar EV accelerates chasing Team 25's Pure Yellow Yangwang V3 Supercar with driver Lincoln Abrams and passengers Ford Geralds and Kennedy Johns.

Antonio oversees the climate control first freezing Team 25 until their teeth are chattering then causing the heat to drench each team member as they sweat profusely having the vehicle's seals start to leak.

After two hours of torturing the team, Antonio decides to light up the Dead President's vehicle as the leaks and the electronics' failure ignite.

With the Yangwang V3 Supercar filling up with smoke exits the highway, the Golden Eagle HQ has already informed a local service station to transport a brand-new Pure Yellow Yangwang V3 Supercar to their GPS location.

The metallic blue Ferrari Enzo 517 Supercar EV driven by the nuclear generation's Antonio Ferrari continues down the highway seeking his next victim.

The Lemnian Deeds Federation HQ reports that the Steele's Tesla has regained the lead in the Eight Tea Days Around Europe race.

The Deeds HQ announcer states to their assassins, "You will soon be approaching Zagreb, Croatia where most racing teams will stop for an hour to have their daily tea ceremony."

As a tow truck trailer is seen on the opposite side of the highway transporting a Pure Yellow Yangwang V3 Supercar to Team 25, Antonio smiles as he sees ahead a road sign pointing ahead to Zagreb.

Ljubljana, Slovenia to Trieste, Italy

Roxanne states, "Leaving Ljubljana, Slovenia traveling to Trieste, Italy takes 73 minutes traveling 59 miles on highway A1 with an autobilled toll."

Stephen says, "In Trieste is where writers James Joyce working on 'Dubliners' and Umberto Saba lived and taught at the Berlitz School."

Roxanne states, "Trieste is a major seaport with several shipyards and its residents speak both Slovene and Italian,"

Stephen adds, "An email from the FA-King states 'Museo Revoltella is a modern art gallery acquired by Baron Pasquale Revoltella has housing of famous artwork and sculptures.'"

Quickly heading towards Trieste, Italy is Antonio in his metallic blue Ferrari Enzo 517 Supercar EV saying, "I am happy to be home in Italy although Maranello is my family's true home."

The metallic blue Ferrari is driving behind Team 27's Porsche 918 Spyder EV with driver Dean Blake and front seat passenger Seymour Moore, and in the backseat the gorgeous, Pamela Fawcett.

Team 30's Napier Green McLaren 517RP Lightweight Supercar capable of accelerating to 300 mph with it hitting 60 mph in 1.35 seconds.

The driver of Team 30 is James Shatner with his co-pilot Nimoy Spock and backseat teammate, Nichelle Uhura.

Shatner tells his team, "This enterprise Eight Days Race is exhilarating but can be dangerous if the other captains get greedy,"

The captain swerves the supercar to avoid hitting greedy Antonio's Ferrari Enzo, having the McLaren spinning out of control onto the highway's shoulder.

Speedily, the driver Shatner regains control of the McLaren 517RP blaring his horn while his teammates show off their middle fingers in response.

Spock laughs declaring "Using only my middle finger is the vulgar peace symbol."

Ten miles ahead, the metallic blue Ferrari Enzo cuts off the Napier Green McLaren Supercar causing it to slide into the highway's left lane where a passing 18-wheeler semitrailer truck catapults it off the highway and into the bushes.

Quickly, the entire team vacates their McLaren as the vehicle bursts into flames having the Golden Eagle HQ respond by sending a tow truck with a brand-new Midnight Purple McLaren 517RP Supercar.

Antonio states, "My doctor always tells me that 'compassion is the one thing no Supercar ever had.' Maybe it's the one thing that keeps racers ahead of the traffic."

Observing the offroad spinning Napier Green McLaren Supercar, he chuckles remembering his great, grandfather who remarked, "Ford makes ugly little cars in ugly factories."

Trieste, Italy to Zagreb, Croatia

Stephen Griswald states, "Racing from Trieste, Italy to Zagreb, Croatia takes 2 hours and 33 minutes to journey 141 miles on highway A2 having an autobilled toll."

Roxanne states, "The Golden Eagle Organization reports 'The Westin Zagreb located in the center of Zagreb, across from the neo-renaissance palace from the 19th century which houses Mimara Museum. The Croatian National Theatre is close by The Werner Herzog Restaurant that serves high tea and scones from noon till 4 p.m."

Stephen states, "The FA-King notes that 'The Art Collection of Ante and Wiltrud Topić Mimara at the museum houses paintings of the Dutch masters Van Goyen, Ruisdael, fifty works to the Flemish masters Van der Weyden, Bosch, Rubens, Van Dyck, around thirty to the Spanish masters Velázquez, Murillo, Goya, twenty paintings to the German masters Holbein, Liebermann, Leibl, thirty paintings to the English painters Gainsborough, Turner, Bonington and over one hundred, twenty paintings attributed to the French masters Georges de La Tour, Boucher, Chardin, Delacroix, Corot, Manet, Renoir, and Degas.'"

The Ferrari Enzo 517 Supercar EV is three miles behind Team 1's BMW Z17 Roadster driven by Cordelia Van Dyke with passengers Bruno Tivoli and Majesty Royal.

As Antonio gets closer and about to use his SuperPower abilities, Cordelia, knowing the Ferrari's dirty skills spins her team's BMW 180 degrees facing the approaching metallic blue vehicle.

She accelerates the 'beamer' at full speed ahead as Antonio using his SuperPower ability to force the BWM brakes to be applied stopping the crazy BMW driver. His ability to control the opposing vehicle is not working so he continues ahead to maximize his SuperPower ability.

Unbeknownst to him, Cordelia has the SuperPower to become invisible and to negate any other person's SuperPower abilities.

Just before the two vehicles collide, Antonio quickly veers off the highway past the shoulder and into the woods as the BMW Z17 Roadster performs another 180 turn heading back to Zagreb. Her teammates who were scared to death begin to cheer.

Apollo jokingly states, "So Ben Kenobi, have you ever been to Zagreb, Croatia before?"

The Professor replies, "My young padawans I have been all over the world even been to tea at the Westin Zagreb on several occasions. Even in our galaxy, having a tea ceremony at The Werner Herzog Restaurant is worth traveling 'into the inferno' for a truly worthwhile experience."

Zagreb Teatime Ceremony

Roxanne states, "The Werner Herzog Restaurant named after the German film director serves high tea and scones and pastries from noon till 4 p.m., The menu list popular German teas such as black tea including Assam, Ceylon and Darjeeling, fruit tea. Chamomile, Fennel, Rosehip, and Peppermint. With pasties served being German apple cake, bee sting cake, Linzer cookies, Sacher torte, German plum tart, dipped gingersnaps, sauerkraut chocolate cake, apple Bavarian torte, Black Forest torte, German apple strudel, German butter pound cake, and chocolate rum balls."

Stephen states, "The Westin Zagreb is in the center of Zagreb, right across from the neo-renaissance palace from the 19th century that encompasses Mimara, one of the largest Zagreb museums. Drinking the afternoon tea while viewing the greenery and multiple parks such as the Croatian National Theater seems as though all of Zagreb is right there in view."

The Tesla enters Westin Zagreb having the valet parking attendant take their vehicle as they enter the lobby.

Professor Steele, who is world-wide recognized even before the iBroadcast Eight Tea Days race is escorted with his nephews by the manager to a private table for afternoon tea and inside the Mimara.

The manager tells the Steele clan, "You have carte blanche as the Mimara museum, the Croatian National Theater, and local Zagreb parks are all at your disposal."

Team 1 's BMW Z17 Roadster driven by Cordelia Van Dyke in second place heads to the Werner Herzog Restaurant for an hour of afternoon tea and scones in a film memorabilia atmosphere.

The Westin Tea Room sommelier states, "Good afternoon, sirs. The Westin proudly serves English Breakfast tea, Keemun black tea, organic Japanese green tea, Earl Grey tea, sweet Moroccan herbal tea, creme caramel red tea, and Yorkshire white tea."

The Steeles respond with their favorite tea variety from the provided list.

The sommelier continues, "The waiter will bring out the three-tiered Afternoon Tea tray where the bottom tray contains sandwiches and appetizers. The second tiered tray has scones served with jam and clotted cream. The top or third tray has small pastries and sweets. Before the next tray is started, feel free to order another tea from our luxury brand list."

He walks back to the kitchen as the teas and three-tiered tray arrives at the private table as a few other racing teams enter the public tea section of the Mimara museum.

Jonathan Barbosa, the younger brother of Brittany who has the SuperPower to become invisible and, like his sister, manipulate time is attending the Autonomous University of Barcelona, Spain for physics. He was recruited by Stormy Weather in the "Stop the Professor!" campaign and volunteered to be the Lemnian Deeds assassin.

In Jonathan's University dorm room are a dozen copies of Jerome David Salinger's 1951 novel entitled 'The Catcher in the Rye' that has been in the possession of six assassins in the USA.

Jon Barbosa is delivered from the Lemnian Deeds Federation, a mint green Jaguar XJR 513 EV Supercar that accelerates to 60 mph in 1.45 seconds with a top speed of 260 mph.

Jonathan Barbosa often states to people, "You may call me 'Jonathan' or 'Jon' but unlike John Wick, who many times is called 'Jonathan' never call me 'John'" as he chuckles.

While the Professor and his nephews enjoy a marvelous afternoon tea ceremony inside the Mimara museum, Jonathan parks is mint green Jaguar in a location where he can quickly escape and drive back onto the highway.

He walks around the Zagreb Westin parking lot where the valet attendants have reserved empty spots for their special guests.

As he gets close to the Tesla SUV EV with the license plate 'Steele1,' he walks around the vehicle pretending to do a vehicle perimeter check. He is unaware that the five Tesla security cameras are capturing his image and actions. The footage alerts the executive armed security HQ. Immediately, the team of eight professional, military-style, anti-terrorist security force jumps inside the ML51 Armed Security Vehicle EV.

Within 5 minutes, the ML51 with their loud mini train horn blasting enters the Westin valet parking lot.

Jonathan promptly runs across the parking lot and jumps in his car avoiding a confrontation.

As the armed security team of eight, secure the Tesla SUV EV and verify that the invader seen on the security cameras poses no threat, they contact their HQ reporting an 'All clear' status.

The team is told by their HQ commanding officer, "Our protocol as stated in the corporate guide is to wait in the parking area having the vehicle in sight at all times. Then, as the vehicle departs the area, our team in stealth mode must follow them for an hour."

Within thirty minutes, the Steeles have completed their Zagreb park and Croatian National Theater tour, returning to the Tesla SUV EV.

Zagreb, Croatia to Sarajevo, Bosnia

Roxanne states, "Zagreb, Croatia to Sarajevo, Bosnia takes 4 hours, 45 minutes traveling 250 miles on E762 with an autobilled toll. Sarajevo is the capital and largest city of Bosnia and Herzegovina."

Stephen says, "The FA-King writes a note that reads 'Ars Aevi Museum of Contemporary Art in Sarajevo, houses a collection of 1,600 pieces, including around 130 works by renowned world artists such as Pablo Picasso, Michelangelo Pistoletto, Jannis Kounellis, Joseph Beuys, Marina Abramović and Joseph Kosuth.'"

Jonathan, driving to flee the Professor's armed security team, gets on the highway as other Eight Tea Days racers stop for their required tea ceremony.

Jonathan travels to Okoli, Croatia having to transport the vehicle 40.3 miles taking him 50 minutes. He stops to wait for the Tesla SUV EV to drive by as he decides to eat at Okoli Pizza 70.

Sitting in the pizza restaurant, his wood burning oven pizza pie gets delivered to his table where the tomato sauce is served on the side.

Then, his pitcher of Zagreb Brewery beer which has a light body with medium carbonation having a sweet, bitter aftertaste.

The chef makes a locally enjoyed pizza containing thinly sliced sausages and prosciutto, with herbs of sage and rosemary.

As Jonathan is charging his early dinner on the Deeds credit card, he sees the Tesla SUV EV passing on E70. He exits the restaurant just in time to see the ML51 Armed Security Vehicle EV pass by.

He gets in his mint green Jaguar XJR 513 EV Supercar and drives far behind the ML51 until it makes a U-turn onto the highway returning to Zagreb leaving the Tesla to continue its journey unaided.

Jonathan accelerates getting closer to his 'Stop the Professor!' mission as he messages Myrena telling her "I am driving the Jaguar XJR 513 EV Supercar being directly behind the Steele's Tesla SUV EV."

He uses his skill in physics to aim and fire a few rounds from his Croatian semi-automatic pistol not realizing that the custom Tesla SUV EV has bulletproof glass and tires.

When he realizes that the Tesla has not been affected, he reverses time using his family's SuperPower to try to shoot the Tesla SUV again.

Back aiming at the Tesla's tires, he shoots a few rounds watching the projectiles bounce off the rubber tires. Again, he reverses time and in slow motion, aims and fires watching the many bullets hit the driver's side tire ricocheting off the back and side of the tire with no penetration or loss of air.

Jonathan in disbelief reverses repeatedly, as he aims, shoots several bullets and in slow motion watches each projectile hit the rubber tire and bounce off with no effect.

He communicates with the Lemnian Deeds HQ to report his observation. The operator tells Antonio, "The Professor must have customized the Tesla to have everything on it made bulletproof."

Jonathan goes back in time to his morning's events and before the delivery of his vehicle, he obtains a magnetic landmine.

Then, Jonathan fast forwards time to when he was circling the Tesla SUV EV located in the Westin Hotel's valet parking area.

At that point, he places the magnetic landmine underneath the Tesla's suspension.

Then, as the security team in the ML51 Armed Security Vehicle EV arrives, he leaves running back to his Jaguar XJR 513 EV Supercar unseen knowing that when the Tesla drives away, an explosion will happen immediately.

Jonathan sitting in his vehicle gloats smiling as he tells himself, "Sayonara, Steeles" as he drives speedily away.

The eight professional, military-style, anti-terrorist security force discovers the hidden landmine during their inspection and using a robot that carefully removes high explosive bombs or improvised explosive device (IED). Skilled in disarming all bombs and mines, an experienced Explosive Ordnance Disposal (EOD) technician opens the landmine casing carefully removing the timer mechanism and detonator.

Jonathan uses his SuperPower to fast forward enjoying his Zagreb pitcher of beer and pizza pie. He thinks that he will either see the ML51 Armed Security Vehicle EV if the landmine worked or the Tesla SUV EV drive by again if nothing exploded.

Finishing the food for his second time, Jonathan walks to his mint green Jaguar XJR 513 EV Supercar parked behind the pizzeria. Soon he watches the Tesla SUV EV followed by the undetected ML51 Armed Security Vehicle EV. Unhappy, Jonathan follows them as the ML51 turns around driving back to Zagreb. He speeds up to the unescorted Tesla calculating his next attempt to stop the Professor.

Driving for another hour, Jonathan has dozens of Eight Tea Days races competing with him as each car attempts to pass.

Sarajevo, Bosnia to Podgorica, Montenegro

Roxanne states, "Racing from Sarajevo, Bosnia to Podgorica, Montenegro takes 4 hours, 31 minutes with a journey of 144 miles on highway E762 to route M-18."

Stephen states, "Podgorica means 'under the hill' being the capital and largest city of Montenegro. The city is just north of Lake Skadar and near the coastal destinations on the Adriatic Sea."

Roxanne adds saying, "Podgorica is the media hub of Montenegro being the headquarters of the state-owned public television iBroadcasting stations including this one. Also, it has the local iBroadcast and iRadio stations and all the Montenegro's daily iNewspapers."

Stephen says, "The Podgorica Airport is located in Zeta Plain, 6.8 miles south of Podgorica City and is Montenegro's main international airport."

Roxanne comments, "The Clock Tower of Podgorica, Montenegro, is located at Bećir Beg Osmanagić square being a surviving Ottoman landmark after WW2's bombing of Podgorica."

Stephen adds, "The Ostrog Monastery is a monastery of the Serbian Orthodox Church situated against an almost vertical background, high up in the large rock of Ostroška Greda, in Montenegro. The monastery is allocated to Saint Basil of Ostrog whose remains are located here."

Team 26's royal blue Praga Bohema Copperhead Hypercar crashes into his Jaguar XJR 513 EV Supercar, he reverses time so that the collision with the Praga Bohema Copperhead backfires sending his adversary off the highway in need of the Golden Eagle HQ to get a replacement vehicle from a local service station.

This mayhem of collisions, rewind time, collision, back in time, off road crash, forward time goes on for the next two hours. Jonathan's mission is never fulfilled as he never catches up to the Tesla SUV EV again.

Chapter 25

Tuesday 'Eight Tea Days Around Europe' Race

"Good day racing fans and welcome to the Golden Eagle HQ iBroadcast of the Eight Tea Days Around Europe Race. I am Roxanne McLaren reporting on Day Four, you are watching live racing iNews."

Stephen states, "The Eight Tea Days Around Europe racing teams continue traveling to Tirana Albania."

Roxanne reads a note, "World Association of Zoos and Aquariums having the acronym 'WAZA' reads 'The Dolittle family from the Galapagos Islands helped improve the Zoopark Tirana healing the original animal including bears, lions, llamas, monkeys, wolves, foxes, and some birds as well as importing species not native to Albania.'"

Stephen remarks, "Former American NASCAR race car driver, Richard Childress said 'Once you've raced, you never forget it…and you never get over it.'"

Podgorica, Montenegro to Tirana, Albania

Roxanne states, "Racing from Podgorica, Montenegro to Tirana, Albania takes 2 hours, 40 minutes racing a distance of 98 miles on E763 to M-18."

Stephen says, "Tirana is the capital and largest city of Albania located in the center of the country, enclosed by mountains and hills overlooking the Adriatic Sea in the distance."

Team 58's legendary Formula 1 racecar driver, Paul Georges states "It's about time for this senior citizen to hit the men's room."

Paul looking out his window humorously says, "Care to join me, Professor Steele?"

The team's Alfa Romeo Giulia Quadrifoglio IV Supercar EV driver Farrah Monroe drives the vehicle into a rest stop restroom.

Farrah jokingly says to Paul, "They say when it's your time to go." as he quickly exits the vehicle and runs into the convenience store.

The other passenger, Sabrina Jackson and Farrah walk into the convenience store to load up on supplies and use the facilities to powder their noses. -

After finishing their needed tasks, Farrah notices that old man Paul has not emerged from the restroom.

She sees three EMTs enter the convenience store and asks them, "Can you check the men's restroom as one of our race members, old man Paul has yet to be seen."

A smile from the beautiful Farrah and her female teammate, Sabrina, who nods in agreement gets the medics to proceed into the men's restroom.

They notice that Paul is unconscious and as one medic is checking his vitals, the other EMT is performing CPR on him,

After a few minutes, Paul is coherent and revived from a near fatal heart attack.

After being helped into the Alfa Romeo, Farrah says to Paul, "When I said, 'when it's your time to go,' I meant go to the restroom not go to the eternal resting room."

Paul and Sabrina along with the three EMTs laugh, breaking up the tense atmosphere.

Jonathan Barbosa drives up to two feuding racing teams as he cannot find an opening to pass them.

In the left highway lane is Team 22's Ferrari 513CM Le Mans Hypercar with driver Ken Cannon and front seat passenger Robin McCarthy and in the back seat, Nichole Thicke.

Their adversary in the right lane is Team 41 having the namesake driver Anita Lamborghini driving her family's factory prototype Lamborghini Essenza SCV51X Hypercar. Her supermodel passengers are Gemma Georgio and Shoshana Amato both sitting together in the passenger front seat.

Anita floors the accelerator pushing her prototype Lamborghini Essenza SCV51X Hypercar to its limits. Passing the Ferrari in the left lane she says, "Guidi come una nonna."

Gemma translates stating. "She doesn't drive as fast as my grandmother."

Robin McCarthy replies, "I tuoi antenati non potevano costruire biciclette."

Gemma remarks, "Even my grandmother could build a bicycle, a motorcycle and a better car than your crummy Ferrari."

The Ferrari almost collides with the Lamborghini forcing it to spin into a pastureland of grazing cows. As driver Anita looks up, she notices two longhorn bulls racing toward them.

Without hesitation, Ms. Lamborghini performs a 180-degree turn having the bulls followed by a herd of cows chasing after the vehicle branded with the raging bull logo, The bull plated Lamborghini accelerates just getting nicked by the bulls' horns.

The Ferrari gets the pasture manure splattered on its windshield forcing its wipers on full speed to disperse its windshield wiper fluid to clean the 'bullshirt' that is blocking her view

Jonathan maneuvers his mint green Jaguar XJR 513 EV Supercar avoiding making hamburgers as he carefully misses the livestock following his two racers in their Ferrari vs. Lamborghini feud.

Jonathan tells himself, "That scenario I refuse to replay with my SuperPower."

Tirana, Albania to Korçë, Albania

Roxanne reports, "We continue our live coverage where the racers leave Tirana, Albania to Korçë, Albania taking 2 hours, 40 minutes traveling 101 miles on E852 to Sh3."

Stephen says, "In Korçë, Albania there is manufacturing of knitwear, rugs, textiles, flour-milling, brewing, and sugar-refining. The city is the headquarters of the nationally famous Birra Korça being the third largest beer producer in Albania."

Team 27's Porsche 918 Spyder EV with driver Dean Blake and front seat passenger Seymour Moore, and in the backseat the gorgeous Pamela Fawcett exits the highways to stock up on the award-winning Birra Korça. Dean purchases a variety of their Blonde Ale, European type pilsner and Dark Ale.

The racers keep their distance remaining in place as Albanian State Police called in Albanian 'Policia e Shtetit' drive alongside the racing teams.

Team 21 has Iris Lille driving their Liquid Petroleum Aston Martin Valkyrie Tarantula EV. The all-female team waves at the law enforcement officers receiving kisses from the male driver, Luan, and his female partner, Boran who winks at the ladies. The team's passengers Demi-Leigh Sedgefield and Bonnie Houston blow kisses back as they accelerate passing them.

The Rimac Team 11 with members Giana Rossi, Keara Karlson and Theris O'Leary try to follow but the Albanian State Police vehicle puts on its flashing lights while having them pull over.

Korçë, Albania to Thessaloniki, Greece

Stephen Griswald reports saying, "The race continues from Korçë, Albania to Thessaloniki Greece taking 2 hours, 53 minutes traveling 154 miles on highway E90 having an autobilled toll."

Roxanne reports, "Thessaloniki is the second-largest city in Greece and the capital of the geographic region of Macedonia located on the Thermaic Gulf, at the northwest corner of the Aegean Sea."

Stephen states, "The Thessaloniki International Film Festival is organized by the Greek Ministry of Culture being held every November."

He says, "Greek gallerist and an important collector of modern art works, Alexander Iolas stated 'Oh yes, no more hospitals and orphanages; a center of contemporary art; that's exactly what Thessaloniki needs.'"

Roxanne continues saying, "According to the FA-King 'Thessaloniki has four art museums the Museum of Modern Art, the Museum of Contemporary Art, Macedonian Museum of Contemporary Art, and State Museum of Contemporary Art Collections. Thessaloniki Museum of Modern Art Costakis collection has Russian avant-garde art by well-known artists like Kazimir Malevich, Vladimir Tatlin, Wassily

Kandinsky, El Lissitzky, and Lyubov Popova, Thessaloniki Museum of Contemporary Art has work by Rolf Escher and the permanent Thessaloniki Museum collection includes artwork by Andy Warhol and Max Ernst.'"

Driving onto the highway is a silver Hyperion XP-5 which goes from zero to 60 mph in 1.45 seconds and maxes out at 276 mph.

Myrena Gorgona iBroadcasts to the entire Lemnian Deeds Federation, "Driving the silver Solar-Powered Hyperion XP-5 Hypercar is my close friend and Lemnian Deeds technology Goddess, Olympia Gort." The worldwide monitors show thousands of dedicated Deeds members giving her a standing ovation. A photo is shown on the iBroadcast screens of Olympia on her computers with a dozen flying droids above her head.

The silver Hyperion XP-5 is following Team 5's Ford Mustang EV Ididarod Edition.

Olympia has her flying drones unveil their Solid Carbide Diamond drill that can easily penetrate a moving car tire.

Inside the Ford Mustang EV, Callon Ferrel is driving his passengers Lazer Cannon, Elowen Redington, and their mascot, an Alaskan Husky.

The flying drone attaches itself to the vehicle's anti-roll bar located underneath that connects to both rear tire assemblies

Then, the Solid Carbide Diamond drill spins against the inner sidewall of the driver's side tire, Soon, the drill moves into the tire causing a blowout as the uncontrollable Mustang gallops onto the highway's shoulder and flips.

Team 5's members get bruised as its racing dog gets hurt as it begins whimpering and whining.

Immediately, the Golden Eagle HQ begins the emergency process as paramedics and the Tirana Veterinary Hospital staff are dispatched to their GPS location.

They dispatch a brand-new Ford Mustang EV Ididarod Edition which is placed on a service station vehicle trailer and sent to deliver it to Team 5.

The paramedics check the human patients and bandage their bruises while the vet assesses the Husky and transports him back to the Tirana Veterinary Hospital.

The Hyperion XP-5 jets down the highway towards Thessaloniki Greece with her flying drones.

The vehicle transportation trailer arrives with the brand new Ford Mustang EV Ididarod Edition.

Team 5 and the service station mechanic drives down the highway resuming their day,

Approaching the feuding teams, Olympia Gort is behind Team 22's Ferrari 513CM Le Mans Hypercar and Team 41's Lamborghini Essenza SCV51X Hypercar.

She programs her flying drones to travel under each vehicle and wait for her instructions.

As Olympia passes the adversaries maneuvering between them at maximum speed, she waves goodbye to them.

Calculating that she is a safe distance ahead of them, she presses the ignite button making the drones explode.

The Ferrari is lifted twenty feet into the air spinning right over left as the Lamborghini is shot above them having the two drivers facing each other windshield on windshield.

Anita airborne gives Ken Cannon and his teammates the bird sign reminiscent to the film 'Top Gun' with Anthony 'Goose' Edwards and Tom 'Maverick' Cruise before both vehicles crash and burn.

The Golden Eagle HQ quickly dispatches two ambulances with EMTs and a tow trailer with a brand-new Ferrari 513CM Le Mans Hypercar and a Lamborghini Essenza SCV51X Hypercar to their crash site's GPS location.

Thessaloniki, Greece Teatime

Stephen states, "The Golden Eagle HQ indicates 'Hôtel Plaza Athénée high tea with Parisian style and flair.'"

Roxanne says, "The Honey and Healing Tea Tasting offers several special honey selection and a warm cup of homemade Ceylon herbal tea with traditional Greek pastry Mekitsa is a dish made of kneaded dough with yogurt."

Stephen states, "The Golden Eagle HQ reports 'The Thessaloniki Tea House serves tea such as English Breakfast, Darjeeling, Earl Grey, Nepal Shangri-La, and Nepal Sakhejung Golden Organic.'"

The Plaza Athénée is in Thessaloniki on Avenue Montaigne, which is known as the 'Golden Triangle' of the eighth district renowned as the epicenter of French luxury.

Professor Steele and his two nephews enter the hotel lobby where Laurence the hotel director states, "Bienvenue à l'Hôtel Plaza Athénée, Je suis Laurence la directrice de l'hôtel."

The Professor replies, "Merci beaucoup."

He tells his nephews, "The hotel director is Laurence, and she welcomes us."

The twins say to each other, "We speak over 20 languages and French was one of our first languages we studied," as they laugh.

The hotel director escorts the famous Steele CEO and his future leaders to 'La Galerie,' a chic space with soothing elegance, as gentle melodies are heard from the harpist and soft conversations.

Immediately, they are introduced to the staff and the sommelier.

The tea sommelier watches, as his staff makes in the kitchen the tea then transfers each order to another silver teapot, so it doesn't overbrew.

The sommelier states, "The finest Parisian tea connoisseurs provide their teas such as exotic Olympic black tea, Darjeeling Goomtee, white tea, green teas, fruit teas, oolong tea, Pu-erh tea, rooibos teas, herbal teas, and chamomile tea. Accompanying the tea are the Foie Gras being a duck or goose liver between two biscuits topped with orange chutney, lobster tartlet topped with Petrossian caviar, Comté Gruyère cheese sandwich with spinach and black truffles, smoked salmon Blini with dill cream and Granny Smith apples, and the Croque-Monsieur that is a hot sandwich made with ham and cheese."

The Steeles order their teas and delicious food as more sponsored racing teams enter the 'La Galerie,' unescorted.

Driving their BMW Z17 Roadster, Team 1's Bruno Tivoli says to Majesty Royal and Cordelia Van Dyke, "Ladies, it is almost 3 p.m. which is time for our 'tea stop in Thessaloniki, Greece.'"

Bruno continues, "There's a place nearby where I told my childhood friend Joe to meet us."

A few minutes later they pull into 'The Venus Teapot Dome.' Standing outside waiting is a short man wearing a leather outfit.

Bruno walks over to him and the two embrace each other like long-lost friends.

Turning to Majesty and Cordelia, Bruno introduces his friend, "This is my childhood best friend, Joe. To his associates, he is known as 'Joe de Pest.'" After shaking hands, they all walk to the establishment for their daily tea break.

Bruno explains to Joe that they need to get their required racing daily tea at three.

Joe proudly states, "The tea is on me."

Turning to the server behind the counter, Joe says, "Kind sir, may we have three hot teas for our three o'clock teatime at 'The Teapot Dome.' I would like a cold beer."

The server fills the tea kettle with water as Joe de Pest says, "Sir, how long will it take you to make our tea?"

The server turns around saying, "Five minutes."

Joe de Pest unsure questions him, "Are you sure about five minutes? Five minutes? Exactly five minutes?"

The server looking puzzled smiles and nods 'yes.'

Joe adds, "I was told by a barista that it takes seven minutes. Perhaps the laws of physics do not exist on your stove. Are we to believe that boiling water heats faster in your establishment than on any place on the face of the earth?'

Embarrassed, the server nods.

The group sits down at a nearby booth. As they are talking, they are soon delivered their three o'clock tea,

The server shyly states. "The teas are on the house."

Cordelia verifies that the event is transmitted back to the Golden Eagle Race committee.

Olympia Gort after driving all over Thessaloniki finds the Tesla SUV EV parked in the valet lot at the Plaza Athénée.

Nearby, she gets a late lunch at Planet Club Thessaloniki and waits looking across the street for her targets.

Olympia, still eating her meal, watches as the black Tesla SUV EV heads towards the highway. She tells herself "We will meet soon, and I will be the exploding pathway behind you Steeles."

Thessaloniki, Greece to Sofia, Bulgaria

Stephen states, "The leaders are racing from Thessaloniki Greece to Sofia Bulgaria that takes 3 hours 29 minutes traveling 184 miles on E79 with an autobilled toll."

Roxanne reports, "Sofia Bulgaria is the capital and largest city of Bulgaria being situated in the Sofia Valley at the foot of the Vitosha mountain. The city is built west of the Iskar River, and has many mineral springs, such as the Sofia Central Mineral Baths. Sofia has a humid continental climate being centrally located in the Balkans, between the Black Sea and the Adriatic Sea."

Stephen states, "Sofia is one of the most visited tourist destinations in Bulgaria with the neo-Byzantine architecture of the Alexander Nevsky Cathedral, a gold-plated dome rising 148 feet high."

Olympia, who uses the Sun to power her Hypercar is unlike Icarus who flew too close to the star and crashed.

She drives approaching Team 1's BMW Z17 Roadster driven by Cordelia Van Dyke.

Believing that the silver Hyperion XP-5 will use her SuperPower to detour their journey, Cordelia starts preparing her negating SuperPower as an initiative-taking strategy.

Olympia programs her flying droids to soar under the BMW Z17 Roadster and deliver it like a transport plane back to Tirana, Albania.

As the BMW Z17 Roadster is airborne, its passengers Bruno Tivoli and Majesty Royal start yelling "Cordelia, can't you do something about this?"

Majesty complains, "I get sick when I fly commercially."

Cordelia, unable to negate the current situation says, "If you feel queasy, there are sick bags in front of your seat," as she laughs while Majesty looks for anything to help.

Being transported at hyperspeed or 'plaid speed,' they arrive at the parking lot of the Thessaloniki Museum of Modern Art within the hour.

Bruno still amazed says, "We have to repeat the 184 miles drive on highway E79?"

Majesty states, "At least, we are back on the asphalt. I am not happy either repeating the 3 hours' drive."

Cordelia unhappily states, "Or paying the expensive autobilled toll again," as she accelerates back onto highway E79.

The Hyperion XP-5 races down the highway towards Belgrade, Serbia with her flying drones seeking the Tesla SUV EV especially Professor Steele.

Olympia remarks, "Professor, come out, come out wherever you are. Is that saying from the Wizard of Oz or old blue eyes?"

Sofia, Bulgaria to Belgrade, Serbia

Stephen states, "Traveling at high speed from Sofia Bulgaria to Belgrade, takes 4 hours, 9 minutes traveling 243 miles on A4 to A1 with an autobilled toll."

Stephen continues stating, "Belgrade being the 'White City.' is the capital and largest city of Serbia between the Sava and Danube rivers and the financial center of Serbia."

Roxanne says, "The iBBC reports that 'Belgrade is one of the five most creative cities in the world hosting the Film Festival, Theatre Festival, Summer Festival, BEMUS or Belgrade Early Music Festival, Book Fair, Belgrade Choir Festival, Eurovision Song Contest, and the Beer Fest.'"

Stephen reads an email stating, "The FA-King reports that 'Belgrade's National Museum houses a collection of more than 5,600 paintings and 8,400 drawings and prints by art masters such as Bosch, Juan de Flandes, Titian, Tintoretto, Rubens, Cézanne, G.B. Tiepolo, Renoir, Monet, Lautrec, Matisse, Picasso, Gauguin, Chagall, van Gogh, and Mondrian."

Roxanne states, "The Nikola Tesla Museum is a science museum located in the central area of Belgrade, Serbia dedicated to honoring and displaying the life and work of Nikola Tesla being his final resting place."

Stephen says, "Elon Musk should be praising him as they are probably in Heaven working together for something inventive for God" as he chuckles.

Roxanne states, "Belgrade is also a fashion and iBroadcast hub. Belgrade's Fashion Week has helped launch the local fashion talents on the international scene."

Stephen states, "The beaches and sports facilities promotes various sports such as golf, football, basketball, volleyball, rugby union, baseball, and tennis. Extreme sports such as bungee jumping, water skiing, and paintballing are extremely popular participated in one of the largest indoor arenas in Europe is the Štark Arena or Belgrade Arena with capacity of 19,384 spectators."

Myrena had the Lemnian Deeds Federation SuperPower members secretly enter the Steele Corporation testing labs. They were able to acquire many prototype items such as the patented 'Maxi Nitrous Oxide' or commonly known as 'laughing gas.' The gas is colorless, and this latest version can be inhaled with immediate feelings of calmness, euphoria, and laughter. Nitrous oxide is harmless, commonly used to blow up floating party balloons and in whipped cream canisters.

The silver Hyperion XP-5 is behind Team 44's McLaren Speedtail Hermes 3 EV who is race feuding with Team 15's Nissan Flash EV.

The McLaren Speedtail Hermes 3 EV has driver Arnold Winkler and his passengers Ronnie Most and Heidi Klumaker.

The Nissan Flash EV is driven by Tiger de Forrest with his passengers Ash Arturo and Winter Sazon.

Tiger growls loudly, "Winkler, how dare you marry my beautiful twin sister, you bastard!"

Arnold yells back, "Me? What about you, you scoundrel! Once you dug your claws in him, you married my twin brother. My parents were shocked! They still are."

Heidi Klumaker on her driver's side says, "And Winter, did you get bombarded by an extratropical cyclone as your hair and make-up looks like an unnatural disaster."

Winter Sazon furiously retorts, "Out of my sight your pig face does infect my eyes. I would challenge you to a battle of wits, but I notice that you are unarmed. You smell like a Vieux Boulogne!"

Ronnie Most exclaims, "Ash Arturo, I no longer love you!"

Ash replies, "You're a bi-otch! You better start playing poker because that's the only place you will see any Queens."

As the verbal fighting continues at 200 mph driving down the highway, Olympia has two of her flying drones filled with 'Maxi Nitrous Oxide' attach itself to the ventilation system of the McLaren Speedtail Hermes 3 EV.

Then, another two flying drone likewise attaches to the ventilation system of the Nissan Flash EV,

Soon Team 44 and Team 15 have stopped arguing and begin acting crazy with euphoria and laughter as they begin driving at 30 mph allowing the silver Hyperion XP-5 to fly past them heading down the highway to Budapest seeking another team to victimize.

Belgrade, Serbia to Budapest, Hungary

Roxanne says, "Racing from Belgrade, Serbia to Budapest, Hungary takes 3 hours, 42 minutes traveling a distance of 230 miles on A13 with an autobilled toll."

Roxanne adds stating, "Budapest is the capital and most populous city of Hungary having the most well-known sight of the capital with the neo-Gothic Parliament that houses the Hungarian Crown Jewels."

Stephen reads "I just received a note from the FA-King where he writes, 'Budapest Museum of Fine Arts' core of the collection is constituted by the seven hundred paintings acquired from the Esterhazy estate. The collection is split up into Italian, German, Netherlandish, Flemish, French, English and Spanish art. The most important works include Maso di Banco's 'Coronation of the Virgin,' Sassetta's 'Saint Thomas Aquinas at Prayer,' Domenico Ghirlandaio's 'Saint Stephen Martyr,' Bernardo Bellotto's 'The Piazza della Signoria in Florence,' Gentile Bellini's 'Portrait of Caterina Cornaro,' Giorgione's 'Portrait of a Young Man,' Raphael's 'Esterhazy Madonna,' Giambattista Pittoni's 'St Elizabeth Distributing Alms,' three works by Corrado Giaquinto, 'Allegory of Painting,' 'The Angel Annunciant' and 'Moses receiving the Laws,' Correggio's 'Madonna and Child with an Angel,' three works by Sebastiano del Piombo, Bronzino's 'Adoration of the Shepherds' as well as his 'Venus, Cupid and Jealousy,' Romanino's 'Doge Agostino Barbarigo Handing over a Banner to Niccolo Orsini,' Titian's 'Portrait of Doge Marcantonio Trevisani,' Tintoretto's 'Supper at Emmaus,' Tiepolo's 'St James the Greater in the Battle of Clavijo,' Dürer's 'Portrait of a Young Man,' Bernard van Orley's 'Portrait of Emperor Charles V,' eight pictures by Lucas Cranach the Elder, Pieter Bruegel the Elder's 'St

John the Baptist Preaching,' Rubens' 'Mucius Scaevola Before Porsenna,' Murillo's 'The Christ Child Distributing Bread to Pilgrims,' Maarten van Heemskerck's 'Lamentation,' two excellent portraits by Frans Hals, and a particularly strong collection of works by Spanish masters including El Greco, Velázquez and Goya.'"

Roxanne says, "Budapest is home to a fashion week twice a year, where the city's fashion designers and houses present their collections and provides a meeting place for the fashion industry representatives."

Stephen says, "The Dohány Street Synagogue is the largest synagogue in Europe, and the second largest active synagogue in the world located in the Jewish district in central Budapest."

Driving their plain white Le Mans Hypercar class Peugeot 13X13 EV Hypercar is Tyrone Dinkler with passengers Lena Lannister and Maisle Stark.

Following them close behind is the Lemnian Deeds female mercenaries Hannah Darryl and Polly Powerpuff. They are driving their chili red Czinger 58T Hypercar that accelerates to 60 mph in 1.35 seconds topping out at 315 mph.

Hannah asks Polly, "So what SuperPower abilities do you possess?"

Polly answers saying, "The ability to fly was my first SuperPower like everybody else. I will show you my second SuperPower, but you must put the car in cruise control so that we don't accidentally crash."

Hannah complies as Polly blinks her eyes three times.

Now, being in a hypnotic trance, Hannah believes that she is in an evergreen forest smelling terpenes of fresh pine scent as though it were Christmas time.

Before the Czinger is steered off the road, Polly smacks Hannah in her face, having her come back to their reality.

Verifying that Hannah is back able to drive, Polly asked her, "Quid pro quo! What can you do with your SuperPowers?"

Hannah says, "My first SuperPower ability is to become invisible. My second is somewhat unusual as it is called 'Serpens Creatio ex Nihilo' which means 'creating snakes out of nothing.'"

Polly says, "That's pretty cool!"

Hannah remarks, "My only problem is when the snake attacks our victim, it vanishes into thin air once it came."

Pulling behind the plain white Peugeot 13X13 EV Hypercar, Polly says, "According to Israel's Weizmann Institute of Science the human-made particle HEX or hexadecanal triggers aggression only to females. I will flood the Peugeot that will drive Lena and Maisle crazy with rage."

Blinking three times, the Le Mans Hypercar class Peugeot is quite normal for Tyrone Dinkler as is two female passengers begin to argue frantically over the color of their lipstick.

Then, Hannah not to be out done says, "Now it is my turn to use my SuperPower."

As she blinks three times, she states, "I conjure up inside the Peugeot a deadly snake extravaganza. Now lying throughout the Peugeot are inland taipan being the deadliest snake in the world that can kill any human in 45 minutes, the coastal taipan that can jump 10 feet in the air to attack its victim, the king cobra that has enough venom to incapacitate and terminate an elephant, the banded krait whose venom causes respiratory failure, the Eastern tiger snake that causes paralysis and death within 30 minutes, and Russell's viper that has killed more Asians than Covid, HIV, and TB."

Inside the pure ivory Peugeot, Tyrone yells, "Like Samuel L Jackson once said, 'Get these damn snakes off the plain white Le Mans Hypercar class Peugeot 13X13 EV Hypercar!"

His female passengers have stopped aggressively attacking each other as they stare into the round pupils' tiny eyes snakes."

Maisle Stark states "The snake's eyes and I don't mean dice with only one dot telling me that these reptiles are diurnal which means that they are very active during the daylight hours."

Inside the Peugeot, Team 51 begin screaming and waving their arms back and forth in pseudo karate motions.

As each deadly reptile with their elongated body and tail attacks each of the Peugeot members, one by one they disappear.

Hannah in the Czinger 58T Hypercar states, "In the book of Exodus, chapter 7 God says to Moses and his brother Aaron 'when the Pharaoh asks you to perform a miracle ' take your staff and throw it down before Pharaoh and it will become a snake' as the Lord commanded, they obey. Then, the wise men, Egyptian magicians, and sorcerers of the Pharaoh throw down their staffs that become snakes too. But the Lord showing his Almighty power has Aaron's staff attack and swallow the Egyptian wizards' staffs."

Polly with her eyes wide open says, "That's impressive! It's like I'm back in Sunday School" having her laugh.

Soaring down the road in their Czinger 58T Hypercar, noticing that ahead of them is Team 31's electronic Shelby Cobra 7 Hypercar with driver Emilio Sheen and passengers Judd Wilson and Molly Ringer.

The team is discussing their favorite movies as Emilio says, "I really like the film 'The Way' with Martin Sheen who I tell people is my father" as he smiles with a Cheshire Cat grin.

Judd Wilson declares, "I really like for cinematography 'A River Runs Through It,' ' Candide 2517,' and the remake of 'The Graduate.' For comedy films I have enjoyed the original Peter Falk in 'The In-laws' and Michael Caine with Steve Martin in 'Dirty Rotten Scoundrels.'"

Molly states, "I like anything done by the late Quentin Tarantino including 'True Romance.'"

Hannah Darryl tells Polly, "Quoting your favorite director, Quentin Tarantino from 'Kill Bill Vol 2' where my namesake has Elle Driver nicknamed the 'California Mountain Snake' says reading 'the venom of a black mamba can kill a human in four hours if, say bitten near the seven bones of the human tarsus or opposable digit. However, a bite to the anterior facial vein or trunk can bring death from paralysis within 20 minutes. Now, you should listen to this."

Hannah blinks your eyes three times while having a black mamba appearing in the electronic Shelby Cobra 7 Hypercar.

Emilio, seeing the snake remarks, "Everybody listen up! We must put a barrier between us and the snakes!"

In the backseat Molly Ringer, out loud says, "According to my favorite movie 'Kill Bill volume 2,' Daryl Hannah as Elle Driver states 'Now, you should listen to this, as this concerns all of us 'the amount of venom that can be released from a single fang piercing of the Black

Mamba can be gargantuan.' The Black Mamba can deliver as much as 400 mg of venom from a single bite.'"

Emilio Sheen remarks, "You know I've always liked the word 'gargantuan' which is so rare to use in an everyday sentence but in our current situation the word 'tiny: or 'miniature' would be a word more to my liking."

As Team 31 shrieks loudly, Emilio loses total control of the Czinger having it spin doing a 720 as though he was snowboarding and not driving a hypercar.

Finally stopped on the highway's left shoulder, the team looks intensely at the dashboard where the black mamba was located.

Judd Wilson states, "The 'Dendroaspis pilylepus' has disappeared. I assume hopefully returning to the sub-Saharan African continent."

Soaring past the temporarily disabled Shelby Cobra 7, is the two SuperPower females inside their chili red Czinger 58T Hypercar.

After the entire Team 31 takes a 5-minute breather, the electronic Shelby Cobra 7 Hypercar returns to the highway as it accelerates towards Budapest, Hungary.

Budapest, Hungary to Vienna, Austria

Stephen remarks, "Racing from Budapest Hungary to Vienna, Austria takes 2 hours, 25 minutes traveling a distance of 151 miles on M1 to A4 with an autobilled toll."

Stephen continues saying, "The Vienna International Centre is the campus and building complex for the United Nations Office in Vienna."

Roxanne states, "Vienna is called either the 'City of Music' due to its musical legacy of many famous classical musicians such as Beethoven and Mozart who called Vienna home or 'City of Dreams' due to the world's first psychoanalyst, Sigmund Freud who lived there. Famous composers including Wolfgang Amadeus Mozart, Joseph Haydn, Ludwig van Beethoven, Ferdinand Ries, Nina Stollewerk, Franz Schubert, Johannes Brahms, Gustav Mahler, Robert Stolz, and Arnold Schoenberg have worked in Vienna. Perhaps, they spent some time at the St. Stephen's Cathedral in Stephensplatz or at the Mozart Haus where Wolfgang Mozart resided."

Stephen remarks, "Vienna is considered the center of LGBTQ life in Austria having same-sex anti-discrimination laws. The city has several cafés, bars and clubs frequented by LGBTQ community."

Roxanne states, "My favorite topic, Viennese cuisine. We all know about 'Wiener schnitzel' which is fried veal. Also, there's Tafelspitz that is boiled beef, Beuschel being a ragout containing veal lungs and heart, and Selchfleisch which is smoked meat with sauerkraut and dumplings. For dessert there are Apfelstrudel being a strudel pastry filled with apples, Millirahmstrudel that's a milk cream strudel, Kaiserschmarrn that's shredded pancakes served with fruit compotes, and Sachertorte being a cake of two layers of chocolate cake with apricot jam in the middle."

Stephen reads an email saying, "The FA-King reports that the 'Vienna's Gemäldegalerie of the Kunsthistorisches Museum has major works by Dürer, Raphael, Pieter Bruegel the Elder, Velázquez, Vermeer, Rembrandt, Raphael, Caravaggio, Venetian artists such as Titian, Veronese, Tintoretto, Flemish artists such as Peter Paul Rubens, Anthony van Dyck, Early Netherlandish artists such as Jan van Eyck, Rogier van der Weyde and Old German artists such as Albrecht Dürer, and Lucas Cranach.'"

Rolex Kronos, the brother to Gabrielle is also a hyperjacker with the SuperPower ability to become invisible.

Rolex remembers graduating high school at age 10 reading 'The Art of War' where Sun Tzu writes, "If you know the enemy and know yourself, you need not fear the result of a hundred battles."

Recent doctorate graduate from the Swiss Federal Institute of Technology Zurich or known as 'ETH Zurich,' Rolex majored in cyber security but as the world's top hyperjacker named 'Morpheus II' desires to get into any valuable electronic device undetected.

While attending the university, Rolex perfected his 'hyperjacker helper' that can automatically reprogram any EV within five hundred feet.

For testing, he would drive by car dealerships and without the key open any car's door, start the car and still in his car drive the empty car around the dealership parking lot,

For fun, Rolex would drive the showroom cars around the interior from the street inside his Bugatti Bolide IV Solar Hypercar so that the dealership manager would arrive the next day to see his twelve showroom vehicles aimed at the exit as though they are seeking to leave.

As Rolex approaches the next car, he uses his Hijacker Helper Device to reprogram unlucky Team 13's Subaru Hypercar 2 EV having driver Echo Windwood and her passengers Pandora Boxlighter and Joddos Canterbury unaware of his intentions and skills.

The Subaru Hypercar 2 EV to speed up 200 mph as he accelerates to stay close behind.

He programs the Subaru Hypercar 2 EV to make a left turn at the next intersection which 10 seconds later where the Subaru Hypercar does turn left with Rolex's car following.

As Echo Windwood tries to turn around heading back towards the highway, nothing happens as the Hijacker Helper Device has total control of the Subaru Hypercar 2 EV.

Three miles ahead, Rolex in control of the Subaru Hypercar 2 EV has it make a right turn heading straight for a Rocky Mountain as Rolex's car stops and watches.

Team 13's Subaru collides into a solid rock wall throwing the passengers thirty feet hitting many trees as the Subaru Hypercar 2 EV is totally crushed resembling an accordion.

The Golden Eagle Headquarters dispatches an ambulance with EMTs as the local service station transports a brand-new Subaru Hypercar EV to Team 13's GPS location.

Chapter 26

Wednesday 'Eight Tea Days Around Europe' Race

"Another great sunny day racing fans and welcome to the Golden Eagle HQ iBroadcast of the Eight Tea Days Around Europe Race. You're joining Roxanne McLaren reporting on Day Five, you are watching live racing iNews."

Stephen states, "The Tesla SUV EV known as the "Steele Team" is still leading the pack. For some unknown reason vehicles keep having tire blowouts, accidents crashing off the highways and one car was transported back to its recent starting position."

Roxanne states, "A legendary NASCAR driver, Jeff Gordon stated 'When you're in a race car, you're going through so many different emotions throughout that race.'"

Vienna, Austria to Prague, Czechia

Stephen states, "Racing from Vienna, Austria to Prague Czechia takes 3 hours, 50 minutes traveling 183 miles on E59 to D1 with an autobilled toll."

Roxanne reports, "Prague is the capital and largest city in the Czech Republic, being the political, cultural, and economic district of central Europe. The city's architecture has remnants of Romanesque, Gothic, Renaissance and Baroque."

Stephen reads aloud, "The FA-King notes that 'The National Gallery in Prague is a state-owned art gallery housing the largest collection of art in the Czech Republic. The collection includes Monet, van Gogh, Rodin, Gauguin, Cézanne, Renoir, Schiele, Munch, Miró, and Picasso who has many works there.'"

Roxanne says, "The must try cuisine in Prague are the Czech homemade palačinky crepes, Trdelník being a traditional Slovak rolled pastry topped with a pinch of sugar, nuts or cinnamon, vepřo knedlo zelo is Czech roast pork, dumplings, and sauerkraut."

Rolex Kronos in his Bugatti Bolide IV Solar Hypercar navigates towards Prague, the road has a few commuters in their vehicles so for kicks he oscillates between turning on each car's lights then their iRadio on extremely loud while scanning through the iStations irritating each of the drivers and their passengers.

After a half hour of doing his mischievous deeds, he accelerates flying past the unaware commuters.

Piloting his vehicle as fast as he can until he is behind a bunch of other commuter vehicles. Rolex seeing that the vehicles on the in the left lane and those in the right lane are not adjacent to each other, he operates his Hijacker Helper Device so that in unison all the cars in the left lane shift to the right lane and those in the right lane shift to the left lane. Although this technical magic trick scares the bejesus out of the vehicles' drivers and passengers, no accident occurs.

Then, fifteen minutes later seeing that the same vehicle situation is still viable, Rolex returns the cars to their original location annoying those in the vehicles.

After another fifteen minutes driving behind the left lane vehicles, Rolex hijacks forcing all the left hand vehicles into the right lane, leaving everyone a distant memory in his rear view dashboard monitor.

Rolex listening for 45 minutes to iBroadcast iMusic of the 'Best of Lovegood Studios,' Rolex can see miles ahead of him an Estrema Fulminea VII Hypercar belonging to Team 4.

Soaring closer to the vehicle, he recognizes the driver Quentin Marron with his passengers Caspian Prince and Torin Shepherd.

Driving parallel to them in the right lane, Rolex waves to them with his left middle finger saying, "The Lemnian Deeds Federation welcomes you to your everlasting peace."

Rolex decides to play some more games with Team 4 by first hijacking with the satellite iRadio from low to high volume then having the car unaided switch lanes from the right to left and back.

Quentin keeps telling his passengers "I have no idea what's going on. There is absolutely nothing that I am doing to make this happen."

After 45 minutes of this foolish behavior, Rolex sees ahead of them a cherry red Lamborghini Sián Supercar.

The manager at the Deeds HQ tells him, "The Lamborghini Supercar currently has driver Dallas Worthington with her passengers Wesley Adams and Morris Williams. Be careful as Dallas is a worthy opponent at the wheel."

Rolex forces Team 4's Estrema Fulminea VII Hypercar to accelerate so that they catch up to the cherry red Lamborghini.

Soon all three cars are in line together.

Rolex forces the Estrema Fulminea VII to get into the left lane to pass the Lamborghini.

Predicting the driving scenario, Dallas jets forward forcing the Estrema Fulminea VII to return to the right lane almost colliding with the Bugatti Bolide IV Solar Hypercar.

This unpredictable event irritates Rolex as he is reevaluating his strategy.

The three cars proceed down the highway in order, Rolex decides to check out the Lamborghini's driver.

The Bugatti accelerates past the Estrema Fulminea VII driving parallel to the Lamborghini.

Dallas looks to her left and views the driver of the Bugatti, she smiles at him giving him a full view of both of her middle fingers as a welcome.

As mad as a Hatter can be, Rolex tries to hyperjacker the Lamborghini by using his device.

Approaching commuter traffic in all the lanes, Rolex programs his Helper Device to force the cherry red Lamborghini Sián Supercar soar ahead crashing into every commuter vehicle in front of her.

As he initiates destruction of the cherry red Ferrari, he witnesses a miracle as Dallas calmly drives through all the traffic not even getting a scratch as she is ahead of the pack.

Rolex screams at himself, "There is no SuperPower in Heaven or on Earth that can overrule my Hijacker Helper Device. That woman has got to be the luckiest SOB in the world."

After three hours driving towards Prague, both the Estrema Fulminea VII and the cherry red Ferrari Sián have left the highway heading to an EV recharging station.

Prague, Czechia to Berlin, Germany

Stephen says, "Prague Czechia to Berlin Germany takes 3 hours 49 minutes traveling 211 miles on A13 with an autobilled toll."

Stephen states, "Berlin is the capital and largest city of Germany with an economy based on high-tech firms and the service sector, such as startup companies, research facilities, media corporations, and convention venues."

Roxanne says, "Berlin Fashion week is yearly in January and July focusing on creative young designers."

Stephen reads, "The FA-King notes "Gemäldegalerie is an art museum in Berlin housing masterpieces from Albrecht Dürer, Lucas Cranach, Hans Holbein, Rogier van der Weyden, Jan van Eyck, Raphael, Botticelli, Titian, Caravaggio, Peter Paul Rubens, David Teniers the Younger, Rembrandt, Johannes Vermeer, Thomas Gainsborough, Joshua Reynolds and Antonio Viviani. Notables are the octagonal Rembrandt room and a room that has five different Madonnas by Raphael. In the art collection are two paintings by Vermeer 'The Wine Glass' and 'Woman with a Pearl Necklace.'"

Roxanne says, "The Berline cuisine are Königsberger Klopse that is meatballs, Schnitzel, and Bratwurst with dessert offerings like the Berliner which is a German jelly doughnut with no central hole and Berliner Käsekuchen being a cheesecake made from curd cheese mass with raisins and rum. Berlin has a long brewing tradition with a fondness for Pilsener, a type of pale lager."

Rolex Kronos driving his Bugatti Bolide IV on the highway to Berlin, Germany begins his first half hour in commuter traffic weaving in and out of traffic to bypass all the non-racing vehicles.

After fifteen minutes, he finally finds Deeds' intel on the Kia Stinger EV that states the vehicle belongs to Team 6 whose driver is Tuile Horvath, having her passengers Took Lux and Ember Azer.

Still furious about not being able to control the cherry red Ferrari, Rolex uses his Hijacker Helper Device to cause the Kia Stinger EV to weave in quickly and safely and out between the commuter traffic.

Catching up to his prey, Rolex using his Helping Device forces the Kia Stinger EV in the left lane to accelerate into the right lane between two classic gas guzzling BMWs.

This hyperjacking action causes all three cars to collide and spin off the road onto the shoulder then being flipped into the forest.

The Golden Eagle HQ immediately sends out three EMT vehicles to aid the potentially hurt members of the vehicles as well as a service station tow trailer containing a brand-new Kia Stinger EV two brand new BMW Z17 Roadster EVs to replace the classic gas gobbling relics.

After an hour of driving down the highway towards Berlin, Rolex finally sees a high-speed racing Audi RP51 EV Supercar.

The Deeds' Intel indicates that driving the Audi is Birch Woodward with his passengers Wolf Kessler, Miss Lincoln Storm, and Avalon Pendragon.

As the Bugatti Bolide 4 accelerates, so does his adversary having the distance between them remain the same.

The Bugatti is too far for the Hijacker Helper Device to be effective. The two high performance vehicles remain a steady distance between them.

Rolex increases his speed to maximum staying in the left lane to avoid the slow commuter traffic.

Each mile he travels he gains a quarter mile to his adversary.

On the way to Berlin, the Bugatti Bolide 4 is closing in on the Audi RP51 EV Supercar as he views five miles ahead of his vehicle the Mazda CC-5 Supercar.

Again, looking at his Deeds Intel report the Mazda is being driven by Razor Braun having his passengers Vulus Tomic and Sherlen Mintz.

After another 30 minutes of pursuing these two racing supercars, Rolex is finally within distance to use his Hijacker Helper Device.

First, he tries to get both cars to crash into each other but to no avail as the drivers can keep control of their vehicle.

Before entering Berlin, the hijacker Rolex programs the Mazda CC-5 Supercar in the right lane to make a sharp left turn as he programs the Audi RP51 EV Supercar in the left lane to make a sharp right turn.

Again, the experienced professional drivers are forced by their vehicles to make the turns what they miss hitting each other as both cars veer completely off the highway ending up on the shoulder.

As the Bugatti Bolide 4 accelerates passing the unfortunate sacrifices to his Goddess also known as Myrena Gorgona he arrives in Berlin, Germany.

The Golden Eagle HQ on a secure iBroadcast connection transmits the entire morning's captured footage of all the morning's action showing what Rolex, who is working with the Lemnian Deeds Federation, had done.

At the end of the footage, Rolex states, "Professor Steele, I swear to my Goddess, Myrena Gorgona that your Tesla SUV EV is my final mission."

Professor Steele watches the footage while his nephew Apollo is driving the Tesla SUV EV while his twin brother rests in the back.

Looking at his Apple watch, the Professor notices that it is almost time for their daily teatime stop at the Ritz Carlton.

The Professor gets a secure iBroadcast connection with the Golden Eagle HQ where he states, "This is Professor Steele, are there any Eight Tea Days racers in close vicinity following us?"

The Golden Eagle HQ operator states, "Team 3 in the Ashton Martin Maxi EV Supercar and Team 8's Volvo XTC90 EV Hypercar are right behind you."

The Professor requests, "Can you give me a secure iBroadcast connection between me and the two teams following us?"

Immediately, he hears the drivers of both teams responding, "Hello?"

He states to the two racing teams, "This is Professor Steele communicating on a secure private line. I am asking both teams to help me."

Apollo and Rocky clearly hear the members of both teams respond, "Absolutely."

The Professor continues, "I would like the Ashton Martin Maxi EV Supercar team and the Volvo XTC90 EV Hypercar team as you get close to the front parking lot at the Ritz Carlton to both want the exact same parking space causing a major collision. Then, my Golden Eagle HQ has been instructed to replace your vehicles while we relax at the Ritz Carlton having High Tea. The entire required Tea Stop is on me, gratis."

Berlin Teatime Ceremony

Roxanne on the iBroadcast channel states, "The Ritz-Carlton in Berlin offers its guests an exquisite noble afternoon tea served by certified tea sommeliers that educate visitors to the mysterious world of tea. A five-star recommendation."

Stephen Griswald continues saying, "The Regent Hotel in Berlin offers Afternoon Tea and the Victorian Teatime which is exquisite and authentically British. Each teapot contains tea leaves with milk served on the side accompanied by cucumber wholemeal tramezzini, salmon with tomato tramezzini and egg salad with basil tramezzini served on a tiered silver tray."

He continues saying, "The wait staff serves a plate of fruit tarts and scones with homemade strawberry jam and clotted cream. Another five-star recommendation."

Roxanne adds, "The traditional Chinese Tea House serves forty selected Chinese tea styles in their garden oasis on a lake. The Chinese tea master demonstrates Chinese tea art dating back to the Ming Dynasty. The guests can enjoy tradition Chinese desserts such as almond jelly with fruit salad, Chinese white pears with Goji berries and Chinese dates, soymilk pudding, Tang Yuan that are sweet rice balls, and Chinese Red Bean Paste Buns. A delicious alternative."

The Tesla SUV EV turns off the highway and parks in front of the Ritz Carlton. Quickly, the head valet runs over to greet his guests as his second attendant parks the Tesla SUV EV.

Two minutes later, the two vehicles are racing down the highway belonging to Team 3 and Team 8. The cameras record both vehicles heading for the exact same parking space in front of the Ritz Carlton. The two vehicles collide with each other as their teams are cheering their driver and each vehicle gets their carbon or titanium bodies severely dented. Once the vehicles have stopped, each team exits observing that their vehicle has been wrecked beyond repair.

A public iBroadcast announcement from the Golden Eagle HQ states, "Team 3 and Team 8 has just collided totaling both vehicles. Luckily, none of the team members of either vehicle have been hurt. Two service station vehicle trailers have been dispatched with new racing vehicles. Have a safe day!"

Professor Steele enters the Ritz-Carlton where he is greeted by the hotel director who knows the notable guests, especially those whose HQ calls ahead for reservations.

The director has a private meeting room for the group and instructs the head sommelier about his special guests.

The sommelier arrives at the table stating, "Ritz-Carlton offers forty selected teas from exclusively in The Ritz-Carlton the French gourmet brand 'Mariage Frères' to exquisite varieties as Lotus Blanc, where each tea leaf is placed overnight by hand in a lotus blossom to absorb its aroma. Our exquisite British-style afternoon tea is unmatched anywhere and served with the finest delicacies from the in-house patisserie. The tea ceremony is accompanied by live piano and harp sounds. While the tea is being ordered, can I start the gentlemen and ladies with a glass of exquisite champagne to relax after a stressful morning."

The Professor and his nephews greet each guest from Team 3, the driver Darcy Austen and her teammates Jubilee Perez and Romy Ruiz and from Team 8 the driver Pelton Nordic and his teammates Joloc Michel and Zelda Arwen.

As the assembly sit inside placing their tea orders, the Professor stands up and says, "I would like to thank both teams for creating a realistic accident that'll benefit all of us."

Both team members are puzzled but they all high five each other.

Professor Steele continues, "A little 'Golden Eagle' has told me that there is an agent from the Lemnian Deeds Federation using advanced technology drones and devices to murder my nephews and myself."

All the attendee's gasp and say, "Oh my God."

The Professor continues, "I have instructed the Golden Eagle HQ to deliver to both teams black Tesla SUV EV vehicles that match the vehicle that we are racing in including the same license plate."

Everyone laughs followed by applause.

Professor Steele continues, "Each of your teams has two members with SuperPowers that I have verified with my HQ technology team."

From Team 3 Jubilee Perez and from Team 8 the legendary Zelda Arwen who have the SuperPower ability to fly and to morph looking like my two nephews and myself. The second SuperPower members with invisibility are Romy Ruiz and Joloc Michel.

Since the drivers of each team will not be traveling with their two mentioned SuperPower members and will stay here enjoying the facilities while waiting for their team's replacement vehicle. The SuperPower members mentioned will continue the race in matching vehicles to ours as a dummy target hunted by the Deeds' assassin. During the race. they will maneuver avoiding any encounter but eventually lose the battle pretending to get killed. In actuality, the SuperPower members in each vehicle during the confrontation will become invisible as the other member flies them to safely before the vehicle is destroyed. The Golden Eagle Headquarters has provided the remaining driver at the Ritz Carlton with a replacement for the team's vehicle. In the brand-new matching vehicle, the rested driver will pick up their SuperPower teammates and continue the race."

Pelton Nordic states, "Professor that sounds like an excellent plan that'll greatly help you and your nephews. My question is 'what is the benefit for us?'"

Professor Steele states, "I have informed the Steele Corporation's legal counsel to give every member of both teams two million dollars US each after the race whether I live or die. The money is guaranteed to each member with an additional 10,000 shares of Steele Corporation stock."

Everyone grabs a scone, takes a sip of their tea, and stands up applauding the Professor.

The hotel director privately tells the Professor that the matching Tesla SUV EVs have been delivered and are parked in the rear of the building.

Professor Steele states, "We received a delivery from HQ so the first Team 3's SuperPower members may depart" as they hug Darcy Austen saying, "See you soon."

Darcy responds, "Good luck. I will be picking you up soon."

Team 3's two SuperPower team members exit the restaurant's meeting room having the first morph into Professor Steele and his two nephews with the invisible second team member following.

Fifteen minutes later, Team 8's two Superpower team members shake Pelton's hand as he states, "Bon Voyage see you soon!"

They exit the restaurant with the invisible team member followed by the other looking like the Professor and his two nephews.

Looking out the restaurant's front window, Rocky tells the two remaining drivers, his brother, and the Professor "I just saw the Bugatti Bolide IV Solar Hypercar driving down the highway after the first black Tesla SUV EV.

Apollo says, "Still parked behind the building is the second black Tesla SUV EV awaiting to follow far behind them. I assume that we can finish our tea and pay everyone's bill after they leave."

The Professor has his nephews, and the two drivers order another tea and a plate of sandwiches and scones.

After finishing the tea and snacks, the Professor pays the bill for everyone having the remaining drivers from Team 3 and Team 8 get in their new replacement vehicles and his two nephews join him inside their Tesla SUV EV.

Berlin, Germany to Hamburg, Germany

Stephen says, "Racing from Berlin, Germany to Hamburg, Germany takes 3 hours traveling 180 miles on B2 with an autobilled toll."

Roxanne says, "Speaking of this city, I could eat a couple of hamburgers" as she giggles.

Stephen remarks, "The citizens of Hamburg are known as 'hamburgers' so like Hannibal Lecter you want to be a cannibal?"

Then, he begins to laugh and impersonates mimicking the famous

Lecter voice, "I ate his liver with some fava beans and a nice chianti," as he mimics the chewing sounds.

Roxanne states, "The Fairmont Vier Jahreszeiten Hamburg is the most prestigious hotel in the city and its restaurants are the recipients of many awards such as having a Two Michelin Stars, Gault & Millau, Golden Teacups. The Wohnhalle Lounge serves a seasonal themed British afternoon tea which the 'UK Tea Sommelier iMagazine' writes it is, "Acclaimed throughout Europe." The Hamburg Fairmont serves a dozen types of teas such as Black, Oolong, Green, White, Yellow, and Darjeeling Spring. The tasty sandwiches are 'Roast beef with truffle remoulade,' and 'Salmon with Horseradish."

Stephen states, "Hamburg is known for its countless bridges and canals as it has more bridges inside its city limits than any other city. Hamburg being a seaport on the river Elbe it has fresh seafood markets, its colorful local dialect, and the amazing architecture."

Roxanne says, "Hamburg has two World Heritage Sites that are Speicherstadt, the world's largest warehouse district and Kontorhausviertel, Kontorhaus district with its imposing brick office buildings."

Stephen reports, "According to the Galapagos Island Dolittle family, 'the Hamburg Zoo has lots of happy residents having the animals seem like they are at home in their naturalistic enclosures with an elephant pavilion and a tropical aquarium.'"

Roxanne says, "The Elbphilharmonie or "Elbe Philharmonic Hall is a concert hall on the Grasbrook peninsula of the Elbe River and home of the NDR Elbphilharmonie orchestra. Hamburg State Opera is a leading opera company having its orchestra, the Philharmoniker

Hamburg. Hamburg is the birthplace of Johannes Brahms, who grew up in the city, and the birthplace and residence of the famous waltz composer Oscar Fetrás."

She continues saying, "Hamburg was an important center of rock music starting with The Beatles who lived and played in the city as well as a major center for heavy metal and nuclear punk rock music."

The first Tesla SUV EV with the disguised SuperPower member who has cloned himself into Professor Steele and his two nephews race down the highway towards Hamburg Germany.

The second Tesla SUV EV SuperPower team awaits in the vehicle. They soon watch the Bugatti Bolide 4 fly past them chasing the first assigned SuperPower team.

They wait in the rear of the Ritz-Carlton until the Bugatti is no longer seen down the highway.

Then, the second Tesla SUV EV exits the parking lot twenty minutes later.

When the Professor signals them, they slowly head down the highway seeking to fool the Lemnian Deeds Federation assassin.

The Professor reminds the second black Tesla occupants, "There is no rush so take your time and when the first Tesla has been attacked start to travel at a faster speed in case the assassin is not fooled."

Rolex Kronos is communicating with Myrena Gorgona saying "I have just driven my Bugatti parallel to the Tesla SUV EV and have verified that driving the car is Apollo Steele and next to him in the front passenger seat is Professor Steele."

Myrena asks, "Are you positively, one hundred percent sure that you saw Professor Steele inside the car?"

Rolex states, "As a member of the Lemnian Deeds Federation, I swear that I got an excellent look at both Apollo the driver and sitting in the passenger seat next to him was the Professor."

Myrena now being assured exclaims, "I want the Professor dead. Not injured, not almost dead on life support, not 'I think he died in the explosion' but cease to live. If his nephews die as collateral damage, I can live with that. Let me know when the deed is successfully completed."

Located in the Bugatti's front passenger footwell and on the seat, two RC cars measuring 21 inches by 8 inches are filled with Trinitrotoluene or commonly known as TNT with a hyperjacker accessible detonator.

Each RC car has been custom made to travel at 280 mph and can attach itself to any vehicle's undercarriage.

Driving down Highway E55, the Tesla SUV EV avoids being directly in front of the Bugatti as it takes evasive action.

Unable to get a suitable location and distance to launch two RC cars loaded with explosives, Rolex keeps calm trying to position himself in an ideal location to launch his attack.

As they play cat and mouse and get onto Highway E26 Rolex realizes that he finally has both cars in perfect position, so he has the robot arms open both sides of the Bugatti's windows and lower the RC cars to the highway.

Rolex using the Hijacker Helper Device initiates his attack having each RC car travel at full speed under the Tesla SUV EV inches inside each of the rear wheels.

When the helper device indicates that the cars are directly under the Tesla SUV EV in an ideal location to ensure no survivors, Rolex stops his Bugatti and sets off electronically the detonator.

Watching a mile away, Rolex witnesses the Tesla SUV EV containing the Professor and his two nephews explode being vaporized fulfilling his Deeds' mission.

Rolex Kronos makes a U-turn driving his Bugatti returning to Berlin, Germany. He sings, "I exploded the Steeles, but I did not harm SuperModel, Myrena."

After driving at normal speed for thirty minutes, Rolex looking across the highway stops his car immediately.

Rolex yells at himself, "What the hell is going on? In the name of my Goddess, Myrena Gorgona, I swear that I destroyed the Steele family. Now, I see on the other side of the highway an exact black Tesla SUV EV with "Steele1" on its license plate. That vehicle is an exact duplicate of the one I destroyed."

Quickly, the Bugatti Bolide 4 drives across the grass medium back onto Highway E55 traveling towards the second Tesla SUV EV.

At the same time, Team 3's driver Darcy Austen in the Aston Martin Maxey EV Supercar picks up the rest of her team who as anticipated survived the explosion using their SuperPower abilities.

As the Bugatti catches up to the second Tesla SUV EV, Rolex is having trouble as the driver Rocky Steele is performing amazing maneuvers making it difficult to get an exact launching position.

Rolex drives his Bugatti parallel to the Tesla SUV EV and again looks to verify that Rocky Steele is driving the vehicle and sitting in the passenger seat next to him is definitely Professor Steele.

Rolex continues looking to be perfectly sure of his target as he takes out his iCommunicator and takes a digital photograph.

The Bugatti gets behind Tesla SUV EV.

As both cars are now approaching Highway E26, Rolex Kronos realizes that he must take a chance on releasing the two RC cars that were extras be used if needed, located on the back seat.

Rolex taking a risky chance initiates the robot arm to grab the two backseat explosive filled RC cars.

Then, he says a prayer to his Goddess Myrena and launches the extra two RC cars having them drive at maximum speed under the second Tesla SUV EV.

As Hijacker Helper Device indicates that the two RC cars are under the Tesla but not in the ideal position, he again stops his Bugatti and prepares to set off electronically the detonator.

Watching now two miles away, Rolex witnesses and records on his iCommunicator that the Tesla SUV EV containing the Professor and his two nephews.

Then, Rolex says, "Say 'hello' to my little RC friends, Steeles!" as he sets off electronically the detonator watching the black Tesla SUV explode being vaporized fulfilling his Deeds' mission.

Rolex Kronos who is overjoyed makes another U-turn in his Bugatti driving back to Berlin,

Driving on the other side of Highway E26 is Team 8's driver Pelham Nordic who is ready to pick up his SuperPower teammates who as anticipated survived the explosion using their SuperPower abilities.

Being ignored by hiding as one of the commuters driving at the posted speed, the real Professor and his two nephews in the Tesla SUV

EV drive past the Bugatti Bolide 4 that they see on the opposite side of the highway.

In the Bugatti, Rolex Kronos communicates with the head of the Lemnian Deeds Federation, Myrena Gorgona saying "Ding, Dong the Wicked Witch is dead!"

Rolex transmits to her the digital recording that he took earlier of Rocky driving with the Professor next to him and then the second recording using the telescopic lens option for viewing a close-up of the distant explosion showing black Tesla SUV disintegrating.

On the iBroadcast iChannel, Myrena Gorgona is seen saying "We interrupt your iBroadcast of the Eight Tea Days Around Europe racing to tell everyone that Professor Steele and his two nephews Apollo and Rocky had a fatal accident on Highway E26 traveling to Hamburg Germany.

Rolex's footage of the explosion is shown to the iBroadcast worldwide audience with the caption 'This is real. Do not try this at home or anywhere.'

Myrena looking solemn states, "It is my duty as a friend to take over all duties of the Steele Corporation and to merge the Golden Eagle Organization with the Lemnian Deeds Federation. Thank you and have a good night."

The Professor communicates through a secure iCommunication network with the Golden Eagle HQ saying, "This is Professor Steele calling from the great beyond. Mark Twain said it best saying, 'The reports of my demise have been greatly exaggerated.'"

Heard in the background are his nephews who are laughing hysterically.

The Golden Eagle HQ uses biometric and voice analyzers that verify that the communicator is truly the Professor.

The Professor continues saying, "As usual the backstabbing bi-otch Myrena Gorgona has preempted our demise and trying to control our Corporation and Organization. We will let Myrena think that we are dead and that she runs the company. Tell this to the Steele Corporation board of directors to pretend to be attentive in dealing with her but do not do anything that she wants as all decisions and mandates must come through me or my nephews."

The deceased Steeles drive to Hamburg's Barley & Malt Deutsch to get a Schorrschbtsu German limited edition BrewDog that cost $300 US per bottle.

Inside the pub, the Professors tells the proprietor "Here is my black card, I want to buy everybody in this establishment a bottle of Schorrschbtsu German limited edition BrewDog."

The proprietor asks, "Is this a special occasion?"

Apollo and Rocky Steele yell out, "Wir starben?"

Gisela tells her English lover "Our rich beer benefactor says, 'We're celebrating our death!'"

As the entire pub cheers on the Professor and his nephews.

Hamburg, Germany to Copenhagen, Denmark

Stephen says, "Racing from Hamburg, Germany to Copenhagen, Denmark takes 3 hours, 19 minutes traveling 206 miles on highways A24 to E47 with an autobilled toll."

Roxanne states, "Copenhagen is the capital and most populous city of Denmark being one of the major financial centers of Northern

Europe with the Copenhagen Stock Exchange and rapid developments in information technology, pharmaceuticals and clean technology."

Stephen says, "The Royal Danish Ballet is also a world famous classical ballet company based in Copenhagen. The Tivoli Concert Hall is a 1,660-capacity concert hall at Tivoli Gardens in Copenhagen. The Copenhagen Opera House is where the Royal Danish Opera has singers who can sing in German, French, English, Italian, Russian and Czech."

Roxanne says, "Copenhagen is amongst the top ten fashion weeks scheduled in January and August."

Stephen says, "Denmark has an international motorcycle speedway racing with its Danish Super League and has won several world championships."

Roxanne reports, "Copenhagen has 33 Michelin-starred restaurants with a total of 52 stars with 3 four stars, 10 two star, and 20 one star. The cuisine in Denmark traditional Danish food is øllebrød, a porridge made of rye bread and beer, smørrebrød, an open-faced sandwich with various toppings such as pickled herring, meatballs, fried fish, or beef tartare, fiskefrikadeller or fish cakes, and cold-smoked salmon on rye bread."

Stephen reading his notes says, "'The FA-King reports that 'the National Gallery of Denmark has in its European Art gallery are the masters Titian, Rubens, and Rembrandt. In its French Art gallery are the works of Matisse, Picasso, Derain, and Braque.'"

Astrid Christiansen from Norway pulls behind a few of the racers in her Koenigsegg Jesko Absolut 3 Hypercar EV.

As she is pulling up to the ebony Chevy Camaro 69 EV driven by Elijah Baggins with passengers Bayberry Fields and backseat passenger, Raven Poe.

As Astrid morphs into an Arnold Terminator clone pulling inches away from the Camaro's driver's window. Wearing the T1 Gargoyles ANSI Classics sunglasses, the Arnold clone indicates to Elijah to lower his window.

He obeys and looks at the Terminator look alike.

The Terminator clone states, "If you want to live tell me where the Professor and his nephews are."

The two female passengers point forward as Elijah states, "I will be back, far back behind you," as he slows the vehicle down.

Astrid in her T1 mode is behind Team 17 Dodge Challenger 55 EV. As the T1 replicant is parallel to the driver Leonard Gooddaughter with passengers Alberto Crowe, Paul Silverberg, and Mistletoe Kringle, she yells out, "Pull over and park your car or I will be forced to terminate you!"

Leonard replies, "We are too fast and furious to listen to your foolishness" as he floors the accelerator passing the next car with ease.

The T1 imposter says, "I do not feel pity, remorse, or fear. I will absolutely not be stopped until Team 17 has been terminated."

As the Koenigsegg Jesko Absolut 3 Hypercar EV approaches Team 15's Nissan Flash EV driven by Tiger de Forrest with his passengers Ash Arturo and Winter Sazon, T1 Astrid says, "Slow your car down or I will vaporize it."

Tiger growls, "You've got balls man I've been told."

The T1 in the Jesko lifts the Barrett RP76 semi-automatic, anti-material rifle that can easily puncture a tank or armored car.

Then, T1 says, "I wouldn't follow me, if you want to live."

The Jesko speeds up to 250 mph yelling out "It's Judgment Day for the Dodge Challenger" the Jesko becomes parallel to the Challenger having the Barrett RP76 pointing at the right-side front passenger window. The driver Leonard and all his passengers in the Challenger all point their S&W .657 Magnums at the Terminator.

Alberto in the passenger's front seat yells out "It doesn't matter if we shoot you by an inch or a mile terminating you is recorded in history as 'mission completed.'"

Responding, the T1 look alike says, "I will absolutely not be stopped, ever, until you are dead."

As the two vehicles begin shooting at each other, the bulletproof Koenigsegg Jesko Absolut 3 Hypercar EV stops the Challenger's incoming projectiles while the Barrett RP76's armor piercing projectiles flatten both the front and rear driver's side tires having the Challenger's driver side tires rapidly deflate.

Leonard Goodman being an experienced racer takes a deep breath as he keeps the wheel straight and gently presses the accelerator to regain control of the vehicle then navigating straight, he removes his foot to slow the car down.

Looking back at the parked Dodge Challenger, the T1 replicant yells out, "Hasta La Vista, baby!"

Driving at high speed, the Koenigsegg Jesko is finally behind the bulletproof Tesla driven by Rocky Steele.

The Professor notices that the Koenigsegg Jesko Absolut 3 Hypercar EV is quickly approaching them after seeing the second place Dodge Challenger has been replaced.

The Professor asks Apollo in the backseat, "Using your Internet connected Mac, please access our special FedUps' flying drones to slow down the second position Jesko vehicle."

Flying towards the Koenigsegg Jesko Absolut 3's rear passenger side and magnetically connecting to the battery block of the electric vehicle. Unaware of the droid's appearance and mission, the Jesko Absolut 3's T1 driver yells at Rocky driving the Tesla SUV EV, "Based on your pupil dilation, skin temperature, and motor functions, I calculate a 95% probability that you will not attack me."

Just then, he speeds the Tesla SUV EV to 250 mph as the Professor nods to Apollo to start the droid's attack.

Looking at the rear view on the vehicle's monitor, the Professor and Rocky watch as the Koenigsegg Jesko's battery block explodes separating the front and rear of the vehicle.

Apollo sitting in the rear of the Tesla SUV EV is seen waving to the highway's shoulder at the stranded Koenigsegg Jesko Absolut 3 Hypercar EV.

Rocky slowing down quotes T3 by stating, "Tell SkyNet that 'The day the human race was nearly made extinct by weapons they'd built to protect themselves. I should have known our destiny was never to stop Judgment Day. It was merely to live after it.'"

Myrena expedites a Koenigsegg Gemera Supercar IV EV to Astrid's last GPS location with a Desert Eagle X Arrow Handgun that can penetrate ballistic armor and protective shields intended to stop or deflect conventional bullets.

Zooming past her parked Koenigsegg Gemera Supercar IV EV is Team 44's McLaren Speedtail Hermes 3 EV with driver Arnold Winkler and his passengers Ronnie Most and Heidi Klumaker.

Astrid, now looking like an Artemisia clone from the 300 sequel, 'Rise of an Empire,' drives the Gemera Supercar IV EV feeling as though she is named after the Goddess of the Hunt, Artemis who uses her bow and arrow in battle.

Myrena calls Astrid asking, "How do you like your brand new Koenigsegg Gemera Supercar IV EV?"

Astrid replies, "I do have a liking of the Koenigsegg Mega-sportscars, so we'll see how the Gemera Supercar IV EV holds up."

Myrena asks, "When you get up to full speed onto the highway, what are your plans?"

Astrid looking like Artemisia replies, "I will attack the Eight Tea Days racers with my entire arsenal!"

The leader of the Lemnian Deeds Federation says, "I trust that the supplied Desert Eagle X Arrow handgun with its armor piercing projectiles will suffice in your battle endeavors."

The Artemisia clone paraphrases 'The Rise of an Empire' film saying, "Today, we will dance across the backs of the dead Eight Tea Days racers."

Myrena ends the call by saying, "Remember my goddaughter, take the gun and leave the cannoli.' Good luck my Persian Warrior Goddess and former Greek Queen," as she disconnects.

As the Koenigsegg Gemera enters the highway, Team 10's Porsche Taycan Sport Turismo 9 driven by sexy blonde Pamela Baywatch passes her with its passengers Holly Woodland and Parker Peters waving 'bye' at her.

Holding her Desert Eagle X Arrow Handgun in her right hand pointed at her passenger side open window; she speeds up catching the Porsche Taycan Sport Turismo 9.

Holly Woodland sees the pointed handgun pointing in her direction as she screams scaring her driver, Pamela. The Porsche Taycan swerves onto the highway's shoulder as the Koenigsegg Gemera flies past them.

Pamela Baywatch yells at her backseat passenger Holly screaming, "Look, you're on the racing team, and, uh. I don't want anyone on the team screaming like this!"

The Koenigsegg Gemera catches up to Team 44's McLaren Speedtail Hermes 3 EV.

Heidi Klumaker gets her entire racing team to show the Koenigsegg their 'two handed flipping the bird.'

In reply, the Artemisia clone disintegrates their back driver's side tire using her armor piercing projectiles from her Desert Eagle X Arrow Handgun.

Pamela is already driving on the highway's shoulder, so she has no difficulty controlling the newly flat tire of their McLaren Speedtail Hermes 3 EV.

Team 44 shouts, "Get 'yam filthy animal' out of our sight. Darn you, Koenigsegg!"

The Golden Eagle judges viewing from the dashboard camera contacts the local service station to quickly replace the blown tire.

The Koenigsegg Megasportscar Gemera passes Team 45, the Evangelista family in their Pontiac Firebird Trans Am Mark 6 Hypercar

Then, the Koenigsegg Megasportscar Gemera jets past Team 58. Their legendary Formula 1 racecar driver Paul Georges switches seats with Farrah Monroe who now drives the team's Alfa Romeo Giulia Quadrifoglio IV Supercar EV.

The Megasportscar Gemera approaches the lucky Team 13 with its driver Pandora Boxlighter driving the team's Subaru Hypercar 2 EV. Her passengers are Echo Winwood and Joddos Canterbury.

The Artemesia clone disguises Astrid who has two of her landmine flying droids specifically designed to disable any vehicle while it hides awaiting to attack under her front bumper.

As the Gemera is parallel to the left side of the Subaru Hypercar 2, the two droids position themselves flying under the Subaru Hypercar's rear suspension.

Then, the clone female warrior waves her Desert Eagle X Arrow handgun shouting, "Race your arses off, for tonight we dine in Hades!"

The Gemera speeds off at top speed as the two explosive droids are triggered destroying the rear suspension.

As the Golden Eagle Organization HQ is alerted to Team 13's emergency where luckily none of the team was hurt.

Echo Winwood says, "I consider it a great day being able to walk away from such an incident."

Pandora explains, "You can easily replace a Hypercar but it's harder to replace a teammate."

Joddos Canterbury remarks, "Reflecting on the Subaru corporate motto, I have an 'uncommon confidence in motion,'" as an auto transport trailer delivers to Team 13 a brand-new Subaru Hypercar 2 EV.

The seaworthy female captain sitting in her Koenigsegg Gemera views two miles ahead is the black custom-made Tesla SUV.

As the disguised Astrid plans her strategy of placing eight lethal landmine drones underneath the Tesla to vaporize the vehicle and its inhabitants.

She begins singing, "Stop the Professor! Stop the Professor! Stop the Professor! Forever and ever."

As she is now behind the Tesla SUV, she notices that Rocky Steele is driving with his brother Apollo sitting in the backseat playing Gran Turismo on his portable PlayStation XXV.

Like a hunter stalking its prey, the Gemera maintains its distance behind the Tesla.

Unbeknownst to any of the racing teams and especially the Gemera, Professor Steele has been in constant communication with the Golden Eagle HQ. He is fully aware of what happened to Team 44's McLaren Speedtail Hermes 3 EV.

The Professor has surmised based on the type of vehicle and the SuperPower ability of his driver that the race is being infiltrated by Myrena Gorgona's best friend, Astrid Christensen.

Noticing that more of the Eight Tea Days racers have appeared in her rearview mirror around five miles behind her, she launches the eight deadly landmine droids to proceed to fly under the Tesla SUV.

Apollo Steele feels a disturbance in his Force placing the PlayStation racing game on pause.

He uses his SuperPower of telekinesis to veer off the undercarriage droids placing them under the high-speed passing Koenigsegg Gemera Supercar IV EV.

The Professor tells Rocky Steele to slow down giving the Koenigsegg Gemera enough room to feel safe regarding the explosion she believes will occur.

As the distance between the two cars exceeds five miles, Astrid communicates with the Lemnian Deeds Federation, "Tell Myrena that I am in the process of 'Stopping the Professor. Forever and ever!"

Astrid initiates her transmission for each of the eight land mines to fulfill their purpose of existence.

The Steeles inside the Tesla SUV well over five miles away hears a roaring booming sound ahead of them from a pulse from the eight landmines that is traveling faster than the speed of sound.

As the Koenigsegg Gemera is torn apart into tiny pieces scattered all over the highway, Astrid is thrown over fifty feet landing on the huge area of thorn bushes in the woods.

Luckily, she survived with some vertigo, tinnitus, and hyperacusis. The thorns still embedded in her buttocks and legs have caused red bumps, patches, swelling, pain, and itching.

While she awaits the delivery from the Lemnian Deeds Federation, she crawls towards the highway's shoulder removing each thorn as she recuperates.

Driving past the wreckage of the Gemera, Rocky Steele yells out the window, "Stupid is as stupid does. Run Astrid run," quoting the old classic 'Forrest Gump.'

The Steeles grab a beverage and a piece of cake each in celebration.

Copenhagen, Denmark to Gothenburg, Sweden

Stephen says, "Leaving Copenhagen Denmark to Gothenburg, Sweden takes 3 hours, 10 minutes traveling on 194 miles on E20 with an autobilled toll."

Within 45 minutes, a brand new Koenigsegg Agera Octo Supercar is delivered to the GPS position of the wreckage. Astrid notices in the front passenger seat a .44 Remington Magnum VI like the one used in the Dirty Harry films.

Getting her new Koenigsegg Agera Octo up to its top speed, she morphs into an Inspector Harry Callahan looking replicant.

The Agera Octo catches up to the pack's slowpokes in their racing vehicles.

The first vehicle that Dirty Harry encounters is Team 5's Ford Mustang 3 EV Special Iditarod Edition driven by female race car phenon Elowen Redington. Ms. Redington is the fifth generation Iditarod Championship racer. Her teammates are Laser Cannon and Callon Ferrel.

As the Dirty Harry clone pulls out his .44 Remington Magnum, he notices in the front passenger seat the team's Alaskan Husky which was helicoptered back to the team. He automatically lowers the gun, placing it on his front passenger seat.

As Team 5 is seen singing the Iditarod 'Soon Hee Newbold' song, the Koenigsegg Agera flies past them yelling out his window, "Mush! North To The Future!"

In response, the entire Iditarod team yells back, "Qanuippit?" which phonetically sounds like "Kha-noo-ee-peet."

Astrid, using her multilingual translator, a device that Myrena Gorgona stole from the Professor's laboratory is told that they asked, "How are you?" in Inuktitut a Native Alaskan language.

The translator tells Astrid to reply "Naammaltsaimt" meaning "Have a good journey" as she dashes past them with her pedal to the metal.

Approaching swiftly to the next car owned by Team 14, the cyan Mazda CC- 5X EV. The driver Vulus Tomic sees the approaching Agera Octo informs his teammates, Razer Braun, Shetlen Mintz, and Wingalyn Bluejay.

Vulus tries to intercept the Agera Octo sliding into the left lane in front of his adversary.

The Dirty Harry clone at high-speed shifts into the right lane attempting to pass the Mazda.

Not to be left in the dust, Vulus preempts his opponent, by gliding in front of him almost causing a collision then without thinking immediately darts back to the left lane anticipating the same of his opponent.

The Koenigsegg driver removes his fully loaded Remington and yells out, "You've got to ask yourself one question: 'Do I feel lucky?' Well, do you, punk?"

Then, two high-speed projectiles tear apart the rear driver's side tire causing the Mazda CC-5X EV to slowly coast the vehicle onto the highway's right shoulder where it stops.

As the Golden Eagle HQ is already sending a tow truck with the replacement Pilot Sport EV tire to their GPS location.

Looking back, the Dirty Harry replicant chuckles saying, "I guess they weren't that lucky!"

Three miles ahead of the Koenigsegg Agera Octo travels Team 2's Audi RP51 EV Supercar. The driver Wolf Kessler is singing the latest Lovegood Records triple platinum song with his passengers Birch Woodward, Ms. Lincoln Storm, Avalon Pendragon who has the SuperPower ability of invisibility and to create mirages.

Quickly narrowing the distance between them, Astrid with her Inspector' Callahan's hand holding the 44 caliber Remington Magnum outside her supercar's window as she drives faster towards the Audi.

Avalon seeing the popular shooter handgun aimed at their vehicle and uses his SuperPower to create a diversion.

Astrid looks out of her windshield seeing an eighteen-wheeler fully loaded with concrete blocks headed directly towards her.

She veers off the road onto the shoulder as the illusion has vanished. Quickly, she gets back onto the highway accelerating to its high speed.

Looking two miles ahead of her is Team 2's Audi RP51 EV Supercar.

The Koenigsegg Agera Octo is thrusted full speed catching up to her adversary.

Avalon again seeing the Agera Octo swiftly heading towards them uses his SuperPowers making the Audi invisible.

As Callahan, she states, "Go ahead, make my day" having the Audi RP51 EV Supercar disappear.

Astrid in disbelief says, "Is that Audi a Transformer like Mirage?"

Unknowingly, the Agera Octo is down the highway at high speed next to the invisible Audi. Together, they travel trying to locate the next racing vehicle while passing normal traffic of cars and trucks.

Chapter 27

Thursday 'Eight Tea Days Around Europe' Race

"Let's begin the day examining our racing fans frontrunner, the Steeles. This triple threat is sponsoring the race, is in the race and currently is winning the race, Welcome to the Golden Eagle HQ iBroadcast of the Eight Tea Days Around Europe Race. You're joining Roxanne McLaren on Day Six with live racing iNews."

Stephen joins stating, "British Formula One World Champion, Damon Hill jokingly stated 'Winning is everything. The only ones who remember you when you come in second are your wife and your dog.'"

Gothenburg, Sweden to Oslo, Norway

Stephen says, "Racing from Copenhagen Denmark to Oslo Norway takes 3 hours, 27 minutes traveling 182 miles on E6 with an autobilled toll."

Roxanne states, "Oslo is the capital and most populous city of Norway and the economic and governmental center where Norwegian trade, Oslo Stock Exchange, banking industry is located. It is the center for maritime industries and maritime trade in Europe where the world's largest shipping companies, shipbrokers, and maritime insurance brokers reside."

Stephen says, "Oslo has a nickname being known as 'The Tiger City' due to Norwegian poet Bjørnstjerne Bjørnson whose poem 'Sidste Sang' from 1870 describes a conflict between a horse and a tiger. The dangerous city is the tiger while the calm countryside is the horse."

Roxanne says, "There are places on my sightseeing list in Oslo like the Oslo Opera House being the home of the Norwegian National Opera and Ballet."

Stephen says, "A place that I would like to visit is the Kon-Tiki Museum that houses vessels and maps from the Kon-Tiki expedition, originally built to house the Kon-Tiki, a raft of balsa wood of pre-Columbian model that Norwegian adventurer Thor Heyerdahl used to sail from Peru to Polynesia in 1947."

Roxanne states, "The Vigeland Park is the world's largest sculpture park with more than 200 sculptures in bronze, granite and wrought iron."

Stephen says, "For the winter enthusiasts, the Holmenkollbakken is a large ski jumping hill located in Oslo, Norway having a hill size of HS134, a construction point of K-120, and a capacity for 70,000 spectators."

Roxanne reading her email, says, "The FA-King notes that 'Norwegian artist Edvard Munch, one of Expressionism's early pioneers has his work in the Munch Museum housing more than 1,100 of his paintings. The National Museum in Oslo besides having Munch paintings like 'The Scream,' has a few works of Claude Monet.'"

Marseille, France's Ruby Bordeaux Chardonnay who has the SuperPower ability to transform objects from one form to another and to become invisible has joined the Deed assassins.

Ruby Bordeaux Chardonnay waits for the Tesla SUV EV with her long-range sniper bolt-action rifle.

As Apollo is driving, he looks behind him seeing the Professor enjoying a Bach concerto on his headset.

In the passenger seat, his brother Rocky is sound asleep.

Ruby takes a shot at the Tesla, but a bus gets in the way blocking her ricocheting the projectile.

As he enjoys the peaceful drive, he hears an explosion from across the highway. He slams on the brakes. The Professor removes his headset looking startled at his nephew.

Apollo blushes and comments, "I guess someone had a blowout. My crazy thought was that somebody was shooting at me."

The vehicle returns to cruising at high speed.

The Professor states, "I once had a realistic dream Where I had died and was in a cloudy bright area. I was standing in a tremendously lengthy line awaiting my turn to check in. As I looked around, I noticed across the way was one of my childhood idols, Nicholas Tesla. I stepped out of line and walked over to him. We chat it for what seemed like an eternity."

Then, wiping a tear from his eye, he continued, "Then, he told me he had a previous engagement with Steve Jobs and disappeared. I was told by other afterlife residents that Jobs was the creator of the Heavenly Information Highway called HIH. I returned to the processing line were standing in front of me was the great, great, great, great, great grandson of Rocky."

Rocky, hearing his name jostles in his seat still dreaming.

Apollo returns a Cheshire Cat smile with a chuckle from the Professor.

The Professor continues, "It was then I heard a voice tell me 'Like the Phoenix Eagle, I return you to your earthly body.' In a flash, I was lying in my bed wide awake and alive."

Apollo replies, "I pray that all of the Steele heirs are blessed with the same prophecy."

Rocky now awake, states to the Professor and his brother, "The members of the Golden Eagle are declaring 'Let's get out of DODGE.'"

Ruby Bordeaux Chardonnay gets into her orange, Papaya Spark McLaren R25 Hypercar EV and accelerates onto the highway to cause havoc to the Eight Tea Days racers.

Team 38's mustard yellow Draco Motors Dragon EV Supercar has a carbon fiber structure with Gullwing doors for its five passengers having it driver, Kilel Kent with front seat passenger, Diana Empress and back seat passenger, Arthur Orin.

The Dragon flies with a top speed of 300 mph able to accelerate to 60 mph in 1.35 seconds.

Chasing the Dragon is Ruby inside her orange, Papaya Spark McLaren R25 Hypercar EV where she reaches into her Grey Zumi Medium Top Handle Bag in Crocodile given to her by Myrena. She finds a package of sixteen individually wrapped Bazooka bubble gum pieces.

Ruby maintains the same speed keeping close behind the Dragon as she begins chewing the bubble gum. She has named the Draco Dragon Hypercar "Kilgharrah after Merlin's dragon."

She makes a bubble filling it with her exhaled breath.

She opens the driver's side window releasing the bubble as it floats upward becoming a hot air balloon with a mounted bazooka that is a man-portable recoilless, anti-tank rocket launcher weapon.

She repeats chewing another piece of Bazooka bubble gum and releasing the second blown piece turning that one also into a hot air balloon having a bazooka weapon inside its gondola or wicker basket.

Looking at her dashboard monitor on the right of her steering yoke; she fires upon Team 38's mustard yellow Draco Motors Dragon EV Supercar.

Kilel Kent acts lightning fast anticipating each projectile's aimed location. His teammates tell him that he a truly a super driver.

Ruby keeps yelling at her modified bubble gum weapon seeking to hit their intended target.

The athletic Diana Empress in the front keeps telling Kilel the direction that the bazooka is aimed at.

Sitting in the spacious back seat is passenger, Arthur Orin who states, "Okay, so we're doing things a little out of order. Quiet, Shhh! It happens."

Unaware of the conflict, Team 46's Cadillac Le Mans TK Edition Hypercar passes the Papaya Spark McLaren. The bazooka hot air balloons readjust their target hitting the Cadillac Hypercar.

The blast overpressure is caused by a shock wave that is heard as a destructive sonic boom that occurs when air travels faster than the speed of sound.

The resulting sound is equivalent to a very loud thunderclap as the sound forces the properties of the Cadillac's tempered glass to explode outward.

The Golden Eagle HQ expedites a two trailer with a brand new Cadillac Le Mans TK Edition Hypercar to Team 46's GPS location.

Oslo, Norway to Karlstad, Sweden

Roxanne states, "Oslo Norway to Karlstad, Sweden takes 3 hours traveling 136 miles on highway E18 with an autobilled toll.".

Roxanne continues stating, "Karlstad is built on the river delta where Sweden's longest river, Klarälven, runs into Sweden's largest lake, Vänern."

Stephen remarks, "Ice hockey is a highly popular spectator sport in Karlstad. The Tingvalla IP is a stadium in Karlstad, Sweden that is the home of the soccer team Carlstad United and the American football team Carlstad Crusaders. Several soccer clubs exist of the highest-ranking teams for men and for women with several Karlstad men on the Swedish national team."

Roxanne says, "Some noteworthy areas in Karlstad are the Stadsträdgården that is an English-style park having a circuit of gravel paths lined with over 800 different species of plants, trees and shrubs. Östra Bron or the 'East Bridge' crosses the Klarälven or 'the clear river' being Sweden's longest stone-built bridge."

Taking the day off from work as a civil engineer for construction in Bergen, Norway is Maya Christiansen, Astrid's younger cousin. She has the SuperPower abilities to fly and emit light from her eyes.

When Maya blinks three times a beam of coherent light is released from her optic nerve which transmits visual data to the brain and for her can send stimulated emissions of photons from excited electrons in atoms from her eyes' optical material forming a long range, thin laser beam.

She has used this SuperPower alone at work to weld metal and cutting structural steel for building bridges, tunnels, as well as residential and commercial buildings.

Maya helping the Lemnian Deeds Federation as the assassin drives a lavender Koenigsegg CCGT53 EV Hypercar which can accelerate in 1.4 seconds to 60 mph having a top speed of 285 mph.

Maya cruising down highway E18 sees using her telescopic ability eyes five miles ahead a maximum orange Aston Martin Valkyrie 5 EV. She reports the vehicle to the Deeds surveillance team that is monitoring the race.

Quickly, the surveillance team operator responds "The spotted maximum orange Aston Martin Valkyrie 5 EV belongs to Team 28 with its current driver Quatro James and passengers Tris Woods and Miles Hughes. Our intel states that Quatro James is an ex-Mossad while his teammate Tris Woods was a legendary Mossad assassin with thirty-six unconfirmed kills.

Maya has caught up with her target and focuses on the left rear tire to create a laser cut puncture in it.

Tris using her keen military skills smells burning rubber telling Quatro "nakit film motqumkat."

James swerves into the right lane passing two commuter vehicles saying, "Evasive action taken. Thanks. Are we safe now?"

Tris replies, "Yes, for now. Watch the lavender Koenigsegg!"

Quattro says, "Prepare," having the two back seat passengers open their windows.

Then, Miles prepares to defend holding his Belgian made FN MAG-4 machine gun as Tris holds in her left shooting hand her Israeli Mossad .22 LRS-3 being the third generation for Israeli Intelligence Agents 'Long Range Special' handgun.

On the rear-view monitor, Quatro views passing commuters as the marked lavender Koenigsegg CCGT53 EV Hypercar is trying to get behind them.

Quietly, Quatro says, "oands!" meaning "get ready!"

Maya now closely following the Valkyrie EV concentrates on puncturing the rear tire using her laser eyes SuperPower, but the two ex-Mossad back seat soldiers begin shooting at her Koenigsegg CCGT53 EV Hypercar. As the lavender Koenigsegg Hypercar is mutilated by the FN MAG-4 machine gun destroying the windshield and making the hood into Swiss cheese as the Israeli Mossad .22 LRS-3 deflates both front tires causing Maya to maneuver onto the highway's right shoulder.

Tris yells out her window at the lavender Koenigsegg's driver, "You are attacking the Valkyrie a 'female figure who guides souls of the dead to the god Odin's hall Valhalla' and tell Odin 'hello from Team 28.'"

Quattro remarks, "You are like your idol from the film Divergent who chooses the Dauntless faction over family."

The Lemnian Deeds' team dispatches a tow trailer that delivers a brand, new Liquid Petroleum (gold) Koenigsegg CCGT53 EV Hypercar.

Karlstad, Sweden to Stockholm, Sweden

Stephen states, "Karlstad, Sweden to Stockholm Sweden takes 3 hours, 37 minutes traveling 189 miles on E20 with an autobilled toll."

Roxanne states, "Stockholm is the capital and largest city of Sweden stretching across fourteen islands where Lake Mälaren flows into the Baltic Sea."

Stephen says, "The FA-King notes 'the Nationalmuseum houses the largest collection of art in the country having works by artists such as Rembrandt, Rubens, Goya, Renoir, Degas and Gauguin.'"

Roxanne says, "Royal Swedish Opera is an opera and ballet company based in Stockholm, Sweden. Call me your dancing queen! My favorite band of all time, ABBA has a museum which is a Swedish interactive exhibition. 'Momma Mia, here we go again!' Distinguished among Stockholm's many theaters are the Royal Dramatic theater and the Royal Swedish Opera."

Stephen states, "On the anniversary of Nobel's death on December 10th in the Stockholm City Hall the Nobel Prize award ceremony takes place in Physics, Chemistry, Physiology or Medicine, Literature, and the prize in economic sciences."

Roxanne remarks, "The Golden Eagle HQ reports 'Professor Steele the CEO of the Steele Corporation holds the annual Golden Eagle award ceremony there on May 17 his birthday.'"

Stephen continues saying "Annually, the Stockholm Marathon occurs also known as the Adidas Stockholm Marathon for sponsorship reasons."

Roxanne says, "Stockholm has 5 three-star Michelin star, 12 two Michelin star, and 24 one Michelin star restaurants. Swedish cuisine can be meat-filled potato dumplings, smoked sausage stroganoff, Smörgåstårta, a fancy savory sandwich cake with prawns, flygande Jakob, a curry casserole with bacon and chicken, potato dumplings with minced seasoned pork belly. Swedish desserts consist of yeast buns, cookies, biscuits, and cakes and often eaten with coffee."

Maya Christiansen is now driving her replacement Liquid Petroleum Koenigsegg CCGT53 EV Hypercar. She drives down highway E20. She receives intel that ahead of her is racing Team 47.

The next message seen after Maya presses 'page up' states, "Team 47 has its driver Brian 'Bohemian' Cruise at the yoke of their midnight black with gold trim Pagani Zonda Trident EV. His passengers are Doug Brown and Ms. Jordan Shue.

Doug tells Brian and Jordan "Here's a non-alcoholic cocktail. My special virgin pina colada recipe as he sings 'If you like piña coladas and getting caught in the rain'"

Maya looks ahead on the highway puddles thinking that using her laser emitting eyes, she can reflect the waves bouncing off the water surface.

Then, she can cause severe damage to the undercarriage of the Pagani Zonda.

Brian 'Bohemian' Cruise will not allow another vehicle to pass his team, so he drives covering the left lane then blocking anything passing by shifting to the right lane.

Maya accelerates getting close behind Team 47's Pagani Zonda.

As Brian shifts lanes cutting Maya's vehicle off, her golden Koenigsegg CCGT53 EV Hypercar nicks the Zonda's rear bumper.

Jordan yells at 'Bohemian' saying, "Brian, you're wandering all over the highway!"

Brian replies, "Yeah, well that driver just slammed into our vehicle."

Doug states, "No, no, she didn't slam you, she didn't bump you, she didn't nudge you... she 'rubbed' you. And rubbing, son, is racing. So, listen to the day's thunder."

Maya decides to use her laser eyes on the Pagani Zonda Trident EV regardless of where on her target she hits causing some damage. Her aim is straight ahead connecting with the rear window.

Jordan Shue feels a warm sensation on the back of her head so turning around she notices a beam of light coming through the rear windshield. She grabs from her Christian Louboutin Paloma Couronnes Seville Calfskin Leather Tote bag, a ten times compact hand mirror. She lines up her ten times mirror with the beam of light returning it to its sender,

Maya, not consciencely watching as she is more concerned with her driving in her lane, gets blinded by the light that is brightly shining into her eyes.

Maya loses control of her Liquid Petroleum Koenigsegg CCGT53 EV Hypercar winding up on the right shoulder of the highway. As the Koenigsegg CCGT53 is stopped, Maya frantically rubs her eyes as tears run down her face.

Afternoon Tea in Stockholm, Sweden

Stephen says, "Every day, tea drinkers take a popular relaxing British-style tea break in the Swedish capital. In Stockholm, there are numerous teahouses, hotels with afternoon tea, patisseries, and restaurants serving delicious tea buffets with sandwiches, scones, pastries, and other afternoon tea treats.'"

Roxanne states, "The Golden Eagle daily bulletin states 'Stockholm Gourmet Tea chain serves a variety of teas such as the classic cream tea, lemongrass and orange tea, Ceylon tea with scones with lemon curd, jam or clotted cream, dainty little finger sandwiches, an assortment of brightly colored cupcakes.'"

Stephen says, "Also noted in the bulletin 'The Grand Hotel Royal Collection Hotel sits the Cafe Royal has afternoon tea accompanied with oven hot scones provided jams and clotted cream, and a variety of pastries and cake. freshly brewed chai tea.'"

Roxanne says, "The bulletin also lists 'The Nimb Restaurant's Afternoon Tea that serves scones with clotted cream and homemade jam, as well as the Danish classic flødebolle, a house-made chocolate puff filled with whipped cream.'"

The Professor and his nephews get valet parking from the attendants at the Radisson Blu Waterfront Hotel in Stockholm, Sweden.

The Steeles enter the hotel's lobby where its director states, "Bienvenue! Welcome, Professor Steele and his nephews. I am the hotel director, Lukas."

The group shakes hands as the director says, "Radisson Blu Hotel is certified as an environmentally friendly hotel. And we will provide the Eight Tea Days Racers with a spectacular Afternoon Tea ceremony. Come follow me, sirs."

The Steeles follow Lukas into the Lady Hamilton room, the entire group is introduced to the chief sommelier.

The sommelier arrives saying, "Bienvenue! Welcome Professor and his gentlemen. As your chief sommelier we offer you Afternoon Tea with your choice of organic loose-leaf teas formulated and hand blended in micro-batches direct from tea gardens around the world such as Valerian Dream, Tangerine Ginger, Earl Grey Lavender, Jasmine Pearl Green Tea, Iron Goddess of Mercy, Vanilla Mint Chai Tea, Da Yu Lin Oolong, and Teahouse Macha."

The waitstaff serves a tray of sandwiches such as smoked salmon with watercress, cream cheese, and tomato confit on German chutney bread, smoked duck with red onion compote on mole bread, cucumber with Swiss cheese and spicy aioli on ciabatta, and Brie with cream cheese and pear compote on French baguette.

Another server places a tray of Swedish sweets such as Sweden's national cake being the princess cake, strawberry cake, chocolate sticky cake, fika bread, Swedish cinnamon buns, and Swedish seven cookies having Brussels cookies, chocolate slices, dreams, raspberry caves, oat biscuits, nut biscuits, and shortbread chessboards.

More sponsored racing teams enter the Lady Hamilton room led by Director Lukas as the Steeles enjoy a few more filled teacups with sandwiches and pastries.

The Professor hands the wait staff his black credit card as they walk up to Lukas thanking him for his hotel's services.

Stockholm, Sweden to Jönköping, Sweden

Stephen states, "Stockholm, Sweden to Jönköping, Sweden takes 3 hours, 30 minutes traveling 210 miles on E40 with an autobilled toll."

Roxanne states, "Notable people from Jönköping, Sweden include the former United Nations Secretary-General, Dag Hammarskjöld, Swedish novelist and 'Sweden's last Romantic' author,

Viktor Rydberg, Carl Lotave was an illustrator, sculptor and painter of portraits having his work of notable leaders of World War I and two well-known portraits of President Abraham Lincoln, Agnetha Fältskog who is the first 'A' in the Swedish supergroup 'ABBA.'

Maya is back scouting victims on highway E40 driving her Liquid Petroleum Koenigsegg CCGT53 EV Hypercar.

Maya Christiansen receives a digital message stating, "Team 42 inside the desert gold Mercedes Brabus Super Rocket EV 3000 is being driven by professional getaway driver, Ansel Judge with front seat passenger, Jodie Glenn and in the backseat, Brooke Butler."

Maya focuses on the rear driver's side tire of the Mercedes Brabus Super Rocket EV 3000.

The famous, never caught getaway driver, Ansel Judge never trusts others as he is 'always looking over his shoulder,' He notices that his team is being closely followed by a gold Koenigsegg, He starts to weave in and out between the commuter's vehicles to see that driver's response,

As suspected, the gold Koenigsegg follows his Mercedes Brabus Super Rocket also weaving around the commuters chasing. So, Ansel accelerates having the Rocket live up to its name by first climbing to 60 mph in 1.35 seconds and then getting to its max speed of 275 mph.

The Koenigsegg CCGT53 EV Hypercar follows as its specs are in accelerating in 1.4 seconds to 60 mph having a top speed of 285 mph. As the two vehicles are traveling alone on highway E40 at high speeds, Ansel warns his passengers of his actions then hits the brakes squealing.

Maya in her Koenigsegg CCGT53 EV Hypercar is shocked by what has just happened as she maneuvers around the Mercedes Brabus

Super Rocket sliding onto the highway's left lane shoulder. Gaining control of her vehicle she stops and takes a breather thanking her Goddess Myrena for helping her.

Team 42 is laughing and congratulating Ansel on his success saying, "That's my baby, driver Ansel,"

Ansel states, "Sometimes all I want to do is head west on E40 in a hypercar that I can't afford with a plan I don't have. Just me, my music, and the road."

Brooke replies, "We are all alone heading to Jönköping."

Jönköping, Sweden to Copenhagen, Denmark

Stephen states, "Driving from Jönköping, Sweden to Copenhagen, Denmark takes 3 hours, 36 minutes traveling 213 miles on E4 with an autobilled toll."

Roxanne states, "Every racer is heading back to Copenhagen which is the capital and most populous city of Denmark."

Stephen says, "Although Disneyland's trademarked slogan is 'The Happiest Place on Earth' while Walt Disney World in Florida is called 'The Most Magical Place on Earth' but Copenhagen is said to be the 'happiest city in the world.'"

Roxanne remarks, "The once Viking fishing village is a green paradise being rated as the world's top cities for cyclists."

Stephen notes that "The tallest building in downtown Copenhagen, the Radisson Blu Royal Hotel, being Copenhagen's first skyscraper."

Roxanne says, "I would enjoy going to the Tivoli Gardens that's one of the oldest amusement parks in the world. In fact, both fairytale writer Hans Christian Anderson and Walt Disney visited the Gardens many times. I would race you Stephen to get on their wooden rollercoaster!"

Stephen states, "The racers are returning back to Copenhagen, Denmark."

Stephen adds saying, "I remember as a child watching the classic film 'Hans Christian Anderson' with Danny Kaye."

The entire iBroadcast team begins singing *Wonderful, wonderful Copenhagen. Friendly old girl of a town.*

The Tesla SUV pulls into a German Tavern to visit the restroom and get a drink.

Rocky asks, "Bierkellnerin, what beer do you recommend?"

The beer server replies, "Sir, do you see that factory across the street?"

Apollo who joins his twin and Rocky turn to look saying in unison, "Yes!"

The server remarks, "That factory is Bremen's Brauerei Beck & Company, perhaps to you fellows known for their Beck's beer."

She continues saying, "Their key logo has our city's coat of arms with the Bremen's patron saint being Saint Peter."

The twins order a Beck's German Pilsner while the Professor orders a costly Grand Old Parr Elizabethan Edition 11 Blended Scotch Whisky.

Playing throughout the tavern is the latest nuclear rock iMusic hit from Lovegood Records 'Jump, Jump, Jump."

As the Steeles notice that they have been relaxing for over 90 minutes, the bartender Couglin states, "Gentleman, it is closing time. You don't have to go home but you can't stay here."

Apollo looks up at him and says smiling, "Mr. Wizard, we live further than Kansas is from Dorothy's Oz."

The trio of Steeles thank him as they get up and vacate the public house.

Maya is back scouting victims on highway E4 driving her Liquid Petroleum Koenigsegg CCGT53 EV Hypercar.

The Deeds Federation messages Maya texting, "On E4 just ahead of your location is Team 8's Volvo XTC90 EV. Their driver is Zelda 'The Legend' Arwen with her passengers Pelton Nordic and Joloc Michel."

The gold Koenigsegg Hypercar soars catching up to her target, the Volvo.

Maya fluent in over twenty languages says, "Volvo in Latin is 'I roll' so let's see how fast the XTC90 EV can roll" as she laughs,

The 'Legendary' Zelda drives like the wind as she plays cat and mouse with the Koenigsegg as the cat.

She tells her team saying, "The Koenigsegg is trying to get our cheese," as they chuckle with her.

Maya tries to get a perfect location to use her laser eyes SuperPower as two vehicles zoom past her almost colliding with her Koenigsegg,

The two feuding teams now in third and fourth place which changes every three seconds are Team 11 in their Rimac Nevera B2 EV Hypercar and Team 12 inside their Lotis Lightning EV,

Driving the Rimac Nevera is Charlie 'Cheating' Chester as his cheering teammates are Giana Rossi, Ms. Keara Karlson, and Ms. Theris O'Leary.

Cheating' Chester states, "That darn Speed Demon Sam Forest! I hate that driver now and when I was beaten at LeMans last year. So, darn you, Speed Demon Sam Forest, and your little vehicle too."

Speeding past them in the Lotis Lightning EV has driver Speed Demon Sam Forest flipping them off. Her passengers who follow their leader by birding Team 11 are Thunder Blitz and Newt Harper.

Maya becomes incredibly angry and re-evaluates her mission's target seeking to dismantle by laser the Rimac and Lotus,

Getting behind them, she has Team 11's Rimac in the right lane and Team 12's Lotus in the left lane soaring at 200 mph.

She cannot get an ideal position to focus her eyes on their rear tires as she is more concerned with her high-speed driving.

After thirty minutes following them as the trio is almost approaching Copenhagen, Netherlands auto toll, she still cannot use her destructive SuperPower on the vehicles.

Copenhagen, Netherlands to Hamburg, Germany

Roxanne states, "We are back in reverse directions driving from Copenhagen, Netherlands to Hamburg, Germany takes 3 hours, 19 minutes traveling 206 miles on highways A24 to E47 with an autobilled toll."

Roxanne continues saying, "Downriver from Hamburg, in the town of Wedel, lies the Willkomm-Höft that is a 'welcome point' for ships arriving at, or leaving the port of Hamburg. There are over fifty ships daily that are welcomed here by playing the national anthem of the country where the ship is registered, or for departing ships saying bon voyage or farewell by hoisting the set of flags that shows 'U' and 'W' meaning 'I wish you a pleasant voyage.'"

Stephen says, "Hamburg has more bridges than any other city in the world that reliable sources state are between 2,300 and 2,500."

Roxanne remarks, "The Dolittle doctors on Madagascar state 'Hamburg's Tierpark Hagenbeck is a different type of zoo as there is not a single cage in sight. The animals live in open enclosures surrounded by moats allowing each group to have a more natural environment where they can move freely. The Tierpark Hagenbeck remains the only large, privately-owned zoo in Europe.'"

Stephen smiles saying, "The Herbertstraße in the St. Pauli district is as Hamburg's shortest street and the most notorious street. The street is blocked from sight by barriers at both ends as it is Hamburg's red-light district. Although it is a fairly popular tourism area for men, women are not welcome here and will be immediately chased away by the prostitutes who work there."

Roxanne notes that "The Beatles-Platz, named in honor of the band whose later fame was forged in the clubs around the Reeperbahn. Even their singer, songwriter, musician, and lead rhythm guitarist, John Lennon once said, "I didn't grow up in Liverpool, I grew up in Hamburg." The young group, the Beatles played around 273 nights in Hamburg between 1960 and 1962."

Stephen states, "The grand, neo-renaissance Hamburg City Hall was built to honor the wealth and independence of the proud harbor city.

The City Hall has 47 rooms, six more than Buckingham Palace in London."

Maya in her Liquid Petroleum Koenigsegg CCGT53 EV Hypercar is following on highway A24 Team 11's Rimac in the right lane and Team 12's Lotus in the left lane.

The two feuding teams keep switching places in race order as they switch lanes making it difficult for Maya to focus on their tires,

As the vehicles get onto highway E47, Maya can put her gold Koenigsegg in cruise control as she has her left eye laser aimed at the Lotus in the left lane and her right eye laser focused on the Rimac's rear tire,

After 30 minutes of having her eye lasers burning into the vehicle's tires, they finally puncture the rubber.

The Lotus with a blown right tire can quickly steer on to the highway's left shoulder.

Then, the Rimac who has a deflated left rear tire is forced onto the highway's right shoulder.

The Golden Eagle HQ immediately dispatches a tow trailer, a brand new Rimac Nevera B2 EV Hypercar delivered to Team 11's GPS position and a brand-new Lotus Lightning EV to Team 12 across the highway.

As Maya passes her victims, she watches as they are bickering still with each other as she laughs singing, "It's been a hard day's night. I've been working like a dog!"

Chapter 28

Friday 'Eight Tea Days Around Europe' Race

"Another day of exciting racing live iNews as we get closer to the finish line. Welcome to the Golden Eagle HQ iBroadcast of the Eight Tea Days Around Europe Race with your host, Roxanne McLaren on Day Seven."

Stephen states, "American former professional racing driver and Indy 500 Hall of Famer, Parnelli Jones said "[In racing] if you're in control, you're not going fast enough."

Hamburg, Germany to Rotterdam, Netherlands

Stephen says, "Racing from Hamburg, Germany to Rotterdam, Netherlands takes 5 hours traveling 312 miles on A1."

Roxanne states, "Rotterdam which means 'the Dam on the River Rotte' is the second largest city in the Netherlands being economically in the shipping industry, the secondly in industries such as chemical, commodities trading, pharmaceuticals, logistics, and electrical equipment."

Stephen says, "The Rotterdam Philharmonic Orchestra is a Dutch symphony orchestra based in Rotterdam residing in the concert hall De Doelen that is also a convention center."

Roxanne says, "Nicknamed the 'City of Sports,' Rotterdam hosts the Rotterdam Marathon, the World Port Tournament, the Rotterdam World Tennis Tournament, the Red Bull Air Race World Championship, and the car racing event Monaco aan de Maas. Some of or Eight Tea Days racers have been finalist in the last event."

Stephen says, "Rotterdam has 4 three Michelin stars, 16 two Michelin stars, and 28 one Michlin star restaurants. The cuisine has changed from the old city's diet of meat or fish and potatoes to attracting a group of younger, diverse, and sophisticated chefs."

Roxanne reads her handed note saying, "The FA-King notes 'Rotterdam is the home of the Chabot Museum dedicated to the Dutch painter and sculptor Hendrik Chabot.'"

The Lemnian Deeds Federation has assigned Stormy Weather to intercept the Eight Tea Days racers as they leave Hamburg, Germany.

Stormy getting to Hamburg two days earlier goes shopping on the streets around Jungfernstieg and Neuer Wall are the best places in Hamburg to discover luxury designer brands and talk with their famous designers. In the center of Hamburg is the elegant Alsterhaus department store with five floors of international fashion designers, high quality perfume and gourmet restaurants that from the fourth floor overlooks the beautiful Lake Alster.

Nearby in Karolineenviertek amongst the vintage clothing shops are famous designer shops featuring Herr von Eden, Bent Angelo Jensen, Wolfgang Joop, Karl Lagerfeld, Jill Sander, Bitten Stetter, Sarah Beutling that dress the young and hip fashionista in Hamburg.

After two days of designer shopping using the Deeds' black credit card, Stormy tells her good friend Myrena, "Just wait until I return and show you all of the great designer clothing that you bought for me."

Myrena has provided to her BFF, Stormy Weather an iconica blu Pininfarini Battista Tre Special Edition EV manufactured by Automobili Pininfarini GmbH having its headquarters in Munich, Germany.

She drives her Battista Tre that accelerates to 60 mph in 1.35 seconds with a top speed of 250 mph.

Stormy decides to start her journey off by blinking her eyes three times having torrential pouring rain accompanied by large hailstones bouncing off the highway.

Commuter traffic drivers lose control of their vehicles having them spin off the road to having the hailstones hitting the top of their vehicle making a large thud sound.

Team 44's McLaren Speedtail Hermes 3 EV has its driver Heidi Klumaker using her vast racing experience to weave in and out of the commuter traffic safely.

Her two passengers Arnold Winkler and Ronnie Most start singing, "Stormy Weather, Stormy Weather go away and don't come back another day."

Inside Team 5's Ford Mustang EV Iditarod Edition the Alaskan Husky howls communicating that it fears the hailstorm noise.

Elowen Redington drives doing her best to avoid the hailstones as her teammates Laser Cannon and Callon Ferrell pet the husky's head trying to calm her down.

Team 25 in their Porsche 918 Spyder EV catches up to the iconica blu Battista Tre.

Former NASCAR and Indianapolis driver, the angelic Farrah Monroe passes Stormy's vehicle then navigates her vehicle to cut off Stormy forcing her onto the shoulder.

Almost colliding, the Battista Tre is forced to go into the left lane that now has eighteen inches of water forcing her to hydroplane onto the shoulder.

The two passengers of Team 25, Dean Blake and Seymour Moore begin yelling, "Hurrah! Pip, pip Hurrah! Pip, pip Hurrah!"

Behind the first place, black Tesla SUV EV is Team 25 chasing after them.

Stormy Weather now angry as she can be, accelerates back onto the highway as soaring behind her is Team 17.

Driving the fast and furious black Dodge Challenger 55 EV is Mistletoe Kringle.

Sitting next to her is professional race car driver Paul Silverberg who is giving her aggressive driving instructions.

Looking in her rear view monitor she sees her backseat passengers, being Lenard Gooddaughter and Alberto Crowe, both drinking their apple spritzer which is also called 'apfelschorle.'

Inside their Subaru Hypercar 2 EV, Team 13 is catching up to the iconica blu Pininfarini Battista Tre Special Edition EV.

The driver of the Subaru Hypercar is Pandora Boxlighter who looks at the heavy rain pouring down upon the deep mauve hood and begins singing Prince's lyrics, *Purple rain, purple rain. Purple rain, purple rain. I only want to see you bathing in the purple rain!*

Then, her teammates Echo Winwood and Joddos Canterbury join her singing *Purple rain, purple rain. Purple rain, purple rain. Only wanted to see you underneath the purple rain.*

Then, as Pandora drives into the left highway lane pointing the front of her vehicle towards the lane's shoulder, she taps her brake extremely hard shooting a tremendous amount of water upon the Pininfarini Battista Tre's driver's side window and windshield blinding Stormy's view.

Stormy turns her windshield wipers on full blast as she slows down. She watches the Subaru Hybrid team fly past her as they point in her direction laughing.

The racers and Stormy drive entering 'La Ville Lumiere.'

Rotterdam, Netherlands to Paris, France

Roxanne comments, "Paris is called 'La Ville Lumiere' meaning 'the City of Light' because it was the first big city in the continent to have gas street lighting."

Stephen states, "Traveling from Rotterdam, Netherlands to Paris, France takes 4 hours, 50 minutes traveling 278 miles on A1 with an autobilled toll."

Roxanne continues stating, "While in Paris, enjoy viewing admiring St. Chapelle, Notre-Dame Cathedral or crossing Pont Neuf which means 'New Bridge,' so named by King Henry III."

Stephen says, "The biggest holiday in France is Bastille Day on July 14th having sky painting fireworks illuminate the Eiffel Tower. Earlier armored tanks move slowly and heavily down the Champs-Elysees in a military parade. In the skies, low-flying jet planes soar spraying blue, white and red smoke behind them. Bastille Day celebrates the storming of the prison Bastille in 1789."

Roxanne says, "Napoleon authorized the construction of the Arc de Triomphe in 1806 which took 30 years to complete. Napolean wanted to erect a large triumphal arch to celebrate his troops called the Grand Armee. The arch is 164 feet in height and 148 feet in width."

Stephen states, "Many visitors coming to Paris suffer from 'Paris syndrome' having them experience disappointment due to unrealistic expectation portrayed by the media of the city. They may suffer from hallucination, dizziness, sweating, and more."

Roxanne states, "Paris has no 'stop' signs and the FA-King writes in an email 'The Louvre Museum in Paris is the largest art museum in the world housing over 38,000 art objects which would take a visitor almost 200 days to see everything."

Stephen trying to be punny states, "My sister met her husband in Paris so 'she came to Paris to find Louvre.'"

Stormy driving her the iconica blu Pininfarini Battista Tre Special Edition EV is in the middle of a deluge of commuter traffic.

She attempts to exit getting free to hunt down the Steele Tesla SUV EV having the highway A1 to Paris transportation stifling her. She drives to the left highway lane and commuters are stopping her progression then switching lanes having her blocked.

Stormy seeking her vehicle freedom to speed ahead causes rain using her SuperPower then freezes the asphalt that turns into black ice. She follows this by conjuring up high winds at 180 mph immediately making the vehicles ahead of her begin to slid and flip over providing a clear escape path,

Then, Stormy generates a tornado spinning at 150 mph having a 30-foot diameter. The twenty-five commuter vehicles surrounding her Pininfarini Battista Tre begin cycling upward.

The entire twenty-five commuter vehicles are arranged as a shish kebab of vehicles as though it were a skewered sculpture on the left shoulder of Highway A1.

Stormy looks out of her window as all the vehicles' drivers and passengers are thrown into the shrubbery within a hundred feet of the highway.

Stormy Weather yells out "I have created an exceptionally large spindle that would make Dustin Shuler jealous. I'm sure Dustin after seeing my 25-vehicle monument would be so angry that he would impale himself."

Ahead of the remaining vehicles, the iconica blu Pininfarini Battista Tre travels alone towards Paris in search of the Steele's Tesla.

Paris, France Tea Ceremony

Roxanne states, "In Paris, France having afternoon tea is gaining momentum which has been a long-standing practice in their frenemy Great Britain."

Stephen states, "The Parisians enjoy everything from very casual to very luxurious Afternoon Tea ceremonies."

Stephen continues saying, "For the sponsored teams having a memorable teatime in Paris starts with the five-star Shangri-La Hotel."

The Shangri-La manager escorts Professor Steele and his two nephews saying, 'Welcome to La Bauhinia restaurant. I am Jules, the hotel manager and next to me I would like to introduce our restaurant manager, Claude Michel, and our certified sommelier, Pierre Jacques.'"

Everyone present shakes hands saying, "bonne journée, Monsieur."

Claude Michel says, "La Bauhinia is an inspirational flower that adorns the Hong Kong flag. It comes from honoring the passion of Prince

Roland Bonaparte who was the heir of Napoleon Bonaparte with a skilled interest in botany."

Claude Michel continues saying, "You are seated in the most excellent table where above is a luminous glass dome created by architect Maurice Gras. I hope that you will enjoy this special moment sitting at an exceptional excitement that overlooks many of the Paris monuments."

The certified sommelier, Pierre Jacques states, "Your Afternoon Tea Ceremony has the sweet pleasures in combination with the delights that you remember from your childhood with our specific selection of hot tea drinks of your choice. It is our pleasure to end your tea ceremony with Paris' best glass of champagne. Our pastry chef, Maximilian Bardot has freshly prepared pink pomelo cheesecake, vegan cocoa lime, the famous profiterole, buckwheat mille-feuile, and exotic fruit plate accompanied by a variety of ice cream and sorbet. Our sandwich selection is comprised of a lobster roll with authentic fries, lobster salad with avocado, mango, iceberg lettuce and ponzu sauce, club sandwiches served with mixed salad and fries, a selection of poultry, smoked salmon or vegetarian delights, and brioche bread with ham or turkey fillets accompanied by a mixed salad and fries."

As the restaurants wait staff brings out the sandwiches and dishes that the sommelier mentioned, he continues saying, "Our tea selection has green tea from Japan and China, Oolong tea with hints of orchid fragrance, white tea from China scented with jasmine flowers, English breakfast tea from India and Sri Lanka, Darjeeling tea from India, chamomile tea, peppermint leaf tea and rooibos tea."

The restaurant's wait staff comes around taking each person's hot tea order as the other wait staff team delivers silver trays of sandwiches and pastries.

Roxanne remarks on the iBroadcast iChannel, "The Prince Roland Bonaparte Teahouse located near the Eiffel Tower serves a variety of tea a company by classic and vegan serve pastries and sandwiches. Nearby the Hotel de Crillon has an enjoyable afternoon tea near the Champs Elysees."

Stephen states, "The Four Seasons Hotel George V high tea in their Galerie Lounge which is beautifully decorated with its Flemish tapestries detail carpet and art decor interior. The Galerie Lounge serves high tea that includes finger sandwiches with cheese, ham, cucumber, smoked salmon, Foie Gras canapés, smoked salmon with goat cheese cannelés from Bordeaux, homemade scones with house made strawberry and orange jam or clotted cream, carrot cake, and chocolate brownies."

Roxanne continues saying, "Other choices for afternoon tea is the five star Le Bristol Paris which has floral decorated porcelain teacups to drink excellent teas with the tastiest petit fours, T' Xuan Chinese Heaven that serves tea Matcha Mille-crepes and Chinese jelly, Le Meurice located right near the Eiffel Tower serving unique tea variations such as green, white, or herbal."

The five-star Ritz Paris in their Salon Prost having their sommelier say, "We proudly serve a selection of teas such as herbal, green, white and English teas. Our selection of sandwiches are vegetarian, being eggplant, zucchini, peppers, and tomato. Our other selection of meat sandwiches are lobster roll with lemon confit, pickles and fried onions, veal ham or truffled goat cheese and chives. Also, elegantly served is our plain scones or milk chocolate served with French whipped cream, marmalade jam or clotted cheese. For caviar, I personally recommend the gold Osetra Caviar or Beluga caviar served with blinis and condiments."

Paris, France to Bordeaux, France

Roxanne states, "Racing from Paris, France to Bordeaux, France takes 5 hours, 40 minutes traveling 362 miles on A10 with an autobilled toll."

Stephen states, "Bordeaux in France is a port city and the capital of the Nouvelle-Aquitaine region."

Roxanne says, "Bordeaux is a world capital of wine having many castles and vineyards that stand on the hillsides of the Gironde, and the city is home to the world's main wine fair, Vinexpo. Bordeaux wine growing area has about 287,000 acres of vineyards having 10,000 wine-producing estates and 13,000 grape growers."

Stephen remarks, "Bordeaux is classified 'City of Art and History' displaying over 362 monuments with its 'Port of the Moon,' being an UNESCO World Heritage site as 'an outstanding urban and architectural ensemble.'"

Roxanne states, "My email from the FA-King reads 'The Grand Theatre of Bordeaux was conceived as a temple of the Arts and Light having a neo-classical facade with its auditorium ceiling being a painted large fresco by artist Jean-Baptiste-Claude Robin.'"

Stephen continues saying, "My FA-King email reads 'The art collection of the Musée des Beaux-Art de Bordeaux has two wings in the museum covering a significant panorama of European art from the 15th to the 20th century with the works of Perugino, Titian, Veronese, Velvet Brueghel, Van Dyck, Rubens, Chardin, Delacroix, Corot, Rodin, Kokoschka, Picasso, and Matisse.'"

Driving through the autopay toll heading to Bordeaux, France are the two rivaling vehicles from Team 11 and Team 12.

Still, demanding to drive the Rimac Nevera B2 EV Hypercar is Charlie 'Cheating' Chester that is trying to outperform the Lotis Lightning EV with driver Speed Demon Sam Forest.

The Lemnian Deeds Federation operator reports to Stormy saying, "The National Weather Service states 'Approximately 21% of vehicle crashes totaling per year nearly 1,235,000 are weather related. Weather-related crashes are defined as those crashes that occur in adverse weather such as rain, sleet, snow, or wet pavement."

The feuding vehicles drive past the iconica blu Pininfarini Battista Tre with the Rimac Nevera in the left lane and the Lotis Lightning EV slightly ahead in the right lane.

Stormy is closing in on the Rimac as she swears at the Lotus having many lightning bolts bombarding it as she yells, "Have a couple of dozen lightning bolts Mr. Lotus Lightning!"

Speed Demon Sam ignores the blinding electrostatic discharges through the atmosphere as she knows that EV vehicles on the highway are grounded.

Then, she cuts off the Rimac in the left lane.

Stormy predicting this maneuver accelerates in the right lane passing the Rimac and then the Lotus.

The Rimac crosses into the right lane chasing closely behind the Pininfarini Battista Tre as the Lotus in the left lane speeds up.

As the trio is approaching commuter traffic, each racer weaves in and out maintaining their position on highway A10.

Newt Harper tells driver 'Cheating' Chester, "If you beat these vehicles to Bordeaux, I will treat our team to wine and dining at the Port of the Moon Wine Restaurant that is set in a restored 16th century palace. They serve on the ground floor traditional French dinners often accompanied with fries since being in France doesn't need the redundancy."

Thunder Blitz adds, "Bordeaux is known for its canelé that is a small French pastry flavored with rum and vanilla with a soft and tender custard center and a dark, thick caramelized crust."

Newt reading the restaurant's web menu states, "Beat these vehicles and we will be having Bordeaux wines, foie gras, oysters from Arcachon Cap Ferret, dishes à la Bordelaise, caviar d'Aquitaine, dunes blanches which are pastries topped with pearl sugar, and cèpes de Bordeaux having Porcini mushrooms, Pauillac lamb shoulder, confit de vin de Sauternes au safran, sel de Château, Puits d'amour, gratton de Lormont1, fish breaded and baked in a sauce involving white wine and lemon juice, and rib-eye steak prepared as entrecôte à la Bordelaise."

As the trio races towards Bordeaux, France, Stormy noticing one-hundred-foot-tall European chestnut trees quickly decides using her SuperPower to have lightning stop her adversaries.

She makes rain pour down as lightning strikes several tall chestnut trees. The trees just struck by lightning are hotter than the sun's surface causing fires. As the wind causes the lit matchsticks looking chestnut trees to blow down the highway, the puddles begin to convert to steam, which can explode.

As the iconica blu Pininfarini Battista Tre flies past the Lotus and Rimac, the fiery chestnut trees are blown in front of the duo entering Bordeaux as several of the chestnut trees block their way causing both vehicles to crash.

The two disabled vehicle teams leave their hypercars smelling like roasted chestnuts. Luckily, the passengers are unharmed, which rarely happens.

Team 11 and 12 walk to the Port of the Moon Wine Restaurant to drink and eat. While their replacement vehicles are being delivered, the teams turn a tragedy into a celebration.

Speed Demon Sam Forest sings, "Chestnuts roasting on an open fire, Jack Frost nipping at your nose."

Not to be outdone, Charlie Chester states, "When I was in grade school, I learned how to play chess. My mother gave me a humorous Christmas card that read 'Chessnuts boasting in an open foyer.'"

Arguing which vehicle is winning, the Golden Eagle HQ expedites a tree service company to remove the fallen logs

Bordeaux, France to Logroño, Spain

Stephen states, "Traveling from Bordeaux, France to Logroño, Spain takes 4 hours traveling 246 miles on A630 with an autobilled toll."

Roxanne states, "Logroño is the capital of the province of La Rioja in northern Spain having the Ebro River located in its north region."

Stephen says, "Logroño has been awarded as a 'European City of Sports' due to the variety, quality and accessibility of its sports and bicycle for transport and as a sports practice."

Stormy Weather heads to Logroño, Spain driving on A630 in her iconica blu Pininfarini Battista Tre.

Soon she sees ahead of her Team 17 with Alberto Crowe driving their black Dodge Challenger 55 EV.

Listening on his multi language Babble Device is Lenard Gooddaughter who is dancing and singing in the front seat as he listens to Tony Bennett, Frank Sinatra, Celeste Bordeaux, Rileigh Michele, Matt Monro, and Des O'Connor.

Their other teammates Paul Silverberg and Mistletoe Kringle sit in the modified trunk that has been turned into a back seat resting.

As they approach the North Region the river Ebro, Stormy using her SuperPower to create super chloride-ion rain that immediately deteriorates the stone bridge's road crossing the river.

Stormy forces Team 17's Dodge Challenger to cross the stone bridge as she accelerates her Pininfarini Battista Tre behind them.

The Challenger enters the bridge when they noticed that ahead of them sections of the stone bridge due to the super chloride-ion contamination has disappeared.

Waking up in the back is professional race car and film stuntman Paul Silverberg who tells his driver Alberto saying, "You must accelerate to the maximum speed, or we will all die."

Alberto floors the accelerator having the front of their Dodge Challenger raise up like a skateboard doing a kick turn.

With only the rear wheels on the ground, traveling at top speed, the Dodge Challenger begins to fly through the air crossing all the bridge sections that are missing.

Behind them Stormy in her Pininfarini Battista Tre gets her vehicle to also soar across the bridge.

Then, both cars traveling back on the highway as Stormy still at maximum speed passes the Dodge Challenger with ease.

Closing in on Team 3's Aston Martin Maxi EV Supercar, which is five miles ahead of her, she heads towards her next victims.

Team 3 with driver Darcy Austin with her front seat passenger being Jubilee Perez who has the SuperPower to morph herself and Romy Ruiz.

Darcy looking in her rear-view monitor sees the iconica blu Pininfarini Battista quickly heading towards them.

She tells her teammate Jubilee that she believes they are being hunted by Stormy Weather who they know is a friend of Myrena Gorgona.

Now parallel to the Aston Martin, which is in the right highway lane, Stormy looking at the driver in disbelief. For sitting in the front passenger seat, she observes Professor Steele.

Rubbing her eyes, Stormy takes out her wrist iCommunication device.

Then, sending digital video back to the Lemnian Deeds Federation she questions them saying, "Are my eyes deceiving me or is this truly Professor Steele inside the Aston Martin?"

Within 10 minutes, Myrena is on the iCommunication device responding, "Stormy, although the person you have captured on digital video looks exactly like the Professor seeing him joining Team 3 in their Aston Martin and not with his two nephews is highly suspicious. Please keep following them and updating us and if you happen to get destructive, I will have no complaints."

As Stormy Weather continues seeing an incredibly attractive gentleman, she tells herself, "Knowing that Professor Steele is older than Gandalf and Methuselah, he is still a very attractive, youthful looking gentleman. Being aware of the fact that he is highly intelligent and has trillions of dollars is also a plus."

Stormy trying to stop the Ashton Martin makes a tornado that should spin the vehicle off the highway but for some reason the SuperPower effort backfires as her Pininfarini Battista Tre is spun like an Oz farmhouse flying first through the air and then tossed like a salad 150 yards from the highway.

The Lemnian Deeds HQ sends a brand-new chic pink Pininfarini Battista Tre to her GPS location as she is black and blue bruised but otherwise unharmed.

Chapter 29

Saturday 'Eight Tea Days Around Europe' Race

"The final day of exhilarating racing is live on iNews as we get closer to the finish line. Welcome to the Golden Eagle HQ iBroadcast of the Eight Tea Days Around Europe Race with your host, Roxanne McLaren on Day Eight."

Logroño, Spain to Madrid, Spain

Roxanne states, "Racing from Logroño, Spain to Madrid, Spain takes 4 hours traveling 203 miles on A-2 with an autobilled toll."

Stephen states, "Madrid is the capital and most populous city of Spain. Since 2005, Spain legalized same-sex marriage having Madrid being one of the largest hot spots for LGBT culture."

Roxanne remarks, "Madrid is the headquarters of the UN's World Tourism Organization and the Standing Committee of the Association of Spanish Language Academies located in the Royal Spanish Academy."

She continues saying, "Mercedes-Benz Fashion Week Madrid has the principal challenge to promote fashion in Spain being held twice a year."

Stephen says, "Madrid is home to two world-famous football clubs and basketball playing at the WiZink Center."

Roxanne says, "The FA-King sent an email that reads 'Madrid's Prado Museum has a collection with works of art by Francisco Goya, Hieronymus Bosch, El Greco, Peter Paul Rubens, Titian, and Diego Velázquez.'"

Stephen continues saying, "Another email from the FA-King reads 'Madrid's Queen Sofía National Museum Art Centre had Spain's greatest masters Pablo Picasso and Salvador Dalí paintings along with Joan Miró, Francis Bacon, Georges Braque, Robert Delaunay, Max Ernst, Vasily Kandinsky, Paul Klee, Yves Klein, Fernand Léger, René Magritte, Diego Rivera, and Mark Rothko.'"

Roxanne adds saying, "A third email from the FA-King reads 'The third piece of the art museum triangle is Thyssen Bornemisza National Museum with paintings by Jan van Eyck, Petrus Christus, Antonello da Messina, Bramantino, Palma il Vecchio, Titian, Tintoretto, Veronese, Jacopo Bassano, Sebastiano del Piombo, Albrecht Dürer, Hans Holbein, El Greco, Caravaggio, Rubens, Van Dyck, Rembrandt, Frans Hals, Gainsborough, Domenico Ghirlandaio, Winslow Homer, and John Singer Sargent.'"

Stephen reading the FA-King note states. "The Thyssen Bornemisza National Museum has on display in the European 19th century gallery the works by Vincent van Gogh, Francisco Goya, Thomas Lawrence, Delacroix, Géricault, Corot and Courbet, Claude Monet, Auguste Renoir, Edgar Degas, Camille Pissarro, Alfred Sisley, Pierre Bonnard, Toulouse-Lautrec, Paul Gauguin, ,Paul Cézanne, and Vincent van Gogh. The diverse collection of twentieth century modern art includes Cubist works by Picasso, Braque, Edvard Munch, Egon Schiele, Kandinsky, Salvador Dalí, Paul Klee, Chagall, Magritte, Piet Mondrian, Edward Hopper, Jackson Pollock, Mark Rothko, Roy Lichtenstein, Willem de Kooning and Francis Bacon. The gallery with German Expressionism has works by Emil Nolde, Ernst Ludwig Kirchner, August Macke, Max Beckmann, George Grosz, and Otto Dix.'"

Roxanne states, "The Auditorio Nacional de Música is the main venue for classical music concerts in Madrid being the home to the Spanish National Orchestra, the Chamartín Symphony Orchestra, and the venue for the symphonic concerts of the Community of Madrid Orchestra."

Stephen continues saying, "The Teatro Real is the chief opera house in Madrid, located in front of the Royal Palace where the Madrid Symphony Orchestra performs."

The Lemnian Deeds Federation HQ texts the Cyber Mistress writing, "You and Juliet will be coming behind the black Dodge Challenger 55 EV with driver Lenard Gooddaughter and his front seat passenger Paul Silverberg and in the backseat Alberto Crowe and Mistletoe Kringle."

Juliet says, "I just came over the hill and around five miles ahead of us, I can see the Dodge and not the DODGE who are our allies," as she giggles.

The Cyber Mistress driving her Dendrobium Z7 EV Supercar remarks, "Let us smack these baddies fast and furiously," as she lets out an evil laugh.

The two female, Leeds assassins accelerate gaining on their victims.

Lenard tells his team, "I see two unknown supercars gaining on us."

Paul states, "Look at all those commuters down the highway. They follow the rules for what? They are letting fear lead them."

Mistletoe remarks, "We do what we do best. We improvise Gran Turismo Hypercar EV and Juliet Capuletty in her Renault Razor 5 Supercar EV."

Both Deeds' supplied Supercar EV vehicles can accelerate to 60 mph in 1.45 seconds having a maximum speed of 275 mph.

The Cyber Mistress tells Juliet, "I cannot wait to give my next slave victim a terabyte worth of bi-otch slapping.'"

Juliet says, "With my day's earning from the Deeds, I will dream of touring the world first class throughout the journey with my love, Romeo."

Juliet tells the Cyber Mistress, "Are we ready to use both of our SuperPowers to challenge by reprogramming the Dodge?"

They blink their eyes three times in unison forcing the Challenger to perform a 180-degree turn, now driving in reverse.

Alberto screams, "Are you serious, Lenard? Is this your idea of 'improvising?'"

Lenard replies, "This is not my doing. Someone is controlling our vehicle and it is not me."

Paul calmly states, "Just keep driving until we slow down, and I will guide you to do another 180 degree turn to drive forward again."

The Dodge Challenger is weaving in and out of traffic backwards as Lenard keeps his hands off the steering wheel and pressing as hard as he can on the brake to no avail.

Paul grabs the steering wheel trying to turn it around, but he is disbelieving what is happening,

Finally, after three and a half hours, as Lenard keeps pressing the brake, the Dodge Challenger begins to slow down.

Madrid, Spain to Salamanque, Spain

Roxanne states, "Racing from Madrid, Spain to Salamanque, Spain takes 2 hours, 22 minutes traveling 129 miles on A-50 to AP-6 with an autobilled toll."

Stephen states, "Salamanca is a city in western Spain being the capital of the Province of Salamanca lying on several rolling hills by the Tormes river being declared a UNESCO World Heritage Site."

Roxanne says, "The local Salamanca dishes are steamed rice with pork, a slow-cooked chickpea-based casserole and meat pie."

Juliet thinks that the silence is killing her, so she blinks three times having all the commuter traffic listening to Rileigh Michele and MaryJane sing their duet of 'Deflowering Cunnegonde.'

Caught beyond the castle walls, you are for me the one.
Half the size of the Queen, your mother, weighs over one ton.
I am the servant of the King, your dad.
I am deeply in love with you, Cunnegonde, the virgin I had.
I desire to be the King's newly adopted son.
Deflowering his huge daughter as he sends me to prison.

Linda Higgins inside her Ford Bronco IV EV states, "I love this song and the movie with Oscar winning actor Robert Leach who was fantastic playing Candide."

Juliet blinks having the music of 'Deflowering Cunnegonde.' on maximum volume as for the next ninety minutes as it plays on and on.

As the Cyber Mistress and Juliet Capuletty follow the two dozen commuters, through the journey all they hear are the loud digital music of Rileigh Michele and MaryJane.

After a while, they laugh as they witness every commuter having a fit trying to stop or turn off the continuous digital music,

Heading into Salamanque, Spain, the music stops playing having Linda Higgins yell out "Thank God, the digital iMusic has finally ended, Enough with this song. I now hate it. I think that Robert Leach, and the film should return their awards,"

Salamanque, Spain to Porto, Portugal

Roxanne states, "Racing from Salamanque, Spain to Porto, Portugal takes 3 hours, 46 minutes traveling 216 miles on A25 with an autobilled toll."

Stephen states, "Porto is the second largest city in Portugal after Lisbon having Port wine being one of Portugal's most famous exports."

Roxanne says, "Porto has the traditional Portuguese cuisine like Tripe Oporto style, cod fish, fried pork meat, pig blood-based dish, fresh fish, and grilled sardines."

Stephen remarks, "Porto's famous resident include J. K. Rowling who was the writer of Harry Potter that taught English as a foreign language in Porto and lived there. Armando Pereira de Basto was a Portuguese painter, illustrator, sculptor, and decorator lived there too."

Maisle Stark driving Team 27's plain white Le Mans Hypercar class Peugeot 13x13 EV Hypercar tells her team, "I am looking forward to stopping in Porto for our tea ceremony where I will start with a large glass of Porto wine."

The back seat passenger Lena Lannister replies, "Make that two glasses of Porto."

Her front seat co-pilot, Tyrone Dinkler states, "While you're having those lady drinks, I'll be filling up on Macieira, the most consumed brandy in that has a fruity aroma of vanilla, peach, honey, and cherry."

Maisle accelerates the Peugeot passing Team 22's Ferrari 513CM Le Mans Hypercar.

Inside their Ferrari, driver Nicole Thicke exclaims, "Darn it! We just got overtaken by the white Peugeot."

Her two passengers are Ken Cannon and Robin McCarthy. Ken states, "Don't let that Citroén merging French automobile get ahead of us. Accelerate it, girl!"

Robin says, "It's time to show the other Le Hypercar class which car has won the World Sports Car Championship and several years winning the 24 hours of Le Mans race:"

The two hypercars are now neck to neck racing towards Porto.

Porto, Portugal Tea Ceremony

Roxanne states, "The Golden Eagle HQ reports 'Elite Café serves afternoon tea in Porto being located on Santa Catarina street near a pedestrian walkway for shopping and for the finest members of society. The café displays Art Nouveau decoration, by architect João Queiroz. Inside are the aroma of tea and the scent of leather upholstery and varnished wood and ceiling of endless Flemish mirrors.'"

Stephen says, "The Elite Café has wonderful teas such as white sky, Emperor Sencha, Moroccan mint, Jasmin Queen tea, silver moon tea, chai tea, English breakfast, Earl Grey, Royal Darjeeling, herbal teas like chamomile and rooibos vanilla bourbon."

He continues saying, "The afternoon tea sandwiches are cucumber with cream cheese, smoked salmon or chicken with bacon, fresh scones with clotted cream and Morang jam. To end the perfect afternoon tea ceremony, they serve everyone a glass of port wine."

Roxanne adds saying, "The Portugal famous pastries to select such as travesseiros meaning 'pillows' or 'cushions' that a puff pastry with almonds and rich cream, malasadas that are Portuguese yeast-leavened doughnuts coated with cinnamon or granulated sugar, pastel de Tentúgal being an iconic Portugese fried extremely thin with powdered sugar, filhós are traditional Portuguese deep-fried treats coated in cinnamon sugar or dipped in brown sugar syrup, Berliner being Portuguese donuts that are sliced in half and filled with sweet and creamy egg-based custard, queijada is prepared with a combination of queijo which is a local cheese, eggs, milk, flour, and sugar, pastel de Chaves which is a clam-shaped Portuguese delicacy made with a puff pastry shell filled with a unique mixture of minced veal, bread, and onions, and pastel de Belém is a traditional Portuguese egg custard tart."

The Steeles enter the InterContinental Porto where a well-dressed man says, "Welcome Seniors Steele, I am Rodrigo Rocha the hotel director," as they shake hands.

He states, "We have wonderful afternoon tea in our Astoria Restaurant. Follow me to your table for special guests" as the Steeles comply.

Rodrigo introduces the restaurant manager Joao and his sommelier Beatrice, having them all greet each other.

The Steele family is seated in a special section of the Astoria restaurant for honored and well-known guests.

The sommelier Beatrice states, "The luxurious five-star Intercontinental Porto has a special selection of our teas that we freshly brew according to your order. Our fine tea selection includes British teas such as Darjeeling, English breakfast, Earl Grey, Sri Lanka flavored black tea, Nepal spring white tea, tea with rosebud or jasmine flavor, green tea from China and Japan, oolong tea, Ceylon black tea, and Assam tea. Our scones are classic plain or mandarin orange with Madagascar vanilla or British berries jam, Cornish clotted cream or Kentish rhubarb and apple jam. Our cake and pastries include blueberry and English lavender eclairs, cherry blossom poached peach tart, champagne, and freesia cube cake. The delicious sandwich offerings include Royal Gala apple with green kohlrabi coleslaw, grilled wagyu beef with organic asparagus, lavender smoked halibut fillets with a tomato relish, and slow roasted Jerusalem artichoke with English peaches."

The Steeles place their tea orders as silver tiered trays of sandwiches and pastries are brought to the table by the wait staff.

Apollo tells the Professor and his brother, "We are almost done with our journey called 'Eight Tea Days Around Europe' and soon I can get back to Amelia who has been texting me every day."

The Professor hands over his black credit card to pay for the luxurious Intercontinental Porto afternoon tea ceremony.

Apollo gets in the front seat to drive the black Tesla SUV.

His brother sits in the back having a bottled water and sitting in the front passenger seat next to him is the Professor who is listening to digital music by Beethoven that is his Symphony Number 5 in C Minor and Bach's Orchestral Suite Number 3 in D Minor.

Porto, Portugal to León, Spain

Roxanne states, "Racing from Porto, Portugal to León, Spain takes 4 hours, 11 minutes traveling 246 miles on A75 with an autobilled toll. León, Spain is the self-governing territory of Castile and León in the northwestern Iberian Peninsula. León is the capital of the León province."

Stephen says, "The FA-King reports that 'MUSAC being an acronym for 'The Museo de Arte Contemporáneo de Castilla y León,' a contemporary art museum and a landmark in the city of León, Spain.'"

Team 10's Porsche Taycan Sport Turismo 9 Hypercar is driven by Parker Peter who tells his two passengers Pamela Baywatch and Holly Woodland, "Ladies, we're catching up to the leaders as we are heading to León, Spain."

Holly says, "It'll be a cool world if we win. Parker, can you think and drive at the same time because I can't. "

Pamela remarks, "I was once in a relationship with another lifeguard named Leon. You don't think that he lives in Spain, do you?"

Team 15's Nissan Flash EV driven by Winter Sazon tries to pass the Porsche Taycan Sport Turismo 9.

Nissan Flash's passenger Ash Arturo states, "I always tell people, 'You must start where you are, use what you have, do what you can.'"

Tiger de Forrest adds, "Monsters come in many different forms. Do you know what I consider the greatest monster of them all?"

Parker replies, "No, I don't."

Tiger states, "Fear which is the belief that's something is dangerous causing pain or threats."

Parker accelerates saying, "I will not be limited by my fears."

León, Spain to Saint-Sebastian, Spain

Roxanne states, "Racing León, Spain to Saint-Sebastian, Spain takes 2 hours, 30 minutes traveling 240 miles on highways A-321 to AP-1 with an autobilled toll."

Stephen replies, "San Sebastian is a city and municipality located on the coast of the Bay of Biscay, 12 miles from the France–Spain border."

Roxanne says, "San Sebastian features a humid subtropical climate having warm summers and cool winters."

Stephen says, "San Sebastián 's motto is 'Waves of people's energy' with city festivals, music, theater, and cinema that take place throughout the year, especially in summer hosting every July the San Sebastian Jazz Festival."

Roxanne remarks, "San Sebastian has fifteen restaurants with three Michelin stars, twenty-five with two Michelin stars."

The Porsche Taycan Sport Turismo 9 as they battle out for position with the Nissan Flash EV, they are both approaching Team 31's Shelby Cobra 7 EV Hypercar driven by Judd Wilson having his front seat passenger, Emilio Sheen and in the backseat, Molly Ringer.

On the highway to Saint-Sebastian, Spain the three cars juxtaposition trying to move ahead of the other two vehicles.

First the Porsche Taycan accelerates to over 200 mph passing the other two Hypercars.

Then, the Nissan Flash floors the vehicle having it pass the Shelby Cobra and being in the left lane parallel to the Porsche Taycan.

Not to be out done, the Shelby Cobra accelerates to its maximum speed passing the Porsche and the Nissan.

Ahead in the distance, the black Tesla SUV EV is heading towards the Chunnel in Calias, France.

Saint-Sebastian, Spain to Bordeaux, France

Stephen states, "Racing from Saint-Sebastian, Spain to Bordeaux, France takes 4 hours, 8 minutes traveling 147 miles on A63 with an autobilled toll."

Roxanne says, "Bordeaux is a port city situated near the Garonne River in southwestern France."

Stephen remarks, "The rue Sainte-Catherine is the longest pedestrian street in Europe being three quarters of a mile as the main shopping street in Bordeaux, France."

Roxanne states, "Bordeaux boasts over five hundred wineries and is famous for its rich reds. Average vintages produce over seven hundred million bottles of wine."

Fast approaching the Shelby Cobra, Nissan Flash, and Porsche Taycan are the two Le Mans Hypercars, Team 27's Peugeot, and Team 22's Ferrari.

In the right lane of the highway, the Ferrari 513CM passes the Shelby Cobra as the Peugeot 13X13 Hypercar flies advancing by the Nissan Flash.

As the cars all accelerate being too close to each other to easily pass, they continue as a unit heading towards Bordeaux, France.

Bordeaux, France to Le Mans, France

Roxanne states, "Racing Bordeaux, France to Le Mans, France takes 2 hours, 30 minutes traveling 276 miles on highway A10 with an autobilled toll."

Stephen replies, "Le Mans is a city in northwestern France on the Sarthe River that hosts the 24 Hours of Le Mans, the world's oldest active endurance sports car race."

Roxanne says, "The FA King email reads, "Musée de Tessé, is the fine arts museum of Le Mans that displays paintings by Philippe de Champaigne, Charles Le Brun, François Boucher, John Constable, Ingres, Théodore Géricault and Camille Corot.'"

Continuing down the highway, the Shelby Cobra and Nissan Flash are closely followed by the Porsche Taycan next to the Ferrari 513CM.

Suddenly, the Porsche Taycan followed by the Ferrari 513CM drive on the shoulders passing the Shelby Cobra and Nissan Flash.

The Ferrari driver, Ken Cannon states, "We are heading to Le Mans, France where in an endurance race with the topmost prestigious sports cars race for 24 hours usually with teams of three drivers per vehicle. Alongside the Monte Grand Prix and the Indianapolis 500, Le Mans makes up the Triple Crown of Motorsports."

Team 27's Peugeot driver, Dean Blake says, "The Peugeot Sports prototype racing car has won several of the Le Mans' endurance races. I expect our team to place among the top ten in this race."

Le Mans, France to Calias, France

Stephen states, "Racing from Le Mans to Calais takes 4 hours traveling 261 miles on A28 with an autobilled toll."

Roxanne states, "Calais is a major port for ferries between France and England and the home of the Channel Tunnel linking nearby Coquelles to Folkestone by underwater rail."

The iBroadcast camera crew watches as the black Tesla SUV EV is clearly in first place heading to Calias into the EuroTunnel.

The iBroadcast iNews having the entire world watching shows the remaining racers driving on A28.

Behind the Tesla SUV is the Lamborghini Essenza SCV51X Hypercar

The Porsche Taycan is feuding with the Ferrari 513CM for third and fourth places.

In fifth place is the Shelby Cobra and the Nissan Flash is in sixth place.

Accelerating down the highway are the two Deeds female assassins, Juliet Capuletty in her Renault Razor 5 Supercar EV and driving her Dendrobium Z7 EV Supercar is the Cyber Mistress.

The Cyber Mistress tells Juliet "Tell me, have you ever taken the Eurotunnel from Calais to England?"

Juliet responds, "I have always wanted to make the trip after seeing many movies where people have taken the Euro rail. If I ever get to England, I assume that using words like 'that's brilliant' or 'you're being very cheeky' might have me passing as a local."

The Cyber Mistress laughs and says, "Bloody hell, you sound absolutely nothing like a Brit."

Myrena Gorgona tells the Deeds board saying, "I remember when I was in Ocho Rios in Jamaica doing a SuperModel shoot near the Dunn's River Falls, I collaborated with a beautiful black model named Cynthia Mitchell. She texted me the other day letting me know that she was visiting her sister in Birmingham, UK. I used my professional influence to get them excellent seats to watch the Tottenham Hotspur football match and afterwards visit the winning Tottenham Hotspur Football Club and its owner."

The Lemnian Deeds Federation strategy team asks, "That was wonderful for you to do but how does this help our current situation?"

Myrena smiles saying, "Cynthia using her SuperPower will simply fly across the English Channel and using our provided Rolls-Royce Phantom 513 EV, she will get a board the Euro Chunnel driving behind the Professor's black Tesla SUV EV. Besides being able to keep the Rolls-Royce Phantom after her mission, the Deeds will pay her $5 million US."

Fifteen miles ahead of them, the Lamborghini and the black Tesla SUV EV having a license plate 'Steele1' are battling for first place in the Eight Tea Days Around Europe race.

Apollo driving the Tesla SUV looks across at the Lamborghini saying, "Each of those SuperModels are like every girl that I've ever dated including Myrena whose personality matched her last name. The snake headed Gorgon that even her looks turned men into stone."

Rocky, noticing that Gemma Georgio was putting on her eyeshadow, decides to use his telekinesis to poke herself in the eye causing her to curse.

Then, looking at the other front seat passenger who is applying lipstick, using his SuperPower he jostles the car having Gemma Georgio miss her lips and smearing it all over her cheek with the classic red lipstick.

As another jostle of the Lamborghini occurs, Shoshana Amato again pokes her eye with the eyeshadow stick as Gemma Georgio slides the red lipstick across her left cheek.

Rocky sitting in the queen size bed located in the rear of the Tesla SUV, opens his window.

Then, Rocky yells out at the Lamborghini SuperModels, "My, my you SuperModels look extraordinarily beautiful today."

The driver, Anita, looks at her passengers saying that the jostling has caused a makeup nightmare and tells her team to check their handheld mirrors.

Ranting like a Mad Hatter waving their arms screaming in their Lamborghini are two females frantically and angerly yelling "OMG, Coco Chanel didn't say "Beauty begins the moment you decide to uglify yourself."

As the SuperModels fix themselves, Apollo Steele says, "Can the Lamborghini members tell me now who is in first place?" as he laughs at them.

Anita Lamborghini says to her team, "Our strategy must be to get ahead of the Professor and let him and his two nephews deal with the two hyperjackers. When we get to the Eurotunnel and Calais, we will be right next to him in our carriage. Then, when we get to Folkstone in the UK that will be our chance to show our racing skills and beat him in our race to Greenwich."

The Steeles watch their Tesla's dashboard monitor observing the twenty blue Tesla robotaxis behind them.

Juliet Capuletty says to her teammate the Cyber Mistress "Our strategy should be to repeat our previous successful attack where our robotaxis surrounded the vehicles and forced them to crash destroying everything including this black Tesla SUV."

The Cyber Mistress agrees as she call the Lemnian Deeds Federation HQ and reports their plans to ' Stop the Professor! Now and forever!"

The Cyber Mistress programs a flying landmine droid to sneak under the Lamborghini to fulfill its purpose.

As the two Deeds female assassins initiate the robotaxi attack, Professor Steele tells Apollo "Now is the time to let Myrena and her Lemnian Deeds Federation know what the Steeles are made of."

The Cyber Mistress initiates the program as the flying landmine droid flies under the Lamborghini Essenza SCV51X Hypercar having a 15-minute timer for its detonation to occur.

As the robotaxis begin to get in position to imprison the black Tesla SUV, Apollo using his SuperPower of telekinesis overrides 'hyperjacker helper' program forcing all the twenty blue robotaxis to drive reverse doing a 180 degree turn at maximum speed.

Juliet says to the Cyber Mistress "I do not know what is going on as my program is still telling the robotaxis accelerate forward."

The Cyber Mistress replies "I agree as far as I can see everything is in working order."

The twenty high speed fleet of blue robotaxis crash into Renault Razor 5 Supercar EV and Dendrobium Z7 EV Supercar pushing them off the road into a solid mountain wall.

Trapped inside their vehicles, Juliet Capuletty and the Cyber Mistress communicate with the Lemnian Deeds Federation "We have been tricked by the Steeles having both of our vehicles crippled and paralyzed as we are between a rock and a hard place. We need help immediately to get back to our real lives. Luckily, none of us are hurt but we have lost the war."

Then, the Lamborghini Essenza SCV51X Hypercar explodes throwing its passengers over one hundred feet into the river.

Anita Lamborghini questions her team saying, "Is everybody all right? Shoshana? Gemma?"

They respond, "We're alive but could use some medical attention."

Inside the approaching Rolls Royce Phantom. SuperModel, Cynthia Mitchell says "I cannot believe what just happened? The Steeles made mushmeat out of two assassin vehicles and the Lamborghini."

The Golden Eagle HQ has an ambulance response unit immediately travel to the GPS location of the Lamborghini Essenza SCV51X Hypercar team.

At the right lane of the Calais Eurotunnel security station, the guard notices that he has a celebrity being Professor Steele and his two nephews who are very well known throughout the world and on the iBroadcast iChannel.

After checking their passports and collecting their toll, she tells them, "Welcome Professor Steele and his two gentlemen. All of us here have been watching the Eight Tea Days Around Europe race. The administrator of the Chunnel has instructed everyone to put you on the first departing carriage and have you immediately pass through security station in Folkestone."

Professor Steele thanks her saying "I believe knowing that my calculations are correct this will give us a 30 minute head start on all the racers who are able to get onto this departing Chunnel."

The security guard smiles saying "You are probably correct since you are a super genius" as they get on to the special carriage the front of the under the sea train.

Rocky asks his uncle, the Professor "How many of the Eight Tea Day racers will be on our departing Chunnel train."

The Professor looks at both of his nephews saying, "There will be us and probably no more than twenty-five other racing teams as the rest of the teams will be on the next Chunnel train."

Calias, France to Folkestone, England (Eurotunnel)

The racers enter Folkestone to travel across the Channel on the Eurotunnel, commonly called the Chunnel.

Spread throughout the teams of security guards on their iCommunicator device, are digital images of Katrina Quark and Leizi who over a week ago distributed exploding nitrocellulose ping-pong balls in every carriage in the underwater train.

The Lemnian Deeds Federation cancels their assignment of their assassins Katrina Quark and Leizi.

Myrena continues saying, "Once Cynthia Mitchell is on the carriage, she will use her second SuperPower which is the ability to touch an object and rapidly multiply it. I have personally instructed her to bring upon the Chunnel a bottle of Tuocon that will flood every carriage having all the passengers fall asleep as though they were knocked out."

In line to enter the Calais connected carriages is a black Tesla SUV EV, then a McLaren Speedtail Hermes 3 EV belonging to Team 44 and then the Deeds' assassin operated Rolls-Royce Phantom 513 EV.

The Lemnian Deeds Federation HQ operator tells Cynthia, "The tunnel under the English Channel is 31.5 miles long traveling under the Channel being 246 feet below sea level. The Chunnel took 13,000 workers to build an underwater railway that measures the distance equivalent to 169 Eiffel Towers making it the world's longest undersea tunnel."

Entering the Eurotunnel Le Shuttle in Calais, France going through the security border check in and having their tickets checked, each car drives into their carriage.

Cynthia looks out of her car once parked seeing darkness which she comments, "Simon and Garfunkel said, 'Hello darkness, my old friend I've come to talk with you again.'"

Exiting the Phantom 513 EV with her bottle of Tuocon, she removes the bottle's cap placing her right index finger inside the bottle's tip having every carriage except hers get drops of Tuocon water seeping on the carriage's roadway.

Every second that passes, half an inch of Tuocon water rises above the floor unnoticed by any of the occupants. A few of them are sitting in the passengers' lounge area while most of them are inside their vehicle.

Paraphrasing Bob Marley, Cynthia sings…

No Tuocon, no flood

No Tuocon, no flood

No Tuocon, no flood

No Tuocon, no flood

In this great future,

you can't forget your past

*So, dry your **Tuocon**, I say*

In 120 seconds, every carriage has three feet of Tuocon water as 75% of the passengers have their eyes closed and sleeping because of Professor Steele's patented 'Tuocon water.'

As the Tuocon water dissipates into the Channel, Cynthia has already fulfilled her Deed's mission by flattening tires, destroying the EV battery, and removing the EV spark plug.

Being unaffected by the Tuocon water, the Professor and his two nephews exit the Chunnel as all his competitors that are on this trip are having the Folkstone England service stations tow each customer's EV vehicle off the carriage to repair the mysteriously caused EV vehicle problems.

Cynthia drives her newly acquired Rolls-Royce Phantom 513 EV back to Birmingham where she finds an email from her bank letting her know that there was a $5 million US deposit into her Jamaican National Commercial Bank account.

.

Folkestone, England to Greenwich, England

Stephen states, "Leaving the Eurotunnel in Folkestone, England and heading to the finish line in Greenwich, England takes 1 hour, 15 minutes traveling 64 miles on M-20 to A20."

The black Tesla SUV EV leaves Folkestone, England heading to the finish line in Greenwich at the posted 70 mph speed limit.

All the other 'Eight Tea Days Around Europe' racers who were able to make the same departing underwater railway tunnel shuttle as the Steeles, must wait in line to pay their toll while the security guards check each vehicle and occupant's passports.

The Steeles, having diplomatic immunity, leave with a thirty-minute head start. Their black Tesla SUV EV has passed Ashford before the next racer's vehicle is repaired and leaves the processing security station.

With less than an hour's drive, Apollo Steele passes Maidstone where the Professor says, "If you look over towards your right which is towards Kent, you can see the Leeds Castle where the Culpeper Gardens and a shrubbery maze are some of the activities to do there."

The tow vehicle and their mechanics fix each 'Eight Tea Days Around Europe' vehicle in the order that they entered the Chunnel according to the Golden Eagle HQ.

Exiting the Eurotunnel after paying their toll and showing their passport to security, is Team 10's Porsche Taycan follow two minutes later by Team 22's Ferrari 513 CM.

Team 10's driver Parker Peter in the Porsche Taycan Sport Turismo 9 Hypercar states, "I always thought that the Chunnel protected vehicles from getting flooded by the Channel."

Having his team chuckle as he soars down the highway in second place.

Fifteen minutes later, Team 31's Shelby Cobra and Team 15's Nissan Flash appear on the iNewscast driving down M-20 still battling it out.

Five minutes later, Team 27's Peugeot 13X13 EV Hypercar accelerates onto Highway M-20 trying to catch up to the other racers ahead of them.

Soon the next EuroTunnel shuttle has arrived as the remaining 'Eight Tea Days Around Europe' racers go through the passport and security check station entering Highway M-20 heading towards the finish line in Greenwich.

The Checkered Flag

At 11:45 p.m., the vehicles are seen racing down A20 Eltham Road heading to the finish line in front of the Royal Observatory.

As all the Eight Tea Days Around Europe racing teams have returned to Greenwich in front of the Royal Observatory, Professor Steele announces, "As the sponsor of the race, I would normally give the trophy to whoever wins but in this case it is the Steele1 license plated Tesla SUV EV, followed in second place with Team 10 in their Porsche Taycan Sport Turismo 9 EV, in third place Team 22 in their Ferrari 513CM Le Mans Hypercar, in fourth place Team 15 Nissan Flash EV with fifth place with Team 31's Shelby Cobra 7 EV Hypercar and then sixth place Team 27 with their Peugeot 13x13 EV Hypercar. Congratulations to the winners and all the teams that spent the last eight days seeing Europe at 200 mph."

As the Royal Observatory museum adds the winning Tesla SUV EV to their exhibits, they drive the winners to the five star Novotel London Greenwich Hotel.

Chapter 30

After the 'Eight Tea Days Around Europe' Race

The next morning after having a delightful breakfast, a limousine from the Royal Observatory transports the Steeles to London City Airport where their Aerion CP513 Super Sonic Business Jet is parked.

Several Lemnian Deeds Federation hired assassins begin shooting their long range sniper assault rifles missing the Steeles and destroying the terminal's windows as the waiting passengers for other destinations duck.

The airport security returns fire, but the shooters are too far away to even hit anything. Airport officials communicate with the local police who take over searching for the shooters, but they are long gone by the time they get there.

Professor Steele along with his two nephews Apollo and Rocky escape in their Aerion CP513 Super Sonic Business Jet flying .home to Reykjavik, Iceland.

Professor Steele decides to be the pilot as his two nephews sit behind him in the comfortable executive seats.

The Steele twins' comment in unison saying, "After two weeks abroad, I feel like I am riding Hidalgo through the longest distance desert."

The Israeli Military Defense Minister has given Myrena Gorgona their best defense weapon since the Steele Corporation years ago gave several of their enemies' assault vehicles and technically advance weapons,

Representing the DODGE Initiative, Myrena with a fully armed King David's Sling System 3 so named after the biblical story where David defeats the Giant Goliath in a mano a mano winner-take-all competition. The arsenal at Myrena's disposal contains thirty-two nuclear missiles each aimed directly at the Business Jet owned by the Steele Corporation.

Currently its only occupants are the pilot Professor Steele and sitting in the two passenger seats are Apollo, and Rocky.

Myrena with her finger on the trigger whispers "You treacherous, lying S.O.B. 'Good things come to those who wait' like me. Ever since my wedding day, I have vowed revenge on the Steeles seeking this exact moment. Then, I only wanted half ownership of the 'Golden Eagle' Organization, now I will have it all."

The mission is being recorded in high definition for the entire iBroadcast world to witness. Myrena is heard stating, "One does not have to be a 'mourning bride' to realize that 'Hell hath no fury. like a woman scorned.'"

Watching on their high-def screens, the world watches as the Aerion CP513 Supersonic Business Jet peacefully travels across a cloudless blue sky as thirty-two anti-aircraft ballistic missiles ricocheting across the heavens accelerate behind.

In one short instant, a bright flash of light indicating a collision followed by a loud thunderous explosion.

From the control room at the iBroadcast station, the sounds are continuously heard as the visuals are played and replayed several times showing an explosion with a mushroom cloud surrounding the Aerion CP513 Supersonic Business Jet,

Then, an empty cloudless blue sky is shown,

Myrena comments, "Ding-dong. The Professor is dead. Long Live Queen Myrena."

With the sound of an announcer's voice the iBroadcast world hears "What you have just witnessed has been the world authorized execution of Professor Steele and his two nephews Apollo and Rocky Steele."

After a five second pause, Myrena interrupts saying, "Hello world, this is Myrena Gorgona the SuperModel, the SuperDesigner and now super in-charge of the 'Golden Eagle' Organization as well as the founder and head of the 'Lemnian Deeds' Federation."

Assuming that all the Steeles are now ashes, Myrena transfers three trillion dollars from the Golden Eagle and Steele Corporation accounts into her 'Lemnian Deeds' Federation account.

Myrena states, "As Reykjavik, Iceland's adopted Chess World Champion would say 'Checkmate Steeles.' Or Iceland's ATP legend Arnar Sigurðsson would often state "Game, Set. And Match!"

On the screen is shown the words "A 'Lemnian Deed' is the cruel slaughter of someone as revenge."

The SuperPower Series Continues…

SuperPower The Ability to Fly or to Become Invisible:
In Ashes, Phoenix Eagles Shall Rise (Book #4)

"SuperPower The Ability to Fly or to Become Invisible: In Ashes, Phoenix Eagles Shall Rise" starts after Myrena Gorgona launched the Israeli David's Sling nuclear missiles directly hitting the Aerion CP513 Supersonic Business Jet plane flown by Professor Steele with his passengers, Apollo, and Rocky Steele

With her enemies dead, Myrena Gorgona assumes leadership of the Steele Corporation as its new CEO.

The combined efforts of DODGE and the 'Lemnian Deeds' Federation in recruiting new SuperPower ability females helps as Myrena has her 'Lemnian Deeds' Federation take over her latest acquisition, the 'Golden Eagle' Organization.

-What effect does the 'Lemnian Deeds' Federation have changing its allegiance with its ally DODGE (Department of Defense Genetically Engineered) Initiative with the SuperPower world?

-In the battle of the sexes, it's the female organization led by Myrena Gorgona against Elijah Wood Jr. and the Martin twins who control the DODGE Initiative. Who wins the war?

-And what about the Professor and his two nephews?

-Their ashes inside three large steel urns are beginning to make a fire crackling (crepitation) sound.

SuperPower The Ability to Fly or to Become Invisible:
In Ashes, Phoenix Eagles Shall Rise
(Book #4)

Chapter 1
Woodpushers

As Glenn Peterson the international chess master walks through the Bobby Fischer Chess Park and observes several chess games being played on the concrete chess tables.

He notices that at one of the tables two chess experts are battling where white has Checkmate in four moves.

After having a meal from one of the food truck vendors, Glenn walks around and notices soon to be mated blackside player. He walks up to the man and asks "I saw that you were playing earlier as black. What was the outcome of the game?"

Without hesitation, the man says, "We drew the game."

The next day, Glenn has a meeting with Reykjavik's Secretary of the Ministry of Finance and Economy.

Entering the birch paneled government office, Glenn tells the receptionist "Good morning Góðan daginn, I have a 10:00 a.m. meeting with the secretary."

She tells Glenn "follow me" as they enter the Secretary's executive office.

As she leaves closing the door, Glenn notices a marble chess board and honey rosewood Staunton chess pieces, The board is in the initial chess set up. Glenn remembering the position where the mate in four should have occurred moves the pieces until that position is now on the chess board.

Glenn returns to the chair across from the Secretary's executive one.

Soon the Secretary of the Ministry of Finance and Economy arrives and greets Glenn with a firm handshake. He asks Glenn "How can I be of service to you Mr. Peterson?"

Glenn asks him "Are you familiar with Professor Steele?"

The Secretary states "Yes, we have a business relationship and can be considered 'friends.'"

Just then, the Secretary notices the chessboard and sees that the pieces have been moved. He gets up and walks over to closely examine the position.

He asks Glenn "Do you play chess?"

Glenn answers "Yes, I do from time to time."

The Secretary asks, "Did you set up this position?"

Glenn answers "I do not understand."

The Secretary tells him "This is the exact position I had in a game that I played yesterday."

Glenn walks over and asks, "What did you play at this juncture?"

The Secretary shows him his played second rate move and says, "We drew a few moves later."

Glenn states "I would have played this move" as he moves his queen.

The Secretary remarks "That's terrible as I can capture your queen like this."

Glenn responds checking with his knight announcing, "Move and I mate you in two moves. "

The Secretary responds, "Not true" then analyzing the board says, "Oh my God, you are correct."

Then Glenn confesses to seeing the game as he was in the Chess Park having lunch.

The two men laugh.

Sitting back at the Secretary's executive desk, Glenn tells him "Is it possible for you to schedule a meeting between us and the Professor?"

The Secretary tells Glenn "It is hard to believe that you're not aware that on every major iBroadcast iChannel and later on the iNews iChannels the Lemnian Deeds Federation headed by SuperModel and fashion designer, Myrena Gorgona used Israeli David's Sling missiles to disintegrate Professor Steele's jet. Luckily his two nephews Apollo Rocky somehow manage to survive."

Glenn with his eyes wide open says " I seem to recall hearing something about that but who can believe the tabloid iNews iBroadcasts."

The Secretary continues saying "Evidently there is a Clash of the Titans between Myrena Gorgona and the two remaining Steele twins as to who will be in charge of the Golden Eagle Organization and the Steele Corporation. There are rumors of sightings of the resurrection of Professor Steele on the front pages of gossip iNewspapers next to stories of extraterrestrials and Elvis observations."

Glenn requests "I'd appreciate any help that you can provide me in regard to a business meeting."

They shake hands before Glenn exits to next meet his investors for lunch.

MOVIES

MUSIC

BOOKS

NOTES

Media Citations

Besides the fair use law, the following sources are referenced in this book.

<u>Film, Book or Song Title</u>   <u>Director or Artist</u>
                                      <u>Production Company</u> <u>Year</u> <u>Medium</u>
The Ballad of Gilligan's Isle   Schwartz, S., Wyle, G.
                                 CBS Productions.   (1964). Film.
Casablanca   Curtiz, Michael.
                                 Warner Bros. Pictures (1942). Film.
Chestnuts Roasting on an Open Fire Cole, Nat King.
                                 Sony/ATV Music Publishing.
                                                        (1944) Record.
Clueless   Heckerling, Amy.
                                 Paramount Pictures.   (1995). Film.
Days of Thunder   Scott, Tony
                                 Paramount Pictures.   (1990). Film.
Dirty Harry   Siegel, Don.
                                 Warner Bros. Pictures. (1971). Film.
Dunkirk   Nolan, Christopher.
                                 Warner Bros. Pictures. (2017). Film.
Escape (The Piña Colada Song) Holmes, Rupert.
                                 MCA Records   (1979). Record.
Finding Forrester   Van Sant, Gus.
                                 Columbia Pictures.   (2000). Film.
Ford vs. Ferrari   Mangold, James.
                                 20th Century Fox.   (2019). Film.
Forrest Gump   Zemeckis, Robert.
                                 Paramount Pictures.   (1994). Film.
Hans Christian Andersen (Copenhagen) Vidor, Charles.
                                 RKO Radio Pictures.   (1952). Film.
A Hard Day's Night   The Beatles.
                                 Capitol Records,   (1964). Record.
Hitch   Tennant, Andy.
                                 Columbia Pictures.   (2005). Film.
The Hitchhiker's Guide to the Galaxy Adams, Douglas.
                                 Pan Books   (1979). Book.
How to Lose a Guy in Ten Days Petrie, Donald.
                                 Paramount Pictures.   (2003). Film.
I Can't Breathe   H.E.R.

RCA.   (2020). Record.

I Kissed a Girl   Perry., Katy.
                             Capitol Records.   (2008). Record.
Kill Bill Vol. 2   Tarantino, Quentin.
                             Miramax Films.   (2004). Film.
Livin' la Vida Loca   Martin, Ricky.
                             Columbia Records.   (1999). CD.
Money, Money, Money   ABBA.
                             Atlantic Records.   (1976). Record.
No Woman, No Cry   Marley, Bob & The Wailers.
                             Universal-Island Records. (1974). Record.
Oppenheimer   Nolan, Christopher.
                             Universal Pictures.   (2023). Film.
Philadelphia   Demme, Jonathan
                             TriStar Pictures.   (1993). Film.
The Portrait of a Lady   James, Henry.
                             Houghton, Mifflin and Co. (1881). Book.
Purple Rain   Magnoli, Albert.
                             Warner Bros. Pictures. (1984). Film.
The Raven   Poe, Edgar Allan.
                             New York Evening Mirror.   (1845). Poem.
The Rocky Horror Picture Show Sharman, Jim.
                             20th Century Fox.   (1975). Film.
Scarface   De Palma, Brian.
                             Universal Pictures.   (1983). Film.
Star Wars: Episode IV A New Hope   Lucas, George
                             LucasFilm.   (1977). Film.
Strawberry Fields Forever The Beatles.
                             EMI.   (1967). Record.
Sudden Impact   Eastwood, Clint
                             Warner Bros. Pictures. (1983) Film.
The Terminator   Cameron, James.
                             Orion Pictures.   (1984). Film.
Terminator 2: Judgment Day Cameron, James.
                             TriStar Pictures.   (1991) Film.
300: Rise of an Empire   Murro, Noam.
                             Warner Bros. Pictures. (2014). Film.
The Wizard of Oz   Vidor, K., Fleming, V.
                             Metro-Goldwyn-Mayer (MGM).

(1939). Film.

Tin Man America.
  Warner Records Inc. (1974). Record.
Titanic Cameron, James.
  Paramount Pictures. (1997). Film.
Xanadu Newton-John, Olivia & ELO.
  Musicland Studios. (1980). Record.